SHAKING THE TREES

Jeremy Tager

ISBN 978 1 7638746 3 3 (print)
ISBN 978 1 7638746 4 0 (ebook)

Shaking the Trees
By Jeremy Tager

Edited by: Crystal Leonardi & Georgie Montague
Front Cover & Interior Design by: Crystal Leonardi

Distributed by Bowerbird Publishing
Available in National Library of Australia

Bowerbird Publishing
Julatten, Queensland, Australia
www.crystalleonardi.com

Lightning Source paper suppliers are environmentally responsible and do not use papers sourced from endangered old-growth forests, forests of exceptional conservation value, or the Amazon Basin. Lightning Source book manufacturing aims to reduce supply chain waste, greenhouse gas emissions, and conserve valuable natural resources. We share this world. We are glad to do our part in keeping it sustainable.

To Danika and Shani, with much love.
And to all activists who work tirelessly and passionately
to protect the extraordinary life on this planet and make
the world a better, kinder place.

CONTENTS

PART 1

I had no epiphany...but...a thousand unremembered moments
produced in me an anger, a rebelliousness,
a desire to fight the system...

Nelson Mandela

CHAPTER 1

A long time ago I stood on the cliffs at Hvar and faced one of my great fears - jumping into the sea from twenty-four metres, into those crystal waters that had no end. I was thirteen and desperate to impress a girl. Lust can bring bravery and foolishness both. I jumped and crossed a boundary that felt important at the time. Other boundaries later would be much harder, less clear and require a whole different brand of bravery.

Crossing into death was the last and it is from here that I watch my great nephew Jake and the boundary at which he stands.

He is in a nondescript patch of Queensland desert with the freewheeling sky above him, pinned to the spot, paralysed with fear, as I was for so long on that cliff face. Everything he has been taught tells him not to act. Everything he knows tells him he must. This is a boundary that cannot be uncrossed, it is like walking through a one-way wormhole into a different life. There are no returns.

Jake knows, just as I do, that it is time. You can see it in his face, see that he's afraid and knows that in these moments before dawn everything will change. That's what he wanted. That's why he stands in the darkness and the cold beneath that immense swirl of space.

But he better choose soon.

At last he moves. Leaning over like an old man, he picks up the sports bag at his feet. When he starts walking I can see the rise and fall of his chest. His breaths are shallow and rapid, but it's not from exertion.

It's cold. You can see his breath leaving his body as though the spirits – or perhaps demons - that inhabit him are fleeing.

Jake can smell the dust he disturbs as he walks. He turns around briefly as though he thinks he is being followed. There must be a breeze at his back. When he finally stops he looks down the tracks to the east and the west. Straight, as far as the eye can see.

He opens his bag and rummages past the ecologist's tools – notebooks, camera, collection bottles, fake business cards - an employee of one of the big environmental consultancies - until he finds what he needs. He begins to work quickly. The welding hood, the torch, the small bars of steel.

The flame and sparks from the welding torch fly into the pre-dawn air. It feels almost peaceful now. He has chosen, but he's not at peace. Fear tears at him. Every few seconds he looks up, looks around, expects terrible. The fear is simple and real; the risk of years in jail, losing Julie and losing all the comforts of his middle-class life.

I don't know that I share his motivations – although we share much – but I won't condemn him. Passion is easy but the courage to act isn't. If a train full of coal ends up on its side like some rough beast, so be it. What others call terrorism may well be an act of humanity, a fight for something that is necessary and right. I won't sit in judgement, not for this.

Not that my judgement matters one iota.

*

He chose to work alone, thought it was safest, thought the only person he could trust with his life, the only person he would ever ask to help him was Julie. And he knows she wouldn't do it. So he told no one, asked no one, not even Julie.

I didn't agree with that either. She's special to him and he is about to become a man who sabotages rail lines and that part of him is going to be hidden from her. Risky. Risky to tell her too, I guess, but I'd rather he told her than have her find out once he's behind bars. Jake did all his research in a library, avoiding the temptations of the internet. It was kind of funny watching a young man learn to use a library. He felt so stupid. He blushed every time he asked the young woman behind the counter a question. You could see she wanted to laugh, but only because she liked him.

He bought all the equipment he needed from private sellers found in the trading post – the hard copy. Hilarious, I don't think he'd ever searched for anything in a trade paper before. He never took off his sunglasses and hat when he was buying something and he introduced himself as Phil – his grandfather's name. He was probably being overly cautious.

I admire him. I said that already. Maybe I envy him too. I once took such a large step, but not by choice.

He is afraid in this moment of what he is about to do. Afraid of failure, afraid of being caught. He's afraid it will make no difference what he does, that humans will decide that killing the planet is okay and continue to hurtle towards oblivion. Afraid that he will never be able to have children. He aches to share these thoughts with Julie and can't stand to imagine what the world will be like in ten years or even five.

He has these recurring visions of a Mad Max future in which desperation, displacement and fear have become the norm.

Ironically, I don't think he would be doing this if it wasn't for Julie. Not that she knows or would approve, but she has slowly defused one form of his anger and strangely released another – colder and more conscious and ruthless.

He would come home after work in a rage. First occasionally, then all the time. He took everything to heart; it all became personal for him. He had no off button. Asylum seekers, education policy, the war in Syria, approval of a coal mine. The environment first and most. That's his work after all. Trying to end the age of coal for a non-profit green group. Every day, he saw how little was done, how little changed, how little anyone with power cared, what a struggle it was even to be heard. He watched the industry pay for 'science' that said climate change isn't happening or it isn't caused by humans or the models are wrong, any foothold of doubt, and his anger became bigger, more unruly, never left him alone.

Julie knew that it wasn't directed at her. She held him or sat with him on the sofa and stroked his leg with her bare foot. She sometimes simply started talking about her day at the childcare centre.

"You should have seen Liam today. He walked in with this crazy big strut and announced that he is the President of the World." Or how one of the finches ate seed out of her hand today. "Just one, but the others all watched. There were six of them on the railing, watching."

"I hate birds that don't get involved," Jake said and they both laughed.

She tucked her bare feet under his bum. They were drinking wine and you could see the anger had drained away and desire took its place, slow and intimate.

That opened the door to a thinking anger. Julie didn't see it and he tried never to show it. So, in a way, it was, is, her love that has brought him here as much as his fear. His love too. He has become so determined to protect her, determined to give her a world better than the one he sees.

He can't speak of it because it is so clichéd. Heroic man saves woman who is the love of his life. But the embarrassment doesn't mean he doesn't like the idea.

I don't understand this young man. He is my blood, but I don't understand a fear – and a passion – that is about the whole world. And I don't even understand a love so profound that he would die for this woman. I don't understand his devotion to work and environment organisations that he believes are doomed to fail.

Actually, I understand that part. They are his tribe.

My tribe was the militia. My mother's tribe was the religious nuts who thought the fracturing of our country and the signs of an imminent war were the beginning of the End Times. She never left the house during The Siege. She closed the curtains, read the Bible and waited. I was rarely home, but she didn't need me anymore. She died in the shelling that destroyed the building – a house she hadn't left for six months.

*

Jake moves down the track, several hundred metres or so, welds, and continues on. He stops often. He thinks he hears a car or a plane. He checks the time again and then again. He is just holding it together. He is heading east towards dawn. It is still dark but sunrise is soon and the light even sooner. He will be a shadow on the tracks, visible if anyone is looking. Twenty minutes, max, he thinks. He starts working more quickly. He lifts the visor and sweeps his arm across his brow. Sweating. Fear. Now there is enough light to see clearly what he is doing. Welding bars of steel to the track, the sparks disappearing into the pink sky.

He finally removes the hood, walks back up the track towards his car. Nice looking lad, even with all that tension in his face. Dirty brown wavy hair, kind of careless, deep set eyes, dark and intense. He bites at a corner of his lower lip. He looks north, finds the small grove of trees where his car is hidden, finds his bag, stores his gear and pulls out his phone. He puts a handkerchief over the handset, calls 000 and asks for the police in a very deep voice with a mild and somewhat muddled eastern European accent. "I am from The Free Radicals. We have just sabotaged East West rail line between kilometre 247 and 252. I suggest you urgently stop coal train that is due to pass in exactly 60 minutes, otherwise it will derail. There are 10 points along the line you must find. Do you understand these instructions?"

He listens. "I ask if you understood?" He finally nods, hangs up, removes the sim card, rubs the phone down with the handkerchief and then pounds it into tiny pieces with a stone. I like the way he does that. There is no anger there, no hurry, just business. I realise as I analyse his every move how scared I am too. He buries the pieces in the soft sandy soil and walks rapidly to his car.

He changes his clothes and stows his bag in the boot. If he is stopped he will look as though he's on his way to work. Careful man. He drives at the speed limit. Now you can see the tension in his hands gripping the steering wheel. He has put on some music, it's classical, maybe Bach, something soft, to keep him calm. A part of him is expecting the sound of sirens any moment.

A press release is scheduled to go out to all media outlets in about ten minutes. He has made sure that it is routed through several IP addresses and will look as though it is coming out of Russia or somewhere. The Free Radicals First Strike Against Climate Criminals.

It's pretty clear what happens next. A high-profile investigation, of course. Promises from the political sector that no effort will be spared in stopping eco-terrorists. Then there will be the broader demands for cracking down on those green extremists. More calls. It has been happening for years but this will accelerate the process.

Jake used to rage about this too – "We keep failing and they keep attacking us. I have no idea what they're afraid of." Maybe they are not afraid at all. They are simply demonising a powerless population because that is what they do best.

The laws will be made tougher. There will be heavier fines, even prison terms for protests and no doubt increased surveillance, less privacy.

He hopes some of his colleagues follow his lead. He expects the big groups to do nothing except criticise his acts, write more submissions, write more letters, sit on more committees, twitter and chatter and avoid hard choices. He's not sure what his colleagues in the Stop Coal and Gas movement will do. They are a grass roots movement opposed to fossil fuels that sprang up and grew rapidly everywhere in the country about 5 years ago, although little has really changed. This is the nub of it. Those who know they have won every battle but are still losing the war may decide that Jake's actions make sense.

Jake pondered the fallout, tried to calculate whether this step will have results that are more good than bad, and ultimately, he decided 'We can't win unless we begin to shake the tree.' For all his thinking, it came to this, sabotaging a rail line – and whatever else is next – with no real plan and no control.

He knows many of his colleagues still believe that their political leaders, their government, will do something, something rational, that engaging with a broken system is the way to fix it. "Be rational. We have a system of endless growth and endless exploitation, a system controlled by corporate interests whose only motivation is profit. We don't have democracy. Politicians shamelessly support coal and gas – they don't even pretend to care anymore. We're in the middle of the most severe existential crisis humans have ever faced and we're still approving coal mines, for fuck's sake," he cries out to the vast desert and his empty car.

It is a debate he has had many times now – both in his head and with others – and over the last year he has become more radical, more dogmatic, less forgiving and more adamant that the world of extreme capitalism must end if anything is going to change, ever.

He grips the steering wheel even tighter. "Remember Kyoto?" he says. "Remember our response – 'it's a good first step.' How many said that? Most of them. Us. And ten years later when the first step had become the last, activists turned away and worked on coal, or finance, or despaired and planted trees or convinced themselves that personal transformation was enough." He'd heard plenty of discussions about taking action – the kind of action he took today – but no one did it. All talk. All as scared – and comfortable – as he was. He is talking aloud again and driving faster as he gets louder. He finally catches himself, forty kilometres over the limit, and eases his foot off the accelerator.

CHAPTER 2

She sleeps curled on her side, her hand between her legs. He thinks this must be the shape of her dreams. Her dark hair tumbles across the pillow. The sharpness of her features – the clear line of her jaw, the aquiline nose, the narrow lips – can sometimes make her face look severe, although he never sees her that way. But when she sleeps she simply looks serene. He stares at her, his shirt still in his hand. He's not even thinking, just swimming in the idea of her, the love of her. He wants to wake her. He wants to slip into bed with her so quietly she doesn't even stir, to run his hand along her hip, slide down to her waist, between her thighs, he wants his touch to enter her dreams, gentle and sensual.

She begins to stir. He awakens from his waking dream and undresses quickly. He has been driving for hours and is knackered. Shower. Bed. Sleep. It's almost time for Julie to get up and head to work.

He told her he was going to be at the office last night painting banners preparing for a demonstration at Parliament and that he might spend the night there.

The water washes over him. He expects a moment of release, when all the tension of the last few days drains from him and his legs go rubbery and he feels elation, terror, collapse...something dramatic. Instead, he thinks about lying to Julie. How easy it was and how much he hates it. How he is going to have to lie to her again and again if he keeps doing this. "By any means necessary," he says aloud, but he knows that isn't true. He isn't and will never be ready to sacrifice her.

It would tear her up if I told her, he thinks. She would think it's about her, that I don't love her enough, that love isn't enough. "That's such crap, Jake,"–' he says aloud to the misted mirror in the shower stall. "You don't tell her because it puts her and you at greater risk, and because you're afraid that she would leave you. You're prepared to risk prison but not prepared to lose Julie, even if it means lying to her."

"Jake, that makes no sense. You have some work to do here. You say you love her and believe she loves you, but you don't trust her."

"I do."

"Then tell her."

"I can't. She'd never forgive me for risking her life, her happiness as well as mine."

"Well, then you're in the proverbial, mate."

The water flows over his forehead and across his lips. He stands utterly still, like a stone on a river bed with the water rushing past him. In a million years he will be nothing more than a million particles on the bottom of a river flowing to the sea. Even that is no comfort.

He can already feel the reality of the rail lines slipping away from him. Parts of the landscape – a termite mound, a tree, the smell of the dry desert air, the whirring of cicadas – are beginning to lose their clarity. Even if he remembered everything, it would feel as though he is forgetting, as though his presence there wasn't real, as though he is allowed to disappear from the scene, even if it leaves him with a kind of terrible emptiness.

He is sure that if he rubbed away the fog on the mirror at this moment he wouldn't even see his own face.

Jake awakens unsettled. His sleep was brief and his dreams, although he doesn't remember them, were crowded and threatening. Julie has gone to work. It is close to noon and he isn't used to the midday light splattering across the bed. He switches on the news. It's there. The lead story. Thank God, he thinks. It was a dread that he never spoke – that they would ignore what he had done. There is an aerial photo of a rail line, somewhere. An interview with the police saying they've found the phone. Another with the head of the Minerals' Council, a despicable man, Colin Sect. He's creepy. A face Jake thinks that speaks of a life spent hurting others. The large lips have begun to droop, the eyes may as well be lidless.

Jake checks the online news. There is the usual yabber about terrorists and he has even grabbed the attention of the PM, whose comments are more of the same. Jake grows impatient. He's not sure what he is looking for, but he hasn't heard or found it. There is an online comment from one of the large green groups repudiating this kind of violence. There is little support for what he has done from what he can see. He expected that, but still he feels the first claw of disappointment. Perhaps he was hoping that this would immediately open the dam gates and out would pour the revolution.

The trains will be running again by late afternoon. He delayed a coal train for twelve hours. He risked, risks, ten years, more, in prison, for a 12 hour delay. He closes the computer and walks out to the verandah. He has risked everything for nothing, he thinks, knowing this is wrong but not knowing anymore what's right.

He hangs the towel on the verandah railing, making sure the ends are even, and waves to a neighbour about to get in his car. He vaguely watches the apartments being constructed across the road. Two of the builders in intense conversation. One pointing towards the skeletal structures and then sweeping his hand to his right. He washes the dishes, even makes the bed. He moves with a kind of steady but passionless determination to be doing something quotidian. He straightens the papers and mail on the sideboard, dusts the top of the bookshelf but nowhere else. He can't settle and he can't find words that explain the weird storm that is swirling inside him.

He finally sits with a coffee at the kitchen table and drinks with his eyes closed. He hums a song that he knows is Boulter but can't remember the title or the words. Something about wolves. When he opens his eyes he looks at his hands as though they might no longer belong to him.

Back to the computer. Brendan Sykes, a reporter for Fairfax, has posted a number of stories. Fairfax has more detail than any of the others and most are correct. He describes the welded pieces, how they are removed and the grinding of the rails to remove all traces and risk. He has spoken with the officer who took Jake's call and with some security expert who works for BHP talking about how the coal industry has been expecting this for some time. "We are well prepared for this, both in terms of protecting our investment and in terms of tracking down the criminals who attempt to use terrorist tactics to further their ideological extremism." Criminal. Terrorist. Extreme. Ideological. All in one sentence. Pretty good, Jake thinks. I wonder which company he's talking about?

Another story by Sykes is about the historical lack of radicalism – and complete absence of violence – in the environment movement, and how this act has apparently caught the movement by complete surprise. Jake feels a twinge of vindication.

Later there is footage of the police walking the rail lines searching for clues. Jake has a moment of panic – have I left something behind without knowing it? Stop it, he thinks. You need to feel nothing, intellectual curiosity but nothing more. When the police come – and they will – you must believe you had nothing to do with this at all.

There's no doubt that the media stories are only the tip of the efforts being made by the police. Jake assumes they have found where he parked the car, assumes that every bit of security camera footage is being watched, every worker at a petrol station that was open is being interviewed. He assumes wiretaps and computer intrusions are being arranged and that the police will start pulling in people for questioning. Jake prepared for all this. He knows the Federal Police will soon start to contact and interview some of the more hardcore activists, the ones they have been tracking for ages now. They infiltrated a number of groups many years ago, but Jake knows the police, the informers and the greenies are all in the dark, perhaps even panicking because they are clueless.

Finally, at around 2pm, Jake calls into work. Garth answers. "Hey Garth, I'm working from home if anyone needs me. Sorry I didn't call earlier – I kind of forgot." It sounds feeble to Jake, but Garth is elsewhere.

"It's gone a bit mental here, man. The rail line thing has all of us running around like chooks. The media calls every five minutes asking if we support violence. Sure, and revolution...and random executions. God, they are stupid."

Jake likes Garth. He is passionate and self-deprecating, cynical but still laughs. He has become a friend of sorts.

"Anything we need to do to hose this down a bit?" Jake asks.

"I think we're okay. Sean's pretty pissed off. He thinks this will hurt the cause. I'm kinda surprised it hasn't happened earlier, you know, and I'm kinda curious. Like, I think it must be someone I know, but I don't have a clue who, you know?"

"Yeah, I know, I've been running through names in my head since I heard and I have no idea who it is. Have the police been there yet?" Jake is amazed at how calm he feels.

"No, we're probably not highest on the list. Rachel told us all to go through our computers and make sure there is nothing there that we aren't happy for the police to see, because they are going to take our computers. Maybe not today and maybe not all of us, but all of us are potential targets and I guess we have to assume that everything we've ever said may well be read."

"Good idea – I hadn't even thought of it."

"It's a shit, really. I mean I found an email from five years ago where I wish some asshole politician dead and I start shitting myself. It might be easier to just throw the computer in the river."

"If they go after everyone who wants a politician dead, they'll have to arrest the entire country."

At some point, this is what it will come to. The point where we begin to censor ourselves and words that need to be heard are silent. I'm sure that it was Milos' words that killed him. He was my closest and last friend. He couldn't stop making jokes even as it became clear that words were becoming risky. He didn't like the Serbs and had one joke about a general that he told over and over again long after it had ceased being funny. And he didn't like the Bosnian Government either, formed when independence was declared. They were weak, appeasers. He made jokes about them too.

We told him to be careful. We told him we didn't want to be part of his rashness. He would make jokes about us then and we tried to pretend we didn't know him. A lovely, foolish man. Perhaps he understood more than we did that words matter and silence can be even more dangerous.

"I'm more worried that they'll use stuff like that to justify a witch hunt," Garth says. "You know. They find something we wrote, something stupid or exaggerated and we become suspects or they even arrest us just to intimidate us. This may be the excuse they have been waiting for."

Jake feels a dark weight move in him. He is afraid. He knows how ugly this can get. "Well, I better start clearing stuff off my computer too. Thanks Garth."

His computer is already sanitised. Days of sifting through the rubbish heaps of his electronic memory. He laughed at one point, thinking, thank god all this crap isn't stored in my head.

He sits and stares at the screen. He wonders if he is ready for whatever happens next. Ready for friends to be demonised. Ready for the internal battles. The work they do will be implicated as well. There will be deep divisions and serious attacks on organisations and ideas.

He thought he was ready, he had thought long and hard about every permutation he could imagine, every possible facet. Logical, analytical. He realises now that he is thinking about it emotionally and it is completely different.

You have to let it play out, he says to himself for the umpteenth time. You have to remember you can't control it and you're going to have to live with whatever comes next.

Jake can't stay away. He tracks the news even when he knows there is nothing there. Some craziness, particularly on social media, like the ones who blame the Chinese or the East Timorese and the ones who want to shoot all greenies. Anger, but a dislodged anger, anger at everything. Angry at government, angry at corporations, angry at the media, angry at being powerless, angry at being cheated in any way, angry that their sport team keeps losing. Angry angry angry. He knows the feeling. At some deep level, Jake knows this is what he wants to harness.

A few stations read out parts of Jake's media release, read out the part about coal and climate change and big corporations controlling our government, but intelligent discussion is in pretty short supply.

Jake knows this is pointless and goes back to work. Ten minutes later he is online again. Just checking.

In the early days of The Siege, we listened for any news that would allow us to make a decision to go buy bread, to brave the square or gather water. We listened too for signs that NATO would intervene, that the US would send us arms, that the Serbs had simply decided to go home. The news was never of any real use, was never true enough to rely on. We began to read between the lines even when there was nothing to read. At some point, we realised the news told us nothing. And so, then, we were afraid to act. The world was changing around us with unbearable speed and we had no good information to follow. Finally, we acted on instinct and the shards of information we had gathered from friends and neighbours. Eventually, we added experience to that mix. In a way, we were back to depending on each other.

There is an interview with the Minister. Predictably, he calls this an act of terrorism. He is blustering. He threatens cameras on every centimetre of track, promises mobilisation of the military if necessary. "They will be brought to justice and the coal industry, which is the backbone of our economy, will be protected."

CHAPTER 3

It's a bit like hole in your life. You're never sure how an absence of something can even exist and whether you can speak to it. Two weeks on and there has been no knock on the door, no phone calls. Jake was sure the police would at least talk to him. He wonders if he should have let the train derail. Was his action so soft that the police aren't taking it seriously?

The police did come to the office, questioned Tina and Garth – climate campaigners – confiscated four computers, all of which were returned within two days, and haven't been heard from since. Jake was meeting with the Greens and missed the fun. Garth said it was a pretty aggro visit. The police were clearly under pressure but were equally clearly working in the dark. "It was like they were angry at us because they didn't have anything to go on and the bosses were saying, 'go question someone, arrest someone, confiscate something'." Garth likes to shake his hands at the side of his head, an artefact of living in France for a year.

Two weeks and Jake's fear is beginning to move into the background. He and Julie are fine, all good, he pretends. He goes about his daily life as though his life is the same. It isn't. He needs there to be more. Weird, he thinks, I wouldn't be happy if they arrested me. Or took my computer or questioned me for 12 hours. And I'm not happy when they ignore me.

Impatient man. I suppose though when nothing happens, nothing changes.

He sits at his desk unable to face the documents in front of him – a long term strategy for coal ports, a submission he has barely started, a letter for supporters to sign demanding a stop to fossil fuel subsidies for Sahan. He is back at work – a funny way to think when he never left, but everything is different. Writing a submission is making him crazy. No matter what he says, or the entire movement says, the government will proceed with laws that will allow all the existing coal ports in Queensland to expand. But no new ones will be built. This is their version of protecting the Great Barrier Reef. Gas wells are still being approved, even though the companies pay no tax and have raised the domestic price to match that of the export price. A submission arguing against a conscious choice made by those in power isn't likely to make anyone think twice.

He wants to sleep. He wants to run out of the room screaming, 'There is no point, no point, no point in doing this'. Later, he tries to read the Department of Environment's paper on water management and coal mines. The words become glazed and slide off the page. At one point whole pages have gone blank, he is sure he can hear the words tinkling to the floor and breaking like meaningless baubles. He shakes his head and forces himself to open his eyes again.

He wants to tell someone what he has done. Not Julie, but a colleague, maybe Garth. Then he gets angry at himself, his neediness. He tries to turn his need into a virtue, shape it into an accusation, a challenge to others. 'Look, it can be done. I was terrified, but I did it.'

He doesn't see the irony or maybe it's the hypocrisy. His pride – or fear – is about what he's done not what he's accomplished. He often points out to his colleagues that they measure their so-called successes in exactly the same way.

*

He and Julie arrive early at Binna Burra. His suggestion to get away. The National Park is special to him, the place where his activism started. He still remembers the moment – sitting at the Gwongoorool pools in a kind of dream and realising that he had to do something to protect a small bit of suburban bush near his home in Brisbane that some developers wanted to raze. He was afraid then too, afraid of conflict, of stepping out of his comfortable world. A small group succeeded in stopping a small project. The ambition seems so small now, but it's how most of his friends became activists too.

It is cold up on the plateau. The mist is still slipping through the trees and the bird chorus just beginning. The rainforest feels stiller and more mysterious than in the full light of day. Jake begins walking as though he is being chased. He leaves Julie behind, not like him at all. He finally stops in a grove of walking stick palms. Something calmer there that slows him down, quieter too, muffled as though the trees are in quiet conversation, and the world around him has become attentive. He waits but doesn't go back up the path. Julie is a few minutes behind. I can see how upset she is, but she doesn't say anything. She just goes up to him and hugs him. She rests her head against his chest and there is a kind of fierceness in the way she holds him. He is stiff, like he expects something bad to come of this. He won't last a month without telling her. It feels like a myth of inevitable loss. One prophecy says that if he doesn't tell her, he will lose her and the second that if he does, he will lose her too. Which prophecy should he attempt to defy?

He finally returns the embrace properly. "Okay, Mr Votek, what was that about?" She gently unfurls from him, takes his hand and waits.

He looks around this grove of strange palm trees. "I was thinking about the decision yesterday to allow the clearing of the forest at Maules Creek for the coal mine. I heard Scott on the radio yesterday. They lie, you know. They just lie." Jake is lying now, although in a way it's true too. I can't tell if Julie knows this. Probably not yet, but she will. She will see it or feel it soon enough.

"Maules Creek? Jake that's not even something you're working on."

"But he keeps lying about everything. I was having this argument with him in my head, and I just started getting angrier and angrier and walking faster and faster."

"Do you really expect them not to lie? Ever?"

He rests his head against hers. I can feel how much he needs to tell her. "No, I don't expect different." And if I did, I wouldn't have sabotaged a rail line, he thinks.

He tries to pull himself back to this place and Julie, but there is this crazy swirl of stuff in his head, a leaf storm, a storm of frantic birds.

He didn't expect that it would be this hard in this way. It's there all the time. He's there all the time. Fear, or memory, or replaying conversations or waiting, or lying and then lying on top of earlier lies. His recent past crowds into his present like occupants of the Tower of Babel. And not only is he constructing a vast lie, he has to be afraid that it will fall on his head. Things fall apart. All the time.

Julie watches him. He has disappeared again, just gone, like that. Her eyes narrow when she's trying to make a decision and these lovely worry lines appear on her forehead. He doesn't notice. So self-absorbed. Pay attention man, this is the woman you love and you're going to fuck it up!

He takes her hand and they walk together. They are quiet. He is trying. She is worrying, knows there is something more. The wind moves at the top of the canopy. They stop at the creek, sit on a boulder with their feet in the water, touching. Julie starts talking about her work.

At one point they stop for a snack and several lyre birds appear. They are feeding in the undergrowth and are soon within meters of Jake and Julie. Jake watches them with an intensity and joy he hasn't felt in far too long. He and Julie remain so still they are invisible. When the birds disappear into the bush Jake's pleasure dissipates.

"Do you find it strange that a bird that is so poorly disguised physically is so well disguised vocally?" Jake asks in a distant voice.

Julie looks at him, again that look of, 'Okay, what's going on, what are you really saying?' "Are you sure they are disguising themselves vocally and not simply calling attention to themselves?"

He breaks into a smile and answers her question with a question. "Don't you think sounding like a chainsaw is a disguise for a bird?"

"Not if you end up attracting a logger."

He laughs loudly, then begins to cough.

Julie is quiet. She leans back to look at the sky.

CHAPTER 4

There weren't really turning points, simply a series of small events, small failures, small realisations that began to weigh more than Jake could carry.

Only several months ago Jake and the Green Earth team had worked on the campaign to stop banks financing coal. They'd gone after the ANZ and it had failed. The bank wasn't interested in changing its policies. It would loan to coal mines if it wanted and if the numbers held up. The public didn't leave the ANZ in droves. The campaign caught no one's attention or imagination and Green Earth struggled for a year, finally letting it go.

Even if it had worked, Jake knew it wasn't the main game. All the banks were going to keep lending to big coal – and anyone else – until bigger forces made them stop. Obviously, climate change wasn't big enough.

What does it take? he asked himself. And he had no answer. If the end of life as we know it, if planetary disruption and global chaos aren't enough to make us change, what the hell is?

It was like Sarajevo. If murder, mass rape, genocide and unimaginable brutality weren't enough to make the outside world sit up, pay attention and act, what was enough?

Jake wondered, as I did many years before, why this happens over and over again in so many different forms. 'This'. What is this? He asked himself. Is it silence? The capacity to deny the undeniable? Forget the unforgettable? Greed? Self-interest? A cultural blindness or delusion that we are all capable of? And does the capacity for denial, faith, belief and delusion all spring from the same well? He found no answers just the dark knowledge that it was wrong and humans could do better.

Then Jake had worked on carbon pricing in 2011 when the Labor Party was in power, only to see the price set so low that nothing would change – and it didn't. Then the government had changed, climate change had become a political poison, and the carbon price was thrown out because climate change was crap.

He and a number of others had tried to stop the climate movement supporting a carbon trading system. Markets were a lousy way to solve problems like these. Most problems, actually, Jake soon decided, but environment groups had supported it because they thought this was the only way a carbon price would be accepted. Jake became convinced that the politically feasible wasn't worth much anymore.

He worked on solar policy and ending the billions in fossil fuel subsidies from the Commonwealth. Tax breaks and special deductions, lost profits and 'interest' on company losses – nose in the trough subsidies and the government refused to eliminate a single one. He'd worked on the effects of burning coal on health and the reappearance of black lung disease amongst coal miners but realised quickly this was not going to change hearts and minds either.

He read everything, too much. He wanted to know even if the knowing gnawed at him. He still believed then that knowledge was power.

Hell, it isn't even truth anymore. And lies have become an accepted form of knowledge.

It was almost as dismal inside the organisation. At a climate team meeting in May, five of them crowded into one of Green Earth's windowless meeting rooms, the one with the lime green walls. Tina, the team leader for the climate campaign, spoke. "We have to come out strongly on this. A 5% emissions reduction target isn't nearly enough. I've been speaking with the other groups and we're going to call for an immediate 15% target and 25% by 2020."

"Shouldn't we discuss this first?" Jake said drily.

"I've discussed it with the CEO, already," Tina said.

"I meant with the climate team...You know, the folks around you who work on this issue. What's the science say? My memory is a 50% reduction in emissions by 2020 if we're going to avoid catastrophic climate change, and that's probably conservative."

"80% of all coal has to remain in the ground beginning now," Garth added.

"It's unrealistic, Jake. There's no point demanding something that is so far out of their head."

"I think there's no point demanding something that won't do the job."

"We'll just be irrelevant in the debate."

"We're irrelevant now – we should take the rational position and try and make it meaningful for government or business or even the public."

"Well, Jake, we're going with the other groups and those are the agreed targets."

Jake fumed. "I want to make it clear that I object completely to this approach and find your lack of consultation with your own team arrogant and divisive. You know what you're agreeing to? You're agreeing to a three, maybe four, degree rise in temperature. You're accepting an ecological and human catastrophe. Tell me how that's good strategy or something anyone should campaign for?"

Jake walked out of the room, out of the office, out into the street busy, noisy and dirty with cars, out into the late morning crowds from the Uni. He was trying to escape himself, but he had – and still has – no idea how to do that.

He eventually stopped dead on a street corner. He didn't know where he was but it looked different. There was a bicycle chained to a post box, a man wearing a gigantic hat that no one seemed to even notice. It looked all wrong. Why am I getting so angry? he asked himself.

Jake stood there at the corner. People moved past him. Some glanced at him – he was breathing heavily and his fists were clenched. I can't keep living this way, he thought, but at the time he had no idea what he meant or what he should do.

He looked at the bicycle again. He looked at a BMW illegally parked. He watched a truck pass spewing fumes, a shop filled with clothes and giant photos of what was supposed to be beautiful people. The noise of the street began to grow louder and louder in his head. He wasn't holding together very well.

"Hey Jake."

Jake turned to face the intruder. He slowly returned to earth.

"Hey." For a moment Jake can't find his name. "Hi Philip." At the time Philip worked at Earth Inc, a group trying to fit the planet into an economic model.

"You look like shit."

"Yup. And feel it too."

"I'm going for a coffee. You want one too?"

At first Jake just vented. Vented about the state of the world, about Tina, about failure.

"Do you remember Malcolm X saying 'By any means necessary'?" Jake asked.

Philip nodded.

"You have kids, right?"

"Yeah, two."

"Would you risk your life for them?"

"Of course." Philip had no idea where Jake was going but it was already clear he didn't want to go there.

"How much would you risk to save a species or the whole planet?"

"I don't know. I haven't really thought about it."

"Would you get arrested?" There is an intensity about Jake that was almost physically pushing Philip backwards.

"I guess."

"Would you put your home and job at risk?"

"I don't know. It depends, I guess, on what I'm doing and whether I'm likely to succeed. I don't want to lose what I have though."

"None of us do, I suppose," Jake said softly, "but it's happening anyway." And Jake's intensity slid away into a discombobulated silence.

"Are you okay?" Philip asked.

"Just wrestling demons. Sorry for being pushy."

They chatted then, mainly about Philip's work. Jake used to think that this idea of giving monetary value to the environment made sense, but no longer. Making everything about money was part of the bigger problem that he was beginning to see, even then, before he acted. It just makes nature into another commodity, he thought that day. He didn't say this to Philip then. He knew he was taking his anger out on someone who thought he was doing good. Jake felt sure that he was right and that too he didn't want to say. An idea not fully formed; an idea that would put him at odds with many of his colleagues. But he still felt it.

"Do you know the story of Cassandra?" he suddenly asked Phillip, once more determined to interrogate. He didn't even wait for an answer – as usual he presumed ignorance. "She could see the future but was destined never to be believed. Do you ever feel that way about what we do? We are seeing a future that is ugly and brutal if we don't change, but no one believes us, maybe not even ourselves."

Phillip stirred the small puddle of coffee remaining in his cup. "I don't know," he said. "I hate to believe we are somehow privileged with foresight or knowledge that doesn't belong to all of us, but sometimes I feel that way. I don't really want to be a keeper of knowledge."

"You mean, you hate feeling as though you know and the great unwashed are ignorant?"

"I suppose it offends my sense of equality, my sense that those who believe they keep knowledge are the most dangerous."

"Do you think what we're facing is ignorance or the learning given by a culture devoted to self and commerce?"

"They might be the same," Phillip said tentatively.

"Probably so. How do you get a whole people to strip that away when the culture that created it remains in place?"

"I don't know," Phillip said and it was clear to Jake that Philip had had enough of this interrogation.

"I better get back to work," Jake said. "Sorry, Phillip, I'm taking out on you a whole world of craziness that isn't your fault."

Jake watched as Phillip waved goodbye and left without looking back.

He remembers that encounter so clearly, months later. His struggles with anger and righteousness. He was aware that he was just alienating people, like-minded people, but somehow he was unable to stop. That awareness struck him for the first time that day. He remembers thinking, 'You clearly need to do this differently Jake – biting their heads off doesn't seem like a very wise conversion strategy.' Another small plank in the decision to act.

*

He'd worked on coal ports and the Great Barrier Reef, but it was clear that all political parties had decided these projects must be approved regardless of the effects. In May another coal mine was approved on some of the best agricultural land in NSW. Jake railed against the broader reality that the environment always lost out to growth and the same vacuous cargo cult claims about jobs, repeated often enough so that it must be true. He began to think, knowledge is whatever.

And all the while the renewable industry – where the jobs were – was being undermined, ignored and attacked.

When he repeated this litany of failure to himself, he kept asking why are we failing? Why at every turn do the forces of darkness win?

One morning Jake sat outside the office on the steps drinking a bitter coffee and watching the early morning life of a city when he suddenly realised the climate movement, or him, was making an assumption that was wrong – that the political debate was a space that could be contested rather than one already occupied and owned by corporate interests. An oligarchy, like Russia. A coaligarchy he thought.

That realisation sent a shock through his system. It percolated into his thinking. It was daunting and depressing but it explained many things. Power was never going to come through the current broken democratic system, he decided. The ruling elite and the political elite were the same elite and greenies had none of the traditional types of power – not political or financial power. Power has many shapes, though, he thought, and ours, if we want it, it is going to have to take another shape. He tried to say this at a Green Earth retreat in July. It was intended to be a celebration of the organisation's hard work and successes in difficult times. But Jake couldn't find a single success. Everyone spoke and said what had inspired them, or impressed them. Jake spoke last and spoke of failure. "Sure, let's celebrate our hard work, or celebrate the planet, but first we need to accept that we are not winning and to understand why."

That went down like an old iron boat. He could still feel it sitting on the rocky bottom of his spirit, a rusting hulk, home to more demons than fish.

Breathe in, he reminded himself and don't swallow the darkness.

CHAPTER 5

There were other things too in that crazy six months before the rail line. Jake and Julie wanted time away together and travelled north, up to the tip of Cape York. Magical, wild country. A place that reminded Jake of why he does what he does. They stayed in a small community, travelled out to islands to snorkel and make love. Sat in town and talked with everyone. Sam the fisherman and Ella the policewoman and Bill a real life croc wrestler.

One day, the third day, a large Islander man came and sat next to them on the pier. Jake said hello. Julie looked out to sea, not rude, just far away with a winged smile on her face. The man nodded, the slightest smile passed across his face. Finally, he said, "People have noticed you here. They have. They say, they don't fish, they don't hunt, they don't get drunk, they sit and talk as though they have all the time in the world. It can take a long time to learn that. They say you come out of love, so I thought I wanted to see you with my own eyes, this miracle!" He cackled, a great laugh. "I am Charlie. Charlie the Mayor. A distinguished citizen of a lost part of the world. Yes indeedy. I am Charlie," he said almost sadly. "I grew up here. In the town, yeah, but here too – right on this pier. Fished here, swam here, wrestled and cried and fell in love here. Got drunk for the first time right where you're sitting and fell into the sea. Middle of the night and I remember the trail of moonlight and I was there thinking 'That is the path, that is the path.' Except it went straight out to sea and I wasn't that drunk. Yes indeedy. Hey, you see that little island over there?" They followed his finger and only see sea.

They shook their heads. Neither of them has said a word yet.

"Right there. 100 metres out."

They looked again. There was nothing there. They began to think this man might be crazy.

"That's where I made love for the first time. Everyone did. Couples would swim across. It became a custom. People got married here, on the pier, and someone, a brother or sister or cousin would take a blanket and some food and flowers across by boat. Later the couple would swim across to make love for the first time or the second. It didn't matter." He paused, deep furrows in his brow. "Really low tides, you can see it still. Used to be there all the time. At first we thought it was sinking." He paused again. "What are your names?" They told him and shook hands. "We're pretty religious here. Christian, but it's never that simple. Lots of old beliefs all mixed up in here." He touches his temple with his forefinger. "Anyway, it started going underwater once in a while, high tide maybe, about three years ago. Five. We thought we were being punished. We thought God was taking love away from us. Some people still do." Charlie went silent, looking out to the island that was still there but wasn't. "Anyway," he says finally, "that's why I wanted to meet you folks. Some were saying you were bringing love back."

"Julie's pregnant," Jake blurted out. He so wanted Charlie's story to be true.

Julie blushed deeply and Charlie stood up, threw his arms out and bellowed "Halleluyah!" A smile as large as the moon on his face.

This is a hard story to think about now. They celebrated that night. Charlie organised a wild and wonderful party. Everyone knew Julie was pregnant by then and while it created a kind of mythical expectation of both of them they could do nothing about, it also opened up lives and hearts and created joy.

Julie wasn't pregnant after all. The home test was wrong, and they never saw the drowned island. But those days of love and imagined pregnancy and the story of the lost island were also part of Jake's decision.

CHAPTER 6

Jake stood at the edge for a long time not able to bring himself to act. Every rational part of him said there is no choice in this. If you believe that we are destroying ourselves and that the only ethical response is to try and stop the destruction then you must do something more. If you believe that it is the coal industry that is the biggest destroyer then you must act against them and the government that supports them. By any means necessary? No, he can't go that far. He rejects violence against others or taking up arms, although he has questioned even this.

He went to a rifle range one day, wanted to find out what he could do and what was beyond him.

Milos brought me a gun one day. He leaned forward in that conspiratorial and slightly caricatured way that he had and whispered, "I have brought you new powers." He smiled broadly. "Guess," he demands.

"An invisibility cloak?"

"No, no, no."

"A beautiful roast beef smuggled in from Italy?"

"I only wish I had one for myself."

"No more guessing, Milos."

"Very well, but you're a wet blanket," he says with great seriousness, reaches into his briefcase and hands me a handgun. I eventually took it. I was scared of it at first and hid it in the freezer.

I was a craftsman. I worked with woods, beautiful oaks and walnuts and ash. How did I come to have a gun? How did I come to use it? How did my hands, dedicated to beauty, come to this?

"I'd like to try shooting. I've never done it before," Jake said to Luke, the owner of the range.

"Rifle or pistol?"

"A rifle."

Jake shot at a target for almost an hour. He hated it. Hated the immediacy, ubiquity of the violence. The noise, the kickback, the thud of hitting a target. He hated too the thought of a weapon so powerful in hands that so often lacked wisdom or restraint. He was a terrible shot and I suspect he didn't care if he hit anything, he just wanted to get past hating it all. He couldn't make it banal. He decided then that he had no capacity for violence against people. I wanted to tell him he was wrong, we all do.

The first time I fired the pistol, I shot at bottles. We saw war on the horizon then. The second time I put down a dog that was hit by a car and was in pain. That was the last time I shot in a time of peace.

As Jake drove back to work, he knew he had decided to act. He didn't know what it looked like, except it wouldn't involve guns. It's as though in finding some kind of boundary he gave himself permission to act. That changed everything. Even before he mapped out what he was going to do or how he was going to do it, many other things changed.

He sat in a room full of friends and colleagues, like minded, smart, passionate and he was barely there. It was an anti-coal alliance meeting. Patrick stood at the white board, drawing out a strategy for making the health costs of coal a bigger political issue, taking advantage of the fire at Hazelwood coal plant and the reemergence of black lung disease in Queensland. He is tall and gangly and has a crooked smile. Patrick has this crazy visual mind and loves diagrams. Jake always struggles to follow them.

Jake met Patrick on a landcare project planting trees along the river in Oxley. Patrick loves soil, it's his passion. It has always made Jake laugh, which only made Patrick more determined to demonstrate that soil, not water, not air, is the stuff of life.

Ellie was there too. She was a doctor and gave it up to become an activist. She is endlessly surprised and offended by what happens in the world and she often laughs out loud. That day, she came in asking anyone, everyone in the room, "Did you hear Trump's election commitment? He wants to put a wall on the Mexican border. If only he knew – Mexicans would love a wall if it would keep the Americans out! He's going to win, you know the Americans are crazy enough. Then we can all take to the streets!" She plonked herself in a chair, looked around as though she was ready to take to the barricades right then, and finally, belatedly, said good morning and laughed at herself happily. She has two children and a Mexican partner and she never stops and never looks tired.

Garth was there and so was Simon, a surfer dude who plays the cello and doesn't seem to feel the weight of the world as Jake does. He works on the Sahan coal projects in Queensland – the mine and the port expansion – and the Great Barrier Reef campaign. He talks about the state of the reef report, the coral bleaching report and the water quality reports, all due to be released early in the new year, and the scientists working on those reports who are leaking information to him almost daily. "They are so pissed off," he says, "and they just give me whatever they've got."

These are Jake's friends and usually he was part of these meetings, heart and soul. He likes to argue and laugh and celebrate a sense of shared purpose. But on this day, the day he decided to act, he barely uttered a word. He must be so far below the radar that no one will ever even think of him when it matters. But he was also silent because he agreed with so little of what was planned and couldn't bring himself to say, 'You're wasting your time.' He had an inkling then, how big his decision really was. He knew he couldn't allow himself to become angry again, knew that he had to watch more carefully what he said and to whom.

Steve came up to him afterwards. "You all right, Jake?"

Steve organises the logistics for all the direct actions that they do and Jake doesn't know him well. Jake is surprised Steve has noticed his distance. So much for being below the radar.

"Yeah, I'm fine, a bit distracted." Jake didn't want to talk about it, didn't want to think about it. This sense of necessary isolation wasn't part of his plan either. He walked out the door, down Spencer Street with the smell of train fumes around him and he kept going until he landed at Mama Sapia's Coffee shop. He ordered a cheesecake and ate it without tasting a thing. He almost abandoned his half-formed plans for action right then.

That evening he opened his email to a barrage of pleas and cries and accusations. Rabbits scream! Elephants slaughtered. Lions, tigers, orangutans, wolves, giraffes, eagles, rays, sharks all going extinct. Stop Sahan. Stop torture. Eradicate ecocide. Stop Coal. Stop this train, I want to get off. He read these email headlines as though he was being bludgeoned. Every day there is more, he was sure of it. The extinctions, the declines, the misery, the desperation all felt endless, hopeless. He flinched when one screamed at him, 'Doesn't Jake care about asylum seekers?' Donate. Volunteer, Give, Help. Sign. We need you. Do more, do more, do more. Do it now. Urgent, urgent, urgent.

At that moment his spirit began to bleed, and he couldn't stop the loss, he may as well have been haemorrhaging. He couldn't read another email, he couldn't hear another plea for help, another disaster unfolding, another story about extinction, or methane or much of anything. He has been pummelled. He turned off the computer and walked down to West End. He tried to browse in a bookshop but he became too anxious. He worried that there are too many books and he can't even read the ones he has. He sat down at an outdoor café for a beer but the noise was unbearable. He walked around instead. Shards of conversations surrounded him – someone going shopping, someone talking about their father, their illness, their children, and nausea swept over him. He had no idea what was happening to him.

He went home locked the door and closed the curtains and crawled into bed with his computer. He sent money to save giraffes. Why giraffes? He doesn't even know the organisation.

He closed the computer again. Anger overwhelmed him. Then loss. Then anger. Then he began to cry. His tears were so sharp he was sure his face was bleeding.

His anger gnawed at him again. At himself, at the world, at the neediness of everyone, at the brutality of humans. An anger against the whole universe, against the big bang because none of this could be happening without that amazing confluence of events billions of years ago.

He believed at that moment that killing would be easy, that suicide would be easy. A reaction to powerlessness. In the absence of any other capacity, in the absence of any other power, he still had the power to cause harm. But the price will be high, he thought. It's a kind of madness and he may have already crossed a threshold to which he can never return.

He was asleep when Julie arrived home at 6. He called his doctor first thing in the morning and made an appointment. "It's urgent," he said. The doctor listened to Jake and then prescribed anti-depressants and anti-anxiety pills. The pills made his stomach churn like an old washing machine.

CHAPTER 7

Jake felt nauseous constantly. He went back to the doctor who ordered a suite of tests. All negative. He tried herbal remedies, he tried to meditate and failed. He became increasingly sensitive to noise and started complaining to Julie about the sound of cars, lawn mowers, leaf blowers, motorcycles, rubbish trucks, loud music in pubs. He couldn't control anything, even his own body. He remembered how in his first months as an activist, he stood up in a packed meeting room, terrified of speaking, and he confronted the council, the developer and his deep fear of conflict. That was easy compared to this.

He regularly woke in the middle of the night, a rogue anxiety haunting him.

He held onto Julie, sometimes woke her. He wanted to enter her dreams where he was sure it was safe.

Julie had seen this in children before, ones who are afraid of everything. She held him and wondered what he had unleashed inside himself and why.

The determination to act was now a way of saving himself as well. In fact, Jake increasingly believed that what was happening to him was because he wasn't doing what he knew must be done. It was now latched on like a limpet. He didn't yet know that he would sabotage a rail line but he knew he would do something.

He prepared a political strategy for the bills on a carbon price. He prepared a talk for a university course on renewables. But he wasn't really engaged. In fact, he could barely complete even the simplest of tasks. One day he visited a library for the first time in forever and went home with a bunch of books on resistance movements. Histories of change and violence, of dissent, silence, revolt. In all of them, those in power attack those who want change. Legal violence. The laws are changed to reduce rights, reduce public information, increase powers of the police, criminalise being a citizen. Arrests, detention, hate politics. Then it escalates to brutality against protests and protesters. Live bullets, torture, rapid deployment of riot police. Even assassination. He reads about the FBI trying to blow up a forest activist in the US in the 90s and then arresting her for carrying the bomb they planted. For much more than a moment he felt raw fear. He was entering uncharted territory. Almost inevitably, dramatic change only occurs with some level of violence in response. What do you do when those in power make it clear they won't change? It happens over and over and often ends in violence and chaos. Is there any way to avoid that? He looked at Ghandi, Malcolm-X, Stalin, Lenin, Nicaragua, Mandela, North Africa and tried to make sense of the disorder that seemed to be the norm in all of those histories.

Sean and Melaina came for dinner during one of those weeks and he spent the entire evening in argument with Sean about whether violence was ever justified. He had said he wasn't going to do this again, he needed to learn to be silent, but he couldn't hold himself back. The argument was too loud and he too aggressive. He knew that and kept going anyway.

Julie went to wash the dishes after they left. He sat alone for a few minutes, swirling in spaces without words, and then went in to help. "What was that about?" she asked without turning from the sink.

"What do you mean?"

"You spend the whole evening arguing with Sean. You don't talk to Melaina at all, you don't talk to me, you drink glass after glass of wine without even offering it to anyone else. You don't help clear the dishes...You want me to go on?"

He looked at her stunned. He had no idea he was wearing his craziness so openly. That scared him at first and then made him angry. He almost turned away and walked out.

"I didn't know," he said, quiet, ashamed.

Julie looked at him first as though that was the most pathetic excuse she had ever heard, but she stopped, saw something in him that scared her.

Thinking about it now, that 'I didn't know' was the first time he lied to her. Not a real lie, not a telling of an untruth but an untelling.

CHAPTER 8

Jake dreams that he is standing outside in the desert, that desert, and the stars are wheeling through space at high speed and they burn through him as they pass. He is in the path they must take, and with each passing another hole is burned through him. Time is chasing him, he thinks as he stands there unable to move on the red, star burned sand. Finally, he cries out as the stars approach him again. He doesn't know if what he feels is pain or fear. He opens his eyes. Julie stirs next to him. He holds his breath and he can feel and hear the sky drain from the holes in his spirit, an emptying that scares him far more than the charred spaces he feared a moment before. He whispers, 'Julie,' then stops and nestles his head next to hers. He can smell the sandalwood in her hair and the even breathing that slowly calms him. 'Don't wake,' he thinks, 'don't dream.'

He wakes later with another jolt, a single rail track piercing him, one violent point of light. He remembers the scratches on the track, cutting diagonally across the surface. What's that about, he thinks? What does it mean? He knows he saw them as he welded those weeks ago, but he didn't register how strange that was. He shakes his head, trying to clear his brain.

He stumbles out of bed and stares into the fridge. He can feel deep sea currents calling him. He imagines the sinuous dance of the dark waters becoming like a tarantella, a mad dance. A human bitten by a bitter divinity now feels the sting of madness and recklessness. He closes the door. Welding pieces of steel to a single track in the middle of nowhere seems awfully small. He feels awfully small. His hand is still on the fridge door but he is whirling through the dark, feeling the rush of the desert wind and the starlight again piercing the carapace of his spirit. Emptiness and chaos both.

He remembers the rest of the dream. He was welding. When he began to weld, the stars and the sparks began to merge and then Julie was there, watching him. Her expression was...odd. Oddly indifferent and distant. She then became airborne, drifting upwards, a look of terror on her face. She tried to speak but couldn't. Her hand moved towards him, but way too slowly. He reached out to catch her, her feet just beyond his fingers. And disappearing she closed her eyes, surrender.

How can I go down this path and expect her to stay with me? he thinks. I will leave her behind. She will leave me. She will see me disappearing into a world she doesn't even know I occupy and she will know I am somewhere else. She already does. She can't find me, can't rescue me, can't help me. I can't take her with me unless I tell her but if I tell her she will never come. This is a step too far. She doesn't have the anger I do. She shares the ideas but not the anger.

She works in a pre-school. She finds joy in children. She hears the stories of neglect and violence and breakdowns, but it is the joys of these children that she absorbs and holds in her spirit. I once felt that way too, he thinks. It was the beauty of nature and wildlife that was a constant source of joy, the source of his will to fight as well. And slowly that anger has crept over him like a shadow. It's hard to stop fighting. She is sleeping on her side, her hands touching each other, intimate, in a way. She will leave me, he says aloud.

He dresses quickly and rushes out into the dark, walks down Amis Street, barefoot and weeping. Should I undo this, forget this, start over but not this way? Should I leave now and try and disappear into an underworld where I can fight the forces of darkness alone? How could I not have thought about these things? He berates himself. He thought so long, so hard, so deeply, tried to imagine every step, every permutation. He learned what he needed to learn and how to learn it. He chose a target well and wisely, did his work quickly and safely. He had so many conversations with himself where he asked whether this was a necessary or ethical or useful thing to do, but somehow he missed this giant part of his life, glossed over it, perhaps thought, 'We're in love, we'll be fine'. He sits on the side of the road beneath a gum tree that glows in the starlight and he doesn't know what to do. Julie, he thinks, when we walked last month in the rainforest, I didn't speak about the ache that such beauty gives me. I remember looking at the buttress roots of a tree so tall I couldn't see over them. I ran my hand along that winged root and felt the pulse of the entire forest. He knows how close it is to what he feels for Julie.

He can suddenly hear the wind pressing through the trees above him. The leaves begin to swirl around him. He catches a faint smell of coffee and a distant smell of rain. For a brief moment he thinks that the swirling in his head has brought the wind and that the wind will then carry him somewhere else, somewhere different.

*

He met Julie on her way to Trieste. She boarded the train in Venice and sat opposite him. That was seven years ago. She was occupied with her book, a novel. He can see the cover but can't remember the title. He was reading a textbook and trying to make sense of the doctrine of estoppel. Who travels with a law textbook? He is muttering to himself.

"What makes no sense?" she asks.

"Excuse me?"

"You just said, 'This makes no sense'. I was kind of curious." She smiles fleetingly. "I think I like things that make no sense."

"You should study law then."

"I don't like big things that make that no sense," she laughs. "Little mysteries will do."

"So, you've never had the inclination to explore the mystery of estoppel?"

"Never even heard of it. It took me long enough to figure out that torts weren't always cakes."

"Well, it's no accident that torts and torture come from the same root."

"What root is that?"

"I don't know. I just assumed they both meant torture."

"Maybe tortellini has the same root too. A torture of tortellini. And what about tortoises?"

"Hang on, I have to look this up." It doesn't take long. "Tort and tortellini and torture all come from the word for twist or distort."

"That explains tortellini. I think tortoises are safe though."

They liked each other right away and talked until he left the train only 20 minutes later. But neither of them was brave enough that first time to suggest seeing each other again. Both accepted that this is the nature of travel. Passing ships and all that.

They run into each other again two weeks later in Verona. They had dinner and the next day walked the city together. They meant to do the tourist thing, but they just walked. They were lost within minutes and didn't care. They laughed, practiced their bad Italian, stopped in squares and watched the world with a sense of shared joy. Just this once, Jake thought, I'm going to believe in destiny. Julie doesn't need such words.

They started to travel together and haven't been apart since.

CHAPTER 9

Julie is American, or was. She grew up in Arizona in a deeply Catholic and conservative family. She was the only child, her birth so difficult that her mother couldn't bear children ever again. Her parents blamed her for this violation of God's law and their conservative, narrow and strict demands were coloured by an anger and resentment that Julie only understood years later. The church was the centre of their community and the source of their knowledge and perspectives – often angry and racist. Julie's best friend in high school was black and an atheist, a mild rebellion perhaps, but one her parents refused to accept. Her parents tried to end the friendship, becoming increasingly autocratic and insistent that it was Julie's duty to obey. She argued, fought, rebelled and eventually conformed until she found a job at age 15, finished high school by correspondence, and aced the college entrance exams. She was offered a number of scholarships and finally decided on Middlebury College – progressive, demanding and about as far away from her parents as she could get in the continental US.

When she graduated with a degree in psychology she went to Europe. It felt like an almost obligatory rite of passage, but in meeting Jake she found the final thread in a liberation that was too long coming.

Not once did her parents seek her out, call, visit, or even write, and Julie was determined not to make the first move knowing her parents would see it as a sign she was ready to capitulate.

When she agreed to come to Australia with Jake, she finally wrote them, explained that she no longer believed in God, could no longer accept their views of the world, was living with a man and moving to Australia. If they wanted to get in touch, they had her email, but she never heard a word.

CHAPTER 10

Ian sits at his desk reading a journal. Since he retired, he forces himself to read, write and prepare articles for publication, at least an hour a day, often more. Often, he just stares off into space. A lifetime as an economist and too often he struggles to make sense of even the language of economics now. It's not as though the concepts have shifted much since Keynes, he thinks, but it's as though the discipline is now intended to serve an ideology more than it once did. Jake is coming soon for dinner. He would probably argue that point. Economics has always served ideology, he would say. Maybe true but it once also had ambitions to understand how this part of the human world works.

"Ian, hon, could you help me in the kitchen?" Mary is growing forgetful, and she is asking for his help more than she ever has. It's strange that Ian doesn't see this change in her no matter how often Mary asks the same question or misplaces the same object.

"On my way."

She said to him recently in her very proper and succinct way, "I don't really like asking you for help, but I do tend to think I'm entitled after all this time, don't you?"

That almost made him weep, although he gave nothing away. "Of course, I do. And it's long overdue."

"I can't find the saffron anywhere," Mary says.

"What's it look like?" Ian asks.

"Don't you know what saffron is?"

"Of course, but I want to know what the container looks like."

"Oh, sorry, dear. I think it's a small plastic box. Smaller than a matchbox."

He rummages amongst the spices. They were once orderly, now some of them are on the spice rack, some on the shelves, some in bags in drawers. He doesn't try to make sense of this either nor does he consider straightening them up himself. "What are you cooking?"

"A paella. Do you like paella?"

For someone who hates forgetting anything himself, he avoids recognising her forgetfulness with deep discipline.

"I love paella, particularly yours."

"I'm doing chicken paella not seafood. I hope that's okay."

"It's the chicken paella I love, sweetheart."

It's not in with the spices and not out on the counter already. He finally finds it in with the matchboxes and small screwdrivers and an odd assortment of nails.

"I found it my love. That's probably my fault. Can I help with anything?"

"Is Julie coming too?"

"Yes, she is. It will be nice to see her. She has been too busy lately."

"Oh, that's good," she says and then returns to her cooking as though Ian isn't there.

Ian sits back at his desk, a neat mess, and stares out the window. He is a bit adrift and a bit sad. His career disappears from him. His status – such as it was – diminishes. He stares at the paper on the top of his reading pile. Yet another economist grapples with the financial implications of climate change. He stares at the title: Externalising the Planet: who pays for climate change and how. Climate change is another reality Ian doesn't recognise. He tells himself that the models are flawed, that the system is far too complex to understand with models. They keep getting big things wrong. He hangs onto these holes – real or imagined – with a kind of grimness that is out of character. Jake has accused him – nicely – of being a conservative, over-educated, ageing, white male stereotype. He wonders if he is losing sight of things he once would have allowed himself to see.

The lawn needs mowing, he thinks instead. The empty lawn that is never used. Maybe I should cover it with gnomes. Peta and Jake used to leave their toys everywhere. He always yelled at them to clean them up. In those days he often yelled. Today he can't figure out why. It's just an empty lawn. Snap out of it, Ian, he thinks.

He hears the car before he sees it. It's labouring up the hill. Jake and Julie haven't come by in what seems like months. They lead their own lives, he knows, but he still feels the resentment of someone who no longer has a centre to his life. He wants them to want to spend time with him – not out of obligation but love, interest, intellectual curiosity. But that doesn't bring them here very often.

He scans the news on his computer and then shuts it down.

He stands slowly. Aching everywhere. Nothing damaged but everything hurts. He isn't prone to complaint, but there is much about ageing that he doesn't like.

"A Bosnian Serb was convicted today of genocide," Ian hands a glass of wine to Julie. "Did you know I was Bosnian too – a Croat though?"

Julie nods, "Jake told me, but that's about all I know."

"Me too," says Jake with a laugh.

"I was born Ivan and changed my name as soon as I got to Italy. I left Yugoslavia, Sarajevo, before Tito died and it broke apart. I hardly ever think about that time. I've never really wanted to remember, but today," Ian drifts away for a moment. "Do you remember me yelling at you Jake for leaving your toys on the lawn?"

Jake nods, concern and curiosity both apparent.

"It just got me thinking." His voice peters out again, as though his past is not a comfortable place for Ian. After a brief silence, he suddenly says, "I had an uncle named Tarek. I last saw him when I was five, I think. I don't know what happened to him. My earliest memories are of him. He used to do silly magic tricks. Pull lollies from our ears. I remember his wonderful bellow of a laugh and these gigantic hands he loved to clap together. He was a woodworker and a merchant. He made me a wooden top once. God, I haven't thought of that in ages. There are others in the family that kind of disappeared from view too," he adds quietly, almost an afterthought. And again, he slips into silence.

That is the most Jake has ever heard his father talk about his origins and some of its demarcations, almost ghostly. It is the first time Julie has heard about his background or name. It is the first time I have heard Ian mention my name in more years than I can remember. It has been a long time since I laughed as he remembers. Jake stares at his father. He has never asked his father a single question about his history, not one. It was off limits, or so he always thought in the remote way that children process the silences of their parents.

"Did you have family that went through The Siege?" Jake almost blurts out.

Ian looks almost alarmed at the question and doesn't answer it. "I know almost nothing about The Siege."

"I don't either, that's why I was just, sort of wondering, you know, were your parents..." Jake see how shaken Ian is and stops. "Are you okay?" Jake asks. Mary too is looking at Ian with a rare intensity. She then stands and quietly goes to the kitchen.

"I didn't follow it. I don't know if Tarek was there. Or anyone else. I didn't want to know." Ian speaks with his head down, almost whispering.

Jake looks at him keenly and with a look of concern, maybe compassion too. "Like with climate change?" The question is asked so gently that Ian knows immediately it is not Jake provoking him. But he still answers as he would have if provocation had been intended. Or because he wants to change the subject.

"I pay attention to climate change, I just don't believe it's caused by humans or that it is the apocalyptic crisis you claim."

And it's on again.

"Are you disputing the reality of greenhouse gases? Or that the build-up of carbon dioxide is caused by humans? Do you dispute the carbon cycle? We know that the system is being destabilised, the evidence is now irrefutable. And we know, as surely as they knew in the Warsaw Ghetto that the time for dying will come. And it will be much worse than...anything."

"I certainly question that conclusion and I think comparing climate change to the Holocaust or even war is just offensive. This 'crisis' is based on models – not Nazi's going from house to house dragging people from their homes."

Julie takes Jake's hand beneath the table. These debates with his father tear at him. He invites them and then they tear at him. There is no animosity, but his father is always so certain, so immovable. So is Jake, but he doesn't see it that way. Facts are facts he thinks, but he knows that his father's denial is not so simple for him or his father.

"Dad, people are already dying because of this. And you have to remember it's an incredibly complex system, with feedback systems we are desperately trying to understand. But we still know a thousand times more about the inputs than you do in any economic system. With each year of data, the models get better – unlike in your field, they actually improve."

Jake stops and squeezes Julie's hand. He tries to find some calm – he feels his own precariousness. Long true with his father, but now more true in the rest of his life.

"Natural variability is part of the system. This has always happened. It just feels like a religious argument... The end is nigh, repent and all that stuff, before it's too late. It's a post-modernist, post-Christian apocalyptic vision that isn't convincing."

Jake doesn't want to argue anymore. At least not tonight. He knows neither of them will change their minds. But if he can't change the mind of a smart, caring man whom he loves, what hope does reason have out there in the world of commerce, greed, affluence and comfort?

"How about we go help Mary in the kitchen," Julie says quietly. "You can continue this later if you both want to, but it doesn't seem like you're enjoying it very much."

What a strange look from Ian. He glances at Julie, as though she is an intruder. As though she couldn't possibly understand the pleasure he takes from such debates. He doesn't look at Jake, doesn't want to know what Jake feels. Ian believes what he says, and he doesn't realise, even unconsciously, that he is ripping at Jake's spirit in ways that would horrify him if he knew.

Jake just looks tired. He has planned his second event, but he has been putting it off for weeks, refusing to even think about it. He has known from the beginning that a single sabotage would never be enough to bring the kind of changes he is demanding. But I feel his ambivalence. I want him to go. I want him to stop. I don't want him in limbo. Could he go back now to the life he had? I think so, but I'm not sure. Not sure he'd survive the self-loathing that can come from giving into fear or failure. I never had the chance to find out.

He stands and Julie follows. "I wish we could hear more about his time in Yugoslavia," Julie says quietly.

"Sorry. My fault. And I would too. He speaks of it so rarely. And I never ask. It has always felt off-limits."

Mary is in the kitchen poised over the pan. Her head keeps dipping down and turning. "Mum, what are you doing?"

Mary breaks out laughing, almost a giggle. "Don't worry, I'm listening to the paella."

Julie joins the laughter.

"Excuse me?" Jake says.

"She's listening to the paella, of course," Julie says smiling at Jake.

He's missing something. "Could one of you mirthful souls please explain?"

"I have no idea," Julie says, "it just seems funny."

"Well," Mary says and then stops and turns the pan 180 degrees on the burner. "I forget what this stage is called but the idea is to brown the bottom of the rice and I have to listen for the sounds of crackling rice which is different from the sound of the water bubbling. I can't let the rice burn."

She finally turns it off, removes the oven gloves and turns to them.

"He said more about Sarajevo tonight than I've heard in almost all our years of marriage. It kind of scares me."

"I stupidly made it about climate change and we just had the same old fight."

"I think he's struggling with retirement. And spending so much time with me," she says quietly. "I'm so forgetful. His past is a touchy subject."

"Within a year of moving to Australia, he was offered a position as a lecturer in the Economics of Eastern Europe. We met that same year. You know, it was the first long term relationship he had ever had. Me too. We didn't really fall in love, we kind of slid towards it until one morning we awoke and in bed next to us was a person we loved deeply and fully. It happened that way for both of us." Mary smiles from far away. "It was never a crazy young love but more like two trees whose roots and branches became lovingly entangled over years.

"But he still wouldn't talk about his past. We used to argue about it. I wanted to know where he came from, who he was. He wouldn't go there. Then we'd argue about what he was hiding or still running away from. Well, we didn't really argue, we never really argued. I wanted to hear his history and stories and he didn't want to speak of them. And that's kind of where it began and ended. I heard a bit but kind of gave up on learning more. That feels like such a long time ago now. We both just moved on."

"There are much more interesting stories to tell," Ian says from the doorway. "You're wrong about you. I love spending time with you sweetheart and you're not as forgetful as I am. I forgot Milton Friedman's name today, Jake will be happy to hear."

"Who?" Jake asks and they all laugh.

"That smells fantastic," Ian says. "Is Peta still coming?"

"She said so, but she always seems to have trouble getting away from work."

Peta is Jake's older sister. It amazes me that the whole family lives in the same town. I am a child of yet another diaspora, I guess.

When Peta arrives, she drops her bags at the front door. It sounds like they are filled with hubcaps. "Mark is a complete asshole and that's all I want to say about it," she says, her voice ridiculously loud. She hugs Ian. "Julie, I'm so glad you've come. Maybe we can talk about something interesting like cricket and stop these two blokes from waging intellectual war that is neither bloody nor bloody interesting. How are you, my brother? You look more like my father every day."

Jake holds her a bit tighter and a bit longer than usual. Peta gives him a look. She lives and acts loud, but she has a very fine radar. This is the first time Jake has seen Peta since his welding 'event'. For a moment, Jake thinks she knows.

"Tea is ready, Peta," Mary yells from the kitchen. She doesn't do loud nearly as well.

Dinner tonight is a bit more jovial than usual. Peta is in fine form. She tells why Mark is such an asshole. Peta has a pierced lip and hair dyed black. She's not quite punk but close enough to startle those she works with. "I have no excuse," is her one and only answer when she's asked why she became an accountant. She would probably say the same about her piercings and hair. Mark is her boss, a partner in a small firm that does accounting and financial advice. "I was doing an audit for one of our bigger customers and Mark comes and stands in the doorway. He finally asks if I'm working on the Barnett account. 'Yes, and if you really want me to get it done today, it would be best to let me work, because I'm leaving at 5. I have a date and I'm not going to be late.' He went away. Then he's back ten minutes later. At least this time he had a folder in his hand. 'Did you check all those deductions? I'm a bit worried about some of those.'

'You can do it Mark, I'm not precious.'

"No, no.' he says, 'I just wanted to check.' Out he goes again. Ten minutes later, he comes back, but this time I'd moved into the conference room. When he found me – bloody Fiona told all – he said, 'Don't do that.' I couldn't believe the jerk was actually angry. 'Mark, piss off.' I told him. He stood there for a minute. Then he sat down, opened the folder and pretended to work. I suddenly thought, maybe there's more to this account than I know. 'So, Mark, is there something you need to tell me about this account? They straight? Or do they do a bit of cooking?' I even winked at him. Asshole. He looked at me in terror. 'I better get back to my office,' I said. 'It looks like you have a meeting.' He didn't follow me again, but I made sure I finished the damn audit before I left. I didn't make it by 5. Sorry."

"Did you find anything interesting?"

"No, I didn't really care to look too closely. Dodgy is so normal."

Jake sits at the table but he is hardly there. He doesn't speak and often looks away, out the window or down the hallway or anywhere but here. He was here a few moments ago, but once again he has disappeared. Julie sees it, of course. She wants to be alone with him and make him talk. She's not the jealous type but it passes through her mind that maybe he's having an affair.

Jake is quiet all through dinner.

When dessert comes, Ian makes a gentle attempt to engage Jake. "I heard Plimer on the radio today. He said you're in it for the money."

Jake looks up from his plate. "Plimer's an idiot." His tone is flat and hard.

Ian is kind of startled and says nothing more. Jake returns to his ice cream, head down and perhaps a bit embarrassed.

Mary begins to fuss. She knows that something isn't right with Jake but doesn't know how to deal with it so she rushes to the kitchen, emerges empty handed and distressed. She goes back into the kitchen and Julie finds her there at the sink just watching the water run.

"I don't know what's wrong with him, Mary," Julie says and breaks out crying.

CHAPTER 11

Ian sits in his office and stares at a paper that he has been reading for twenty minutes without completing the first paragraph. He sits up straighter in his chair, brushes his hand over his head and takes a deep breath, but it's no good. As soon as he starts to read, he thinks of his time in Yugoslavia. When he mentioned me earlier tonight it's as though an attic door opened in his head and out wafted memories, histories, words and scenes. What he doesn't know pours out too. He doesn't know what happened to his sister or parents or all his various relatives. This is his distress. How can he not know even whether they are alive? Why does this suddenly, out of nowhere, feel like such extreme neglect? He wonders. For 40 years I didn't care, at all, not even a little, and now I feel as though I've committed a crime.

He assumes his parents are dead. They were separated when he left, both bitterly angry with each other and both determined to enlist their children as allies. He saw them rarely in his last years there. I saw them rarely too.

The last time I remember seeing Ivan was when I was thirty-five and Ivan was five. He was a funny boy. I taught him to swim in the local pool and I remember him standing on the edge of the pool with his hands together stretched in front of him, yelling at me, "Watch Tarek, watch, I am going to fly across the pool." He would jump in and each time he would swim, then swallow water then begin to sink and I would pull him out. Ten minutes later he would do it again. Is this what economists do?

I wonder if he remembers this? I left Sarajevo for many years and lived in Zagreb. I came back now and then but Ian had already gone. I didn't see him again until well after my death, until I was attached to Jake, almost five years ago. The last time I saw my brother Josip, Ivan's father, was before the Siege. We sat in an outdoor café, he in suit and tie and me prepared to go to my workshop. He saw what was coming and was determined to leave, although he wouldn't leave without selling his business and his properties. We had little to say to each other by that time. We embraced, said our farewells and went back to our lives. I heard he had made it to Germany at some point during The Siege, but never heard from him. Kata, his wife, returned to her family home in Tuzla in 1990. She wanted Sofia to come too but Sofia said no.

Ian stands and goes to the closet next to the bookshelf. He takes a deep breath. Seven shelves stuffed with boxes and papers. Uni stuff, I presume. It is all very orderly in an overfull way. Ian stands on tiptoe but can't quite see what's on the top shelf. He brings the chair over, stands on it and only stops himself from falling – it's a swivel chair – by hanging onto the door. Eventually he brings down a cardboard box, a standard book box.

He puts the box on the floor in front of him and sits and looks at it. Fifteen years it has been in the closet without ever being opened.

He sits there for ages leaning forward in the chair, elbows on his knees, looking. Finally, he cuts the tape away and pulls off the lid.

Letters, notebooks, some loose papers, photographs, dust, smells that Ian can't place.

He puts on the lid and then takes it off again. I am increasingly curious.

One last deep breath and he reaches down and pulls out a handful of documents and begins to scan them. The first is from a hospital in Sarajevo. A death certificate for Kata, Ian's mother. She died in 1991. Cancer. Ian stares at the certificate, an image of his mother in his mind. Standing on the front stoop of an apartment they lived in when he was 10 or 11, smoking, waiting. She wasn't beautiful but she was striking. Even though he cut off all contact with his family the day he arrived in Italy, it is hard to imagine they disappeared completely from his mind. Ian is shocked at himself. He puts the certificate down gently on the floor. A photograph of the extended family, including both his parents. That must have been even earlier just outside of Sarajevo, a place in the mountains the family rented once or twice a year. Ian looks at it only briefly then puts it in a separate pile. There is a bundle of letters that Ian puts to one side. There are 11 notebooks, all the same. Black covered artist drawing pads, filled with fine pencil drawings and pages of tiny handwriting. It looks like filigree or lace. He browses through these a bit. The drawings are obviously by Sofia, Ian's sister. His lovely, estranged sister, my niece. She was an artist before The Siege. Well-known in Yugoslavia and not much beyond. A few of her paintings were sold to Italians. He stops at a drawing of me. My hands folded in front of me made to look even larger than they already were. Another of an old monastery and a castle that I only vaguely recognise.

He pulls out a letter and this one he reads and then reads again. It is dated November 1994 from the police minister's office in Sarajevo.

Dear Mr Votek, we regret to inform you of the death of Mr Tarek Votek.

The letter is written to my father who was long dead at the time of the letter.

He was apprehended trying to cross the border without papers, pulled a weapon on the police and was shot and killed. He died instantly. No further charges will be brought.

There is no signature, just an office stamp. I haven't seen this before and it is like dying a second time. Of course, the letter is a lie, but it still feels as though they have violated me not only in life but in death too.

I stood at the border that day, my phoney passport in my hand and an overnight bag at my feet. I wanted to be anywhere but here, heading across the border to yet another job, another problem to be fixed. I wanted to be back home, even though by then my home was rubble and in the midst of war. I wanted to cross another border, maybe into Italy and disappear, not feel responsible for a war I had nothing to do with starting and which demanded of me things I did not want to do or be. I looked at the mountains behind me and the militia in front of me and came so close to walking away right then. But I chose to do nothing. I waited in line. I remember the silhouette of mountains to the north, the call of the crows, the woman in front of me with her chickens and basket of corn.

When I made it to the front of the line, a surly young soldier took my documents, looked at them, then walked away without a word. He came back with an officer, who asked me about my family, my town, the job I once had. I could feel the first stirrings of fear. They brought me into the guardhouse and started asking random questions. I was confused, then realised they wanted a bribe. I assumed that they didn't know anything about me. I offered them what I had. They would have taken it anyway. These young men, even though Serbs, also lived in difficult times.

They left the room; I thought I could go and started to gather my things. I was going to head home. I walked out the door and was placed under arrest but with different guards and a more senior officer.

I was badly beaten that night and in the morning I was thrown into the back of a truck and taken to prison, a filthy, rat-infested hell hole where I was tortured until my suffering no longer gave them pleasure. After the torture stopped, I was dragged out into a courtyard and executed, shot in the head without even the most trivial of ceremonies of death. Finally, I was thrown into a mass and unmarked grave with 22 other men, presumably murdered in the same way.

Ian looks stunned. He didn't know of my death either and it is unlikely he will ever know the full story.

Ian remembers that the box came with a brief note from the Australian Embassy in Rome. *These materials were received by the embassy in 1993 and 1994, apparently by a relative or friend of your sister Sofia. We have only recently realised that they were being held here and at the time we were given no address only your name, Ivan Votek, and that you were likely to be an academic in Economics in Australia. If you are not the correct recipient please contact us to arrange return.'* The note is dated 2001.

Quietly, Ian returns the letters and photos to the box, replaces the lid and leaves the room. He knows he can only face this in small doses.

CHAPTER 12

Mary is in the kitchen, always in the kitchen, but with the light filtering through the jacaranda and washing across her hands and the bland grey of her dress top, she looks at peace and at home. Jake watches her from the doorway. She called and asked if Jake would come over. Ian is out shopping. He came right away – she has never made such a request before.

"I am dying," she blurts out quietly. "I have throat cancer and I'm likely to die before my forgetfulness gets too bad. A bit of consolation I think. I dread Alzheimer's more than dying." She looks up but not at him – out the window. "You know I planted that jacaranda tree? I can't even imagine it ever being a small seedling but it was." Jake is about to speak or to try to, to say something or ask something that a loving son would ask, but he can see she has more to say.

"Your father knows. Odd I call him your 'father' rather than 'my husband' or 'Ian'. Anyway, he knows, but he pretends he doesn't know. He even pretends not to know that I am getting forgetful. I think he would take my place if he could and if he could ever figure out how to ask me." She laughs from a deep well of affection. "I feel the need to speak now in ways I never have. I guess I expected it would all come out in time – my histories, stories, life. Although I have no idea how." Mary has stopped clinging to the edge of the sink. She could be speaking to herself and she is so different from the Mary he knows that Jake wants her to keep speaking, just to open up in ways he has never imagined and never done himself. "Did you know I trained as a physicist? I think I told you that, at least. I was offered a post doc at ANU and even a job at CSIRO. I suspect you didn't know that. I had children instead. No regrets, but I was thinking about how for a lifetime I've been loath to speak and wondering if it's because I am essentially a watcher and one who believes that we are the tiniest, most irrelevant motes of matter in the universe and what could be more liberating than watching and understanding the miracle that is the creation of the universe." She laughs again. "You've definitely never heard me say that. It took me too long to realise that being a good physicist is not the same as being a good mother. Pity. I was a good physicist. I could speak about and understand something of the mysteries of the universe, but not the mysteries of children and emotions and the tangle of our histories that makes the universe seem simple. Ian knows, but he can only watch and he hates being so powerless. I went to a number of doctors for a persistent croakiness and slight cough. Only the third one had any idea and had me tested. Ian wanted me to go see another doctor. He was an economist for way too many years. The answer you want is there somewhere, you just have to find it." She drifts briefly into silence. "He knows, but he still does battle with the idea, won't accept it. When he spoke about Yugoslavia the other night, I knew how hard this is for him.

"We used to argue when we were students together. It was fun. Do you know the joke about an economist, a chemist and a physicist stuck on a deserted island with a can of soup? Both the chemist and the physicist devise ingenious ways to open the can and the economist sits back in his deserted island deckchair, smiles in triumph and says, 'Just imagine a tin opener'."

"Ian liked that joke," she says kind of sadly. "I always thought it gave too much credit to economists. They have very poor imaginations." Jake smiles and hands her the cup of tea that has been sitting on the table going cold. She looks at him, the briefest nova of surprise that he is there passing across her face.

"I watch you and Ian sometimes, you know. When you argue about climate change it reminds me of then. It's funny, economists are some of the most stubborn thinkers in the universe and they are in a field that wants absolutes that just aren't there. Mind you, you're pretty stubborn too. I studied dark matter. Do you know about it?"

"I've heard of it, that's all."

"In the 70s scientists were getting more and more excited because the velocity of planets was showing there had to be matter or something out there that we couldn't see. And the theory was that 80 percent of all matter had to be dark matter in order to hold the universe together. But dark matter doesn't emit light or reflect light. It's invisible, at least to us. If it exists, we can only know it indirectly. Uncertainty dominates, not only in our own thinking but perhaps in the wider universe as well. It's probably true for me as a mother too," she says quietly. "For a lifetime I've struggled to speak of inner worlds – mine, yours, Peta's and Ian's, of course."

"None of us are very good at speaking of our emotions," Jake says. "Dark matter. I am discovering some of it inside me, I'm afraid."

Mary doesn't catch the moment of fear. "You were always so self-reliant. Stubborn really. When you did something wrong,

I'd kneel down to you – I think you must have been six – and say something like 'Do you know why that wasn't a nice thing to do?' You'd give me a look that said, 'You know nothing', turn around, go to your room and quietly close the door. When you came out, if I tried to talk about it again, you turned around without a word and went to your room again. I kind of respected that or maybe appreciated that I didn't have to deal with your emotional and psychological states. I could tell myself that you had it all under control. Physics should be good grounding for children and non-linear realities, but it didn't help me very much. Ian and I never really struggled with this. It was as though we always knew more about each other than we ever had words for. You know we have loved each other well. You know that, don't you?" And now she looks at Jake as though this is the most important question she has ever asked.

Jake feels untethered but he nods and whispers, "Yes, I know."

"When you came to dinner the other night, he was going to tell you. Or that's what I thought. And Peta. He was going to tell you both, but now I need to tell her separately. She is more fragile than you."

She turns and sits at the table. Jake joins her. After a moment of silence, Jake asks the question that has been sitting here the whole time.

"How advanced is the cancer?" he asks finally.

"The cancer?" she asks from far away? And then she returns. "Inoperable. Some things I can try, chemo, probably a tracheotomy, but the chances are slim. I'm not sure if I'll go through that."

It's clear she doesn't want to speak more. She's tired and also moving far away inside her head.

An abyss opens inside Jake. It's a physical feeling that he is splitting vertically. It begins at his navel and spreads like a jagged crack in the oldest of stones. It's not quite his spirit but some essential gas that hisses out and dissipates in the growing silence. The crack widens as he walks to the car, it becomes a canyon as he drives, barren and harsh. He gets lost going home. He begins to cry and pulls over. A panhandler asks him if he's okay and Jake asks him where he is. The man looks at him as though he's crazy. Jake gives him all the money in his wallet and asks again. The poor man stands there muddled by circumstances far too strange for him. He offers Jake half his money back. Jake shakes his head and drives off. It's not only her dying, it's that he has accepted this woman as his mother without ever knowing her, without even thinking about knowing her. Just my mother, he thinks, and that feels unutterably stupid. How can he undo that now? He knows the silence ran both ways, and the same with Ian really. Parents but not people, and now it may be too late.

"Why didn't she tell us?" He realises the irony of him asking that question of Julie. No, it's not simply irony, he can always live with irony, it's the impossibility. He almost confesses his secrets at that moment, but instead he walks off and Julie is left there in the living room wondering what just happened.

Denial is a kind of faith and faith denial. Jake thinks of his father and perhaps himself. Ian has to believe that Mary will live on because he cannot allow himself to imagine anything else. Love is a kind of faith too. Does that make it a form of denial as well?

Jake comes back five minutes later looking even worse. "What do we do?"

Julie isn't sure which question she is answering. She decides to keep it as simple as she can for now. "We take care of them as much as we can and as much as they need."

Jake looks at her as though she has just kicked the cat across the room. "It's complicated."

"Not really." She stares at him and it's almost cold, as though she's not going to let him wriggle anywhere on this. Not a millimetre of space, she thinks.

"No, I guess, it's not," he says finally.

*

The 'talk' the next night with his parents is incredibly difficult. Ian doesn't deny Mary's illness but insists everything is fine, that they are managing and they don't need help. Peta sits in shock, in a silence so deep, that it is well beyond words. "Mary's doctors are quite optimistic," Ian says a few times. It's not true. Ian keeps trying to pretend all is well. Some weeks ago, Mary insisted he come to her weekly medical appointment. Mary wanted him to hear the stark reality and he did.

The doctor was clear that Mary was right – her chances were slim and the cancer was aggressive meaning her time is also short. She thought Ian got it, but sitting now with his family he seems stricken all over again, as though he has never heard this before.

Jake starts to work from his parents' house two or three days a week. He doesn't need to help look after Mary yet, but he's there to chat or make her tea now and then. He wants to talk to her about physics, what she loves about the world she once studied. He suspects that she, like him, sought and chased love, not only in her human relationships but everywhere. For her it was in the deepest space and the whole of time.

But he doesn't ask. He worries that these are painful not joyful places for her to go and he doesn't know where to begin, doesn't know what words to use. He waits for Mary to speak but he soon sees her past, even who she is, has less and less meaning for her.

He sits in the living room, his computer on his lap and the papers he needs spread on the coffee table, but it's not comfortable. He is surrounded with artefacts that either seem old or that remind him of a childhood that no longer belongs to him. Mary moves around this room and the house generally in a kind of weary ghost-like fashion. He can't tell if his presence is changing the patterns of her day, but he thinks it must be so. He waits for her to speak and otherwise tries to be a useful and sort of innocuous presence. Not the same, but yet another pattern of silence grows.

She mentions her concern for Peta, her 'lost' daughter, once. She tells a story of an eccentric uncle who gave her a telescope when she was 11. Growing up on a farm in Western Queensland the skies were stunning but the morning chores were unforgiving and unrelenting. 'Sleepless nights were good training for Uni,' Mary says. But she's not maudlin, not dwelling in an idealised past. These are just passing stories, harmless asteroids, fragments that Jake quietly collects knowing it is probably too late to expect more.

Ian, who still has an office at the uni, can now go in one or two days a week and spends most of that time in one of the uni coffee shops chatting with old colleagues. It brings some relief if nothing else, although Jake knows there are ghosts there as well.

Julie comes over at least one evening a week and she and Jake, and sometimes Peta, cook for both Ian and Mary. There is unexpected pleasure in that. They try new dishes. They rummage in Mary's extensive collection of cookbooks. Roast pork calypso with flaming rum and coq au vin and an awful attempt at chicken kiev.

Not happiness, but not just grief either. In an odd way, it has seen Jake find a measure of equilibrium. His focus is now family and not work, not the precarious state of the planet.

*

"So, Dad, what would you do if you were certain that climate change was happening? If you knew and no one around you – or almost no one – was doing anything to prevent it, to change things?"

Mary is having a nap and Jake and Ian are sharing lunch in the kitchen. Jake's question is not an attack but a search for a way to be in a world that is making little sense to him.

Ian shrugs his shoulders. "What can I do? I'm a nobody. I have no power, no influence, no friends in high places. I'm old."

"Dad, you can speak up. You can write letters, call people, write. You're not powerless, none of us are and this has to begin somewhere." Jake can hear the pitch of his voice rising. Don't get angry he thinks, hold yourself together and listen. His father is speaking of Mary as much as he is of climate change.

"But Jake, I don't believe in the predictions of doom."

"Do you think you don't believe, maybe, because to believe is to demand we act?"

"You mean I delude myself because I don't want to act or don't have to courage to act, don't you? I think about Nazi Germany or paedophilia in the Catholic Church, East Timor, times where intervention should have occurred – at least in hindsight. But for every intervention, there have been others that have been disasters. Like Iraq or Afghanistan.

"Belief is surely a dangerous blessing," Ian says more softly. "That doesn't mean don't believe, but we need to be more careful with belief. It's always mixed up with history and personal ambitions, baggage and desires, as well as ignorance, all the things we don't or cannot know."

"Not believing is also a belief," Jake says. "There is belief that is based on evidence, belief that is based on experience and belief based on wishful thinking. They're very different," Jake says.

"It is very strange, Jake, to be lectured to by one's son. I'm not sure I like it very much."

Jake begins to cry. Just like that. "Dad, the last thing I want is to lecture you, attack you or hector you. I love you and admire you, but I am struggling to understand how such a smart and thoughtful man can avoid knowing what is going on."

"Jake, do you remember the line, 'The best lack all conviction and the worst are full of passionate intensity'?"

Jake nods. He already knows that passionate intensity is too often his country.

"It is about the dangers of belief, of certainty. There are those who say greenies want climate change to be real because you want the world to end, you want humans to disappear. Others say you want one world government. Belief gathers bits of knowledge around it, shards of evidence that are enough to hold the structure together. Belief terrifies me and I approach it – both within me and outside of me – with extreme caution. Maybe that's why economics attracted me – I never believed in it very strongly." Ian stops and looks out the large bay window, past the front lawn empty of life, past the street and over the house across the road.

"You know, I don't want to believe in climate change being real, it's true. I don't want to think about millions being displaced or our whole planet becoming an inhospitable place to live. I hate the thought – for you and Julie as much as us, but I believe that I don't believe for other reasons that are rational. Maybe a belief in forces bigger than ourselves – not god – that tell us there are limits to our knowledge and our power. Maybe I believe we don't know as much as we think. Our ignorance has always been greater than we have been willing to admit." Ian stops briefly, flirting with the idea that he is talking about himself too and his knowledge of climate change.

"An obligation to act? I don't think it's that simple. I have an obligation to take care of your mother, but to stop climate change or end war? I don't know, I don't think so." Ian drifts into silence.

Jake stands, goes over to his father and embraces him. Ian's distress is so familiar and so painful. "Dad you're a loving and honourable and decent man. I'm not judging you. You know, I too often feel like an alien from another planet and it's you I turn to try and make sense of things that perhaps don't have sense."

Jake knows that this isn't entirely true. He is judging his father even as he tries not to.

Later Ian sits in his office, staring at the box he has had next to his desk now for several weeks. He hasn't been able to open it again since he read of Tarek's death. The box of silence, he thinks, Pandora's box, the box of beliefs and wishful thinking and wilful ignorance. Jake's words still hurt – the more so because this box from his past tells him that to some extent Jake is right, he prefers forgetting or ignorance, because sometimes it is too dangerous or too painful to know.

He wants to talk to Jake again, differently this time. "How far do you go? How much do you sacrifice? What are the limits to this belief in acting?"

His son is an activist, as I was in a very different way, and for the first time Ian kind of, maybe, understands why and understands how hard it must be to take on your shoulders a whole world of problems.

CHAPTER 13

Jake knew better. He was in no mood for a party but Julie needed to get out, needed to hear laughter and silliness, even gossip. Maybe he did too, but what he heard instead was...nothing. People, too many people, drinking too much, making too many bad jokes, having conversations so devoid of substance he could see the words floating away into the air like ash, like fluff. He sits at the fringes of the room. He doesn't remember how he agreed to come here. Too angry, too dour about everything. He knows how stupid he's being – gatherings, sharing food or drink, jokes or stories give pleasure, harmless pleasure. It doesn't mean they don't care.

He walks out into the darkness of the backyard and stands beneath a tree spalled with moonlight and he thinks this tree must be as old as white settlement and the moon much older and the light reaching him from the stars older again. Does light have a memory? he asks Mary in his head. Do trees have memories? Will this moment or any other have meaning in a thousand years? Jake is trying to reach somewhere, find something in these almost random thoughts, but he doesn't know what it is or how to get there. Looking for peace.

A hand on his back, breath on his neck. He doesn't turn but feels the touch pierce him and travel through him like moonlight. A second hand on his chest. He can feel her face between his shoulder blades and she is pulling him closer and tighter. Her hand moves under his shirt, across his chest and belly. He can feel each of her fingers, each electric in different ways, each emitting, giving light and heat and love. He closes his eyes and he can hear the sounds of the party behind him and the sounds of the night around him and the beating of his heart and Julie's and the susurrus of their breaths that are the breaths of the whole world.

He slowly turns like a waxing moon and holds her in his arms, in his branches, in his light, in his vast memory. He aches with love so acute that he knows he is at the border of pain.

They make love. Create love, mould love into a thousand shapes that float into the night sky and will travel across the universe meeting all the light and dust and motes and memories of all times.

In the feeling of being diminished, even dwarfed, a liberation, a growing into a larger world seems to occur and for a brief time the world is much easier to understand and withstand.

They walk out from the dark into the party, arms around each other, quietly absorbed in their shared and private joy. Dave starts laughing when he sees them and gives them both a hug. "Lucky ones" he says. They nod.

They stay a little longer but don't once let go of each other.

PART 2

A great deal of intelligence can be invested in ignorance when the need for illusion is deep.

Saul Bellow

CHAPTER 14

July 2015 was the hottest month ever recorded. Jake reads the story of global floods, droughts, extreme storms and heatwaves with temperatures in some parts averaging over 50 degrees centigrade for the entire month. It is the poorest who die, who can't escape, can't get help. Thousands die of heat in India and Pakistan. California has its worst drought ever and the Amazon has dried 25% since 2000.

How can we as humans, citizens, ignore these events? Jake wonders. We are allowing our life support systems to be killed; we're brutal to each other, to other living things, to our humanity and yet nothing seems to change.

Jake listens to the Greens on radio. They are becoming more strident, as bewildered by our official indifference as any thinking soul. This is so beyond your garden variety cognitive dissonance, Jake thinks. Jake doesn't know how to make sense of a reality that by any rational standard is senseless.

I've seen it before. How do you explain the capacity to ignore a war? To forget a war? Even to fight a war? To see your friends and neighbours start killing friends and neighbours. To accept unbridled violence as normal because normal is more valued than sanity. I have seen it before, seen an upright citizen tear out her hair in the face of circumstances over which they have no control and which no human should have to endure, then go back to her normal life even if that normal is mad, even if that normal is the madness.

Ian faces something else that defies easy explanations. He hasn't read the news today but sits in his study, a pile of papers in front of him. Most are handwritten and show signs of over fifteen years of sitting in a box.

April 1992
Dear Brother

And so it begins as it had to. The war has come to Sarajevo. I am not sure why I write to tell you this – perhaps an attempt to repair the hurt we caused each other, a fear of death, a hope that you will bear witness should I be unable to do so. Most likely it is the recognition that our 'war' was not so big, so violent or so important that we cannot put it aside for things that matter more – like family, like love, like peace.

We, the community, the little people, worked so hard to prevent this but our leaders saw the fracturing of a country and its communities as an opportunity to gain power or wealth. They made hatred our new currency, violence our new market and so we arrive here.

The first death was a Serb. A Muslim shot and killed the groom's father at a wedding. A wedding. It was not a politician spouting hate nor a soldier prepared to go to war. It was not an argument that turned ugly or a neighbourhood dispute that ended in a death that only because of the times ended up being so important. No. It was a wedding and so not only was a man killed today but we were all given a message that even joy is not permitted.

The next two deaths, the same day, were two women, a Croat and a Muslim, shot dead by snipers. They were part of a march of Bosnians, Croats, Serbs all opposed to war. It is almost inevitable now. Janos has joined the militia as have most of his, our, friends. At least amongst those who remain here. Many have left. We have decided to stay, although I wonder every day whether that is the right choice.

So many, for so many days, have been trying to find a way for this day not to happen. They have failed.

For the moment, Janos is home every evening. I suspect the time will come when that is no longer possible.

Sofia, my lovely niece. That first letter was written in 1992. It is almost 25 years later that Ian reads it for the first time. Ian's decision to depart had been the final wedge that split those two apart. He was a shy, introverted man and his sister was loud, political and passionate. She had insisted he stay. 'You can't run away, this is your country.' He didn't want to fight for his country but for his spirit, or so he told himself.

In those days leaving Yugoslavia wasn't easy but at least one wasn't surrounded by war. He was a budding academic and in 1980 received permission to attend a conference in Venice. He never returned. And Tito tended to forget those betrayals unlike others in the eastern countries at that time.

Ian tries to remember the three deaths on that day in Sarajevo, but can't. Why should he? He didn't want to know about a country that he abandoned. That is harsh perhaps, but those of us who remained, all of us, we tried to make our new country into something good. And failed. Failed badly. We resent, or perhaps are jealous of those who left.

May 1992

Dear Brother

I write to you uncertain if these letters will ever be sent or if they are sent that they will ever arrive. The first letter I wrote to you weeks ago now sits in a box in a wardrobe.

I am afraid I will die here. I am writing to you somewhere with no idea of who you are, where you are, what you do each day or who with. And yet, writing to you takes me away from here. Briefly.

The death of the two women has been followed with shootings in the street, brawls, riots and Serbian troops moving towards the city. We have many soldiers but few arms. There are many people leaving. Some people preparing for war and others who still believe that reason will prevail, although our history since Tito died does not suggest this is a reasonable probability.

After these first two letters, Ian comes back from the Uni with an armful of books on the death of Tito, the breakup of Yugoslavia, The Siege, histories of the Balkans. It's kind of funny to see Ian try to make sense of his split with Sofia and his dying wife in words about times and places that seem so unlikely to offer any redemption.

May 1992

Dear Brother

We are under siege. The Serbs not only surround the city and control all roads, they are using artillery to bomb us and snipers to kill us and the Serbs that live in the city to bomb temples and churches and to burn down places where people gather or buy food. It is getting difficult now, but we are also beginning to organise. Our Jewish networks have set up an underground for medicines and drugs, which are in short supply and more needed than ever. Others are setting up food kitchens and places to care for orphans and the elderly.

We receive little news but many rumours. NATO is going to intervene. They will send warplanes, they will send troops. Any day now. Tomorrow. Soon. Janos is spitting mad. He doesn't believe they will ever come – and cannot understand their recalcitrance. Janos never gets mad but he is mad now. I worry that the worst in others will bring out the worst in him. I am more concerned with building a community that resists despair and false hope and provides food and comfort wherever it can. That too, no doubt, is filled with false hopes.

I have begun to take my drawing pad wherever I go. I see much that is heartbreaking and much that fills me with wonder at the vastness of the human spirit. Today, after several hours of shelling, all was quiet. People came into the street. A man with an accordion began to play near the fountain. A few children began to dance, then many, then adults as well. Someone brought a table out and food started to appear. A fiddler joined the accordion player. It was a celebration, an act of defiance. I drew madly! As evening came the shelling began again and we dissipated, but only after we proved that joy isn't dead!

Ian searches for and finds the drawings from that day. Quickly done sketches, but with such a sure touch that the joy shines through as does the war. Janos is in one of the drawings. He stands watching a woman dancing, his rifle slung over his shoulder, but his hands, both hands, are on the rifle. Sofia has captured both joy and tension, the readiness for things to go wrong.

I remember Ivan being forced to sit still by Sofia while she drew him one afternoon when he wanted to go play football. He must have been six or seven. She was incredibly bossy. And after all that she even refused to show him the drawing.

*

Mary is deteriorating quickly. She sleeps much of the day now. She is on heavy drugs, hallucinating regularly and speaking randomly – finding words unattached to anything in the world that Ian knows. Ian is not sure she knows he is there or recognises him or his voice or his touch. She calls out now and then, and Ian goes to her side. Sometimes she settles and sometimes not. It is hard enough to watch her die, but he has to watch her disappear as well.

He stays home every day now. He bathes, feeds and reads to Mary. He is attentive to her in ways that are new to him. He finds pleasure in touching her, folding her diminishing body in his arms, making her bed and then tucking her in. She is showing signs of carphology and her distress becomes his.

He is trying to learn to cook. Julie and Jake both help but he is completely clueless. Mary doesn't eat much. Soups – made by Julie – are in the freezer and will last for days. Ian isn't eating much either. He is rarely hungry but eats out of a sense of obligation, little more.

He grabs a piece of bread or fruit or eats a bowl of soup at random times. When Jake and Julie come, they sit at the table, but Ian is clearly distracted and picks at his food with little interest.

He often disappears after these 'dinners' back into his office.

He no longer reads academic papers. He reads the letters from Sarajevo, still in small doses, and the histories, his histories he now says, the ones that he never knew. He has decided to write all of this into a paper or story. He doesn't yet know how, but he feels the need to atone in some ways for his blindness for over 20 years. He has not been a deeply self-reflective man so turning inward, particularly as it is driven by an imminent death, is a daunting journey.

Jake watches these changes – Ian learning to care for others and learning to question himself – and knows that what is driving those changes is too dark to easily be considered good.

One day, they are sitting at the kitchen table and Ian suddenly says, "Did you know I had a sister, Sofia?"

Jake looks over at Ian, startled, shocked, but Ian is looking elsewhere. "I had no idea."

Ian's hands are clasped together, his head down, his voice filled with shame. "I put it in the past tense, but I don't know if she's alive or not. She wrote me a bundle of letters during The Siege of Sarajevo. I never read them, never even opened the box until a few weeks ago. I only received them fifteen years ago," he says with a dose of self-loathing Jake has never heard before.

Ian then gets up and walks back into his office. Jake thinks Ian is going to get something to show him – a letter, a photo, but no, he just quietly closes the office door and goes back to his papers.

CHAPTER 15

Except for the Lakers' hat pulled low and the cheap oversized sunglasses, he might look like another early riser out for a walk or looking for a coffee shop. It is before dawn and he is on Canberra Street, a day pack casually over one shoulder. It is quiet. An occasional taxi goes past but there are no buses and no pedestrians, not for at least another two hours. A few of the buildings have security guards, but the Mineral House building is quiet and dark, as it has been on the two occasions he has checked out the building over the last four months.

The reconnaissance is such a pain. He had to find time to get away from work, lie to Julie and then spend the time in a place where he doesn't want to be seen or recognised. No meetings and he can't stay with friends. Way too risky. He is camping up in the Brindabellas amongst ghostly white trees, ghost monuments to the unprecedented fires that roared through over ten years ago.

He waits in the darker shadow of a tree across the street. He is not really waiting but listening, gathering courage, thinking of Julie, curled on her side asleep in bed, with one hand between her knees. The haunting hour. His father is standing next to him. That disapproving mouth, the words chosen so carefully that his attempt at neutrality is even worse than criticism. He's not like that anymore, but this is often how Jake pictures him. He wonders briefly why that old image of Ian persists and when and how this changed. It must have been when Jake and Peta left home and Ian no longer felt put upon by his children. He wonders if he will ever be able to talk about those times with Ian. It's not only Ian's problem but his. We, none of us, ever learned to talk about the things that mattered, he thinks. And I still don't have the slightest idea how to open that door.

It is more than three months since the rail line, and one of the few things Jake can show for it is that ghosts are real. Nothing has happened to him, not even a whiff of suspicion, and yet his soul is now inhabited by fears, demons, and voices that aren't his. He feels no closer to accomplishing anything. He feels no path is open before him except the one he started on – and it's not one he wants to keep travelling. His isolation haunts him. His distance from Julie is physically painful. Even his impatience for change makes him impatient with himself. All bound up with lies that stick to the surface of his life like a skein of twine or wire.

He hates to use the word 'sabotage'. For some reason he finds the word wrong. But he has no words for what he's done or what he is about to do. It's not sabotage. It's not terror. But all the words that come to him are euphemisms or distractions. He's not sure why this bothers him, but as he stands there he wants to find the word that fits.

He pulls on one of the straps of his day pack nervously. He lied to Julie again. He has lied to her more in the last two months than in all their years together. "I have some political meetings in Canberra tomorrow," he told her. He waited until breakfast when both were, as usual, rushing to get out the door in time for work. "Green Earth is flying me down," he said. Actually, he is flying to Sydney and then renting a car. That's the riskiest bit, but he can't be seen in Canberra.

"After last time? You said you weren't doing political meetings ever again. Why'd you say yes to that?"

He is prepared for the question. He shrugged his shoulders. "I didn't want to, but I have more experience than the others."

Julie looked at him and he knew that soon she would see right inside him, would see the grinding of his bowels, the slow rotting of his spirit, the dark shadows of his lies. "I'll be back tomorrow night. Sorry, I didn't tell you earlier," he added as though his tepid apology might help. It just added to the heap of lies he's already told.

Julie doesn't know what the lies are, or what they are hiding, but it happens so often now that she begins to feel that everything Jake says is tied up in lies, even if the words at that moment are true. The demons have grown larger inside her and wrestling with them has become harder and more tiresome. She debated whether to speak or spit out an accusation, but she stayed silent instead. She keeps waiting, hoping that given space the truth inside him will open up like an old door and the fetid words he hasn't spoken will come tumbling out. That hasn't worked either. Instead, Jake has hidden even more. His solicitude is real but also dishonest. His evasions transparent to Julie if not to him. She is far more patient than he, perhaps too patient. She gave him a hug, harder and quicker than usual. "Maybe we can talk when you get back," she muttered into his shoulder.

"Sorry?"

"Nothing. Just...love you."

Jake has watched Julie struggle with how he has changed and he has struggled to pretend that all is normal. He knows the pretending isn't working but he can't change it or invent another pretence.

The silences between them have become both deeper and heavier. More than they ever have, they watch movies together or play scrabble or cards – things that allow silence. Things that she did in childhood. She remembers the clicking of backgammon dice, loud, insistent, and a constant reminder of how little her dour father had to say to her.

He feels nauseous almost constantly and she keeps imagining that rats are gnawing at her spirit, like an old rope slowly eaten away until only a thread remains.

They make love rarely and it's less intimate and more desperate – louder, harder as though for Jake it's an exorcism of sorts. Julie lies on her back afterwards and stares at the fan. Jake goes to the bathroom to stare at the person in the mirror. I wonder how much longer before the fabric that holds them together – even at a distance – ruptures and it all falls apart.

They both know that the space between them is growing wider. The crossings no longer simple and direct but planned, fretted over and often not taken. Julie is tired of it. She calls it a game but knows it's far more dangerous than that. And Jake? How many times has he been on the verge of telling all?

He better move or it will be too late.

He crosses the street quickly. At the front door he ignores the camera. He won't be identified from above and nothing he is wearing will belong to him by daylight. He takes out the glue gun and squeezes the resin along the point where the doors join, along top, bottom and sides. He takes out the poster, The Indictment for Crimes Against the Planet and tapes it to the window. He takes out the video camera and shoots for less than 30 seconds. He has already done the voice over explaining that The Free Radicals have targeted the Minerals Council and their members because of their large investment in preventing action on climate change. Five minutes and he's gone. His car is a few minutes away on the darkest side street he could find. He has changed a few numbers on his plates, passable but still a risk.

The last time I watched with a kind of pleasure, today with fear. He isn't focused. He is fighting in his head and is going to make mistakes.

He pulls out the disposable phone and calls all four television stations. They'll share the footage, but he wants them all there, fighting for the spoils. "I am calling from The Free Radicals. You might want to get a crew down to Mineral House before 9 am," he tells them and hangs up. The phone is wiped clean and thrown down a stormwater drain in the dark lane.

He gets out of town heading north and then pulls off the road to upload the video and voiceover and sends it to a long list of media contacts.

He listens to the news on the drive back to Sydney. It is already running by 9:30. 'Over 60 people who work in the building are locked out this morning,' says the ABC 'by a radical group angry about climate change. They have posted a manifesto on the window in which they accuse the mining corporations of crimes against the planet. This is the same group that sabotaged a rail line in Queensland about 3 months ago and police say that significant resources are being put into tracking down these terrorists.'

Jake had hoped they'd read out some of the indictment he posted on the window and the website. He worked on that a long time. 'We are at a turning point not only in human history but in the history of the planet. And if we don't start acting for the future, we won't have one.' It's probably a little bit portentous.

The television footage, which Jake doesn't see until the next day, shows a passing image of the indictment and people milling about. They do a bit of vox pop. The point is rapidly lost.

Later that morning the Prime Minister was rolled by one of his ministers and by the time he was back at Sydney Airport the story is long gone.

CHAPTER 16

June 1992

Dear Brother

It is amusing – in a gallows humour kind of way – to realise that while we are resisting the Serbs we are also paying obeisance to the criminals amongst us. The black market thrives now and we all want their services. Guns, drugs and food. No doubt when the war is over, they will be the elite amongst us, like the Kennedys. Amnesia or denial will strike us all. I find that amusing. The elite before the war once railed against these criminals – they will soon be attending their cocktail parties. If I am lucky I will still be here, still learning to laugh again.

Someone has painted on the wall on our street a message in English. 'Welcome to Hell.' I do not speak English but this we all understand.

How right Sofia was. The black marketeers became the nouveau riche and the new powerbrokers in the country. People I fought with and against, bought industries and properties at fire-sale prices, the stuff the Americans didn't want. They wore waistcoats and grew fat on this modern form of plunder. I doubt Sofia would have laughed at all.

June 1992
Dear Brother

We are sheltering a friend of Janos'. I probably should not even put this in writing – justice here can be random, summary and presumptive. He was wounded in attacks on Serb positions inside the city. The Serbs do not have the numbers to conduct door to door searches as the Nazis did, but still we remain terrified. All the rhythms of life that once were normal are alien now. We pretend to enact them as we can. We have dinner at the table, or at least try. It is now by candlelight but two times in three we will be interrupted by shelling. We must either go into the cellar or we keep eating as though nothing is happening, our conversations now punctuated by explosions. "Ah, a full stop," Janos jokes. "No, no, merely a comma," I protest. "It was not loud enough for a full stop." We are desperate for such 'normal' moments as these.

His friend, Irin, was hit by a bullet and by shrapnel from an explosion. He is in much pain and he too makes jokes. He claims the bullet wound is Russian and the shrapnel wound Serbian. The Serb wound always hurts more. I am learning to be a nurse. I clean the wound, change bandages, even pick out pieces of shrapnel.

I am out of canvas and almost out of paints. I draw instead.

We are getting hungry.

Ian stands next to the bed. The curtains are closed and Mary sleeps fitfully in the half-light, curled under the blue doona that they have both slept under for years. She's almost due her meds, he thinks. And she needs a bath. I wonder if he recognises that like his estranged sister, he is learning to be a nurse too. Sofia would probably appreciate the irony more than Ian.

July 1992
Dear Brother

The UN now controls the airport and has begun an airlift, bringing us food and medicines. Not enough but certainly welcome. The planes are fired on. The smugglers, now more organised crime than anything, have control over much that arrives from the UN, which doesn't do more than leave it at the airport. We struggle to get the medicines we need without buying them at exorbitant prices from those who steal them. On the other hand, without such crime many more would suffer and die. Such is war and life.

Some journalists have made their way into Sarajevo. They stay at the Holiday Inn. You can imagine the jokes we make. We are not sure if the stories we give them are ever told again or if the stories they write are ever published, but we admire them in a way. We are not quite sure who would come to Sarajevo willingly.

The doctor has suggested reading aloud to Mary, even when she's asleep. A small pile of books by the bed includes a book on physics, a novel about bees and A Brief History of Many Wars, the story of the breakup of Yugoslavia. He read that to her today and kept interrupting the story to explain more about The Siege. His words may have never reached Mary's consciousness, but he wanted to believe that she heard, understood and forgave him.

CHAPTER 17

Jake is growing a beard. Julie asks why. "I'm hiding," he says. A joke but not. Julie runs her fingers through the wispy growth.

"I don't know you like this," she mutters. She feels she is being pushed away in yet another fashion.

"I just thought I'd try it. I've never had a beard." He knows she doesn't like it, but he doesn't offer to get rid of it. She knows. He knows. Silence sits between them like some impenetrable stone.

Jake spends the morning at work preparing an overview of the environmental issues that are currently pressing in Australia. Green Earth is trying to restructure, again, this time to integrate climate work into coal work, biodiversity issues, and reversing an epidemic of anti-environmentalism. The list of issues grows way too long. 'Issues' thinks Jake. What an odd word to use. A word without character, like 'event'.

At some point he stops, stares at the wall, stares at Denise out on the verandah having a cigarette, stares at Jessica head down talking on the phone. Simon is in the meeting room, again, writing on the whiteboard. It's all somewhat unreal to him. It's not enough, he finally mutters aloud. The sealing of the doors of the Mineral Council entrance lasted less than six hours. A few Liberal politicians jumped up and down about it and demanded arrests and new laws to control terrorist greenies, most left it alone.

The media enjoyed it. It amused them, briefly, but in Jake's head now it had no point. He can feel the extent to which his thinking is now being driven by his need to be heard in the mainstream corporate media. He knows they will never support him, but they will report him if he does his work well, if it's loud enough, daring enough, stupid enough.

When life in Sarajevo began to get grim; when violence was common and food wasn't, we felt desperate to be heard too, convinced that no one knew what was going on in the city. If only they knew, we thought. When the truth was told it turned out they simply didn't care to know. I suspect Jake will find the same. We were desperate to get the story out to the west. This was before YouTube and video cameras on phones. When we realised the rest of the world didn't care about the war, we worried that what we had experienced and seen would be forgotten because too many witnesses had died, too many voices were now silent. It wasn't the voices we needed but the ears of the world.

We received bits of news of course – it was the nineties and we couldn't be entirely cut off from Europe, but the news was always a partial meal. The Siege was sometimes mentioned, sometimes not. Sometimes there was talk of intervention. We listened to the radio – sound very low – and always, always demanded more than we received. We knew that what we heard, we heard with hungry ears that could not be relied on. Every mention of The Siege or the war made us feel intervention was that much closer, when really it was just the noise of the morning news, thousands of stories rising in the air like the smoke from an unattended fire.

Each day I would say, NATO is coming soon. The pressure is increasing. They have no choice. And Milos would say, they are getting ready to fart – that is the only pressure they are feeling. We would laugh – in part because our humour was becoming more juvenile by the day. Ah well, these were the small pleasures one takes from such times.

CHAPTER 18

"You just can't justify violence. It's always counterproductive. It always results in more repression not less." Garth is sitting at morning tea, a cup of steaming coffee in his hand and arguing with Denise. It's still early in the office and only a few people are there. Jake listens, standing by the window and looking out past the Plane tree and the delivery truck idling on the corner.

"I dunno," Denise says, in her mild Scottish brogue. "India was liberated by violence as well as non-violence. And both were responses to a violent system. We all know what the Brits are capable of. And as resistance began – like in Scotland or Ireland – the repression grew more violent.

At some point we have to say that we no longer accept such violence. It's not gonna stop by working within the system. Nothing's gonna change that way. I dun't think anyone looking rationally at climate change, not to mention the trashing of the entire bloody planet, can find any evidence that people power is going to get the capitalist system to stop doing what it does. And no evidence either that the current system can solve any problem caused by the current system and certainly not climate change." Denise taps her empty cup on the table. "But as soon as you say that we have to face the problem of how to undo a system that dominates the entire globe. I dun't know the answer but I know it's not by writing submissions."

Jake listens in grim silence. He wants to speak but he doesn't dare. Maybe this is how violence works, he thinks. First it pries open a door – not of violence but of thought. He never would have imagined Denise saying these things. She comes across as so proper. She wears dresses and makeup and looks almost corporate. She has a two year old daughter and she loves to dance. He has to stop assuming he knows anything.

"You really think we've reached the point in this country where violence is justified or will work?" Garth asks. "In India people were dying and starving. That's not what's happening here. We're talking about a kind of destruction that most people don't see and don't care about. How many people could name five endangered species, could say how much habitat is being destroyed each year, could tell you why ocean acidification matters?"

"No, you're right, it's not the same in that way, climate change is unlike any threat we've ever faced – it's not only existential but it comes upon us by stealth. But it is the same in the sense that the divide between those who rule and those who are ruled grows wider and wider. The efforts to silence dissent are gettin' more severe. The rights to legal resistance are bein' eliminated. I mean we had a Minister say to a bunch of us two weeks ago that the right to seek judicial review of government decisions was anti-democratic. And he was from the bleedin' Labor Party! We have greenies called eco-terrorists simply because they oppose a port or a coal mine. Fines are getting higher, penalties more severe for stuff we always took for granted, including prison terms, serious prison terms. Getting arrested is no longer a rite of passage but a serious risk."

"But we still have the democratic tools to change this."

"I guess that's the rub and where we disagree. I don't think we have democracy any more, we have a corporatocracy and like the US it's getting worse and worse."

"So, are you saying that you agree with The Free Radicals?" asks Jake tentatively. "Maybe you shouldn't answer that," he adds quietly.

Denise looks at him oddly. "Why shouldn't I answer?"

"For the very reasons you pointed out. Even expressing support for that group may not be legal."

"Well, I'm all for a revolution, as long as it's a good one," Denise says laughing. "And I assume it's still legal to say that."

Poor Jake grasps at such straws. I am afraid that he is approaching the point where he sees salvation – not just necessity – in violence.

When Sarajevo was under siege, surrender, flight or violence were our choices. And all of us at some point wanted others to do violence on our behalf. At first we begged Europe and the US to do more. How many times were we told that the bombers were coming – and we literally waited outside, staring at the sky? Now that seems no less foolish than the cargo cults. Yes, NATO intervention would have slowed the daily bombardment, given us time to bury our dead or wash our clothes, but it was not a solution, was never going to solve the problems that led to war. Sometimes, though, as Denise argues, when we are being violated, when violence is the norm, violence may be the only response.

CHAPTER 19

August 1992

Dear Brother

Almost every country outside of here has recognised Bosnia as an independent country – that we are not part of a greater Serbia, yet nothing changes. The recognition of our status was an anodyne not a step towards protecting us. Now that the world has shown that they care; nothing more needs to be done seems to be their view. There are those, including Janos, who still believe that step had more meaning, but I am of little faith.

I often think that Bosnia was an invisible country, a forgotten country. How does a country, a region, an idea, come to be made invisible? It reminds me of a story of a man who after an automobile accident had brain damage and a paralysed arm. He refused to believe that his arm was paralysed no matter how often he was told, although there it was, all the time, his lifeless, motionless left arm. Is there anything we can't forget, reimagine, make invisible?

August 1992

Dear Brother

The world as much as it knows anything of this war knows it as a siege. That is true but it is not all of the truth. The city itself is divided and there are areas that are controlled by Serb forces and where all Muslims and all Jews have been killed, cleansed.

There are those few who have escaped from the Serbian quarter who tell of executions, brutal beatings, rapes and theft. There is never six degrees of separation here. A raped woman will have been raped by someone that a friend's friend knows. It is hard to describe how disturbing and imminent that feels.

Even worse I suspect the Serbs over there say the same about us. Janos has told me little, but enough for me to know, that some in our militia are capable of similar acts of brutality. Janos says if it happens, the punishment is severe.

We know we are not safe, but we do not even have the luxury of feeling that we are secure, if that makes sense. I have learned to use a gun. I carry it with me if I must go out. That does not make me feel secure or safe either, but it does make me feel I will not die quietly, I will not surrender without a fight to whatever madness it is that drives this war. And so, I become part of this war, this madness. I am pushed to the edge of its violence. It's not where I want to be but it is also no longer an imaginary, impossible place.

Ian tries to imagine what he would do, have done. He has never held a gun. He has heard gunfire but it was never real. He has never seen a building crumble under artillery fire. He has never had to think that his friends at Uni, his neighbours may have been the ones to rape a woman, a girl, a boy he knows, to execute a young man or beat him to death. He understands that the horror of such acts is made worse by its proximity.

He stands at Mary's bedside. Mary is tangled in her sheets again. The curtains have been closed for days. A different kind of horror for Ian and yet another about which he can do nothing.

*

Three weeks after his action in Canberra Jake goes up to the Darling Downs. He went out there last year with the anti-coal group Six Degrees and talked to dozens of landowners whose properties had been invaded by CSG companies. If companies have an exploration licence – and almost anyone can get one – they can come on your land, put in exploratory wells and if there's gas down there, they are almost inevitably granted a drilling licence. They can frack the hell out of the earth, poison the water system, even if it flows all the way to the sea or just to your kitchen.

He met a guy named Frank, a long time National Party voter who had begun to realise that he had lost control over his land and his life; that his entire view of the world and his place in it had gone out the window. Frank was both angry and bewildered, and for whatever reason he latched onto Jake in the days Jake was out there. In the evenings, Jake hung out with him in the Regal and had a few beers. Frank had a 3000 hectare property and several gas wells on this property that were already producing. The water was getting worse every day. At one bore, he showed how bad it had become. He set the water on fire. Jake took a video, posted it on YouTube with Frank explaining how this used to be drinking water. It went mildly viral, but nothing changed. Frank's moment of optimism faded as he read about his local member, a man he voted for, claiming that there was no evidence that the CSG company was responsible for the problem; that they were using best practice, that the new water laws would change all that, blah blah blah. I have heard it all before, just lies, shamelessness, callousness. It sounded no different than world leaders expressing sympathy for the dead and dying in Sarajevo.

The next day Frank took him on a tour of the Downs and showed him a bunch of wells. "Go further west and it's a lot worse," Frank said. "CSG companies can't clear veg without a permit, but the farmer, he can clear pretty much whatever he wants if it's regrowth. Most of the bush is regrowth – cleared at some point in the past. So, the CSG company pays the farmer and it's gone. Lots of giant trees the farmer had no cause to clear are gone and now when there's rain the creek banks are collapsing, the water is now a muddy brown. A lot of things going, a lot of things already gone."

Almost everyone Jake spoke with were farmers, almost all of them from families of farmers and almost all of them wanted to stay on the land, but many were getting close to giving it away. He went to Acland, a farming town bought by a coal company, now down to a single resident who wouldn't leave unless they dragged him away. And he wouldn't go quietly. Once a week he would mow the grass at the RSL memorial in what used to be the centre of town.

In Toowoomba Jake saw the offices of Santos and others, and the site where a bunch of rigs were stored waiting for the next round of final approvals from the State. "They move them in as soon as they apply for a drilling licence. No one says no," Frank said. "The government doesn't even know what chemicals are being used in the fracking. We certainly don't and we're drinking it and feeding it to our livestock and crops and sometimes to ourselves and our children."

A week after that visit, more than a year ago now, Frank's six-month-old child fell ill.

*

It used to be sugar in the exhaust but with complex and computerised equipment it's different now. Jake has bought hydrochloric acid. There are no restrictions and no registration requirements yet for that stuff. After tomorrow maybe. Jake has been up only once to see if he can get into the yard filled with rigs. Security isn't there full time. Security came at 9pm and then around 1am, then it was quiet until 7. He's amazed and then realises that with thousands of wells and not a single incident in over a decade, why would they bother.

There are cameras but they are up on the shed and looking down. As long as he wears a hat or a balaclava he'll be fine. He doesn't think there's an alarm system on the fence or on the rigs. The shed probably has one, but he's not going in there.

At 2 am he cuts a hole in the fence and then waits, prepared to flee. Almost immediately the wind picks up. He can hear it gathering itself in the distance and then beginning to roar across the Downs. Soon it is howling and seems to come from all directions. And then it gets worse. Branches, leaves, debris, rubbish fly everywhere. And Jake barely moves. He looks up and tilts his head trying to hear something more than the sound of the wind galloping across the landscape. I am so tense. I hear the wind as a sign, as a messenger, but Jake is probably right to ignore it because nothing happens.

After 30 minutes, he crawls in through the fence.

He demolishes the console coverings with a small crowbar and pours the acid into the electronic heart of the 7 rigs. He then pours acid into the hydraulic intake as well. Fifteen minutes is all it takes and these machines won't be used again. It seems so simple – much easier and more permanent than the rail lines.

He leaves a blunt message from The Free Radicals, with a small dose of irony, on the shed door. 'No more destruction', and then he leaves.

He has little of the tension that he had the first time but moves with an assurance that worries me.

He looks at his watch. Not even 3 am. He looks again and begins to move quickly towards the car. His plan is to head home. He'll be there by 6 am or so.

But he doesn't head home. He still has half a litre of acid remaining. It's only 3 am and he makes a crazy choice. He starts driving north, slowly and carefully but he knows exactly where he's going. I watch with a kind of horror. This is a mistake and one he promised never to make. I can see a drilling rig in the distance. There is a security light and a fence several hundred metres in front of him. Jake gets out of the car and stares for a minute. I don't think he's waiting or listening. Just staring because this particular rig has a history he knows too well. It is Frank's property. I should have known. Jake leans back into the car and pulls out the acid and then something else. He puts on the balaclava again and then straps a video camera to his head. Shit. Not good. Not smart. Too cocky. When he gets to the fence, he turns it on and he starts talking. "This rig is built on a property owned by a family that has been here for almost 200 years. Last year, six months after the rig had started up, their infant died. Cause of death unknown, but the parents asked for an autopsy and it revealed a child with lesions, disease and toxins throughout her body. He steps through the hole in the fence. "A month before, the water coming from the kitchen sink was so contaminated, that the father, put a match to it and it exploded in flames. The water was tested. It cannot be drunk, but they drank it – every day until that moment. They don't know all the chemicals that are in it. The health department refuses to conclude it's because of this rig, even though they admit they don't know which chemicals are being used by the CSG company."

"When the government lies to citizens, when corporations are willing to kill people in the name of profit, is it wrong to destroy the instrument of that poisoning? I can't arrest the CEO Barry Long, even though he is a criminal and a killer. I can't force the government to act on behalf of the public. So, my choice is this. I want them to know that their crimes will be punished in ways such as this." He pours the acid on the console and is silent as it begins to smoke, then the drill begins to shudder as though it is having a seizure and finally it stops with a terrible grinding sound. I almost feel sorry for the beast. "This punishment is not nearly enough. But this is also not the end of it."

Jake walks back to the car. He has rolled the balaclava up on to his forehead. He looks unapproachable, kind of dangerous. I don't know what to say to him, I think, even though he can't hear me. I feel as though I am his advisor and friend and protector and at the moment I am speechless. Jake gets in his car. He doesn't look around. He doesn't have that precise and careful air he had before. He forgets to take the balaclava and video camera off his head. It isn't until he is entering Toowoomba that he realises. He pulls over, puts the camera and balaclava at the bottom of his work bag. He brought a change of clothes but he can't change now. He curses under his breath. He shakes his head as though trying to clear a fog. He turns on the radio, puts both hands on the steering wheel and begins to drive again, slowly and carefully. If a policeman sees him, he'll be stopped. Too cautious – like a driver who knows he has had too much to drink.

He is home a bit after 7 am. I didn't think he was going to make it. He started speeding up heading out of Toowoomba and down the range. Way too fast, dangerously fast. He finally caught himself in a screech of tires. And then he slowed to twenty km below the speed limit. Wake up man! What is going on in that boy's head? I want to shake him by the shoulders.

When he gets home, he goes to the computer first. He uploads the video, edits a bit of it, but not much. He alters the voice, but I don't know if it's enough. It's pretty dramatic, actually. He sends it out and then a media release. He deletes the video from both the camera and the computer. When he's done he takes off his shoes and crawls into bed still dressed, gives Julie the gentlest of kisses on the head, turns over exhausted and is asleep in seconds.

*

"Hey Jake, where you been?" Sean is sitting at his computer. "I've been feeling lonely, here, man. You find some other work?"

"I've been away a few times for work and spending a fair bit of time working at my parent's house. Is that your photo?"

Sean's screen saver is a stunning photograph of a black kite poised in the air above the photographer. Each feather is crystal clear and the yellow and black eyes stare right through him with an amazing singularity of purpose.

"Yeah, I went out to some cane fields after burning. The raptors go off. Sat in a field with my tripod for hours and this shot made it worth it."

They sit and browse some of his photos. They are mainly nature and landscape photos from a week Sean spent on Fraser Island. They are fantastic. It's clearly his passion. Not for the first time, Jake is amazed at the hidden talents of so many people he knows.

"Even Tina noticed you were gone," Sean says finally.

"I told her I was taking leave. I had to help out with my mum. I don't know how much longer I can do this," he says, almost to himself.

Sean turns to him. "What's up?"

"Personal stuff. But also frustrated, confused. Angry. We tell the whole world to pay attention to the science. Science gives us the truth or as close as we can get. This is real, this is a runaway train, then we act as though it's just one more 'issue', you know?"

"We're trying to do what we can." Sean sounds defensive.

Jake stares out the window. "The possible rather than the necessary?" he asks quietly.

"I guess."

"It's eating me up. I mean last week our former PM went west, opened a new coal mine and said coal is good for humanity. It's not only what we're doing to the planet. It's that the whole system – Government, business and even us – aren't taking care of what we know needs to be done. And it's not going to change with a new PM."

"Oh come on, Jake, you can't put us in the same basket as the others."

"I can. I do. I don't risk much of anything in this fight. I don't risk my car, my family, my possessions, my life even though they are all at risk from what we as a society are doing. I cruise in here, say the right things, do more good than harm and go home at the end of the day. Paid for my services."

"So, you want us all to be martyrs to the cause?"

"No. Don't cheapen it that way. I don't know what I want. Revolution, maybe."

"Peace on earth. Shit."

Jake is skating further and further out, onto the thinnest of ice. These are not innocent discussions anymore. They are no longer the words of a privileged white man allowed to say whatever the hell he pleases. These are words that put him further at risk. So shut up, Jake says to himself.

The exhilaration he felt yesterday, his sense of power, has dissipated, perhaps consumed by his almost endless anger.

Sean thankfully changes the subject a little. "You know they are coming after us big time because of this group, The Free Radicals," Sean says. "The media is going feral. Then the police came in again yesterday – right after the drill rig stuff went viral. They didn't even have a warrant but demanded we hand over all our computers. They questioned everyone on the climate team. It was pretty brutal, man. They assumed that we were guilty and if we hadn't done it we would have, could have. Nothing friendly at all. Brutal. Whoever is doing this is making them mad and ugly. They want to talk to you too, by the way. You should probably call them before they break your damn door down. That's how bad it was. We didn't give 'em the computers, but they'll be back with warrants today. So, when you say we're not doing enough, I look at that. They don't even want us doing what we're doing. I don't think I'm ready for much uglier. They're going to arrest someone soon. They have to. They're getting hammered because it keeps happening. It's getting weirder here too. Like everyone is tense.

More arguments, more caution. Yesterday we argued for ages about a media release attacking government. The Comms team wanted to tone it down. Garth was yelling, man, saying, no, we can't. I've never seen that dude even irked before."

"Yeah, I noticed how tense it felt when I came in."

"And on top of the media we're getting called eco-terrorists as well. A few people have been yelled at in the streets – they were wearing Green Earth t-shirts. Go figure man."

*

The video has gone viral. It is played over 70,000 times. Reactions are all over the place, but for the first time, there is active support for The Free Radicals. Greenies are all scum, but the group was speaking up for farmers and that's okay, almost, sort of, sometimes.

The big environment groups denounce the violence and nothing more. It is undermining the work they are doing, creating a climate of fear and antagonism in which common ground is even harder to find. They think that will save them. A bit like Jews not speaking out against Hitler or Serbs against Karadzic. Silence like that never seems to protect you nor does it win you any friends. At least that's my experience.

Politicians – not just the usual suspects – are falling over themselves to denounce the entire environment movement. The Greens are generally silent, although they are curt and unequivocal when forced to answer: "We don't support violence, no matter how much we support change." That's probably the most Jake could expect.

The extremists in government, and Jake is convinced their numbers have been growing for years, want to wipe away the environment movement. Jake nods at this kind of language with grim pleasure. We can now join asylum seekers as the lowest of the low he thinks. The middle ground is disappearing. He knows he was reckless that night. He knows he let his anger control him, but in hindsight he thinks it was smart. The CSG industry is about farms and food and water. People pay attention to that. Climate change is only about the entire damn planet. He laughs at the ridiculousness of it.

With any luck farmers will start taking matters into their own hands and then the politics gets much more interesting, Jake thinks. The industry could probably safely shoot a few greenies, but not farmers.

Jake is worried though. His voice was altered on the video but it's still his voice and it's still him talking about a family he knows personally. He has no idea where cameras might have been on that part of his trip.

Frank is interviewed by several television stations. "I'm glad it's gone. I'm glad I don't wake up in the middle of the night with the sound of that rig part of my nightmares, but I didn't do it and can't ever approve of others taking the law into their hands – even if I believe that's what the gas companies are getting away with."

When the police interview Frank, Jake knows his name will almost certainly be one of those mentioned. He needs to prepare for this.

CHAPTER 20

The police finally interview Jake. He called them after his conversation with Sean, told them he had been camping at Mt Barney, but it's almost a week before they talk to him. They come into work. He forgets their names instantly. They look much the same to Jake. He sits with them at one of the conference tables that is in the open and very public. The officers clearly don't like that.

"Sorry we missed you last time, Jake," all friendly.

"Well, I can't say I missed you – I was over at Mt Barney discovering some pretty special places. What can I do for you?"

"What do you think about the emergence of this group, um, The Free Radicals?"

"Do you mean what they are doing?"

"That's right."

"Honestly, I think it's pretty stupid. It's not going to change anything; it diverts us from more important work and it means we're more likely to spend time doing this than work."

"Do you own a car?"

"Of course, I'm a greenie."

"Excuse me?"

"A joke."

Not even a hint of a smile in return. "You think this is a joke?"

"I think that if you were investigating the criminals causing and allowing climate change it would be much more useful." Jake cautions himself.

"What colour is your car?"

"Blue," he says straight up, but I can see the jolt, the moment of terror quickly suppressed.

"Can we have a look at it?"

"Sure. It's in the lot. I assume you passed it on the way in."

"Inside?"

"If you have a warrant, of course."

They ask him where he was on various dates – dates he knows well. He knows this is a potential problem for him and he tries to keep it simple. "I assumed you'd want to know that. I checked my calendar – any dates, social or work I put in there and it's clean for all of those days. It means I was at home. Julie – my partner – and I share the calendar and as far as I can tell she was home on all those days too."

"And the days and times before and after?"

"I didn't specifically check that. I can do that if you'd like."

"We'll let you know." No friendliness here. "You said you've been camping at Mt Barney. When were you there?"

"Last week, Sunday to Wednesday morning. Got back yesterday."

"Did you go with anyone?"

"Sorry, on my own."

"Any proof you were there?"

"I don't know. I was bush camping and I spoke with some people on the way there, when I stopped for lunch, but don't know their names."

"Did you buy petrol on the way?"

"No, I filled up here before going."

"Any leads so far?" he asks as they stand to leave.

"A few," the older one says.

"We'd like to take your computer for a few days," one says casually but not.

"Once more officer, you're going to need a warrant. Organisational policy."

They nod, in tandem.

"Good luck," Jake says.

They take several photos of the car and the licence number on the way out. He watches them from the first floor window. They didn't ask a single question about Frank and the Darling Downs.

*

The CSG industry is nervous. Investors are nervous. The price of CSG has been tanking for over a week. Publicly listed CSG companies are being hammered. The industry can't afford this. The muti-billion dollar export facility on Curtis Island in the Great Barrier Reef Marine Park can't afford any drop in exports – it's in debt up to its eyeballs. Jake assumes this is the reason investors are scared. A prolonged period of below projected and needed exports and Curtis Island investments could become worthless. At least that's the line one financial group is taking.

The police haven't been back to see him, which worries him more. It has been oddly silent. It makes no sense to him that he hasn't been interviewed again. Surely, they can't have missed his visit to the

Downs last year and his acquaintance with Frank.

He wonders if they are waiting for him to act again because they don't have enough evidence yet to do more than suspect him. His paranoia escalates. He tries to determine if he is being followed. He looks in windows, makes sudden changes of direction, goes into a store, leaves by the back door then goes around to the front to see if anyone has tried to follow. He laughs at himself – the pretence that he knows how to detect or dump someone trailing him amuses him, but he doesn't stop. He tapes over the video camera on his computer. He checks and double checks his computer for anything that could suggest his involvement. But it's all clean. He is certain his phone calls are being monitored, but that doesn't worry him. He doesn't take his phone with him on these actions.

He stops wondering whether he is being successful and simply worries about ensuring that everything he does is safe, that everything he plans is watertight.

He knows he can't see what is happening beneath the surface – the surveillance, the hidden cameras, the wiretaps, the increased security, but he must assume all of those things are happening and it will only get harder from now.

He knows too that his biggest weakness is his alibis. He told the police that on the dates they asked about he was home with Julie.

He hasn't told Julie that, and he doesn't even know whether she'll remember those dates and tie his absences to the events that were in the news. He told the police they share an online calendar. She has never used it. His stomach churns. What a cesspit it must be in there, he thinks.

He doesn't know what to do next. He is trying to plan his next action in his parents' living room. In front of him a photo of him when he was nine or ten, riding a bicycle, a look of joy on his face. There is nothing in that photo that reminds him of him. There is not even anything from his childhood that he carries close to him, or that's how it feels. All far way and long gone.

He knows his next step has to be an escalation – either in intensity or frequency, but he can't do this on a weekly basis on his own. And the other escalation – bigger, more spectacular, more dangerous, more damaging. What? Derail a train? Scuttle a coal ship in Newcastle Harbour or Abbot Point? He swore to himself that he would harm no one. It would be completely counterproductive. More to the point he couldn't live with that. Sometimes he hates that – a deeply embedded belief in the sanctity of human life, of all life, but it's the human part that disturbs him. If humans are such destroyers why hold those lives sacred? With around eight billion people on the planet – high level predators and consumers – Jake wonders who could argue that each life should be saved when in doing so many other lives of many other living things are then sacrificed? And what about those responsible for climate change. CEOs and billionaires will be responsible for the deaths of millions. Criminal, but he can't yet bring himself to consider the logical conclusion of that knowledge.

During The Siege people went to extraordinary lengths to save others. We harboured people, shared food, made room in our houses for those without homes, including many we didn't know. It was in part a determination to show our spirits couldn't be broken and in part to show that life was sacred, simply because the war said it wasn't.

A young family stayed with me for three weeks before their escape from the city was arranged. I can't remember the names of any of them. I have no idea whether they escaped and once they left my house I never asked. In very real ways they meant nothing to me, but at the same time if they had been captured or killed under my care, I never would have forgiven myself.

CHAPTER 21

September 1992

Dear Brother

Over the last year the shelling has become worse and worse until it is virtually constant. In those few moments where silence arrives, it sits heavy and suspiciously around us. It seems no building is free of injury. All the lovely old government buildings and grand palaces and houses have been particularly targeted. Many are completely destroyed. I have heard several people say that along certain parts of Branilaca Sarajeva they see only rubble, no familiar landmarks, no street signs, no monuments. Perhaps they were on the wrong street. It can be difficult to know. One no longer gives directions as we once did. Instead we say, 'turn left at the church with no steeple.' Our world daily becomes smaller. First it is a city, then a neighbourhood, then a street and for many a room in a house.

Tarek's mother is in such a small world. She was in line waiting to buy bread when a shell landed across the street and the woman next to her was killed and she was spared – if huddling in a room waiting for the next explosion is to be spared not cursed. She will not leave anymore and it is only rarely, mainly at night, that she pulls the curtains aside and peeks out.

I see Tarek rarely these days. He is an organiser and perhaps a fighter too, I am not sure. He is looking old and tired, and like all of us has grown somewhat harder. When I do see him he says little about what he does and where he goes. He has become very secretive. He apologises and says it protects me too. Instead he talks politics.

The Serbs plan to declare and create a greater Serbian Federation. Why do a people feel such a need to be imprinted in ever larger fashion on the minds of people who should be people and lovers first? Why the impulse for empire? They are more burden than boon, I think, but then I am content with a small life.

We do not understand the inertia of the West, their reluctance to become involved. Theories and conspiracies abound and have become like a kind of bread here. Tarek's view is simpler. "We are of no particular use to them – either in a greater Serbia or apart as Bosnians. So, why would they intervene?"

We want them to care but they will only care if care and self-interest intersect. We do not need a conspiracy to understand this.

One time, several visits ago, I insisted we talk about something else. Tarek, Janos, myself. We sat down with some god-awful brandy smuggled in from nowhere salubrious and I said, "Okay, today, no politics, no tragedy. Today we must gossip, only gossip."

As I hope you can imagine, there was a wonderful storehouse of stories to tell. Boundaries tend to disappear in war – and lonely people in war do many things they will try and forget later. Anyway, we were in stitches quickly. There was no cruelty in our words – instead it was a kind of love of others and a real gratitude because we had found such childish pleasure and laughter.

I remember that day well. It had been a hellish week. We were in the early days of digging the tunnel and smuggling equipment under darkness, spreading false rumours, hiding from our own people because no one could know. And then we had raging arguments with the smugglers. We had to work together but their cause was too different from ours. There was one man, Vlad, a powerful, smart and scary man. I negotiated with him. Who paid for the tunnel? Who controls it? What effect on the price of food and guns? He was a dangerous man and the negotiations were long and difficult. We gave away too much. The smugglers knew they had all the leverage.

He was the first man I killed during The Siege. He was paid to smuggle a young family across the Adriatic to Italy. His minions did the work for him and they abandoned the young family near the border. They scattered, believing they had been found out, and the family unsure what to do, hid in the woods, hoping the smugglers would return.

They didn't, but the Serbian army found them and executed the father and raped the mother in front of the two kids. Vlad needed to know that no Bosnian could be treated like this, no Bosnian family could be abandoned.

We – the informal leadership group – agreed that in this case no second chances. I was selected because I knew him, had negotiated with him, I could get access. And I volunteered. And so it was done.

But that was later. After negotiating with Vlad and feeling angry and tired, nothing could have been better than to sit down with my family and tell many stories. My favourite was of two ageing neighbours. One night Elanka began to dance naked in front of her window. Soon, Miroslav, across the lane, started doing the same. She turned up the volume, opened the window and they danced naked to traditional Balkan folk music. Sexy, ridiculous, wondrous.

September 1992

Dear Brother

We met a man from the other side today. That is what we call a westerner now. Another of our dark jokes. We sat down eagerly with this man – we were ready to feast on him. Seriously, I felt like a cannibal. Sadly, though, the meal was bitter. The man was a writer. He had come in with the smugglers. He told us there is little interest in Sarajevo in Europe and even less in America, where the feeling is if the Europeans aren't going to do anything why should we. The Europeans are deeply divided – although all of them are wringing their hands when public attention demands a response. It is terrible, terrible, terrible, but we cannot intervene. Alberto suspects that the unification of Europe – for which so many have worked for so long – is making any intervention here much more difficult. And so, while they unify, we disintegrate. We should not be expected to pay this price.

He was desperate for our news too. We passed him from house to house where he gathered stories and photos and after a week disappeared quietly. We still do not know if his stories were ever printed.

*

These letters bring back so many places, people, histories. I can see Sofia standing at her window singing softly to herself as she did when she worried. The tea pot sits on the table, a filament of steam dissipates in the sunlight. The faded flowers on her sofa – which once belonged to her parents – were sad even when Ian was there. They were barely discernible the last time I saw them.

She told me that she read little during The Siege but there were books everywhere. She never told me she was writing to Ian.

I loved Janos. A man who found joy easily but with his eyes open. He liked to recite poetry. Dismantling the Silence was one of his favourites. It begins, 'Take down its ears first.' Janos would stand in the middle of the room pretending to hold ITS ears in his hand.

Is dismantling silence, taking down its ears, the same as learning to listen, to hear?

I wonder.

There is much to hear.

*

When Jake walks in – no one answered his knock – Ian is standing at the foot of the bed, watching Mary. The crepitations of her breathing sound like a spirit walking lightly on broken glass. Jake joins his father. He takes his hand and together, but still without a great deal of strength, they watch a woman die, watch a person being pulled from their lives, a messy, sticky business. She won't let go easily. They won't let go easily. I have seen scenes like this too many times in Sarajevo and will never get used to it.

Ian is losing weight. He is almost gaunt and the shadows under his eyes grow longer each day. Jake is more worried about him than Mary. "Dad, you can't kill yourself to look after Mum. That doesn't help anyone."

"I'm okay."

Jake wants to throttle him. "You're not okay. You look like shit. You haven't slept, you aren't eating. You're suffering and pretending that nothing is different."

"I don't need a parent, Jake."

"You do need a carer though."

Ian turns away, back to his office and closes the door.

Jake stands in front of Mary and desperately wants her to open her eyes and speak with him, tell him what to do. She is on her back, her hands crossed on her chest and she doesn't move. Her breath is regular if not deep and behind her eyelids there is no movement at all. She doesn't dream. And why should she? What could she want to know – at any level of consciousness – about who she is and where she goes?

Jake begins to weep silently. Parents are a complicated business, like mazes that as children we learn to navigate but rarely to solve. But dying changes that. Now there is just the rawness – the space between two souls unmediated by ritual or habit or history.

And the guilt and sense of loss. How could he have paid so little attention to who this woman was for so long? Is. I always assumed she was just my mother, Jake thinks, but he knows now, too late, that this isn't even close to the truth.

Even more he struggles with his sense of being besieged. Every part of his life is tenuous and uncertain, a mix of trying to influence forces bigger than he can ever be and accepting he has no real control over his life. He stands at the end of Mary's bed, as Sofia stood at her window during the siege, dread and wishful thinking choking his spirit.

CHAPTER 22

Ian told Jake about the letters but has told no one Sofia's story of The Siege. He has decided he can't until he knows how this ends. He faces the end of the letters with a deep dread, a sense of doom – both Sofia's and his own. He reads one, maybe two letters at a time to slow down her inevitable disappearance. He knows she cannot write about her own death – but he is convinced that is what she has done, that this is what these letters are about. A small part of him hopes for a different ending. He hopes she is alive, living quietly in a small village, but too much in that ending doesn't make sense.

October 1992

Dear Brother

There are now snipers regularly on Ulica Zmaja od Bosne. The cry of 'beware sniper' has become too common. We all walk close to walls and doorways into which we can duck if we are lucky. It is strange to have our main street the most dangerous place in Sarajevo. It is like a boundary, a chasm that has been built in the city to divide us into two or perhaps more. There are friends, colleagues, parts of our underground that live on the other side and we must learn to cross this dangerous river quietly.

We are, at a deeper level, also aware that we are surrounded, stuck in the middle, like wearing a noose that very slowly tightens.

We sense a growing number of Serbs are inside the city. It is not only the snipers but last week there was an assault in the market – the one nearest my house – that left seven dead and many wounded. We hear tales of a tunnel out of the city. Perhaps there is one into the city as well.

It is strange that the shelling and sniper fire have become so normal that I speak of them in the same tone as Irfan's affair or Marta's cancer.

Food is becoming a problem – scarce and expensive. Most of us share what we have. We give our goods to the black marketeers to sell or trade and share the food once it comes. It is now mainly processed foods, potatoes and bread. I never thought I would feel a powerful urge for cabbage, but this is what it has come to.

I have met many new people on this street. Many become friends. That happens quickly, because they may disappear just as quickly. I remember all their names though, me whose memory for names has always been so poor.

There are so many injured now. The shelling brings ugly wounds – shrapnel, glass, clothing melted into wounds. The smell of blood – and necrosis – is with me constantly now. I am fine with the sight of gore but when I get home and cannot leave the smell behind, I begin to go mad. I have searched in every room for the dead body; have slept on the bathroom floor – the only room free of the smell. I sometimes wish I'd joined the militia too; felt some sense of control over my life. Treating the wounded in a never-ending stream of misery feels like more symbolic gesture than meaningful change.

We have not seen Tarek in a long time. We are worried.

I saw Sofia as a nurse only once. Funny, her face scared me. Intense, focused, angry, helpless but most of all determined. She had a powerful presence. Hardened militia soldiers wouldn't dare defy her. I will not fail. I will survive. Whatever it takes. Each time I saw her she grew harder, thinner, her eyes hooded with horrors she would never speak, but she was never going to stop.

October 1992

Dear Brother

Tarek is alive but we only found this out in the worst of circumstances. His mother died in her apartment. She had not left her apartment in months and Tarek thinks she died of sadness. Tarek found her. She had been dead almost a week and no one had checked on her. He did not tell us the condition of the body, but we suspect the worst. How could this man who gives so much to resisting the Serbs not feel guilty, feel as though he abandoned his family in his efforts to protect us all?

He is looking very thin and gaunt. Spiritually gaunt as though he has seen or perhaps done too much. He talks little of his time out there except to say he is optimistic that this war will end soon. Janos and I, we do not believe him and we don't even humour him, we know him too well for that.

The shelling has become relentless. Milos says it is over 1000 shells per day. I try to imagine the sky over our home filled with that many bombs and cannot or won't.

*

Ian decides he must find out what happened to Sofia. He doesn't need to finish reading the letters to do that. He calls the Bosnian Herzegovinian embassy in Canberra and asks how he can get help finding family lost during The Siege in Sarajevo.

There are several ways he is told. There is a register, a Book of the Dead. Both survivors and searchers register the names of those they know died and any details – dates, addresses, friends they may have. When The Siege ended, there were many dead and many missing. The city government wanted to honour them and asked for citizens who remained and those who had safely departed to search their memories for as many names as they could remember. "This list is in Sarajevo" the woman says. "The register has thousands of names – but many are not there and may never be there. Because your family is Jewish, there is a non-profit organisation that searches for Bosnian Jews. "Many, but not so many," the woman says. "It may make your hopes bigger." Finally, there are some official records of deaths in Sarajevo. Hospitals, cemeteries, even temples and churches are worth looking into but the records are incomplete. One hopes that a name is missing from these lists but it tells you little, except that hope remains.

Tarek Votek and Milos Danon are the only names Ian has. I could give him many more. If only.

January 1993
Dear Brother

We have seen in the new year. 1993. It was a quiet night. We wonder if this a joke by the Serbs – they must need their moments of humour too. We won't shell on the one night when fireworks are expected. Not very funny, really.

I have been thinking of you. Until now, I think I have been writing to my brother almost in the abstract. I have no idea of who you are now. I don't know if you are even still called Ivan. I barely remember the last time we saw each other or the words we exchanged in such anger. It not only seems far away but foolish too. War creates a different perspective. I hope I see you again. I hope we can become brother and sister once more.

*

Mary is asleep. Ian waits quietly on a chair, hands folded in his lap in false calm, waiting for his family to shed their stuff, get a drink and join him.

Peta, Jake and Julie finally sit, his old impatience surfacing briefly for the first time in years. "I want to tell all of you something," Ian says without preface. "My name is Ivan. I am a Jew from Sarajevo and I've been hiding from this for too long. Today I began to search for my uncle and sister. I believe Tarek, my uncle, is dead, but I don't yet know the full story. My sister wrote me many letters during The Siege that I have had for years and never read, until now. I haven't finished them yet, but I know these letters can't be the whole story. And I have only begun to learn the story of the war. I learned today that Sarajevo was one of the few communities in Europe that accepted Jews after they were expelled from Spain in the Middle Ages. It was a part of the Ottoman Empire then – so Muslim, Christian and Jew. Twenty percent of the population was Jewish then. A real juha of peoples," he says with a small self-conscious grin. "Juha is soup in Bosnian."

"Dad, hold on. You have a sister and an uncle? Did anyone else know this?" Peta asks.

"I found out about the letters and the sister this week," Jake says quietly, "and I had heard a little bit about the uncle only a few weeks ago."

"We had a falling out," Ian says softly and then falls into silence. "I have a box of her things, her drawings and letters. I don't know if she's alive."

Peta, more than Jake, wants to know more, has endless questions. "What's her name? Why'd you fall out? What about your parents? Are they alive? What were their names? What do you mean you didn't read them? Where were they? How many letters?" You can see Ian isn't prepared for such a barrage and you can feel him withdrawing, like a turtle pulling its head in as far as it can.

Jake feels utterly bewildered, even though he knew more than Peta. He is less curious about Ian's past than about what is happening to his father and why.

Finally, he asks the only question he can give shape to in this moment? "Why now, Dad?"

Ian looks at Jake, initially grateful that the questions from Peta have stopped and then realising Jake's question is even harder. He isn't sure, firstly, whether Jake wants to know why he's telling them this or why he has suddenly started caring about a family he left behind long ago. He doesn't really know how to answer either.

"I remembered the box, the one with all the letters up in the cupboard."

Peta kind of rescues him from his non-answer. "Can we read the letters?"

Poor Ian. He so wanted to make the confession but not to explore what it actually means. He stands up, "I'm sorry, maybe I shouldn't have said anything, but I don't know what to say, am not ready to say more yet. Please give me a bit of time," he mutters and walks back into the office, a place once again that is his refuge.

Jake, Julie and Peta sit in a kind of stunned silence. Ian's words, brief as they were, swirl around them. They have caught a glimpse of his past, they know it's now alive in the present, but they are even more in the dark than they were before.

*

Ian left at the height of the cold war. Yugoslavia was bad but not as bad as East Germany or Russia. Tito had united a disparate country with his own brand of brutality and kept a peace that was as real as it was shallow.

Only weeks before The Siege began, Sofia told me the story of their falling out. Ian was a quiet man but believed he needed more academic freedom. That's what he told himself but perhaps what he needed was the opportunity to reinvent himself from a shy, fearful young man into someone else. He was unhappy, painfully shy. An academic, but not prominent. Smart, but not challenging smart, not wise, not rebellious. He wanted more, but the truth was – according to Sofia – that he never had the slightest idea what it was he wanted or how to find it. Sofia said he mistook what was a personal desperation for an act of courage and rebellion both. She thought he was being a coward.

It is only now, many years after my death, I see that his flight, no matter if it was cowardly or deluded, actually worked, allowed him to transform his life in almost exactly the ways he wanted.

Within a year of moving to Australia, he landed an economics position at university – there weren't many experts then on the economies of Eastern Europe. In that same year he met Mary. It was the first long term relationship he had ever had. They didn't really fall in love, they kind of slid towards it until they awoke one morning and in bed next to them was a person they loved deeply and fully. It happened that way for both of them. It was never a romance abundant in lust and crazy young love. It was like two trees whose roots and branches became inextricably and lovingly entwined over years.

He started a new life and thoughtlessly put the old one away. With every passing year, it was further away, less a part of him, or so he thought. It wasn't a past abandoned in anger but left behind carelessly like an old trinket no longer needed. Perhaps another delusion.

I suspect now that he never spoke of those he left behind from a sense of shame. And the longer he remained silent the more ashamed he felt, the more he ran away, determined to forget we had ever existed. And eventually he convinced himself he had forgotten.

January 1993

Dear Brother

How can such horrors become worse? Yesterday the Deputy Prime Minister was assassinated here in Sarajevo by Serbian soldiers. He was being escorted to the airport by UN soldiers. They did not act to protect him. The Serbs stopped the UN convoy, demanded the Deputy Prime Minister and when the French soldiers obligingly opened the door of his vehicle, the poor man was shot multiple times. The UN soldiers did not return fire and didn't attempt to detain the shooters. There are some today who think the Serbs have crossed a line that the UN cannot ignore. They can ignore it. The line was crossed long ago and many times since. After the killing the shells rained from the sky, it was a sight that brought terror, awe and a profound sense that we had not yet hit bottom.

Today Janos and I asked about getting out, going to Italy and trying to do our part there. We could fundraise, organise, speak out in ways we cannot do here. It is hard to know if that is already happening or not. Hard to know whether it is being done well. You will have to teach me English quickly!

We both feel a sense of elation at allowing ourselves to leave, mixed with grief, disbelief, a host of new fears and impatience.

CHAPTER 23

The first arrest occurs on the day Mary is hospitalised. She has had a fit of some sort – perhaps the drugs, perhaps the cancer consuming her from the inside. A young man, Brian Howland, is paraded in front of the media, accused of terrorism and membership in The Free Radicals.

Mary returned home the next day, thinner, exhausted and even less present than before.

Howland is unlikely to go home for some time.

He is being indicted specifically for an attack on a coal train. He didn't actually attack the train but the coal itself. He boarded the train outside Newcastle and sprayed the coal with a foul mixture of ingredients that may or may not have made the coal unusable. It certainly couldn't be offloaded until it was tested and probably cleaned. A costly undertaking,

Following the attack, The Free Radicals circulated a media release. We must stop climate change and all that.

Howland looks like he hasn't slept in days. He looks both stunned and terrified. To some, no doubt, he looks unsavoury and therefore guilty. To me he looks tormented.

Jake knows him from Beyond Coal meetings in Brisbane and Sydney. Quiet guy but intense. A musician or music teacher. Jake can't remember. The police press conference reveals little. Jake starts asking around at work if anyone has more details.

No one wants to touch it. Not a single group puts out a media release. Assumed guilty.

He finally calls a colleague at The Nature Foundation and eventually gets the number for Brian's family. He calls that evening with Julie sitting next to him and dark clouds scudding across the horizon. "Hi, is this Fiona?...I just, um, I'm a colleague of Brian's and I wanted to know how Brian's doing and if there is anything I can do?....Thanks...Does he have a lawyer and all that?...That's good, I wasn't sure they would step up... You don't think he'll get bail?....No, you're probably right....Could you give him my best when you speak with him...You take care too."

Jake hangs up and takes Julie's hand. "They're terrified. He faces a lot of years if he's convicted."

"That was nice of you to call."

He almost says 'I'd want others to do the same for me'.

*

The CSG industry cannot be happy. The support for Frank is causing them potentially serious problems. There are now National Party members in Queensland and federally calling for an inquiry into the death of his child.

Behind the scenes, Jake is certain that the CSG industry is demanding results. They want the entire police force to drop everything to deal with this attack on their rights. After all, they've sponsored the damn police, Jake says. Their logos are on Queensland police cars.

The Premier is in a squeeze, poor woman. The media is in one of its feeding frenzies. The Premier no doubt gets daily briefings, basically telling her the obvious – that she's in a terrible political position. The damage Jake has done is worth close to 10 million dollars, and Frank's well is out of circulation for the foreseeable future. The police and the politicians know though that it isn't the money or the delays that matter, it's the audacity, the sense of uncertainty and concern that is creeping over the industry and the growing support for The Free Radicals that worries them. The industry knows that investors and even, more importantly, financial institutions don't like instability and if this continues for longer or gets worse it will become far more serious.

*

Jake calls Frank ten days after destroying the rig. "Hey Frank, Jake here. What have you done, mate?"

"Well, if the bloody police and pollies can be believed, I've single-handedly torn shreds off democracy."

"I can imagine the police are right up your ass."

"You have no idea. I get I'm an obvious suspect, but surely, I'm too bleeding obvious. They've questioned me twice, searched the house, taken all three computers – my bloody kids are about to tear down the walls without their games– and taken a whole swag of documents I need for the farm and tax."

"After the rail line and other stuff, the police have been questioning everyone in the greenie world. I think I'm a suspect because I have a blue car."

"You're kidding. The bastards asked me if I'd painted the car recently. I'm sure I looked at them as though they were crazy. Now I get it."

"They must know all you did to try and stop the rig in the first place."

"Yeah, they know. And everything I ever said to anyone in anger is going to come back to haunt me. Fuck, I must have threatened someone, somewhere."

"Well, you had a few arguments in the pub, that's for sure."

"And said a few things to you folks that I can't say I'd like repeated."

"I don't remember you saying anything, Frank."

"Thanks mate, but if they come to see you don't lie. I didn't destroy the damn thing so I'm going to keep believing that truth will have at least one victory in this miserable shit of a saga."

"Well, I wanted to see if you're okay. I hope you can get a bit of pleasure from not having the rig there. And look, if you need any help or media or a lawyer, I'll help however I can."

"Thanks mate. We're right for the moment, but fuck, you know, if they arrest me and hold me for any length of time, the farm's going to start bleeding bad."

"Call, seriously, if you need anything."

*

It's strange. Jake has stopped watching the news now. Of all the strange changes in Jake, this is the one that seems to confuse Julie the most. She watches for him. She tells him the things she thinks he would like to hear. He listens, at least that, but there is a kind of screen between him and events that only a little while ago would have engaged him fully. He cooks dinner or reads a novel, but he won't sit with Julie and watch. He doesn't go on his computer and trawl through the various news and commentary sites he has had bookmarked for years.

His sense of confidence, growing since standing at the rail lines over four months ago, dissipates, dissolves into the rashness of taking out the drill rig on Frank's property. He has almost inevitably and stupidly made himself a suspect. Why haven't the police come back and asked him about Frank?

I remember when we began to organise after that first month of The Siege. We realised that there were informers all over the city – on all sides – and behind them enforcers. The Siege wasn't just outside the city walls but all around us. We needed to organise food, medicine, information, escapes, retribution, defence, communication with the outside world. I was both a soldier and a kind of leader, but more than anything I simply wanted to find a way to make life as normal as possible, an attempt to deny what was undeniable. I think now that I was too afraid of dying, too afraid for my family and too unable to accept that the life I had before The Siege was completely gone. But I should have known. Every day I awoke afraid, I went out of my apartment afraid, I visited my family or the bakery afraid, I did my enforcement work afraid. I tried to make my fear normal, but it's still fear and still eats at you from the inside.

It's not true. Even worse than the fear was not feeling fear, feeling powerful or in command, feeling that the violence all around – and inside – was normal and okay. The very act of fighting fear is to court brutality. Feeling indifferent to the pain of others. There were times when I could not recognise myself. I became hard and probably a bit heartless. I told myself it was necessary, I was necessary. I told myself it would all be different, I would be different, once the war was over, as though fighting a war was like going on a diet.

Jake is afraid, afraid of arrest, of losing Julie, of his mother dying, and it sits in his stomach and may never go away. Not watching the news allows him to hold his fear for the planet at bay, at least a little. But it won't go away, he can't shoot it into submission. He should be more afraid of feeling nothing.

*

Jake is sitting on the verandah. He can hear Julie speaking. She must be on the phone. How long since she has gone out with her friends? Jake hasn't seen Cath in months, hasn't seen Mel either. They both used to drop in, but they don't come now. Mel is a lovely woman although drama and chaos seem to follow her everywhere. She has a child by a father who is insane. They have been in a legal and psychological battle for the boy for a decade. She takes care of injured animals and abused women and has had the shit beaten out of her a few times by angry, angry men. She learned self-defence and is now a dangerous woman to cross. But where is she? And Cath. Cath seems so entirely happy with life except three times a year, maybe four, when she breaks off her latest relationship, goes through an existential crisis for about a week, eats copious quantities of chocolate, finds another man and all is well with the universe. Jake can't remember the last time he saw either of them or the last time Julie spoke about either of them. He feels the weight of that on him, squarely on his shoulders. It feels like Julie's life has been sucked into Jake's vortex, into his darkness and his secrets. Made worse because he isn't sharing himself with her and just keeps lying to her.

He stands up and walks inside, ashamed and astonished both.

Julie is still on the phone. He waits. She smiles at him, her little smile. She can see he is waiting and he can tell she is in the middle of what must be an elaborate story. Maybe it's Mel.

When she hangs up, he blurts out, "Where's Mel? Is she okay? And Cath?"

Julie looks at him as though he's crazy. "You probably didn't have to loiter there looking like a boy needing to pee for ten minutes to ask that, did you?"

"I just realised I haven't seen or thought of Mel or Cath for a month, maybe two. That I've been so self-absorbed that I don't know what's happening with you, or your friends or even your work. Can we go sit together and for the next hour or two or four we don't talk about me at all?

"It's not very exciting," Julie says, but she is saying yes!

"I must have missed at least three Mel dramas and at least one Cath romance."

"Probably more of both."

"And after we talk, you talk, can we invite them over and whoever else you want and we'll have, I don't know, a picnic, a party, a gossip session?"

Julie feels relief, a hope and a fair bit of uncertainty. For months she has been holding on, holding on to Jake, to being together, waiting for him to come back. And she was losing hope and suddenly he is there, standing in front of her, in her arms. Belief is tricky.

*

Later, after talking and laughing and making love, Julie sleeps and Jake sits in the dark in the living room, still, but afraid again. He can feel IT coming back, this life that he lives that doesn't include Julie and it becomes larger, hungrier, more demanding.

It's as though too he can feel footsteps in his spirit, the shuffling of hard feet through leaves, the whispers in darkness, the words that he can't yet discern. They're coming. The police, the men in suits, his other selves...

He was so calm when he was being interviewed by the police. Maybe this is what scares him most right now. It was as though he hadn't done anything. He closes his eyes. He thinks he could beat a lie detector test and that means he has the makings of a sociopath, someone who can lie to anyone, will soon be able to hurt anyone, be able to murder without feeling.

Poor man. I sit watching him and I am holding my breath.

Jake opens the computer. He wants to write a letter to his mother. A letter that says all the things that have been unsaid, alluded to, forgotten. 'Dear Mum' is as far as he gets. He closes his eyes again and begins to press keys randomly. Surely somewhere in the universe of the possible there are answers. Instead, all he can think is that somewhere there are men waiting for him.

CHAPTER 24

"I have to go to North Queensland next week," he says to Julie. "We're meeting with the traditional owners at Abbot Point. We think we can get them to refuse to sign the Land Use Agreement – that will make it hard for the Sahan coal project to go ahead. I'll be gone for 2 or 3 days depending on who else we can get meetings with."

Desultory conversation, darkness, attempted sleep. God, it's tiring watching this.

Before he leaves, he takes his car to a garage that he hopes can detect a GPS tracker in a car. He feels a bit crazy. He watched a YouTube video explaining that trackers can be as small as an aspirin and electronic detection is the only effective way to find them. The mechanic, Phil, says, "yeah, get lots of folks coming in. Mostly don't find nothing, though. Usually it's partner crap, jealousy or stalking by an ex. Mind you, you're lucky you ain't got a new car. So many damn computer systems, tracking all sortsa shit and you can't take 'em out. You just have to pay for the info."

"If there's a tracker on this car, it's likely to be government property," Jake says and hopes that Phil asks no more. He doesn't.

It takes an hour and he finds one. Jake stares at this tiny black object that can talk to satellites and feels so out of his depth. This explains why they didn't question him further.

Jake drives home clutching the tracker in his hand. What does he do now? He will have to leave the tracker at home – well hidden – then put it back on the car when he returns. He has to hope they don't become suspicious if the car doesn't move for 3 or 4 days. That's not unusual, but the police may want to do a visual check on the car.

He almost cancels the trip. He is torn. They suspect him, but he doesn't believe they have any evidence except maybe the colour of his car and that he knows Frank. And he's a greenie of course. It's not much. He needs to strike again soon. The door is open, he keeps saying to himself, and the opportunity to increase the instability and fear in the industry is real.

*

Two days after the Federal Government approves the Carmichael mine in western Queensland, which will be the largest coal mine in the southern hemisphere, Jake is on his way to Bowen, just around the corner from where the coal will be shipped.

Bowen jetty is easy to reach by boat. It is around the headland from the Abbott Point coal terminal and at night it's very quiet. The tugs are easy to spot. Coming into the jetty by dinghy late on a weekday, there is no activity. The tugs are quiet and dark, as they have been all evening and the jetty lights are feeble. The tugs are all moored in line on the south side of the jetty. The tugs are the only ones serving the Abbot Point coal terminal. The operators are locals and are either at the pub or at home. The tugs are wooden. It's a hot, still evening.

Perfect conditions. He doesn't wait or hesitate. He takes his dinghy to the end of the jetty and as he gets close, he starts the video camera. "These boats make exporting coal from the Great Barrier Reef possible. But not for long," he says. He then empties twenty litres of fuel in the wheelhouse of each of the three boats. "The mining, export and burning of coal is killing the Great Barrier Reef. This year's bleaching is the worst ever recorded. If it happens again – as is predicted – it is likely to die." He tosses a knotted, burning rag into each boat. "Who is responsible? Who is going to take responsibility? These tugs are part of a crime that is against all of us, not just the Reef." Jake turns the video to the back of his head and heads towards the end of the bay and Doughty's Creek. He is there in less than ten minutes. He turns to watch and film the flames. "I wish we could do more," he says. "Destroying a few tugboats barely touches the surface of what needs to be done. But we've only just begun. It is time for those responsible for these crimes to listen. They are now on notice." He wants them to be afraid.

He deflates the dinghy and within another ten minutes has it in his car parked on Quay Street. He hears the first sirens and looks back again. The fires are ferocious and out of control. He gets into his car and within another ten minutes he is on the Bruce Highway heading south.

He drives only for a few hours to a campsite in Dryander National Park. Midweek and there is no one there.

He has no tent and from his swag stares at a sky clotted with stars. It makes him slightly uneasy. He leaves before dawn and arrives in Brisbane an hour after dark.

He sits in the car outside the house and searches the internet briefly for news on the tugs. The story is big and is carried in dozens of papers. All three tugs burned to the water line. No one was injured. The jetty suffered some damage, but the tugs are a write-off. There are no other tugs to service the coal ships at Abbot Point. No one seems sure how long it will be before replacement tugs can be found.

He didn't send out a media release this time, but the video goes online and is even more dramatic than the oil rig. The media has no doubt it is The Free Radicals. He is pleased.

Julie is curled in front of the television, a hot tea on the floor. He embraces her with pleasure and desire.

She pushes him away, almost gently. "Your mother had a fall today," she says. "No one could reach you. She's okay – in hospital but okay." She can barely look at him.

He stands immediately. "I better go," he says.

"Too late. Visiting hours are over. She'll be released tomorrow morning."

"I can't tell you," he blurts out, with an intensity that surprises even him.

"Tell me what?" She looks at him for the first time, hard curiosity.

He turns away, startled by that look, shaken – again – by the distance between them – a distance he didn't think could ever happen. He walks into the kitchen, grips the edge of the sink, looks at the shards of moonlight dropping from the trees. He thought he was managing it, that they were doing okay, but it's clear papering over the relationship isn't solving anything. He grabs a beer and pours Julie a wine.

"I don't want it, thank you," she says a bit more harshly than she intended.

"You will. Come and sit."

She knows he is going to tell her now and is filled with dread, worse, a feeling that this may be the end, of something, of everything.

"Did you watch the news tonight?" he asks.

She gives the slightest of nods.

"Did you see the story about the tugs burning up at Bowen?"

"Hard to miss." Not a hint of warmth.

"That was me. I did that. And the drill rig and the mining equipment and the train." He speaks with no pride – he doesn't feel any. He tells the story as dispassionately as he can. He doesn't try to justify or excuse himself but he doesn't apologise either and there is no remorse, only dread. He doesn't look at Julie directly the entire time, although he keeps trying to glance at her surreptitiously to read what she is thinking.

Julie watches him with an intensity that disguises her confusions. A thousand questions flap around the room, one-winged craziness. She is horrified, amazed, bewildered, angry, furious, clear for the first time in months what has been happening. A part of her is even relieved. A ten winged creature really. She struggles to hear or to listen – she wants to beat the crap out of him, hold him, tie him up in the cellar until he comes to his senses. You can guess all of this from the wild weather of her face.

Jake finally stops speaking. His hands are clenched together. He looks at Julie now and knows, as he knew when he began, how messy this is going to be. Julie's turn to look away. She picks her wine glass off the floor, empties it and walks out of the room. It's not anger, he thinks, give her some space. And so he sits there drinking beer for an hour before he walks to the bedroom like a condemned man.

She is curled up in bed, the lights out, her back turned to his place in the bed. He is sure she isn't asleep, but she may as well have a 'do not disturb' sign on her. He whispers, "I love you," and walks out again.

He sleeps on the couch, awakens early and can't decide whether to go out and give Julie the house. He makes a coffee and sits on the verandah, listening for the slightest sound of her stirring.

Julie emerges late. He watches her through the glass door and it's as though she is moving through the trees reflected in the glass. She doesn't look at him, but busies herself in the kitchen, disappears and then reappears dressed and looking ready to leave.

She finally leans out the glass door and says in a voice as flat and arid as a stony desert. "I have a doctor's appointment. I may be pregnant. We'll talk when I get back, if you're here."

And then she is gone, disappearing from the treetops, disappearing from the house. He leans over until the car has passed and tries to calm the swirling nothingness that threatens to drown him. He hasn't put the tracker back in the car.

*

Mary is home from the hospital but in bed. "Everyone makes such a fuss," she says. I just fell. I bruised my hip and head. I'm being treated like an invalid."

Ian is sitting by the bed. "You were knocked out, honey, and you have a rather large gash on your head. You bled all over the dining room floor."

She looks at him slightly bewildered. She doesn't remember and perhaps Ian shouldn't have corrected her. Some part of him still believes her dying is simply a passing phase.

"Ian is trying to get me to watch daytime television, can you imagine?" she says to Jake.

The television is in fact on. A bushfire somewhere.

Later Mary naps and Jake speaks with Ian. "What are you going to do, dad?"

"I'm going to take care of her, what else? If that gets too difficult, I'll hire someone to come in and help me. And you and Julie have been helpful already," he adds. "She was apparently heading to the kitchen to cook dinner. That was the first time she had wandered from bed in a while. I don't want to increase her drug dosage to stop her, but I dread the thought of her heading out the front door instead of to the kitchen. I probably don't need to close the office door," he says softly.

Jake keeps thinking that, if Mary survives long enough, the day will come when she forgets his name. He worries for himself he realises as much as for his mother. Physics, he thinks. How could I not have paid attention to that? He is not even sure that he knew. And when he thinks about it, the lives of his parents are largely unknown. A few stories, a few travels, Ian's career, but neither of them thinks about their lives as stories that are worth sharing. Even that may be wrong. Maybe they simply think their children don't care or shouldn't. Maybe lives don't become stories until after they have been lived. And maybe too, we have disconnected from the stories and forces that hold us together – families, communities, nature, people.

Julie should be home now. She didn't come back after the doctor's appointment. He waited until noon, apprehensive and restless and then came here. He texted her but no response.

He should go. But he wants to wait until Mary's asleep. Pregnant! He can't believe it. All his resistance to having children was a sham. When Julie said that – like when she said it in the Cape – he wanted nothing more. No, not true. He wanted Julie more. Most of all. He knows that's what he says, but it's not what his actions say. He wonders how he would react if she'd done what he has done. Betrayal is the first word, the truest word, that comes to him.

He should try and get a bit more work done before going home.

How will I protect a child? he thinks instead.

Julie isn't home. She has left a note. "I need a bit of time. I'll be back in a few days."

Jake stares at the note, looks around the room, bewildered. He rushes to the bedroom. Her clothes are still there. Her toiletries are gone. The book from the bedside table, gone. He circles the house again, looking for something that he can't name. A missing photograph perhaps, a random clue to something, a set of keys. He finally stops in the kitchen and holds on to the table until the swill in his mind begins to clear. Just a few days, he thinks. Is she pregnant? Is she planning to get rid of the baby, then me? Moment of panic. Where is the phone? Did she take the phone? Here's the phone...Where is she then? How can I call her? The words scud across the tundra of his brain until nothing is left moving, the landscape barren and silent.

He sits for a while. He makes a list in his head. Don't forget garlic. Don't forget to call the RACQ. Don't forget to pay the rent. Beer? He stuffs the random list in his shirt pocket. Likely to be forgotten.

*

Jake is struggling with work. Disengaged and restless, other things on his mind. Julie, Mary, his other 'work'. He struggles to complete tasks. He has too many calls to make. He drifts out of conversations and strategy sessions.

Garth and Simon notice and ask if he's okay. The climate team is struggling too, somewhat lost.

"Some personal stuff," is all he says.

Only a few hurdles now remain for the Carmichael mine. The courts have refused to consider the impacts of the burning of the coal overseas, what activists call 'the drug dealers' defence'. We are not responsible for what happens to the coal once it's exported, once it's sold to foreigners. If we don't sell it to them, others will, and our coal is cleaner, better. We are cleaner, better. The court agreed. There are not many remaining grounds for litigation. Carmichael needs final approval for the port expansion and a water licence. They need to finalise the route of the rail line and complete Native Title negotiations. They need to secure funding, but that's not likely to be a legal matter. Jake never really believed such a stupid project would make it this far, but governments have fallen over each other for this one.

Tina provides little leadership for the climate team and has taken to travelling extensively, going to conferences, talking at events. Denise and Sean have left. Sean is going back to photography; Denise has a job saving animals. Before she left, she said what so many of his colleagues were feeling. "Saving an animal's life feels like an accomplishment. I know it's not much, not even close to enough. I don't even know in the long term if it matters, but my spirit finds joy in such simple things and joy is in short supply here and in this campaign."

The team needs to sit down and do some talking and planning. The team is adrift working on random climate issues and inspiring no one. The communications team is angry because they have nothing to say and the campaigners are angry because they aren't campaigning. There is another restructuring underway – money is tight. Green Earth doesn't take corporate donations so it's street work and bequests. The frontliners who beg for money on the street are working harder and getting less. At least fifteen staff are likely to go and the two climate campaigners that have gone may not be replaced.

The CEO thinks that The Free Radicals have made fundraising harder. The frontliners are certainly copping more abuse.

Jake has never seen the organisation so flat. He does what he wants and no one seems to care.

He is flat too. The elation from his action in Bowen didn't last a day. The news was dramatic. It is the first of his actions that went international. The video has had hundreds of thousands of hits and the talk on social media is intense. The number of voices calling for more open rebellion has increased significantly. Jake reads it all but he is thinking of Julie. He feels no pleasure, no vindication. He wants to feel something akin to joy, but he doesn't.

He and Garth have lunch together. "I'm beginning to think that what The Free Radicals are doing is actually working in ways none of us expected. It's as though the investment community is quietly walking away from the scenes of these crimes," Garth says. Jake wasn't going to raise Bowen.

"Yeah, but the political establishment is getting even more extreme."

"True, and they're going to try and make this painful for us. The police returned all our computers after the drill rig was done. They didn't even come by after Bowen. We sat and waited all day for them to appear, our laptops prepped, our alibis in place. They seem to have no idea."

Jake should feel some pride, but he doesn't. Avoiding arrest is not an accomplishment. "It feels like The Free Radicals have kind of taken the wind out of our sails. What do you reckon?" he asks.

"It's weird. If I have to face another pointless submission, I'll vomit. It has brought home how much stuff we do that is pointless and has been for a long time. I sort of feel as though it's a chance to question ourselves and rethink some things, but it's not happening. Not yet."

"How can we make it happen? I mean Green Earth is one of only a few groups that has the experience and orientation to become more radical in what we do and to question ourselves in some fundamental ways. If we restructure and become more cautious, less willing to risk what we've got, we're going to slowly disappear."

"Well, we've got planning and reimagining coming up soon," Garth says. I was chatting with Brian Peters – you remember him? He used to be with the Wildos and then ran for a council seat in Brisbane?"

Jake remembers him.

"After the Carmichael approval, he's suggesting we start organising a nationwide civil disobedience campaign. He wanted to know if we're interested."

"How does he deal with the blowback from The Free Radicals? Doesn't he worry we'll be lumped in with the terrorists?"

"It was kind of interesting. He's suggesting this is an opportunity. That a non-violent outbreak can be a valuable counterpoint to violence. I'm not sure, but I think it's worth exploring." Garth dumps a bowl of fresh chillis onto his lunch. "How about we write a letter to Alex and cc the staff indicating that as campaigners we need to discuss the campaign needs of the organisation and how we're going to accomplish what we need – and any restructuring has to support that, including the possibility of becoming involved in serious civil disobedience?"

"You happy to have a tilt at a draft?"

"I'll get it to you today."

The letter is sent off that afternoon and Jake sits in the office waiting for the end of the day. He wants to be home. Julie might be back. He can't believe he doesn't even know if she's pregnant. He wants to be with his mother before she is gone.

He walks out. For the moment other things matter more.

CHAPTER 25

March 1993

Dear Brother

How this war infects the spirit of all of us. Today a group of young Muslims beat three young Jews to death. These three – two men and one woman – have been part of the network of Muslims and Jews, providing medical care to the people of Sarajevo. All the people. These Muslims were in a gang – one of a number sanctioned by the Bosnian Government. They try to take the high moral ground, but are becoming part of the rot that infects this city. It is scary how quickly we give credence to those divisions then begin to make them part of ourselves. Already in response a Jewish man shot at a young Muslim boy. He missed, fortunately, but he is still on our streets, still with a gun and still prepared to bring yet more hate on us all.

Another attack and we will distrust all Muslims and vice versa when really we should distrust those who are not to be trusted. We must give them names and understand who does what and why.

There is an assassin amongst us. He is on our side but sometimes it doesn't feel like that. Today he killed a commander of Serbian forces in the city with a long-range shot. It is not his first execution. He has killed several informants, executed them with a shot to the back of the head. It seems this is one man. He is known as dzelat – the executioner.

I suppose in war men like this are useful, even necessary, but I increasingly confront how dangerous it is to sacrifice our humanity for even a short period no matter how useful.

I wonder if this is a question that Jake has asked himself. I suspect he believes that his humanity demands that he act, not that his actions compromise his humanity. It is a question all of us asked at some point during the war. There are always choices to be made. Sometimes the necessary trumps the good and sometimes the choices are all bad.

April 1993
Dear Brother

Another part of our family has died. Milos' mother is gone. Like Tarek's mother, she wasn't so much afraid as sad, a sadness that became larger and larger. Everything she knew was being torn apart and so she retreated into her house. She couldn't cook as she once did – there is not enough food and certainly not the foods she remembered. She could no longer read because her eyesight had become so poor, so she knitted, every day. At first she knit real things – sweaters, children's wraps, a shawl. Then one day she just knitted and knitted, a prayer shawl, a burial shroud, that became longer and longer. A shroud of many colours. As she ran out of one colour, she used the next. And when she ran out of yarn, she pulled apart things she had already knitted. The last time Milos saw it, the shroud was five metres long and a metre wide and it covered the floor like a river leading nowhere.

She died quickly, or so we like to believe. A shell hit her house directly. The floors collapsed. She was later found still clutching the knitting needles. The shawl is still buried, although we wanted it found so that she could be buried with it.

You probably don't know that Milos' father died some years ago in an avalanche. He was on military service. His body was never found.

Ian weeps when he reads this letter. He knew Milos' mother but not well. I think he weeps for Mary and weeps because he does not know how to give her death meaning. In some ways he has been knitting a shroud for her too. It is not a real shawl but a fabric of history, words, old letters and memories.

I weep too. But I weep for me.

April 1993

Dear Brother

Milos was arrested today. He broke up a fight – or more accurately an attempt by a man to steal bread from a young woman. The two began to wrestle and then Milos pulled a gun on him – even saying that shocks my sense of this man – one of the most peaceful men I have ever known. The man dropped the bread and fled. Two hours later Milos was arrested by Bosnian authorities. It is hard to know what the law means in a time of war. It is hard to know what arrest means. There are no laws except when there are, and it is never clear until it is too late who owns them. When the police come for a man doing a good deed, we know better than to think that it is simple or that justice will prevail.

Janos and I tried to visit, but we do not even get an admission that he has been arrested. Tarek tried and failed as well.

We call the few influential people we know. A police officer, a mid-level public servant in the Department of Justice, a lawyer friend. Eventually, it is the lawyer who finds him and agrees to represent him. He has been charged with theft, possession of a weapon, assault. We assume the man who went to steal the bread has friends in high places.

Such corruption was so common and Sofia so endlessly naïve. She came to accept the war to a degree she never accepted human behaviour. She was like this even when she was young. She came home from school one day furious because a teacher had punished her for something she didn't do. For days she demanded her parents take it to higher authorities. When they laughed at her, she accused them of being corrupt, which made them laugh all the more. I suspect Jake would say things have not changed a great deal.

I sometimes wonder why Sofia didn't join the militia. She was tough, with an almost fanatic sense of justice and yet she chose a different kind of involvement, one that never gave her a sense of control over a war, but provided an endless flow of misery. I wonder too why I didn't choose as she did – did I choose to carry a gun because I wanted power? Because I was angry? Because a gun was thrust in my hand and so it was decided?

April 1993
Dear Brother,

Milos has been released after only two days. A judicious bribe by Tarek was all it took – a bribe worth more than the bread that started this whole thing. I am impressed by Tarek. He has a quiet authority now that he never had before. He navigates this crazy time with both decency and assurance – rare combinations in these circumstances.

We are sheltering a Muslim family. A mother and her two children. They have escaped from Omarska, four hours northwest of here when the roads are open to travel. Already, in only one day we have heard the most horrific stories. Her husband, a haberdasher, was murdered by the Serbs. At first there was no killing in Omarska, then one day a mob of Serbs – probably a militia group – took ten men out of shops, coffee shops, cars and killed them in a field, cut off their heads with chain saws. They collected the heads in one pit and poured some kind of acid over them and in another pit the bodies were buried.

Zurha and her family began preparations to leave that day. Vedad, the husband, went that afternoon to the mosque both to pray and to say his farewells. Soldiers came to the mosque while he was there. They beat all the men with rifles. They made them urinate and defecate inside the mosque. They shot several men and dragged the rest away to a camp, and there they were killed, all of them but one. Zurha could not – or would not – say how they died.

Later, the one survivor, a bloody mess was burnt to death in the middle of the town square.

Whatever you think of me dear brother, don't let this story be untold. Please.

The family will stay with us for as long as they need. They are safer here than in Omarska but Zurha's story makes us all the more fearful for what will happen here.

Ian stares at this letter with a horror he cannot even begin to understand. This could not have happened, this could not be true. He left a repressive and brutal country, but not this. Different religions and cultures had lived together well. Yugoslavia was egalitarian in its oppression. It was a civilised country. How little that word seems to mean now. He hears Mary calling from the bedroom, a note of desperation rising in her voice. He stands. Do people know this happened? He wonders.

'I didn't know. I didn't hear a thing. I didn't read these letters for years, I didn't follow the news of The Siege and the war. I remained blissfully unaware. And now I feel such a dark need to tell a story that I failed to hear when it should have been heard.'

Ian is beating himself up. Ian, Ian, my nephew, you could not have changed this by telling a story. It wasn't that the truth wasn't out there, it was that too many with too much power decided they didn't care, or didn't care enough.

The truth was never going to be enough. Jake knows this already but Ian is only just seeing the world through new eyes.

Sofia, my niece, how little she knew about me. I was a decent man except when I wasn't. I was also brutal and ruthless. I had no way of avenging Vedad, but I avenged others and did so without regret and without hesitation. I tried to remain honourable in what I did and how I did it, but it was always hard to hold both the anger and hate at bay. They were constant presences, yapping dogs or howling demons depending on the day.

I lie. The first time I killed was horrible, liberating in the worst of ways – as though I became untethered from a way of knowing the world that I had had forever; horrific but so simple.

I cannot remember how many I have killed. I cannot remember more than one or two faces and they will never leave me in peace. I am horrified by what I remember and shamed by what I have forgotten. I can't remember what they had done, why summary justice was right or necessary. I cannot even say that what I did mattered one iota – and that too is a haunting. Jake too will have to live with this. Even though he chose not to kill, others did.

Ian walks into the bedroom, lies down next to Mary, who is speaking gibberish and is quite distressed, and holds her. At first her eyes become wild, like a panicked horse, but then she begins to settle. She stares intently at this man in her bed, feels his arm with her hand, touches his mouth, his cheek as though to ask, who are you, nice man? And then, finally, she returns the embrace, slowly and hesitantly, her arms complete their circle of arms. She closes her eyes and smiles – a smile that Ian would have called magical had his eyes been open to see it.

CHAPTER 26

David, the CEO of Green Earth, decides that the discussion proposed by Garth and Jake is not necessary. The staff meeting is acrimonious. The broader questions of why the organisation exists and for what purpose are not discussed. Jake watches staff angry with management. Management defensive, arguing that they are the appropriate body to manage the restructure although the financial difficulties have been caused by them. People worry about their jobs, their friends but also about the lack of democracy within Green Earth, an organisation that they want to be loyal to.

Seventeen positions will go. The campaigns department will lose five people, a third of their current capacity. Fundraising is untouched.

The process will be finalised within ten days and followed by three days of planning and attempted rejuvenation at a lovely spot on Mt Glorious.

*

Jake sits at his desk facing his computer and he has no idea what to do. He can hear Laura, who works on chemicals and food, on the other side of the partition talking on the phone: "No, you can't say it's safe. I keep hearing this and say where's the evidence? And don't tell me it's based on industry data...Do you really believe that?" Jake waits for the computer to begin functioning so he can close down a bit more. He scans his emails, opens a story on the renewable industry in Cameroon – probably a bigger industry there than here. He has 40 new emails. He is falling way behind. He has to follow up on a freedom of information request that the Department of Environment is insisting is too large and they won't process. He has phone calls to make to organise a strategy meeting next month. The report into policy options to take to the major parties before the election is barely started. His email is filled with information, news, updates, requests for more information or help – the small groups always need training and financial help.

Instead, he checks out the stories on Bowen. It will be at least a month before they can get tugs to Bowen. One will come from Darwin, but won't be able to leave until next week. One is coming from Port Philip, but that won't leave for ten days. And these are just temporary. New tugs are being purchased but that won't be finalised for a week or so and then they will be brought over from Asia.

The ships that are scheduled to pick up coal at Abbot Point are told to leave. They can't be rescheduled yet and there is nowhere else they are needed to pick up coal.

This is a serious blockage. The coal stockpile at Abbot Point can't accommodate much more coal and the mines in the Bowen Basin have been told they will need to stockpile at the mine site. The day after tomorrow no more coal will be accepted at Abbot Point.

It's an odd and empty kind of pleasure. One that sits briefly on the surface but quickly withers and blows away.

He spontaneously does a google search for Julie Harber and finds several thousand hits. There are images of a number of Julie Harbers, but his Julie isn't there. There is a psychic, an accountant, a paralegal in a real estate firm, a nurse. He stares at them all wondering how they are connected to his Julie. 'Mine' he repeats with a dull thud.

He finally finds her. She spoke at a conference last year. She made a proposal to council for a council run childcare program. He knew this but seeing it here, out there in the widest of worlds, changes the way it feels – bigger and more important somehow.

Jake has never looked Julie up before. It strikes him at this moment as a bit strange and as though he is learning something new when he isn't.

He begins to imagine what he'll do if Julie leaves him. His stomach churns. He imagines becoming more and more reckless, a destroyer, violent, no longer working for change but to feed his fury. He can feel his body tense like a single spastic muscle.

'Violence is therapy'. Jake writes the words on his computer. A blank page isn't blank anymore and this is the message he has given himself. He stares. The words stare at him. There is a stand-off of sorts. Jake is terrified those words are true.

"Hey Jacob, Tina wants to know if you've done the letter to Senator Parkes?"

Jake almost falls out of his chair she turns so suddenly. He looks at Garth with only a hint of recognition. "What letter?" he mumbles.

"I think it's the one about the solar thermal plant in South Australia. Are you okay? You look terrible, man."

Jake has a vague memory he promised to get a letter done last week. "I'll do it now," he says quietly and turns back to the computer. Garth stands behind him, Jake can feel his concern burning his skin. "I'm okay, Garth, just some stuff going on at home," he says without turning. He hopes Garth gets the message that he wants to be left alone. He feels Garth's hand gently squeeze his shoulder as he walks off. He hopes Garth hasn't read those three words on the screen.

*

Two days later he comes home and Julie is sitting on one of the lounge chairs, stiff and somewhat grim. Jake isn't sure what to do. "Hi," he says and then stops. He doesn't know whether to give her a hug and kiss and he needs to pee and he wants a beer. Instead, he stands near the door. "I'm glad you're home," he says. She watches him, not angry, not curious, not anything, just patient and observant.

"Would you like a glass of wine?" he asks.

"No thank you," she says somewhat formally.

"I have to pee, I'll be right back." It's almost as though he's asking permission.

He finally sits down on the couch across from her. She still has her shoes on. He's never seen her wear her shoes inside. She's leaving me he thinks with excruciating certainty.

"How are you?" Nervous, he laughs at how stupid the question sounds to him.

She looks at him. "I'm angry. I don't think I can ever forgive you for this. I mean, here you are saying you want a family and you're living a secret life of an eco-terrorist. It's as though you don't get how those two might be connected. It's like you think it's all a damn lark – children, blowing shit up." She is getting louder and then suddenly stops as though he can feel her spirit hitting the steepest part of the hill. "And then there's the lying, the lack of trust of me...You know I get so angry at you doing what you're doing but even angrier that you did it without talking to me first, without showing any trust." She empties the glass Jake had brought her. "Fuck," she says quietly, "I was going to say this so differently. And I'm pregnant. Bloody overjoyed in the circumstances." She stares at him – mainly defiance and anger, but Jake knows there's more. She is here. She is sitting with him, drinking wine.

"I love you, you idiot," she blurts out. "Can you stop?" she asks suddenly and now stares at him, a challenge, a hope.

Jake looks up, then away, then out the window. Fool, he never even thought about this question in the days Julie has been gone. He can tell that Julie expects an immediate 'yes', but he can't say it yet, not so quickly and after so much. He looks at her again, again close to breaking.

He finally knows what he needs to say. "I can, I can stop, but I don't know if I can do that for good, but if I have to start again, I'll talk to you first. No more secrets."

"Not good enough Jake. Telling me what you're going to do is more honest but no fairer. What say do I have? Am I expected to be the dutiful partner, like Mary?"

Jake feels trapped, absolutely fucking hoisted on his own petard.

"I don't like doing it, Jules, I hate it. It scares the hell out of me – and nothing scares me more than losing you, of going to prison and losing you. But, but I didn't choose to do it lightly. I think part of the reason I didn't tell you was because I was so scared that you wouldn't accept it, and I understand that. I've put you in a shit position."

"This is bullshit Jake. You've put me in an impossible position and your understanding is pretty worthless. If you have a higher moral duty to continue destroying stuff for the greater good then you're making a decision that you can't have a relationship at the same time. Your attempt to do both is completely dishonest, and I think the fact that you didn't tell me proves that." For the first time, Julie begins to cry, silently. "And it hurts, because it says to me you don't love me as much as you say and as much as I love you."

Jake is lost for words. He was so clear in his mission and now he feels so obviously wrong, misguided, stupid. He isn't ready to say that yet. Words are swirling in his head, a sloppy sea of broken sentences. He knows he has to say something but nothing emerges. He looks at Julie and his look of utter bewilderment, hopelessness, silence, pulls her up. He is suffering too, she thinks but hates cutting him any slack. She waits. She's not going to let him off.

Finally, he starts to speak from far away. "The first time, I was standing on the rail line before dawn watching the sky. I was thinking about you. I wanted you to be with me. It felt kind of romantic there in those first minutes. I wanted you to be part of it but I wanted to protect you too. I wanted to save the world – for me, for you, for a child. I wasn't angry then. I thought this is the only way to change anything." He drifts into silence again. He has no idea how to navigate the waters he's in. The currents are crazy, the boat is defective, the captain lost.

Julie stands and walks from the room – but not towards the front door. She goes to the back verandah and stands looking out over rooftops. In the distance the television towers and below her the usual sounds of an evening in the city. She wants to leave again, she wants to be alone. She can feel Jake watching her from inside the glass door, his own reflection touching her. She can't quite imagine the way out, a panic setting in that there is no answer. There is always an answer, she thinks, even if she doesn't know what it is. Even if she doesn't like it. He has to stop, that's the first answer. I have to forgive him, that's a second one. He acted stupidly, but it was out of love. Maybe that's all, she thinks with an odd thrill, maybe it's that easy after all.

He just has to promise.

Julie leaves shortly after, whispering as she walks past him, "I don't know what to do next."

CHAPTER 27

July 1993

Dear Brother

We still have not heard from those who smuggle people out. We have been told they are incredibly cautious. That is good.

We still have not heard a peep from the UN in response to the assassination. Well, that is not true. They have apparently criticised the Serbs, who have issued an apology that was closer to a contemptuous dismissal. Shame is all that will remain on their side and we are not sure what, if anything, will remain here.

We spend more and more time scrounging for food and spending more of the little money we have on the food we do find. I am getting scrawny. I have never thought of myself as vain, but I look hollow, old and tired. My eyes bulge, my clothes don't fit, my breasts sag. I find myself fussing about my appearance in ways I never have.

Ian stares out the office window. The guilt he has felt since the first letter grows larger and heavier. I left for good reasons but I also abandoned them, and I no longer understand why, he thinks.

Perhaps when he left he thought that if he looked back, he would be returned to that place. It didn't happen then but is happening now. The curse of Eurydice. He was weak then. Both his ambition and his departure were forms of fleeing from himself. It worked, Ian. You've become a good man, strong enough now to take measure of your failures.

Ian looks through Sofia's notebooks again. Not a single self-portrait. He wants to see her. He wants each letter to come in images – her face, her house, those she cares for. He likes his sister more now than he ever did when he was young. She was just his older sister, a bit bossy, opinionated and always stronger and more powerful than he could hope to be.

He has a vague memory of a political argument they had. He stood up to her for the first time. He defended Tito he thinks, at least a bit, even though he wasn't sure what he believed. He was in uni, a scrawny, shy kid and she took him to task, gave him an intellectual mauling. He'd forgotten that, forgotten that side of her too.

August 1993
Dear Brother

How much I have come to depend on you – or at least the idea of you – in surviving this war.

Janos has come home today in tears. He is in the militia and has seen more than anyone should have to – and I am sure I do not know all the stories. After the assassination, his militia and Croat militia are angry and prepared to stop, shoot and arrest anyone. A friend of his killed a young Serb he thought had a gun. It was a chisel. Janos learned later he was going to his workshop to chisel the name of yet another dead child into a headstone.

He tells me, 'We now patrol the streets not to protect all of us, but to do battle with the Serbs. You can feel this change, it is as clear as changing shoes.'

CHAPTER 28

Mt Glorious was not, as it turned out, very aptly named.

The mood was always going to be grim. The corporate consultants trying to achieve team building through juvenile and simplistic games on the conference centre lawn were told to leave at the end of the first day, following a quite open revolt by staff. "What idiot conceived of this and thought that this would paper over the firing of a bunch of passionate and needed people?" one woman asked.

It wasn't much better when what remained of the campaign team began planning. They sat at picnic tables overlooking rainforest with the sound of a small creek audible if everything was quiet. The climate team argued from the beginning. Both Garth and Jake called for Tina to resign, which didn't go down well at all.

Tina came in with a proposed renewables campaign that no one wanted to touch. She simply assumed it would be accepted and that assumption irked the rest of the team. Not a happy bunch.

Rather than take the time to talk through the current science, the trends in campaigns globally, the role of Green Earth and how Green Earth could best influence an outcome that would avoid catastrophic climate change, there was a lot of posturing and passive-aggressive confrontation and self-serving righteousness. Everyone dug in. Ugly, but at least it never became bloody.

It was also difficult because they all knew there could never be a single answer to climate change. Each member of the team – there were only four now – had very different ideas of what needs to happen and what they were passionate about.

Do they campaign on the Great Barrier Reef? On coal? What about CSG? What about offshore drilling? BP is waiting on an exploration licence in the Bight, with at least two other companies prepared to follow if BP clears the way.

The Paris Agreement was only just reached, preceded the week before by 140,000 Australians who marched around the country demanding more be done. 'How does this fit in?' they all asked.

'We can't do everything,' they told each other over and over again. 'We have to do more,' they say just as often. What about free trade, corporate control, subsidies and tax avoidance by the zillionaires, many of them fossil fuel companies? What about transport? When they weren't arguing, they were dumping another problem, another possible campaign on the table.

There was yet another lengthy session about supporting the renewable industry and how to overcome the political support for fossil fuels. The new Prime Minister, who once supported renewables, has more recently attacked them as an ideological technology.

Some wanted to go for legal reform, others litigation and political work, others wanted to work on public resistance and denialism.

Jake argued that instead of supporting the renewable industry, they should oppose the corporate state. "We all know that climate change is another symptom of a system of consumption and exploitation that infects every aspect of our lives. If we don't change this, we're missing the point," he says.

No one disagreed but no one supported a campaign against the corporate state. It is too large a demon to wrestle.

Jake said his piece and then remained quiet. He tried to find his peace, but it was a bit elusive. He stared at a small rainforest tree being slowly throttled by a strangler fig and tried to make sense of the metaphor.

Wendy, who does media work for the campaign, stood up late on day one, somewhat formal. "If this is the best we can do, we're in deeper trouble than I thought and I'm a pessimist. We have been going for seven hours and all I can see is that we've all dug in and each of us hopes that through attrition we get our own way. I don't know the answer. We have to be practical – we can't take on work that we don't have the capacity to do or to do with others. On the other hand, there is no point taking on a campaign we can win if it doesn't have significance. It has to be a campaign that changes what is happening or what will happen. It has to be something that captures the imagination of people. It doesn't have to be winnable in one step – that's not going to happen – but it can't be a thousand steps. Our steps need to be large." She pauses. "You're all passionate and smart and on the same side and you all have different views of what we need to do. Perhaps we need to get out of our trenches and think about this differently."

Jake piped up. "Wendy's right. Can I make a suggestion?" He looks around until it's clear that they are waiting for him.

"Perhaps we need to understand our differences a bit better and rather than fight about them, shape a campaign – and roles – that take advantage of them. Perhaps we could begin by each of us writing on a piece of paper answers to a few questions. First, what are the three problems that you think are most important to campaign on? Second, what are the three most important parts of that? So, if renewables is your thing, what are the three things that we need to work on most to make the switch to 100 percent renewables happen. I'd suggest too that whatever we write down, it's based on what the science is telling us needs to happen – like about transition speed and carbon emission reduction needs."

Tina frowned in that way she has – with one side of her mouth pursed briefly. That last comment of Jake's was a dig at her, but the suggestion was supported by the team.

The impasse broken, the group began to work together. Their strategic views differ widely, but at least they recognised that their enemy doesn't sit around this table.

By the end of the second day, they agreed that the focus of the campaign will be stopping the Galilee Basin coal mines and preventing the expansion of the coal Ports adjacent to the Great Barrier Reef. Jake will be responsible for investigating corporate issues, political corruption and looking for a court case that is winnable. Jake felt happy, vindicated. He sensed too that he became the de facto leader of the team over that weekend. He wasn't sure that he wanted or needed that.

*

Jake wakens with Julie next to him. He is surprised and amazed and grateful she is there. The morning light is gray and skittish. He strokes her back. "Coffee love?" he whispers.

"Mmm. Thanks."

"Or should you be off coffee?"

"Uhuh."

He wakens for real this time. He is alone in bed; the radio is blaring in the kitchen. He has no idea why it's so loud. Maybe Julie is there.

Julie isn't there. He turns the volume down, starts on coffee, gets some fruit. The smell of her, the shape of her...that dream was so real. You can see he feels a bit overwhelmed by her presence in his dreams and in his spirit.

He stares out the window and simply disappears. And then he's back. Breaking news on the ABC. Someone has derailed a coal train in New South Wales. Two people in hospital, tonnes of coal lost. It will be days before the tracks are cleared – over 100 carriages. One other minor injury. The Free Radicals are claiming responsibility. "This is an escalation," says their communique to the media. "Earlier activities were warnings, an opportunity for those in power and those with money to act. They have utterly failed, relying instead on widespread searches and interrogations, making out that those who care about the planet rather than those who destroy it are the terrorists. We regret any injuries but we also are clear that those who work for the coal industry, those who are involved in the destruction of a safe climate for all living beings are responsible too. They are engaged in criminal acts that will be worse than the genocide in Nazi Germany, worse that the genocides in Armenia, Burundi, Rwanda, Bosnia. Worse than the genocide in Australia. The crime is ecocide and it is time to choose sides – there is no longer any middle ground and those who try and stay in the middle of the road will be road kill."

The toast burns and Jake ignores it. Completely over the top, he thinks. Comparing coal employees to Nazis. It's not the first time he's heard the comparison, but it's not yet ready to be heard. And the death threat at the end is crazy.

He walks back into the bedroom and forgets the coffee. He walks back out to the kitchen and forgets why he's there and puts on more toast.

He's excited, scared shitless, completely bumfuzzled about what this means and what's next and what he should even be feeling.

Most of all he feels elation. He calls Julie. She doesn't answer. 'Come on answer, come on.' He leaves a very brief message. "I can stop now. I can promise that now."

*

Julie comes over that evening. She doesn't bring her bags.

"Tell me what happened," she says softly. "Why can you give up now and why can you promise?"

He wants to make love with her. He wants to get on his knees and tell her how much he adores her.

"Did you hear about the train derailing?" he asks.

She nods. She clearly thinks he did it.

"I didn't do that, but it means I can stop. No hesitation."

She looks at him. A challenge, question, hope, distrust, all of it in that intense and brief moment. Jake meets her eye in the gentlest way, as though he has pulled open the doors to his spirit and said, 'Look all you want, it's all there for you to see now.'

I have more hope for them than I've had in a while.

CHAPTER 29

October 1993

Dear Brother

Tarek visited today. We did not talk of the war or the latest deaths or the latest rumours about NATO. We talked about you. I have become so adept as a nurse, my hands were covered in blood, I was binding and stitching wounds as we spoke.

How did it come to this? We know you went to Australia – an academic at the University of Sarajevo found reference to a paper you wrote in 1990, but that is all we know. And so we talked about finding you, embracing you, teaching you to speak Bosnian again if you teach us both English. I stopped trying to send the letters to you – I had no idea whether my time and money was being wasted by going through smugglers. Today Tarek offered to get my letters sent. He has friends, he says. He can get them to a friend in Italy who will send them on as soon as that can be arranged.

Tarek suggests I send the letters to the Embassy in Australia. They may have the best chance of finding you.

I do not even know if Bosnia has an embassy in Australia. Australia has recognised us, but that doesn't mean we have an embassy there. In fact, it seems unlikely to me now, as I write. I suggested sending the letters instead to the Australian embassy in Italy. Tarek is going to arrange it.

Tarek sends his regards. He has no family remaining except you and me and is feeling the weight of his losses, as we all are.

We walked down to the square this afternoon. I cannot remember how many times this square has been destroyed and rebuilt. It is still one of my favourite places in the city. It has been a living part of this city for over 500 years. In more peaceful times, I have imagined this square during the Ottoman Empire, occupied by the commissars and tax collectors and court miniaturists.

Now it is mainly rubble and vendors who move — or try to — across the square with their carts in those quieter moments. Every morning Ibram walks across the square. He dresses exactly as he has for the last 30 years. He is a lawyer. He has no job, but he walks there each morning regardless. Two weeks ago, his office was gone, turned to rubble. He still walks there. We are both sure that this, in Ibram's quiet way, is an act of defiance.

There is a coffee shop of sorts. It has adapted to war too. When the shelling is elsewhere, it suddenly appears. One table or three. A few chairs. Coffee is for sale but little else and even the coffee tastes less and less like coffee each time.

But this is how it is. Life goes on in whatever ways can be found. Tarek and I had a coffee. We asked for the newspaper and the owner laughed with pleasure and handed us a paper that was nine months old and said, "I only allow good news here."

I am determined to find you.

CHAPTER 30

Christmas and New Year pass almost invisibly. There is not much celebrating. Jake has worked the entire time following the most recent approval of the port expansion at Abbot Point two days before Christmas. He didn't even visit his parents, unwilling to talk about why Julie wasn't coming. Ian tries to make it a special day for Mary, but she is on such large doses of painkillers Ian has no idea if she has any idea what's going on.

Julie moves back in while Jake is at work early in the New Year. She's glad she waited until after Christmas and New Year, but now she stands at the bedroom door thoughtful but more happy than concerned. She looks at the bed with longing. She wants to be holding him, her hand nestled around his scapula. The smell of him. It's a smell that reminds her of the redwood forests in California. Earthy. Jake has never seen those forests. He should. We should go, go to the redwoods and maybe Yellowstone and we can look for wolves. She wants him to herself. She wants him away from here, away from the things he feels so responsible for. He needs to feel joy again, that most of all. To see that the world is still an amazing, mysterious place and that love is as big and important as anything else.

She will suggest it tonight. Maybe Alaska. She has never been and they could discover that together, although bears scare her and there are lots of bears there.

She smiles to herself. She camped once in a park in Oregon, or maybe it was California. At the entrance to the park was a mutilated esky.

DON'T LEAVE FOOD IN YOUR CAR.
BEARS WILL BREAK INTO YOUR CAR.
DON'T LEAVE FOOD IN YOUR TENT.
USE THE STORAGE BOXES PROVIDED.

That night – she was with a boyfriend, she thinks, although she can't remember who – she waked to the sounds of something going through the rubbish bins, turning them over then throwing them. She knew it was a bear. She desperately wanted to get up and have a peek. She'd never seen a bear before, but she was too terrified. Her boyfriend slept through the racket.

The memory tastes kind of bittersweet. A bit of nostalgia. For what?

Odd because she so rarely thinks of America. It's not family and it's not America but a few places that are held deeply inside. Smells again. And nature and wind. She can't remember the name of the tree but when the wind blows the leaves sing, kind of like chimes.

Maybe we'll go after the child is born, she thinks. Easier to travel with when they are that young.

She suddenly grinds to a halt in this gentle reverie. Jake has committed serious criminal acts. He could be in jail before the baby is even born.

A sudden wave of nausea overcomes her and she rushes to the toilet to vomit. Welcome home she thinks, although she has been vomiting for days.

CHAPTER 31

Two police officers come to their house but only Julie is home. They have come to question Jake again. This time they want to take him downtown. She stands in the doorway and doesn't invite them in.

"Are you going to arrest him?" Julie asks. She is terrified and hopes she doesn't show it, which terrifies her even more.

"No, ma'am we just want to question him."

"If it's about Bowen, you know he was with me the whole time," she blurts out.

"Thank you ma'am, but could you ask him to come with us?"

"He's not here," she says, an attempt to stop the whole situation.

"May we have a look please?" The woman officer is hard. Even when she's polite Julie feels she is ready to bludgeon her because she can.

"Not without a warrant. And I told you he isn't here." She stares at the woman officer with all the hardness she can muster. One day, perhaps, she'll laugh about this.

The male officer puts two fingers on his colleague's elbow. "Could you tell us where he is?" he asks. No 'please' but no baggage either.

Julie looks over at him. "He's at work."

They ask about his alibis. "I told you, he was with me all those days – and nights," she says.

They ask her about his political views. She tells them a version of the truth. "He's incredibly frustrated at how little is being done about climate change. Like every person who works in that area and every thinking, caring person that doesn't."

"How does he think that can change?"

"That's the question we all wrestle with. Change our system, make politicians more accountable, make people more aware. Change the laws so that the police can't arrest and interrogate innocent people for as long as they want. You know, the usual marks of a democratic system." She is getting angry and knows she needs to stay calm.

They don't question her long.

They come back in the afternoon with a search warrant for the house and car. That takes much longer and is nerve wracking and intrusive. Nothing is off limits. Two men, polite but not nice, go wherever they want without even glancing at her. She is clammy and anxious the whole time. She calls Jake but has to leave a message. They take a pair of shoes, some papers, lots of photos of the office. They go through their office papers in the spare room, but not in detail. They leave a small mess but nothing is destroyed. They go through the garage thoroughly, particularly Jake's tools. They take a book on Marx.

"Does Jake like Marx?" they ask.

"Oh, please," Julie replies. "Is this what it has come to, reds in the bed?" She thinks at that moment she could easily become violent. She stares at their necks and wants to throttle them, press her thumb into their Adams' apples until they choke. She has never felt anything quite like it. Their presence is an assault of sorts and her sense of her capacity for violence horrifies and invigorates her both. Better than being a silent victim, she thinks.

They finally leave. She watches them from the window, watches the police car move out of sight. She collapses on the bed and stares at the ceiling fan.

*

The police take Jake's computer. Mind you they take half a dozen computers from the office. Jake makes a fuss – how long will they keep it? He needs it for work. There is personal information on there he doesn't want them seeing. Others do the same, although for Jake it is a routine he knows he should go through. The police are sullen and not happy. He again suspects they are getting enormous pressure and are making little progress on the case. He wants to mock them and then gets mad at himself; this is no game, he thinks. It's not about proving how clever you are.

Jake is the only person they take for questioning and this time they begin to push. They don't arrest him, they don't have to, but put him in an airless interrogation room, make him wait, then two men, one scrawny the other beefy, come in. The big one seems to occupy the whole room. So stereotypical he wants to laugh, but he is clearly intimidated.

The only preamble is the younger man identifying himself, his partner, Jake and the date and time for the benefit of the recording equipment. Their first question is where was he on October 17 – the date the tug boats burned?

"I'd like my lawyer here please."

"You're not entitled to a lawyer. You're not under arrest and you're being questioned under counter terrorism laws. Where were you on October 17?"

"I was home. What sections of which counter terrorism laws are you relying on. And I still would like my lawyer present."

"We are asking the questions. What is your partner's name?"

"As I told you the last time you asked, her name is Julie Harber, and we live together. Would you like the address again too?"

Jake isn't sure why he wants to provoke them or maybe he wants to attack them, but he feels as though he is barely controlling himself. He has to do better.

The police ignore his question.

"Have you ever been to Bowen?"

"Several times, but not for at least a year."

"What were you doing there?"

"I was there for work. The last time I was meeting with the Birigabba people about an ILUA." Jake knows they won't know what an ILUA is. He wants to make them look ignorant. Provocation and little more. The beefy one looks at him with contempt. He knows what an ILUA is or he has seen this kind of sad attempt at provocation before.

"Who did you meet with?"

"Duncan something – sorry I can't remember his surname – was the contact with the Birigabba. I met some local greenies too. Ellen Rivers and Patricia Keyes. I stayed with Ellen."

"Do you own a dinghy?"

"No I don't." At least not anymore. He cut it into pieces after returning from Bowen and put it in four different bags and four different dumpsters.

"Would you mind if we searched your car, the blue one?"

"I don't mind if you have a warrant. Look, this is the second time you've questioned me and if you don't mind me being blunt, it's clear you don't have any evidence against me – which makes sense because I haven't done any of the actions you're investigating. I didn't do anything and I don't know anything about who did. None of my friends or colleagues have a clue. And all of them say the same thing – you keep questioning them when it's clear you're in the dark. I have a theory that The Free Radicals is a right wing free-market nut job organisation doing this to get the environment movement shut down or at least too occupied with stupid questions to do the work we're supposed to be doing."

I'm amazed. He has actually embarrassed them.

Jake knows the police will have pulled every bit of CCTV footage from 100 kilometres around bloody Bowen, but Jake didn't stop at any of the big stations. He pulled in at a roadhouse with a single pump that had seen better days and certainly didn't have a security camera. He didn't stop for food – in either direction. He brought food with him. He knows they may be able to inspect traffic camera footage – if they have kept it or the cameras were on – but that's low resolution. It might show car colour but not licence numbers and even makes of car can be difficult to distinguish.

They question him then about his views of the fossil fuel industry and the politics of climate change. He is blunt but there is none of the passion, none of the diatribes to which he is prone. He is in control again. Not nervous, not angry and absolutely clear on what can be said and what not.

"Is this going to take much longer," he asks. "My partner is pregnant and we have a doctor's appointment at 2."

"It will take as long as it takes," says the older officer. The words are curt.

They go over the same event again and again, slightly different questions, some coming at random times, where were you, where did you stay, where did you buy food, petrol, do you have petrol cans, do you own a dinghy, do you know how to weld?

They finally give him water two hours after he asked for it. Then they let him go to the toilet, after making him ask four times and wait 30 minutes.

"I want a lawyer," he says again.

"You aren't under arrest."

"Can I leave?"

"No, we're not done questioning you."

"I'm not answering any more questions then."

"Then you'll be here a lot longer."

"What time is it?"

"Why, do you have somewhere to go?"

"Yes, I told you."

He is getting tired and short. He knows they are pushing for him to make a mistake, to blurt out something that opens the door. Clearly, they don't have anything except suspicions.

"Could I have some food please?" he asks.

"When we're finished."

Jake forgets their names again. He asks to see their ID for the fourth time. This time they refuse.

"Forgotten our names again?"

"Yeah, can't imagine why."

"You being a smart ass?"

"Just a tired grumpy citizen sick of being detained and borderline tortured for no reason and with no rights."

"We want to go back to the welding work on the railway line. Do you have a welding ticket?"

"No, I don't." Jake knows that there are no records of this in any one place and it was a long time ago, when he was sixteen. He did the course at a TAFE that has since closed down. He called TAFE months ago asking for his records and they couldn't find anything. He's hoping the police look no further than he did.

"Have you ever taken a welding course?"

"No, as I've now told you four times. Or is it five?" They ignore his sarcasms.

"When we search your house, will we find any welding tools?"

"I'm sure you've searched already."

They have and found nothing. No tools, no shoes with dirt in the soles, nothing in the car – clean, too clean for a young man. Not a speck of dirt on the floor, not a bit of rubbish, not a book, not a map. They find some mud on the wheel flaps and some tiny stones in the tires.

"How many kilometres on your car?"

"No idea. 200,000 or so."

"Do you keep a service log?"

"Nope."

"Where do you get it serviced?"

"No place in particular. Last time was some place in Wooloongabba, but they're too expensive."

"When did you clean your car last?"

"Not sure. I do it pretty regularly."

They don't believe that. His office at home was a mess. Nothing useful there, but it was clear he wasn't quite as fastidious as he makes out.

And they keep asking questions, hours of questions. Jake can barely focus, barely remember what the last question was. He often forgets the present one. The first two people have been replaced by two more. He thinks they are different. One of the others was a woman, he's sure. He knows he is becoming disoriented and is struggling to stay alert. One of the men has hairy hands and crenelated fingernails. He stares. That's a vitamin deficiency, he thinks, but I can't remember the vitamin. He's about to ask but they are asking him something. He doesn't understand the question. They repeat or ask a new question, he's not sure.

Finally, he pulls himself out of his delirium, briefly. "I'm not going to speak anymore until I get some food and a lawyer."

"We've already told you, you can't have a lawyer. You're being detained under security legislation and we're entitled to detain you and question you for 24 hours."

"How long has it been?"

"Do you favour overthrowing capitalism?"

"Bring on the kool-aid!" he yells. "And one can't overthrow capitalism. It's not, despite appearances, our system of government." Every word is slurred and covered with contempt. He was going to shut up. He knows that is the only way to approach this, but he can't. He has to.

Finally, he puts his head down on the table and closes his eyes. They ask him something but he doesn't try to understand. Another question, their voices coming from so far away. He is beginning to drift into a dream when someone grabs him by the hair, pulls his head back as far as it will go. "You'll sleep, when we say you can sleep, you fuck. Now answer the questions." He is whacked on the side of the head. He doesn't feel pain, only the swirling of space.

He has no idea how long this goes on. At some point he has no idea if they are asking questions, if he is answering, if he can even speak English. At one point he keeps repeating his entire three word repertoire of Croatian, boli me kurak. Blood of my blood! At some point they pour a hot liquid down his throat and play loud music through the speaker system. Every time he tries to sleep they wrench him upright and soon he is neither asleep nor awake.

Finally, they drag Jake out of his chair and tell him he can go. He sits back down and tries to sleep at the table again. They drag him out of the room, then out of the station. They tell him he needs to surrender his passport within 24 hours. He forgets instantly. He is in the City on Roma Street, it is early morning, first light and Jake may as well be in another country.

Jake can't remember how he arrived here. Does he have his car?

He waves down a taxi.

Does he have his wallet?

Does he have his phone?

*

Julie is frantic when Jake finally arrives home. Garth called her and told her he'd been taken in for questioning, but every call to the police was met with ignorance, indifference and prevarication.

She realised how few friends she had with any power in this system. She called Ian but hung up before he answered. She called Chris, a lawyer friend, who referred her to Steven, a civil rights lawyer.

"They can hold him for 24 hours without charge or lawyer," Steven said. "I'll call and see if I can get any information from them."

He called back thirty minutes later. Julie was staring at her dinner unable to eat. "They finally acknowledged he's there, but beyond that they're not telling me anything. And don't have to."

So Julie waited, dozed briefly in front of the television, awakened confused – there is yelling on the television and then shooting. She had a moment of panic that this was a message for her.

When Jake walks in he looks awful, shattered and bewildered. They hold each other without a word. Neither has any – nor do they need them right now.

*

The detention makes it into the media. Jake has no doubt that the news is leaked by the police although he's not sure what they hope to gain by admitting that they can detain citizens at their whim. He returns to work and when he lets them know what happened, he becomes both hero and pariah. It's as though his ordeal is symbolic of the risks all of his colleagues face and at the same time, his detention makes him a real suspect. He may have done these terrible deeds which are causing the movement such harm. He tells the story half a dozen times. After speaking with the CEO and the Director of Communications, he tells the story to the media in an exclusive interview. "By every accepted definition of torture, I've been subject to torture without charge and without a lawyer."

"Yes," he admits, "it's legal – but these laws making it legal themselves are violations of basic human rights. Calling it a law doesn't make it just."

Later he consults Steven, the lawyer Julie spoke with yesterday. He is amazed that he feels so wronged – he wants to take on this battle too – a legal system that hides behind a terror of terrorism – in part manufactured by the system – to justify state sanctioned abuse of its own citizens. He doesn't care that he's done the things he has been questioned about. Without clearly articulating it, Jake thinks the laws are a part of the system he is fighting. They sanction environmental destruction and climate change as well as insulating those in power from any kind of responsibility. He not only thinks that their crimes are worse than his, but that ignoring their crimes is a crime on top a crime.

There is little he can do, Steven tells him. The detention was within the broad reach of the law. The treatment is a clear breach of international law and borderline under Australian laws, but it isn't a fight worth taking on Steven tells him.

He doesn't tell Steven the truth. Steven doesn't ask, but does say that his release doesn't mean he is off the hook. "It's likely that they have some reason for suspecting you and are fishing for evidence they don't currently have. They may well be back, and with new evidence they can do the same again."

"Or even without new evidence," Jake adds with a touch of bitterness.

*

Someone puts out a media release on behalf of The Free Radicals, claiming that Jake's detention proves how corrupt and broken the system is. "Those who are destroying the planet in the name of profit and greed are heroes of industry and those who give their lives to create a better world are subject to torture. We know who should be in prison."

Jake doesn't want to thank them even if it reflects, kind of eerily, his own sentiments.

Four days later in the early hours of the morning, a fire breaks out in Santos House in Brisbane. The blaze is quickly controlled and there are no injuries, but the office remains closed for the day. Increased security, there and particularly at the adjoining courthouse, causes all sorts of chaos in the family courts. The following day, the car of Liam Beselman, CEO of Santos, is torched in his driveway. No injuries but Beselman is clearly shocked and afraid. He puts on a brave face, but only two days later The Free Radicals – not Jake – put out a release that Beselman's family has returned to South Africa for a 'holiday' and that anyone involved in the CSG industry should do the same.

Jake watches with a grim pleasure and a lurking horror that it is all wrong, taking shape in ways he would never have wished. He also has this odd feeling of being pushed aside, as though he has some ownership over what is supposed to happen. Perhaps he never wanted it to be bigger than him.

CHAPTER 32

The targeting of CEOs and members of the Boards of the gas and coal companies gets worse. An email circulates with the names, addresses and even phone numbers of dozens of mining and CSG executives. They are inundated with calls. Wanted signs – for crimes against the planet – are planted in front yards or front doors. Activists are used to this kind of anger, but CEOs definitely are not.

Mineral House, where Jake glued the doors shut, is broken into and a fire set in the lobby, using the corflutes from recent elections. Richard McFarlane, a former federal Minister for Resources and now director of the Bula Coal Company is shouted down at a speaking event at Sydney University and then isn't allowed to leave. The police don't arrive for an hour and when they do arrive, they start beating all and sundry – including, accidentally, an advisor to McFarlane. McFarlane's car is vandalised in the meantime.

Things fall apart.

A small explosion at the Brisbane Convention Centre sees the cancellation of a conference of gas producers. The Free Radicals – whoever they are now – take responsibility for that too, but much of what now happens is simply unattributed and labelled as The Free Radicals by the media or the police.

The first death occurs in January. Michael Cook, Chief Financial Officer at BHP is driving his BMW too fast down the range from Mt Nebo when a wheel falls off and he crashes down an embankment. He isn't found for several hours and is only just clinging to life. He dies in hospital and the police are quick to identify his death as a homicide.

This changes everything.

In Sarajevo a single death during the war meant little. Even when the Deputy Prime Minister was killed, it was the lack of power and will of the UN that meant the most, not the death of a prominent politician.

But here, when one of the elite is killed by a group that appears to be determined to eliminate the elite, it is an earthquake. You're certainly permitted to speak against such people but not to act. In any way. Those in positions of power are hysterical; the media is hysterical, but elsewhere things aren't so clear. The elite aren't well liked even if violence is abhorred.

The Free Radicals take on a reality that at first doesn't belong to them. They become the focus of all evil and the sum of all fears – at least for those in power.

But that also means that this group, that doesn't exist, now has power itself. And this power has no centre, no master and no controls.

The police and political responses are pretty predictable. Run around, arrest a bunch of people, proclaim the wonders of their intelligence arm and hope that everyone goes back to their television.

I'm so cynical.

Patricia, a friend of Jake's and now with the Wilderness Society, emerged after a long night in custody, found a lawyer, went to the media and within a week filed a lawsuit. One she loses almost 2 years later.

When wars begin, they take over the mind, they become the filter through which we see everything. They exert an ineluctable gravity that few can resist. It's almost like that now. Everything is about the greenies and violence.

Climate change remains quietly behind a great wall – barely a part of this debate at all. Jake isn't surprised, but he hoped for more. Making problems into conflicts where hate not solutions are the currency is always the easier path.

At first Jake feels the liberation of not having to maintain a secret life and the joy of Julie's return. Jake goes into the office three days a week and two days he works at his parents' home. He is home at five, before Julie, and cooks dinner, invites Mel and Cath over, arranges a games night with Sean and Melaina. He is so attentive to Julie, she is almost embarrassed. She feels the mixed blessing of being worshipped!

He has returned to work with a kind of new-found passion. He is no less fatalistic, but it is love driving him and not his despair.

*

A farmer assaults and badly beats a driller who ignored the farmer's requests that he leave his land. The driller was hospitalised but the farmer became an instant hero to many.

He is arrested and charged, but the Rockhampton judge lets him out on nominal bail. That doesn't cause even a stir in Canberra, where politicians of both persuasions insist that it is up to the judge. When it comes to the greenies though, it is loud. Radicals, terrorists, haters of democracy, the full weight of the law must be brought to bear.

The first change in laws that passes Parliament prohibits an organisation from getting tax deductible status if they support, endorse, or allow their members to engage in any illegal activity or if the organisation fails to report illegal activities of which they are aware. The second, which passes only a week later, gives the Attorney General the authority to delist an incorporated association if it has engaged in illegal activities or supported such activities in any way. Delisting means organisations will almost certainly have to fold. The third law makes directors and board members liable for an organisation's unlawful activities and prohibits them from acting in any capacity with a new non-profit if they were part of an organisation when it engaged in illegal activity. Illegal activity includes even minor trespass or protesting without police authorisation. This causes the biggest uproar as everyone knows that corporations can and do kill people with absolute immunity from individual liability. Fourth, the penalties for unlawful activities are dramatically increased. A criminal conviction can now result in five years jail time. This includes interfering with critical infrastructure or critical economic activities. This also includes blocking traffic. Fines for convictions increase by a factor of ten. The option for community service instead of paying a fine is removed. Those unable to pay will have to serve jail time.

The Greens and a few cross benchers oppose the laws, but they are passed easily in the early hours of the morning.

CHAPTER 33

Green Earth is in turmoil. Management is trying to accommodate the police and the politics. They want to have a low profile, so they speak out against violence and illegality, but many aren't happy. Green Earth has never engaged in violence but it does use trespass and other minor crimes as part of what it has done for over twenty years. No one has ever been injured.

A message circulates on all the numerous climate, coal and gas e-lists. 'The time for civil disobedience has come. We can neither surrender to a government determined to destroy democracy, the movement and the planet nor those who advocate and practice violence. We are going to focus on the Sahan coal project as a symbol of everything that needs to change. Training begins in three weeks. Contact Jon Byrnes for details.'

Jake is pleased and intrigued. He wonders how many in the movement will support them.

The various green online discussion groups are split.

The cracks in the fabric of the climate movement widen daily. Jake sees it could all fall into a kind of pointless civil war. He rarely speaks when the debates rage at work. Simon, a softly spoken radical and Garth an outspoken one look at him askance. It's as though he changed character overnight without changing his mind.

Garth finally corners him at the coffee pot. Coffee number eight for the day and not an ounce of it has helped clear the fog in Jake's head. "Okay, Jake, what's up?"

"What do you mean?"

"Come off it, dude. The Free Radicals are forcing the hand of the environment movement – and it's an opportunity to push for more serious dissent, a chance to stop being a flat-assed movement that thinks sitting around a table is activism and you're not here. You've been arguing this is necessary ever since I've known you and now you're silent."

Jake stirs his coffee. A whirlpool forms in his brain. He stirs some more.

"Look, I'm thinking of signing up for the training, but I have personal things I have to take care of. Julie and I are working some things out and, well, my mother is dying." He shrugs his shoulders and looks away from Garth. He just wants to break into tears and hug this lovely man. "I don't think though that the movement is ready to be radicalised. And if they're not ready now I can't imagine they'll ever be. My personal stuff is the big thing but a part of me can't be fucked."

"Jake, I'm so sorry about the personal stuff. I had no idea. Is there anything I can do?"

"No. Thanks Garth..." Jake has no idea what to say. He feels the only place he can look is into his coffee cup.

"Look, that's a standing offer. Whatever I can do. And think about doing the training. We need you. It's important, it's what you've been calling for. A real groundswell of peaceful non-violence will take the wind out of The Free Radicals, give us back a purpose and may even drive Sahan out."

"Garth, how many Environment organisations that spoke out against The Free Radicals did that without a word about climate change?"

"I don't know. Most of them, I guess."

"All of them."

"And do you think that climate change is the greater crime?"

"Yeah, I guess. Absolutely."

"This is why I hesitate. Are you thinking of signing up for the training?"

"Yeah, I called Jon. I'm pretty sure that Jon is really Brian. He wants no more than 20 people for the training from all over the country. He has money for meetings, a few experts, and buying equipment. Two weeks and then we go forth and multiply."

"I'm glad you called. I can't possibly go away for two weeks at the moment. I'd like to take care of my personal things and then be enlisted by you. What do you reckon?"

"Fair enough, I guess." Garth gives Jake a kiss on the forehead and without another word goes back to his desk.

*

Jake, working with a young Green's staffer, Ethan, finally convinces the Greens to introduce a private members bill for crimes against the planet. "After WWII, we as nations and states acted to ensure that genocide would not go unnoticed or unpunished. That historic law began with a single man. And bluntly, the crimes being committed daily by corporations and their political lackies against a planet that is their home too are even more serious and more dangerous." He loves Senator Sam Lattimer! But the Bill will never pass, will probably never even be debated. But that's how the debate about genocide began too, he thinks.

Mind you, debate in public and in Parliament is increasingly ugly, racist, hateful. He tries to dismiss extremists like Watson or what's-her-name, Pattison, by simply calling them fascists, but the reality is they are speaking to someone who is listening. It may be that once a system begins to collapse, to enter a critical state, the centre falls out and life moves to the extremities of a system, like two crazed enemies hanging on to the opposite ends of a mechanical arm spinning randomly and wildly in space.

Jake's climate work – looking for scandals and legal cases – is keeping him busy and interested. Strangely, he thinks it might matter, when only a few months ago, he thought violence was the only thing that would bring change.

Scandals and stupidity are not hard to find. The money coming into the political arena from industry is an endless flow – campaign contributions, events, trips, conferences in exotic locations at which favoured ministers speak, contributions to projects within an electorate branded with an industry logo and its expectations. When a politician who has done his corporate duty retires, she or he immediately moves into their corporate chair. The revolving doors aren't even thinly disguised anymore. It's much harder to get anyone to care enough, or to believe it will ever change.

When a billionaire comes to visit, though, the media jumps. Rajeesh Sahan's announced visit has politicians falling over themselves to give him public money, public assets and public land to build a coal mine. They want to be seen with him because it means – in their minds – that they are supporting that weird creature, 'the economy'. Jake doesn't even begin to understand the mindset that says this is good, reasonable or even wins votes.

A colleague of Jake's finds the due diligence conducted by Treasury into the Sahan mine in his inbox one morning. It is dynamite. India is reducing its coal imports, dramatically cutting back on plans to build coal fired power stations. Combined with a price that is unlikely to rise high enough to even cover the costs of mining in the Galilee Basin, the prospect of the coal mine even proceeding without heavy subsidies seems very low. Treasury notes too that in the unlikely event that coal prices rise sufficiently, then the coal will be much more expensive than renewables. A no win situation.

But both the Labor Party and the Coalition defend the mine, defend Sahan and continue to proclaim there are thousands of jobs in this – despite admissions in court by Sahan that there are no more than 1400. Jake shakes his head at the miraculous absurdity of life in the era of climate change, which has become the rude house guest who will not be named.

Garth has gone off for his civil disobedience training. Jake has received one brief email, 'This is great!' and smiles at Garth's deep well of optimism.

*

The second death occurs only a month later. Some lunatic unbolts a high tension power line tower and brings it down with a truck and chain in the middle of nowhere Western Australia. A grazier drives over a live wire in his ute – on the way to hospital for a routine x-ray no less – and is fried. The Free Radicals claim credit or responsibility and dismiss any notion of remorse. 'We do not seek to cause injury, but we cannot be held responsible for the stupidity of others.'

Didn't that set the dogs barking. Baying for blood, they were. They are running out of ways to make the laws even harder – or ways that aren't completely insane, but the voices are there. Some call for unlimited detention of suspects – why not, that's what's done to asylum seekers. Some even call for instituting the death penalty.

The police make numerous arrests and numerous detentions but not a single case has been brought to trial yet.

Simon was detained again and this time was beaten badly. He tried to stand up for his non-existent civil rights. He refused to talk except to insist on having a lawyer present. He kept trying to walk out saying the police had no right to hold him under international law. His injuries weren't from torture, just pissed off police. When he came back to work, you could see he was traumatised – by the beating, by the anger towards him when he has done nothing, by the violence now simmering in too many places. He quit three weeks later. Jake and Julie both tried to help. They talked, they shared meals, Simon came over to the house, they went for a walk in the Border Ranges, but nothing Jake or Julie did could protect Simon from his demons. When Simon walks out of the doors of Green Earth for the last time, Jake knows that could have been him so many times.

*

Jake keeps his head down. He is drowning in documents released under Freedom of Information. He is uncovering more and more on the influence of the electricity, mining and coal industries over everything. He is trying to follow the money. He reads these fragmented stories – many documents are withheld or whole pages are blacked out – with an intensity that drains him. He tracks dates and meetings, follows clues that often lead nowhere. He finds an advisor to the mining minister is taking money from BHP as a consultant. The advisor will eventually be reassigned but nothing else changes. He knows he needs more.

No one talks about it now, but the disaster of the Balkans was made much worse by arms dealers – French, German, American, Russian. Then afterwards, the reconstructionists arrived – French, German, American, Russian – bribing every level of government to get the rebuilding contracts and to ensure that formerly public assets were now privatised. Those who stayed watched the Bechtels and Halliburtons of the world become even wealthier while the displaced waited in line for the basics. Janos saw this coming. Many people did. It's not new, but it's worse now, much worse. There is a kind of shamelessness about it all as though this kind of corruption is the norm.

CHAPTER 34

Jake has started following recipes and his cooking is becoming more elaborate and adventurous. He cooks Thai and Mexican, Indian and Spanish. Julie watches him with a wariness that surprises her. Trust is slow to come – and this change in him – as generous and gustatory as it is – feels somehow wrong. Her wariness, I think, is that even with her return Julie doesn't believe Jake is happy. At first Julie thought this was about her – about him wanting to focus his attention on her, on atoning. Now she isn't sure. He tries to be cheerful, but he isn't. It's not that he is trying to con her but to fool himself, to convince himself that Julie is all he needs. He has become almost doting, Julie thinks, and it feels as unreal as those days when he was lying to her.

"Are you having regrets?" she asks one evening.

Jake looks at her with horror and fear. "Why? No, not even once. Why? About what?"

"You try to be cheerful and it feels unreal, not a pretence but as though you're trying to convince yourself. I see you trying to hide something again and I wonder if you want to go back to destroying things or if you're struggling with me being home. I'm finding it hard enough to trust you without this."

Jake starts to cry. His expression doesn't change, it freezes in place. Everything in him freezes except the tears streaming from both eyes.

They hold each other then. Later they talk, talk properly, for the first time since Julie returned home. Jake is as emotionally fragile as she's ever seen him. Her distrust is one part of that. He is trying too hard and she tries not to show her wariness and so they both act with each other.

They both understand they are on brittle ice – personally and with each other. They move slowly, but at least they are trying to do that together.

*

Julie is four months pregnant and still nauseous most of the time. Jake's cooking sometimes makes it worse. There are some meals that she finds inedible. Certain smells and certain tastes are too extreme. The worst is anything with cloves. Five-spice isn't much better. At first, before they knew, she tried to eat these meals but couldn't.

Jake laughs it off. He simply walks around the table, embraces her belly and kisses that wondrous moon of flesh. "You, baby child will like my curries. Maybe not today, but it will happen."

She wonders why he suddenly took up cooking when she has so little appetite. She likes certain smells though. She likes the moment when she walks through the door and she can smell cardamom, or cumin or lime. Random.

Four months pregnant. I watch her stomach moon and it

reminds me of floating naked in a bay in the Adriatic beneath a gibbous moon in the days long before Tito died. The house is beginning to swell with baby stuff – clothing, cribs, carriages, jolly jumpers, mobiles and stuffed animals. Jake buys puppets – almost weekly. A giraffe, elephant, monkey, possum, crocodile. Several times a week he greets her arrival home with a new creature peering around the kitchen wall, always with a new voice. "Welcome home, Ms Harber, Jake is very excited you're here."

Julie doesn't buy anything. She sorts it and stores it in the spare room. She'll get to it eventually. She wonders at this distance sometimes, but it's not yet real. Nausea is real. Fatigue is real.

One of my neighbours was pregnant during The Siege. She struggled. Every day, whether it was waiting in line, on her feet for hours or the sound of shelling and alarms, she felt this life inside her was doomed to be a child of war. Not just born in war but gestated to the sounds of war rather than song or love or birds.

I have no idea if that child was ever born.

Julie likes visiting Mary and Ian. Mary in particular. Mary strokes her belly with joy and something that feels like reverence, even when she isn't sure who Julie is. One day, in a rare moment of lucidity, she says, "You know, physics didn't even think about new dimensions until the 20th century, but women have lived with it for thousands of years. A life within a life."

At dinner one night with Ian, Mary and Julie, Jake turns to Ian. "Dad, remember when I asked what you would do if you believed in climate change? I upset you. I wanted to ask a similar question, but no lecture this time."

Ian nods. He's curious. Maybe it's the tone, almost deferential.

"If you believed in climate change, would you agree with what

The Free Radicals are doing?

Ian ponders this for some time, head down, chewing. "You know, there are points where you have to defy the laws or the culture or the people in power to do what's right. I know that. I know that's also when great wrongs are done too, like in Sarajevo. That point is in different places for different people. It is why the Jews in Warsaw died in such large numbers – too many were too late, too slow recognising and responding to what was happening. I suppose as an ageing man, that point should come earlier for me. In theory, I have less to lose, but the thought makes my bones ache. This laksa is fantastic," he adds. "Hard to give up the creature comforts I suppose." He is sounding kind of melancholy. Jake wonders, not for the first time, how much of his answer is actually about Mary and what he would do to protect her.

Mary eats little and is ready to return to bed early.

The evening light begins to wash over the table. There is a warmth there that has been absent for some time and everyone feels it.

Julie takes Jake's hand under the table.

CHAPTER 35

January 1994

Dear brother

Dzelat, our executioner, has taken revenge for the death of our Deputy Prime Minister, exactly one year later. He killed an ultra-nationalist Serbian Mayor in Sabac, a town not far from the Bosnian 'border'. I say this with certainty only because others say it to me with certainty. I have no idea if this man exists, if he is only one man or many. He is a hero to many. He resists in ways that are ruthless. He does not initiate acts of hate but he responds in kind. It is this I find difficult. Responding to violence with violence is always dangerous.

On the other hand, silence, passivity and compliance are not very useful responses to what is happening here. Perhaps ethical dilemmas such as this are luxuries that we can afford only when peace returns.

*

After the hottest year on record in 2015, 2016 is looking worse. Each of the first three months of the year were the hottest on record. Record snowstorms in the United States were followed by record floods and here Australia had the hottest March on record. Serious bleaching of the Great Barrier Reef is occurring now.

Jake learns that the violence he started here was already happening in too many countries around the world. Water wars in Bolivia, sabotage and murder common in Russia, property destruction barely reported in Alaska, North Dakota, California, Texas. In Florida attacks on the waterfront homes of the wealthy have become the message of choice as rising waters have seen seawalls built with taxpayer money in wealthy areas but nowhere else.

In Australia, the few local councils trying to plan for climate change and sea level rise are stopped from instituting planning laws preventing development in low-lying coastal areas by State governments. Developers are by far the biggest contributors to State election coffers. They will continue to plunder the landscape and no one will ever be liable when these homes begin to disappear underwater. And as the houses sink, developers will be there selling the new waterfront.

Little of this is reported in the mainstream media, as though not speaking of these upheavals will make them go away. But social media has changed the nature of communication.

CHAPTER 36

Jake is getting almost no work done when he stays with Mary. Even with high doses of painkillers, she is in constant pain. Today she began to hallucinate. She started yelling from the bedroom. Jake ran in and she was sitting up in bed, a look of panic on her face. "My necklace... my necklace it fell off... all the... the things fell off and rolled under the bed. Hurry before it's gone." Jake got on his hands and knees and looked under the bed and there was nothing there. "I can't see it Mum."

"It's there. Look again, look again." She was almost hysterical. This time he pretended to find the pieces and gathered them in his hands. "I've got them, Mum. I'll go into the kitchen where the light is better and fix it."

Without a word Mary collapsed back onto her pillow and Jake walked out with a sense of dread that he has lost his mother before she has died.

Ian is bone tired. He has been staying up late, after Mary has gone to sleep, working in his office. The story of Sofia and me, like his caring for Mary, is both sustaining and consuming him.

Peta has been coming by as much as she can after work. She's not much of a cook but she cleans and sings pretty well. Not much joy around but it's not despair either. It's busy.

For the first time since he left Sarajevo in 1971, Ian is trying to make contact with someone, anyone, who knew me or Sofia. He looks at the old photos and struggles to remember names and relationships. There are several photos of the extended family. He has remembered two of about twenty names and both times he wakened in the middle of the night, sat bolt upright and rushed out of the room to write down the names before they were gone.

Some of the people in those photos are family I haven't thought about in many years. A niece I last saw when she was eight. She liked to dance; a cousin who would clamp himself to my leg like a limpet and yell at me to lift him in the air. I remember many more names than Ian, but there is too much I no longer know – the fates of most of these relations are unknown to me and that ignorance is another kind of loss.

The only reason Jake knows any of this is because Ian asked how he could best use the web to find some people from Sarajevo. Jake looked at him with curiosity and a bit of concern.

*

The Just Disobey civil disobedience movement plans rallies in all the major cities and Mackay and Bowen in order to remind the public that this is ultimately about climate change and a massive new coal mine and port. They will take place in April, hoping to attract families and children.

Garth has spent weeks enlisting the help of prominent citizens to participate. They want politicians to face the difficulties of arresting and jailing prominent scientists, soldiers who have fought in wars, farmers who provide food, sportsmen and women who have been called heroes.

Jake goes. It is the first rally he has attended in months.

He longs to feel a sense of festivity – something he feels little of as Mary slowly makes her way to death. It's a large rally – very large – for Brisbane. There must be close to 10,000 people.

Everywhere he turns he sees someone he hasn't seen in too long. It feels like a homecoming. He has a brief conversation and then moves on and starts another. These are friends, even if they aren't close friends, but it isn't a simple feeling for Jake. There is pleasure, true, but he also feels further from these people than he ever has. The shadow of his solitude is large.

He is scared. He is seeing how deep his roots go in this life he has occupied for a long time, but not now. Each of these friends or colleagues speaks to him of histories that surround him, define him.

There is a counter rally at the same time, calling for an end to environmental extremism and no tax breaks for environmental organisations. It's small, but large enough that the police are there in force. At some point it goes wrong. Off to Jake's left and slightly behind him he can hear yelling – not chants or songs but a fight. He turns but can't see anything.

Then they are in front of him. Around twenty counter-protestors are wrestling with around the same number of marchers. The police are cut off by the rest of the counter-protestors, who probably know as little of what is going on as Jake does.

Then a man is pushing him and yelling at him. He can feel the man's breath on his skin, menacing and inexplicable. He is powerless to stop this man, change his mind, even understand at the most basic level what he is saying, what he wants, why he is so angry.

He pushes away and tries to escape into the crowd but it's getting harder to move.

He turns and the man is now in a fist fight with someone Jake can't see. The march – or this small part of the march – is now like a system in chaos. It has no direction, no front or centre or back. It no longer even feels quite human.

Jake pushes his way out. He can feel himself shut down. He hears a babble of voices, registers colours and movement, but he can't identify words or people. They have disappeared. He is simply pushing through space until he arrives at the edges of chaos and then disappears into a narrow lane, where he suddenly stops and howls at the sky from his narrow canyon, just howls.

It was all pretty insignificant in the end. The stoush was controlled and the rally finished. The organisers were admonished for breaking at least five minor laws – traffic laws and breaching the conditions of the rally licence. But the police chose not to use their new arrest powers. A wise choice but only the first step in what will be an escalating campaign to confront the draconian laws that are now in place.

Jake walks homes thinking more about his fear as he was squeezed by the crowd, about his complete absence of control over events. He has said this is what the world must come to – chaos – but today brings doubts. Chaos can be brutal.

CHAPTER 37

February 1994

Dear Brother

We have had one day only since 1992 when there were no casualties in this, what used to be our home. I feel hate crawl inside my womb, I feel her claws and her heavy rank odour. I do not want to hate but perhaps there are too many emptinesses inside me now that must be filled and hate is closest to hand, easiest to breed, fastest growing.

A week ago, the Serbs bombed a marketplace. Many civilian casualties. For three days without rest we dug the bodies out of the rubble, did what triage we could, then men would carry the wounded to the hospital, or a clinic or a house, wherever room could be found. I have no idea if anyone was keeping track of who went where. I wasn't. My hands were raw and bleeding, my lungs filled with the dust of what used to be a building in a beautiful old city. The wounds were endless. Crushed limbs, wounds from shrapnel or stones, delirium from thirst, collapsed lungs, abdomens torn open by who knows what. I worked for hours or days – literally I don't know. I stopped, or was forced to stop, only because I began to hallucinate.

I am bored of writing of war, but there is little else. Shelling, deaths, rubble – so much rubble – injuries, fear – more fear than rubble, waiting in line for food, for water, for a public servant. Even love is interrupted, diminished and sometimes lost because of war. At least we don't have to wait in line for that! Janos and I will always love each other but it isn't always easy to show this.

I don't know how much longer I can do this. I am not solving anything, not changing anything, not making the war end faster. I am part of the assembly line of misery, fixing what I can fix, then doing it again and again. I can't remember the face of a single person I have treated. I keep busy, do more good than harm, but ultimately it has no more meaning than the shroud knitted by Milos' mother. I wonder why I chose to nurse not fight during this war.

I asked myself the same question over and over – and Jake has done the same. Did I choose to carry and use a gun because it was necessary or because it fed a dark and private need? Did I even choose? I remember staring at my hands one night, thinking, these are the hands of a surgeon, but they never were.

Ian thinks that Jake filters everything through a lens of climate change, just as Sofia does with war. Jake says it's no filter, to be afraid is not a choice but the world we live in and in that way it is like living a war.

Ian realises with shock that he has been reading about the war, living it, for over six months, since before Julie became pregnant.

He tells Mary about Sofia now. Stories that show her strength not her despair. Then he picks up a book, always a novel now, something magical or fantastical, and reads aloud.

Mary has been very unsettled and the new drugs are making her incontinent, but his reading now calms her – and him. Jake too likes to listen to Ian read. He puts down his work in the living room and even if he doesn't hear every word, he listens to the warmth and love in Ian's voice. It's funny though – Ian now hears Sofia's voice when he reads, a voice slightly husky and masculine.

June 1994
Dear brother

Today I write of something other than war!

Of course, I have heard about Vedran Smaljovic, the 'cellist of Sarajevo', but he left a year ago and now others are willing to take his place. A mortar destroyed the front wall of a house three doors down. The mother was killed. Her two children and the father survived. All the furniture remained intact, even the piano survived. It was like looking into a doll's house. A cellist sat at the edge of the destruction and played a Beethoven cello sonata with the father – who played so well – on the piano.

I cannot tell you how much such moments of affirming life and resistance and art and joy matter. People gathered below the destroyed wall and kept gathering. The children sat quietly on the sofa and afterwards people left small offerings, as much as they could. Food, medicine, money, even flowers which may be the rarest of all.

I was there that day. I can still hum that Beethoven tune, so filled with pain but also a joy that sits even deeper, as though ultimately that is the very core of life. It rained later that day, a gentle summer rain. We were all still there and the rain made us laugh.

July 1994

Dear Brother

We thought it was all so easy and clear. The Serbs are enemies, NATO and America our friends. We should have known better, we should have known better from the beginning even if we didn't have facts in front of us.

Even now, it is only rumours – but rumours that are persistent, consistent and very possible. America is actively supporting the fracturing of the Yugoslav state. They are supporting independence not because this matters to them but because they know that war will come, that disruption, disunity, dislocation will provide opportunities for America and American corporations.

I know, my brother, that you are an economist. I can only hope you don't subscribe to the views of Mr Friedman. Three members of the Chicago School came here, not to Sarajevo but to Belgrade, to discuss the opportunities during and following the war. Or so Janos was told.

We have also been told that American diplomats are gently pushing the countries that have suffered so much to adopt certain leaders and sell off certain assets. Companies are already looking to buy those assets, clearly expecting that they will be sold. When this war ends, we will have no money, no infrastructure and the vultures will be roosting. Or feasting. This is the grand plan of the Chicago School – the modern form of plunder.

Most conspiracy theories are foolish, but it is difficult to believe we are not being handled.

You can't imagine how this makes us feel. We fight for the basics – food, water, shelter and medicine, our country, our lives. We think that good and evil are simple truths in war and that ultimately good will prevail. Instead, those we support may have other agendas. Those we oppose may not be as bad as many voices have claimed. Reality begins to blur, truth to become soft.

We become even more afraid – not only of now but of later. None of us has the means or the energy to prevent this. We whisper about it, urgent whispers, in coffee shops and doorways, but we know that at the moment little can be done and by the time the war is over it may all be too late.

Janos thinks, and I agree with him, that the end game in the war is near. The war is no longer needed. We will give everything away, our institutions, our infrastructure, our souls.

Ian knows as little about Sarajevo post-war as he once did about the war itself. One more plank in his house of ignorance. He learns that it was only after the war, when the western financial powers moved in, that the plunder began. How did I know so little? he asks himself. Guilt, anger, self-loathing all circle him.

He can hear Jake's voice in his head. 'Welcome to the world, Dad.'

August 1994
Dear Brother

The Serbs have raided a weapons facility in breach of the UN exclusion zone. After the bombing of the marketplace, the UN called for retaliation. It never happened, but today the unthinkable occurred. An ultimatum was issued to return the weapons and when the Serbs refused to do so, bombers came. I have only heard this second hand and this is so miraculous there is little doubt the stories I have heard bear little resemblance to reality – except that the UN has acted.

I know that cynics would say, of course they didn't come for civilians but only for weapons –and I am one of those cynics – but they have come. Even if it was only a little biplane with a sputtering engine and stones thrown out of the cockpit, they came! Once again, we fill with optimism and imagine that the endless might actually end.

Ian realises with horror that this is the end of the letters. He rummages in the box, empties it on the desk. It can't be. He is desperate.   He goes through every letter again. He turns all the notebooks upside down and shakes them. It's not only that the story isn't finished but that without these letters, his sister will no longer be with him.

He knows that the war lasted almost two more years, almost two years before NATO planes finally intervened. Almost two more years before the massacre at Srebrenica, a story Ian read about only recently.

*

Julie is heavy, slow and aching everywhere but also feeling a joy that wasn't there in the early part of the pregnancy. Less than two months to go! Jake strokes her belly and feet each evening and sings to her belly until the being almost ready to emerge kicks or moves and then grows still.

Julie is now on leave and moves at the pace of seasons and still waters. There is no hurry and although she aches, she often sits and tries to understand or at least feel everything that is going on inside her. Her breasts are already full. They ache too. Milk is leaking out.

She is overflowing. Julie tastes her milk and is kind of disappointed that she can't taste herself, her love, her joy.

One day after work, when Jake steps inside the door he can hear Julie sobbing in the living room. He rushes in and she is sitting staring at her computer screen. "Julie, what's wrong? What happened?" She looks up at him, her face red from weeping and wet from tears.

He takes her in his arms and holds her until her breathing begins to still. Finally, she reaches out for her computer. "You have to watch this," she says.

He feels immediate relief – it is something in the computer, not something wrong with Julie, the baby or Mary or Ian.

There are several short videos Cath sent. The first is of a crow herding a hedgehog across a busy road and another of ravens skiing over and over down a roof covered with snow. There is a cat perched on the front of a pram protecting the child and finally a dolphin swimming up to a scuba diver asking for a fishhook to be removed from its dorsal fin.

"She sends me these videos every day and I either cry hysterically or laugh hysterically," she says through her tears.

Jake watches with her and laughs and holds Julie until she is laughing too.

*

The arrest of suspects is occurring almost weekly now. Jake thinks that the police must have finally stopped obsessing about greenies and realised that most of those involved are those who feel on the fringes of an unforgiving society.

A young man is arrested for the death of the CEO and the next day is charged with murder. His parents speak of a troubled young man who spent much of his time alone and online. He didn't belong anywhere he often said. He left school because he was bullied. His friends were all virtual. He was eighteen and had never had a girlfriend. He had no known political views, no strong ideology. He liked to feed birds and he didn't like to have the success of others rubbed in his face. Michael Cook was ostentatious in his success. Fast cars, beautiful women, big house, fine teeth and smile. Jake suspected this was the key, although he knows that to some extent, he probably opened the door for this young man.

Jake feels sadness for the young man more than anything else. He doesn't know what this says about what he has done or the hopes he has. He knows, in some ways that this is deeper than climate change.

Disintegration may bring nothing. It may see all of the sick, lonely, disturbed, broken beings attach themselves to a cause that slakes their anger, their loneliness, mediates their feeling of being lost and out of control.

There are five arrests in May and June. It is the hottest May on record for Brisbane and even here voices are beginning to speak out about climate change as a current reality not a future possibility. It is the hottest autumn on record in Australia and the hottest spring on record in the northern hemisphere.

The tower toppler is arrested. Another loner, another young man, but this one a greenie. Jake met him once, he thinks. He worked briefly for Greenpeace in their actions unit. A climber. He loved the adventure of direct actions. He remembers now – he met him in Brisbane. He gave a workshop on climbing buildings. It wasn't long after that that he hung off the coal loader at Abbot Point. Graeme seemed happy to be in the limelight. When he came down from the coal loader, he gave the victory sign and smiled a lot for the cameras.

The train derailers are arrested too. Two union men who are angry about climate change, tax evasion, corporate bullies in the workplace, the cutting of jobs. Just angry.

Jake watched each of these arrests with mixed feelings. He wants their acts, their lives, whatever wisdom or intelligence they have, to give him hope or joy. Instead, he just feels sad. This isn't what it was meant to look like.

He is amazed that he hasn't been arrested or questioned again. He has returned the tracker to the car and part of him thinks if they haven't arrested him yet they are unlikely to. Another part of him feels how close they are every day.

The police are optimistic that there will be more arrests soon. They claim to have broken the back of The Free Radicals.

Scientists warn that our understanding of the Antarctic ice sheets now suggests that areas of western Antarctica are susceptible to rapid melting of ice and sea level rise of between three and six metres in decades not centuries.

Another coal mine is approved in New South Wales. Gas is rapidly becoming our largest export.

The winds come from the west and are dry, smoky and lifeless. Julie tries to walk a bit every day but it is too hot – regularly over 30 even as winter approaches. Litigation to link the mining and export of coal from Reef ports to bleaching is thrown out. Once again, the courts have decided that the coal industry is not responsible for the climate impacts of the products by which they live and profit.

Julie stands in a cool shower and lets the water flow over her head and cascade down her belly and she doesn't care if she is wasting water. Afterwards she lies on the bed, the fan on full and Jake gently massages her tummy with rosehip oil. Slow and sensuous, that wonderful waxing moon of her life-begetting belly.

*

Julie gives birth the day that Mary dies. It's a boy. Both Julie and Jake were hoping for a girl to name Mary.

Mary dies at home in Ian's arms. He could feel it coming, you could see. It was early evening. He had spoken with Jake. Julie is in hospital, waiting. The baby looks like it doesn't want to be born just yet. The doctors expect it to be a while. Ian comes into the bedroom to tell her the news – if she's awake and coherent – and to see if she is hungry or needs toileting. She is on her side, her breathing shallow but not out of the ordinary. But he knows something is not right. He strokes her hair, that once beautiful thick black hair now just whispers – single strands of a life coming to a close. He puts his ear to her back, pulls back the covers. He is looking for what is wrong. He feels her pulse, her forehead and suddenly he stops and it's as though his entire spirit drains from him in that instant. He stares at her, then begins to stroke her, tears falling silently. Finally, he undresses and lays naked next to her for the first time in many months. He cradles her from behind and stays there well into the night, keening and shepherding both, until she dies, barely a breath between her life and death.

He misses the call from Jake saying it's a boy. When he rises, a part of him wants to straighten her, to brush her hair, to dress her. He does none of these things, but calls the hospital, slowly dresses and waits on the kitchen stool.

The ambulance takes them to the Mater Hospital. He is told it will be some time. Doctors will have to sign a death certificate, identify the cause of death and arrange for her body to be sent wherever it needs to go next.

He calls Jake who is across the road in the maternity ward. He tells him that his mother is dead. Jake cannot tell him that he is the father of a boy. They have named him Tarek. Julie's idea.

I am shocked. I am afraid that this child will also carry, even repeat, my history.

Jake tells Julie only that Mary is back in hospital and he is going to see her. Julie is exhausted and radiant both. Jake is in a kind of double shock and can feel himself shutting down, a machine that cannot reconcile two completely contrary sets of instructions.

Ian is shattered. Jake holds him and Ian allows himself to be held. Ian thought, he was sure, that the sheer force of his love and care and attention would cure Mary. And now nothing remains, a shell broken on the last part of the journey to shore.

Peta arrives and immediately breaks down and begins to sob. She clings to Ian first then Jake then Ian again. In other times, women would ululate for the dead on the streets of Sarajevo. Grief given the shape of a giant and twisted bird calling out in pain. Peta's grief has no shape. It is an outpouring, the breaching of a dam that holds untold stories and words and silences.

The only words Peta says for hours – and she repeats them over and over – is, "I never believed for a moment she would die."

Jake tries to say goodbye to Mary, but she smells of medicine, mould and death. He can only hold her, cold and already almost abstract. He wants to tell her about a story he read recently about the entwinement of black holes with space, but he has forgotten why it should matter.

Jake needs to return to Julie. He lets go of his mother. What was once his mother and is now something else. Julie is probably asleep but he needs to be there for her as well. He finally tells Ian he is a grandfather and Peta an aunt and hugs them both. There are no celebrations, no demonstrations of joy but Jake doesn't need that now, that time will come.

Jake stands beside Julie's bed and watches her sleep. She dreams. She smiles in her sleep. The baby is in a cot next to the bed, swaddled and virtually invisible. He leans down to make sure he is breathing, as parents have done forever. He breathes. Jake is overflowing with both love and loss. "I can't protect you from many things in the world, but I can promise that you will always be loved, you will always have a family, a house, several hearts where you can breathe in deeply and know how much love there is for you." A promise he may not be able to keep.

PART 3

Everywhere the ceremony of innocence is drowned.

W.B. Yeats

CHAPTER 38

Peta isn't quite sure how to be a shadow, but she is trying. Even my reflections are loud, she tells a friend, but she doesn't want to impose herself on the house and on Ian.

She appeared at his doorstep two weeks ago with an overnight bag and asked if she could stay for a few nights. A week later she brought another bag and her mortar and pestle. Ian has been like a ghost, although some part of him is beginning to return to the land of the living.

Peta cooked for him, although he barely ate. One morning, with the mist sitting heavy in the trees, everything he ate tasted foul, bitter. Coffee, eggs and toast and even maple syrup tasted like lemon seeds and bitterness was the only thing that remained in his mouth and on his tongue. It persisted through lunchtime. When he ate an apple in the early afternoon, it tasted repulsive. It continued through dinner. He hasn't imagined it, but he has little doubt the universe has sent him a message. It is a punishment for failing to keep Mary alive. It is the beginning of his dying.

Dysgeusia. It has a name. Its closest relative is disgust.

Ian returns to his office and stares at the box of letters, some newspaper clippings, and two notebooks he hasn't looked at yet. He stares at Mary's Will. He knows what it says but he knows he can't read it, and can't discuss it with his children without falling apart again.

Five days later, taste returns, but he still isn't eating well. He doesn't like chillis. Peta does. He doesn't really care for Asian flavours. He doesn't complain though. He is glad she is there, although he rarely talks, and spends most of his time in the office.

Peta's grief, very differently shaped from Ian's, is curling through her like a fishing net adrift in open waters, a ghost net, binding her in profound ways to the absences around her.

She has little desire to go out and drink or dance. She used to a couple of nights a week. She visits a few friends, spends a bit of time on the phone and learns to use Facebook. She is growing her hair out and not dyeing it anymore. It looks completely chaotic.

She gets up early and walks for an hour before coffee. At first, she thinks that becoming an early riser is a kind of penance, but she likes it, drawn to the quiet, the emerging signs of human life and the early morning light that is almost fragile and almost numinous.

She is still working but down to three days and thinking of going back to uni.

Mary's death and her own breakdown shook her. Her world was ostensibly pretty simple until then. She worked, she partied. She covered over some large cracks with punk and loudness and it was all good. But it's not all good now.

Sometimes after a period of intense shelling in Sarajevo, you could see the smoke from the guns sitting in the hills, then sinking into the trees and hanging there like a large unformed spirit sleeping in the treetops waiting to capture birds. That's kind of how I see Peta's grief. It is quiet at the moment, waiting, but it is still very much there.

Jake and Julie and Tarek come over a few times a week. The baby is one of those miracles that feeds easily, cries little and sleeps most of the night already.

Jake is all over the place. He seems to have no middle. One moment, he is pensive and removed. The next burbling at the baby or nuzzling Julie's neck with open affection. He has moments of joy and moments where he shuts down so far, he may as well be an asteroid.

Julie notices but lets it pass. She has been absorbed into babyland. A lovely mother. Relaxed and simply joyful.

Ian is funny with Tarek. He seems a bit repulsed and deeply drawn at the same time. He holds him awkwardly, away from his body, as though he is a breakable object he can't be trusted with. Tarek vomits on him once, Ian smiles, Tarek cries. I can only wonder how often he held his own children when they were young.

One Saturday, Peta wakens late, has coffee and is sitting quietly, when she hears Ian in the study. There is a crash from the study and then silence. Peta rushes in and there is Ian sitting on the floor surrounded by the contents of the closet and an overturned chair. Boxes, a few children's toys, books, papers.

"Are you okay?"

Ian nods. "I was trying to get some things down from the top shelf and I started an avalanche."

She offers him a hand. He stands and out of nowhere hugs her, tighter and tighter and doesn't let go.

"Would you help me?" he says finally.

"Of course. What are you doing?"

"Making a mess."

"You want me to help you make a mess?"

"No, no, I've already done that."

"What then. You want me to help you clean up?"

"No, no, I've only just made the mess." Ian begins to laugh. "Thank you Peta." He crushes her again, but only briefly this time.

They sit together on the floor and sort through the papers and boxes. "I'm looking for anything from Bosnia. Before..." He still can't speak Mary's death. "Before Sofia's letters stopped and I want to make sure I have everything from her and there."

He tells her the story as far as he knows it. She understands pretty quickly that Ian is struggling to understand what happened to Sofia and Tarek because he will never understand what happened to his Mary.

They find a children's drawings by both Jake and Peta, report cards, school photos, which Peta has no desire to inspect. They find all the academic journals in which Ian has ever been published There are several photos from Sarajevo. One appears to be a group of men and one woman in a militia. They are armed and smiling. It's a bit menacing. Ian has no idea who these people are. The photo is unlabelled and undated. There is another photo of a woman smoking a pipe in her doorway. She has a wonderful toothless smile. A businessman standing with his bicycle and behind him the rubble of what once was a house. There is one of a woman cooking at a stove seen from the street – the whole side wall of her house is gone. Life goes on.

One photo is a woman with long black hair, tied back loosely and deep-set eyes that are challenging, soft, wary. It is Sofia, older than when he left, but unmistakeable. He stares at her for minutes, this woman he abandoned so many years ago.

He later finds a photo of me with a man he correctly assumes is Milos. And one of me shortly before the war. I was a large man. I never had a moustache unlike so many in Bosnia. It was because women told me I had sexy lips and I thought it would be foolish to hide them. Milos, round-faced and looking, as he always did, as though he was on the verge of laughter. I loved that man. There is a photo too of Janos and Sofia together. It must be before the war. Janos is a handsome man and happy. A kind of joy in being alive suffuses him. Sofia, who is almost as tall as Janos, is smiling. It's self-assured and a little self-conscious. She is turned towards Janos, loving and loved. Apart from the notebooks and some newspaper clippings that were in the original box, there is nothing more in the mess.

They repack the boxes, stack them neatly in the cupboard. "You sure you want to keep all of this stuff?" Peta asks.

"Of course. You never quite know when it will become a history, a story, or a gift."

Later, she finds Ian sitting at his desk staring at the photos that he put aside.

CHAPTER 39

Three weeks after Tarek is born Jake is arrested. He answers the door, is immediately handcuffed and virtually dragged from his home in front of Julie while she is breastfeeding Tarek in the living room. She doesn't even have time to say goodbye.

They are rough with him. He recognises one of the officers. Maybe the other as well. He searches for their names but he is getting foggy, going into shock. Why are they rough with him? He can't remember the interview he had with them. Was he cocky? Did he mock them? He knows that this time they have something. They are not fishing now.

He is processed and put in lockup. They waited until the end of the day – he knows Julie will have called a lawyer, probably Chris, right away, but he won't get in to see him tonight.

He has been arrested under Commonwealth Counter Terrorism laws. They are harsh. He will be charged with terrorism, perhaps multiple charges, including committing, planning, financing, receiving training for a terrorist act, possessing things connected with a terrorist act and even having collected documents likely to facilitate a terrorist act. He will likely be charged with membership in a terrorism organisation. And then there will be the criminal charges too. He faces several lifetimes in prison.

*

He is transferred to the super maximum security jail in Goulburn, like many terrorism suspects. Twenty two hours a day locked up. Twenty four hour surveillance. For his two hours in the yard he is accompanied by four guards. He is in leg chains and handcuffs. Jake didn't imagine this. There is so little time outside his cell, there is little time to be afraid of being raped, beaten up, and all the other things that are supposed to happen in prison. Instead, he must deal with no privacy and the constant presence of guards who tell him he is a danger to the world. He didn't imagine that, and didn't imagine how quickly confinement would begin to work on his brain and body.

His lawyer Chris appeared at the end of the first week. His first visit since Jake was transferred here. "At the moment they are only charging you with the one terrorist act – the CSG rig, but are going to try to link you to at least another six. They are also looking at charging you with the intent to commit various acts even if you never did. They're equally serious. The Free Radicals has been named a terrorist group, so belonging to the group is a criminal offence and you're going to be charged with that as well. Once you're a member of a terrorist group, you can be held responsible for all the crimes committed by that organisation. And you can be deemed a member of a terrorist group even if the group hasn't been listed as a terrorist group."

"How do we even know The Free Radicals exists as a group?" Jake asks. "Is declaring it on a media release enough?"

"I don't know Jake. I'm not a criminal lawyer or an expert in counter terrorism laws. I'm a friend who will advise you in the early stages but you're going to need some experienced help. We're looking for someone now."

He has made one appearance in court – to be denied bail. Julie was authorised to visit in the fourth week there, although visits are rarely permitted. They spoke across a screen with guards present and too close. They are not allowed to touch. He is cuffed to the table. He is strip searched twice a day; the grubby hands of guards who seem to hate him are allowed to touch him but he can't hold Julie.

Tarek is crying. He's afraid of Jake, or afraid of the prison which has nothing friendly about it. He cried, Julie cried, Jake cried.

He has books. He reads and writes. His language becomes stranger, more abstract. He uses words that are real but not as he uses them. Boundaries in his brain are broken by some part of him that knows the only freedom he has is there. But it also feels like a mooring has come loose. Freedom is only one word for what is happening.

He wrote to Julie recently.

Dear Julie

My hands grow hard, thigmotaxis disappears. My brain is slow, not thinking but a searching for agnosia. Words scud around. Images careen around corners and then disappear into a mist. I beat the walls with my hands. They grow hard. The wall just grows. I hope my anger and despair live only here, in this small space, otherwise it will eat me.

Julie devours his letters but this one tells her immediately that Jake is in trouble.

She and Tarek have moved in with Ian, while Jake has generously been given a redundancy. Julie wants to save money for the trial and she knows Ian cannot be alone in the house with Mary's ghosts. Peta moved out, happily, and is rethinking her life. She is thinking of studying medicine, psychology, biology, buying a campervan and becoming a road hippy. Very lost – but also very clear that her life is going to change.

Julie is working one day a week at the childcare centre, just to get out of the house. She is allowed to take Tarek with her. Living with Ian is hard work. Cooking, cleaning, looking after Tarek and Ian too. He's grieving still and simply doesn't care very much about anything. Julie feels that she and Tarek have kind of taken over the house – it is their voices and things and patterns that seem to now define that space that still so deeply belongs to Ian and Mary.

Ian is thinking of going to Sarajevo to find out what happened to Sofia. He tells her about the book of the dead. "He could hire someone to do that for him, someone who is there, but he feels he has to go," Julie says to Jake on her second visit. "He's worried about leaving me and leaving you. I've told him, he can't do much at the moment. That time will come, but it's holding him back."

"Could you tell him I want him to go? I want him to come back with their stories and a feeling he has reconciled with Sofia."

"He put a large amount of money in our bank account for the lawyer."

"How much?"

"Fifty thousand dollars. I told him we couldn't take it. I sent it back and he deposited it again. He knows the trial will cost us more than that. A lot more."

"We'll need it," Jake mutters. "Thank you Julie for not hating me," he says suddenly and they begin to cry again. "I thought I knew, I thought I understood what it was I was doing. I was so ignorant. I don't know if I was wrong, but I wronged you in so many ways."

"You're getting lots more support now that you're in prison. People are criticising the laws, the harshness, the conditions you're put in, that I can't visit you every day even though you are supposed to be presumed innocent. You know Today Tonight contacted me and want me to go on tv to talk about what has happened. I might do it. I'm talking with Else – she's the head of comms now at Green Earth."

Jake nods, but he is struggling to care. He knows the penalty he faces if he is convicted of even one terrorist offence is a minimum of 15 years, more likely 25 and a good possibility of life. He can't remember how many charges there are and more are likely to come. If he begins to think about that, about his cell and a lifetime in confinement he will simply kill himself. Except even that won't be simple. The prison takes a number of steps to make that difficult. We want you to suffer is the message, it is the message every day.

Jake suddenly realises that Julie is speaking. "...around. I couldn't believe how many people came. Garth has become my friend too. He is a sweet man and he feels incredibly guilty for no reason at all. He really pushed for the fund – and made sure people came to the launch. He spoke too. He sounded like you. I was a blubbering mess. Even Ian came and when it was over, he sat at this empty table surrounded by wine bottles and plates and looked off into the distance nodding his head. I finally went up to him and put a hand on his shoulder. "Good people," he said and then went silent.

"No one has much money, but there's a bit there. There haven't been any more arrests since they charged the men who derailed the train, but The Free Radicals are still going. It's not as often but it sort of feels like it is better organised and consistent. Did you hear they sank a dredge? It was heading to one of the coal ports. Then they set a fire at a coal mine. And there was one more. It was last week. That's right, they released video of the Managing Director of Woodside shagging an employee. They put it on Facebook, on a corporate responsibility site. He fucks his employees and his planet both. A good man. Something like that."

Jake actually smiles at that. "An inventive brand of activism," he says. "I heard about the dredge" says Jake. "One of the guards came up to me and said, 'One more for your charge sheet mate,' and showed me the paper. Nasty man. I don't read the paper very often," Jake says in a voice that is filled with such deep loss, that Julie reaches out for him.

The guard steps forward, hand on his truncheon. What a scum bag. Tarek begins to howl again. Julie pulls him closer until he settles.

"Tarek is so loud at home. Ian is being so good about him." Julie just starts talking, anything will do. "He sits up well now and he likes to sit on his mat in the middle of the living room, wave both his arms up and down and shout or howl at the top of his voice. He's not upset, he seems to want to fill the room with himself."

Jake smiles thinly. He has barely been able to look at this young child who is his blood. His failures seem so many, but this one, having a child who will grow up without him, seems the worst. The worst failure, the most despicable abandonment, the indictment he makes against himself that hurts the most. He is sitting in the prison's common room, but when he thinks of Tarek, he wishes he was curled up in a ball under his bed, keening and rocking and inconsolable.

It is lucky Jake cannot hold Tarek either. I think he would simply die of sadness on the spot.

"Garth said to tell you that the Just Disobey movement is doing well. There are rolling activities across the country. They have so many celebrities that are keen to be involved and even arrested, it's very cool. They've had about five office occupations, several lock-ons on rail lines. A flotilla of small boats locked on to a coal ship that was being loaded at Abbot Point, chained themselves together and then chained the entire mess to the prop of the ship. I think they arrested around 20 people for that one. The politicians are having conniptions. They want to come down hard but they can see that these aren't extremists but voters who might matter."

Julie is interrupted by the guard who tells them their time is up. Those 30 minutes pass far too quickly. There is so much more to say, discuss, laugh and cry about. I can't be in prison, it's not possible, Jake thinks. Surely, I can collect my things now and the three of us can just walk out the door.

They cannot even kiss goodbye. This moment is as hard for Jake as being taken to prison in the first place. Harder.

The walk back to his cell is like a slow freefall into a hole, falling further and further into his own mind, which itself is falling too, shedding its understanding of itself, Jake's understanding of his self, his selves. How could that not happen? He is no longer a greenie, but a prisoner. He is no longer a partner, but a prisoner, a single male. His only companion is himself, day after day in a relentless exposure of the emptiness that is his new life and being, his decisions, his past, and the path that led here.

He has become a creature of extreme emotions – paranoia, self-loathing, bitterness, extreme anger, extreme shut down, but it is only pain that moves him and only so far. He feels safest when he feels least and he knows when he reaches that point of feeling nothing at all he will be utterly lost.

*

Jake being in prison throws Ian's life even further into confusion. Haunted by Mary's death, Sofia's unknown fate, the war, what he now sees as his abandonment of his family, the imprisonment of his son – a young man prepared to sacrifice his life for a cause Ian isn't even sure he believes in – feels like a weight he cannot bear. Sometimes he struggles to breathe. Sometimes he cannot sleep and he walks around the house talking to himself in a quiet but grim threnody. A part of him is aghast that his son may have done these things, and like many of his generation, arrest in his mind is not very different from guilt. Instead of denial, perhaps a more normal parental reaction, Ian can't stop believing that Jake probably did these things.

A part of him wonders what he did wrong, how did he fail this time? And a part of him tries to make sense of how a young man reaches the point where he resorts to such acts.

Ian has not been given permission to visit Jake, but Julie tells him all she knows. She tries to be positive about Jake's state of mind, but she won't lie and the reality is she is scared for Jake. She watches him fold in on himself like a snail disappearing into the darkness of its shell.

Ian sits at the vacant dining room table and covers the surface with what feels like the sudden wreckage of his life. Talk about a train wreck. His career is done. He has lost the love of his life. He has found and lost his sister. His son is facing a life in prison. His once certain and stable life and self is suddenly rudderless. What sustained him is gone and what now must drive him has changed utterly.

He knows a few things. He wants to protect and help Jake any way he can. He wants to go to Sarajevo and find out what happened to the remains of his family. This feels, oddly, as if it is something he owes Mary and maybe even Jake.

Apart from giving Jake money and letting Julie and Tarek stay with him – which is more for his benefit than theirs – he isn't sure what to do.

And so he does what academics do – he begins to read. He goes from dry economics to the history of a forgotten war and now to climate change. He starts with James Hansen, the NASA scientist who first raised the alarm in the 1980s. He reads the basic science of the carbon cycle and the holding of greenhouse gases in the atmosphere which was known over 100 years ago. He gets that. He gets that carbon dioxide has dramatically increased in the atmosphere and it tracks with the increase in industrial activity over the last 200 years.

He gets that the global average temperatures have risen inexorably.

He finally understands why scientists say that the current increase in temperatures is almost certainly caused by humans – the increase in carbon dioxide directly matches increases in the burning of fossil fuels. He reads why cities and solar flares and natural variations in temperature can't possibly explain what is happening to the climate.

He goes back to those who deny climate change and looks at their claims with new eyes. He ignores the more colourful conspiracy theories, but everything else is open.

He reads the reports on extreme weather events in the last fifteen years and that these events, which are already killing large numbers of people, reflect the predicted change in climate caused by emissions twenty years ago. The system is going to get more disrupted.

He reads voraciously. It's almost an act of self-flagellation. He reads angrily, condemning himself for his blind resistance. Within three weeks, he truly cannot understand the man who argued with Jake about climate change. The science is so overwhelmingly clear – even to an economist. And as an economist, he is horrified at the implications. The cost of doing nothing will be so enormous that no economic theory could ever justify it.

And yet, doing nothing is being justified on the grounds of cost.

He is a converted man and begins to speak with the fervour of one who now possesses the truth and one who must atone for his previous denial. I think he senses that his conversion is also a necessity, a part of how he must care for Jake and his relationship with him.

Julie laughs at him regularly. "Jake better not hear you say that, Ian. He'll think someone has taken over your brain." Ian laughs too and they become closer through this transformation.

Ian writes a long letter to Jake. He describes his conversion on the road to Damascus. I have been such a mumpsimus! It feels unreal and disturbing that it has taken me so long to learn what you already knew. I have now booked my trip to Sarajevo. I leave in a week. This is another journey that it appears I must take. When I return, I will do whatever it takes to see you freed from jail, returned to your lovely partner and loud child and your loving if somewhat slow father. I love you Jake.

*

It's more than a month before Jake's gets his first visit from his barrister, Steven Kaal, QC. Jake was prepared to be angry with him for taking so long to visit, but he's an immediately likeable guy and Jake doesn't need to fight an ally.

Steven has worked on a number of environmental cases and more recently he has worked on asylum seekers and human rights, including David Hicks and his torture and detention at Guantanamo. He knows the counter terrorism laws well. He has agreed to work as close to pro-bono as he can. Even so, he tells Jake, "This is going to be an expensive process. We not only need to call our own experts but will need to counter theirs. Depending on the evidence they have, that can get very expensive. And there's no doubt they will design this case in part to break you financially. We are very likely to need an investigator. Counter terrorism cases are a great investment for a government that wants people to remain afraid. They are fought in the courtroom, in the media, in social media and in Parliament.

"I know a bit about you. You have an important role in this case. Firstly, you need to put together a plan for outside the courtroom. You will need to have a media and social media strategy. Together we'll put together an investigations strategy. And you need to stay sharp, sane. Prison and a trial can drain you, kill you. Don't let it. This is a fight you need to be part of.

"My initial view is that from a public and political perspective we want to attack the Government for misusing counter terrorism legislation to go after innocent people. We show its anti-environmentalism and ideological extremism and how they've ignored expert advice that these laws cast far too wide a net."

Jake is getting caught up in Steven's enthusiasm. At first, he wanted a lawyer to do whatever he had to do and leave him alone, but he realises his self-pity needs to end now. "I'm going to need secure and confidential internet access."

"I will inform the court that you're participating in the defence preparations and I want you to have full and secure internet access and access to any court related documents. We'll see how that goes. Now, I need to explain the process to you. I should have done that initially. Chris gave you a broad outline of the charges. There have been a few changes since he saw you. A few charges dropped and a few added. I won't give you the details – they're likely to change again.

"There is no defined limit to how long they can hold you prior to going to trial. The Government argues that the law is clearly preventative, so arrest of a suspect when the evidence is not yet sufficient to take to trial is okay. They argue as well that the Government must be given all the time it needs in order to build the case as strong as it needs to be to ensure a conviction. A wonderful bit of presumptive guilt at work in these laws. We will certainly look at challenging the laws as well as the charges."

"Steven, thank you. I can't tell you how glad I am to have you as my lawyer. I feel like you've single-handedly and without even intending to pulled me out of the proverbial prison pit. I know I need to be patient. I know the laws are bad. I trained as a lawyer and if I can get secure access on my computer I can perhaps help with that side as well. Anything you can do to speed the process along would be great. I'll include that in my media strategy. I'll have that done in a few days."

"Okay. So, you know what you have to do. I will try and get you secure internet and email and will begin to look into the legal, media and political dynamics of this. I'll be back next week."

Jake watches this slight and intense man leave. He fights for good in an entirely different way. Jake always calls the law 'end-of-the-pipe activism'. By the time a social or political problem arrives at the legal system it has travelled a long way, veered off into many tributaries, has many dead, many voices and much baggage and the law will only deal with one small bit of this history at a time. End of the pipe. But as Steven disappears, Jake thinks, this man, just with the force of his will and character, gave me hope. Fuel for activists!

CHAPTER 40

When Ian leaves for Sarajevo, Peta moves in. Julie doesn't know Peta very well, but she's happy to have Peta join them. Jake is gone for the moment, she says to herself, but my family is still growing.

Peta adores young Tarek. She has always said she never wants children, but it's certainly not because she hates them. It's as though she finds in Tarek something she has lost in herself. Peta insists on collecting all the stuffed animals and puppets and taking off on these wild stories and adventures that become crazy complicated. All the while Tarek happily chews on a bear's arm or whacks the dinosaur against the ground.

At night she and Peta share a bottle of wine. "I'm going to quit my job and then the entire family can be virtually unemployed. We will be the modern dole bludgers, except that none of us are getting the dole."

"Have you decided what you're going to do?"

"I'm going to go to work getting the dole. Parliament is currently arguing about delaying the dole for the unemployed for six weeks, so they can experience the value of starvation in finding a job. I don't know what I'm going to do. Still."

"You're great with Tarek. You could take my job at the childcare centre."

Peta bites her lip. "This is going to sound kind of crazy. It doesn't even pay. I'm thinking of going to Borneo and volunteering in one of the orangutan orphanages."

"Peta that sounds fantastic. Maybe they'll understand your crazy animal stories better than Tarek."

Peta laughs. "Tarek understands them, he's just disguising it. It kind of runs in the family."

"Jake used to tell me how the two of you would rescue every bird, animal, creature great and small and bring them into your bedroom."

"I don't know why we tried to hide them. Mary loved them and was much better at rescuing animals than either of us. Ian had no idea it was going on. Too many of them died though. I did a wildlife rehab course during uni. Birds, possums, wallabies, but never rescued anything. I only had a bicycle so I couldn't go pick them up quickly unless they were very close. God, that feels like a long time ago. Things that once mattered. You put them aside and then they disappear. One day I awakened to find I was an accountant. The more I think about it the less I remember why or how that happened."

Julie ponders that. "I wanted to be an explorer most of all. I would go out into the desert – I grew up in Arizona – and return with a bagful of stuff. Skeletons, flowers, stones. It was a bit like you, actually. I would gather these things and then imagine the secret history that they represented and the histories I would create. My stories weren't as crazy as yours, but they became complicated and elaborate. I haven't thought of that for years. And then I wanted to be an artist. For twelve months I drew anything and everything. I think I was around thirteen and painfully shy. But then hormones happened and I wanted to be stupid. I was so ignorant and so socially inept but imagined myself so differently. My mother and father never told me anything – not about boys, or periods, or adolescence or sex. I was so clueless. I had a boyfriend – briefly – who played the trumpet. He was terrible, but I decided – also briefly – that I'd be a drummer. Fortunately, my father refused to buy me drums. You know I've never had an abiding passion, only passing fancies. That kind of makes me sad. I'm kind of jealous of that side of Jake, although I know how hard it can be too. And I watch your father move from a career towards things he cares about. It's not a simple process." Julie drifts off into silence. Talking of her past reminds her too of her adolescence, and the awful ambivalence of her sexuality. Moments of attraction and sexual tension followed by repulsion – both of herself and the other and then the longing to experience sex the way she imagines it is supposed to be. Her body aches for Jake. She can feel his hands on the back of her neck, she can feel his full lips and taste the coffee and the warmth of his tongue. She can feel him inside her and around her and quietly, then quickly, her body lets go, her spirit surrenders to pain, to tears, to a whole world in front of her that she can barely imagine or tolerate.

CHAPTER 41

11 August 2016

My dear children

I arrived last night. Strange, strange being here. This morning I visited my childhood home. It is gone. In fact, there is little to recognise. A minaret that somehow survived the shelling, the staircase up to the local church. The church is gone but I remembered the steps. There is a fountain that partially remains. When we were very young we played there on very hot days.

The strange flow of emotions is relentless. Memory mixes with loss. Forgetfulness with nostalgia. My desire to leave and my departure so many years ago are like strangers at the moment. I seek out the familiar and at the same time wonder what I am trying to find. I know the answer of course. I am trying to find Sofia or at least the rest of her story, but it is not that simple either.

After I arrived, I heard the calls to prayer, a sound so familiar from childhood, so much part of childhood, that I haven't thought of or remembered in any way in forty years. How did I put so much of my life away, stored in some locked cupboard? Why did I put it away so deeply? I can feel this journey ripping the doors off of that place and it is not pleasant but not painful either. It is daunting though. Already I feel a deep fatigue as though I have to confront all my histories at once – both here and there, at home.

I watch Ivan more than I ever have, perhaps because he is searching not only for Sofia but for Jake and Jake needs him. I am almost holding my breath. He is jumping from a great height now and perhaps it is long overdue.

It is very strange to be watching him in my country not his, searching in a past that belongs to both of us in completely different ways. Now I am calling him Ivan again – it took me ages to get used to Ian and in some ways, I no longer know him or what name fits.

He is being forced to relive one past, excavate another and to try and make sense of his future – a demand he certainly didn't expect or want. A hard journey. I feel quite silenced by it, as though there is nothing to say, nothing to regret or do. I just watch with hope and a certain joy that he has found his way back here – even if the circumstances are so poor. I cannot see him as clearly as Jake, cannot understand him as well. I am peering out towards the edges of the universe that are open to me and it is blurred and confusing.

I don't even want him to know all the stories that are here. There, in Sarajevo. Particularly mine. He needs to find Sofia or find out what happened to her. I do too. I have not seen her since the day before I was arrested at the border so now Ivan's search has become as important for me as for him. I need him to come back to Jake stronger, more openly loving. We both need to put some things to rest, but neither of us need more horror or fear or pain.

13 August 2016

My dear children

It is the end of my second day here. My fatigue is deep. I am getting too old for travel and this trip is one that is long physically but even longer emotionally. This return is like digging in soil so heavy with histories and emotions that each spoonful seems to weigh tonnes.

I have been terrified of meeting myself, I think. Terrified of what I will find, what I will see and also what will find me.

I went to the Palace today. That building is fully restored, although it is difficult to believe how much restoration is still to be done in this city over twenty years after the war ended. I have walked many places already. It's a vibrant city. There are many people of all descriptions, too many loud vehicles, many street vendors, many people sitting in squares or at street cafes, many people walking. There is laundry hanging from windows and all the signs of life that one would hope for.

My Bosnian is rusty. People are at first amazed when I speak. 'You speak Bosnian so well! Where are you from?' 'I was born here,' I say and they laugh at me. 'You have an American accent,' they say. I look offended and tell them it's Australian. Then they say, 'But don't worry about it. You speak well for a foreigner' and laugh at me again.

Sarajevo and the surrounding hills are so deeply familiar. There is a drought here – the worst in memory and the hills are tinder dry. Fires have been breaking out and it is only the beginning of summer. Although no fires are burning today, the smell of burnt trees is still in the air.

Peta and Julie read these emails together, shoulder to shoulder. They only know some of the history that Ian has just learned; only know the outlines of his departure and Sofia's days of war, but they know clearly how important this journey is, how important that he find Sofia or take the much longer journey of grief and forgiving himself.

*

Jake can feel the hardness growing on him, like a carapace or a tumour. After a little over a month in prison he has shut down much of himself. He is more distant, more calculating, distrustful, wary. He has a kind of imposed catalepsy. He does not make friends but cultivates alliances in the short time he has with other inmates. He eats with them now. He has time in the cage with one or two others. He uses his legal background to buy himself safety and to foster some allies. He helps inmates research the law, helps them to write letters or draft appeals. Most of it will never work, but in knowing the law he has potentially magic powers. At least that's what many of the inmates think.

He exercises now as though his life depends on it. He runs, lifts weights, pushes beyond exhaustion because it is one of the ways he stays sane. He is becoming muscular, bulky even. He likes it but doesn't. It is what he wants to be in here, in this place, but it is still not who he is. At least not yet. The hardness is like a shell that protects him, but it sucks the life from him too. He can feel the dry leaves of his other life – all the empathy, care and love – blow around in the empty shell that he is becoming.

He reads the newspaper headlines online, but doesn't dig deeply into any story. He scans stories about the latest climate disaster or news of The Free Radicals or Just Disobey, he follows the latest climate stories, but with none of the passion he once had. He has more immediate concerns. And those realities out there are now well and truly beyond his influence or responsibility. He knows this but doesn't know if this is a change that is permanent or a change that he needs now in order to survive.

He still doesn't have a court date. He has made another court appearance to plead not guilty but nothing else happens. Steven says the prosecution has still not provided discovery. They are building their case and it is hard to force the government to court in counter terrorism cases. They often take years to compile the evidence they want, and the accused – supposedly presumed innocent – can rot. Jake has read all the counter terrorism laws and cases and he knows he is in trouble if they can produce even a minimum amount of evidence. A big part of justice has been killed by these new laws in the war on terrorism. Once upon a time he would have raged against the coming of fascism, where freedoms and rights are sacrificed to a state of fear. Now he simply turns away and looks for loopholes, defences, ways around not through the law.

He and Stephen have finished the plan for using social media to push for a trial sooner rather than later and to demonstrate the abuses of law and power that the counter terrorism laws represent.

Steven passes information on to Julie who passes it on to Garth who has anonymously set up Facebook, Instagram and Twitter sites. The sites are a platform for demanding to see the evidence against Jake, demanding that they bring him to trial. Arrested without evidence and held while the government desperately searches for something to justify their abuse of power. There is a calendar and clock on the Facebook and Instagram sites. One month. Three days. Seventeen hours without a trial date. Every hour it ticks over.

There are at least two global petitions demanding that Jake be brought to trial now and if they don't have the evidence Jake should be released. Each one has over 50,000 signatures. The law presumes you're innocent. Or used to! the sites scream.

The Government dismissed the first media questions about this. It's a matter for the courts they said, refusing to answer questions about laws they demanded, drafted and passed. They then attacked the Greens when they raised it in Parliamentary speeches.

Even within the first month, this social media campaign has begun to bite. Jake is characterised as a political prisoner by some. His case is seen as the first real test for the Government's terrorism laws and the Government's attacks make them appear defensive.

Jake sits with Farouk in the library. He explains that the grounds for appeal from a terrorism conviction are very hard. Farouk was convicted because his brother, who lived with him, was convicted of having the materials for building a bomb and planned to use them. The materials weren't even at the house. And there is no evidence Farouk knew anything of this. Farouk was finishing his university degree in accounting. There is no evidence that he was radicalised, although there is certainly evidence that he hated American militarism against Muslims.

Farouk is serving fifteen years. It could have been worse.

"Farouk, you can appeal, but the law is so broad, it is unlikely to work. I think the only appeal you can make is to the broader public. And you need to be a model prisoner. Never do anything wrong."

Farouk looks up and away, across the prison yards and past the fences and the cameras. There is nothing out there that belongs to him anymore. He is not a citizen of Australia, not a citizen of Iraq, not anything, not anyone, not anywhere anymore. A part of him thinks, prison is my home and there are worse places, definitely worse.

Jake speaks to Steven about Farouk. He knows the case and says there is little that can be done legally, "But a social media campaign like yours might help."

Steven knows enough people in the asylum seeker and Muslim community to get this underway.

Jake can't do much more than give Farouk legal advice and offer to help him set up a media campaign. He cannot rescue him, cannot inhabit his histories and wrongs, cannot embrace him as a brother wronged by circumstances, life and the corruption of human communities. In other times, perhaps, Farouk, would be a friend. He is a thoughtful and smart man whose perspective is very different from Jake's, but friendship is not what Jake needs or seeks now.

He is hard. It is only Julie that steps through his hard shell without the slightest problem. He cannot keep her out, doesn't want to keep her out. At the same time, he hates knowing that he is vulnerable, that he is weaker than he needs to be.

She visited yesterday for the third time. They again had only thirty minutes and he could feel himself dissolving. When he saw her coming up the walk and then into the visitor's room, his whole body began to shake. He felt the ache of desire, the impossibility of flight, the stinging in his deprived flesh, as though he has no words to express love anymore but through pain that occupies every part of his body.

It was a difficult thirty minutes. "You've changed," she said with a hesitant smile. "You're buff, a hunk." She was trying to be nice, make a joke but why, Jake thought, are we talking about the shape of my body. That doesn't matter. She told him about her friendship with Peta and news of Tarek and about Ian in Sarajevo. She just talked and hoped he felt how bound he is to these people, to the quotidian and normal. He felt only sadness and a deep loneliness.

She handed him – via the guard – copies of Ian's letters and his adventures in looking for Sofia but that isn't what he wanted either. He just wanted to be with her. He wanted to touch her, to stroke her hair, to kiss with his eyes closed so tightly he cannot breathe. She asked about prison life. He didn't want to talk about prison life. She asked about the case. There was nothing to tell. He wanted to say, 'I can still see every inch of your body, your nakedness. I can smell you, taste you. I am lonely. I am horny. I don't want to talk at all but to curl up with you in a very large bed and love, sleep, talk, love and hold on to you, just hold on.'

Life grows hard. Life reduced to some simple things and simple impossibilities.

He doesn't ask about Tarek, who hasn't come this time.

When she left, she was weeping. He raised his hand in farewell but gave nothing away except his soul. When she was out of sight, he breathed deeply and turned away from the door and waited to be led back into the prison's bowels. His face was masked, his anger and pain hidden beneath the shallow surface of his hardness.

Julie is shattered. He is so different. He looks so different. She already feels, as she leaves the gate and opens her car door, that she doesn't want to come back. Not like this. Not with him like this.

Later she reruns what was said, seen, felt, intimated. She sifts through every one of the thirty minutes forensically and she knows she has it wrong. She doesn't yet know what is right, except that there was more in those thirty minutes than she understands.

CHAPTER 42

24 August 2016

My dearest children

I cannot find Sofia anywhere in the Book of the Dead. I begin to hope. I went to her neighbourhood and the place where her house once stood and began to ask anyone and everyone, 'is there anyone here still from the war?' I show them her photo, the one from before the war.

No joy, yet, but I have many more people to ask. It is very strange walking the streets asking about the war. This is way outside my comfort zone, but I am learning rapidly it is making those I question uncomfortable as well.

Most want to forget. At first, they look at me as though I am breaching the most basic of manners. Then they realise – quickly – that I am searching for someone. They respond even if they know nothing.

Once others know I suffered from the war too, they begin to talk about the war, about the street, pointing out the buildings destroyed, the people who lived there, their histories.

I extract myself from these sad monologues with difficulty. 'I am sorry sir, I must continue my search.'

After getting back to the hotel room I write down all the stories I can remember, all the names. I don't know if that has a purpose but it feels important to do so.

How is Jake? I am thinking of him often.

Julie writes back with news and gossip. Chatty but not very substantial. The case against Jake looks weak. Steven is a great lawyer. Jake is lifting weights. Peta is learning to dance.

1 September 2016

My dear children

I learned a bit more about Tarek's death. I spoke with a guard from the prison, who is now in a wheelchair with severe arthritis and deep guilt that makes his pains worse. He is Serbian but he stayed in Sarajevo after the war and started an orphanage to atone. He was there until his arthritis became so severe that he couldn't work at all.

He told me that he remembers Tarek arriving at the prison because his escort called him a filthy Jew murderer. This was in late 1994. Not many Jews about in Sarajevo anymore. He remembers Tarek talking with him, asking about his family and how they were faring in the war. He remembered how tough he was. He was not an aggressive man but in jail a few prisoners thought they could test him. They backed off quickly. And without any violence at all. He was capable of killing, the guard said. He was one of those men who could look at you in a way that said I can kill you quickly, easily and without hesitation. Don't even think it. This is so different from the picture that Sofia painted, but I am learning that there are many faces of war, even on the same man.

He didn't have many enemies though.

He was imprisoned for trying to cross the border with phoney papers. This was a border controlled by Serbia and due process was not their priority. At least that's what the guard heard. It didn't really matter – there were rarely trials and frequently the stated offences weren't the real reason at all.

In other times the rules of law are clear. In war, they were replaced with other rules.

The guard thinks someone in the prison informed on Tarek in order to secure his own release. Authorities learned he was in the militia. They believed he was quite senior, perhaps involved in the trade in medical drugs into Sarajevo.

He disappeared from the prison soon after. Probably taken for questioning in one of the many interrogation areas in Serb controlled Sarajevo and likely killed there. They are still uncovering mass graves and identification is difficult at best. I don't hold out much hope that his remains will be found.

These stories are hard for me to hear. Grains of truth and whole rivers of lies or mistakes or deceptions. Often deceptions. I fear that Ian will find too much.

*

I can see that Julie's spirit is beginning to flag. Tarek is sleeping badly and whingeing frequently. Julie is haggard and Peta is not much help. She is working and playing and reinventing her life. Jake remains in limbo. Julie wants to be in her own house. She is spending Ian's money and she doesn't want to be dependent and doesn't want to feel in debt. She knows it is Jake she needs and with every passing day she feels angrier – angrier with Jake, angry with the world, angry with herself and Tarek. She knows she should go out, walk in the park, meet other mothers, engage in endless chat about the minutiae of children. Too tired, too far from the reality that she is living at the moment. 'Oh, my partner is in prison for terrorism – would you like to come over for tea?' She snorts at the thought.

She invites Mel over. She is small and well-coiffed – pure deception; she has this crazy energy around her, like a wind-up toy that never runs out of steam but never goes in any particular direction. When she falls off the table she keeps going, under the table and chair and when she hits a wall she keeps trying to go through the wall. She's a smart woman who has still not found what she wants to be or do. She started law but didn't finish, started counselling but didn't finish. Worked as an actress. Gave it up. She does a bit of modelling, some tv ads and edits academic papers. "Hey honey mum, you're way too smart to be having babies," she says before she even gets in the door. "You should be out with me living the good life, indulging in excess and pretending everything is peachy. Okay, who is this munchkin? Hello Mr Tarek."

Mel is way too loud for Tarek, who although he is in Julie's arms, breaks out crying immediately. Mel laughs. "He thinks I'm trying to steal you...Well you might be right Mr Tarek."

She embraces Julie, who hangs on. She hasn't even told Mel about Jake; it doesn't take long before it all comes pouring out.

"You always said I lived a crazy ass wild pointless life and now you're putting me to shame, Julie girl. I'm just a boring old semi-employed something or other."

Mel knows that it isn't just sympathy that Julie needs but moments of normalcy, moments of forgetfulness. They don't talk long before Mel stops. "If I can get us a babysitter, fancy going out dancing with me?"

"I can't Mel. He's feeding every three hours and isn't very settled."

"If I can find a babysitter who is willing to brave your child, can you express milk into a bottle and put on some damn dancing shoes?"

Julie resists. Every part of her says no, hide, hide, flee, flee, but she relents because Mel is relentless. Mel calls her mother. She had six children and has seen it all. "Even better she lives 5 minutes from here."

Julie gives Tarek a quick feed, expresses some milk, then gets changed, even puts on a bit of makeup. She feels a twinge of guilt – both for going and for feeling excited about going out.

They dance until past midnight. Then drink until 1, both flirting with the coterie of men on the prowl in the club. Mel wants to take one home, I can see it, but she knows that is not on tonight.

Mel's mother, Sharyn, is asleep in the spare room with Tarek next to her and Julie and Mel crash on Julie's bed.

When Julie wakens, feeling somewhat grim, Sharyn has breakfast waiting, Tarek is fed and looks ready to do it over again. Julie hugs Sharyn, hugs Tarek, hugs her coffee, black and strong.

CHAPTER 43

Jake waits for Steven, who came on Tuesday but wants to see him again only two days later. Something has happened and Jake feels anxiety, hope, restlessness all moving through him like a migratory herd uncertain where it's headed.

He has been rereading the counter terrorism laws. They are draconian in so many ways. In efforts to eradicate terrorism through law – a dubious proposition at the best of times – the laws throw a net of suspicion over an entire society, build a system that is outside of law to which the entire society is subject. It is a shadow regime that is neither democratic nor able to counter terrorism. Instead, it creates its own terrorism, a terror more powerful in some ways than that to which it is responding.

One of the provisions of the criminal code allows the attorney general to ban and label an organisation a terrorist group merely for 'praise' of a terrorist group where that might lead another person to engage in a terrorist act. How did that ever get passed?

Jake isn't surprised but he finds a certain admiration for the ease with which those in power convinced voters that this was the best and necessary way to solve the problems of terrorism. Politically no one in the two old parties was prepared to vote against these laws no matter how bad. Soft on terror. The political accusation akin to a hanging offence.

Ten years later, the evidence is pretty clear that these laws are acts of violence not justice. Claims by government that the new laws – and more secretive powers of the police – have prevented numerous acts of terrorism, are offset by the reality that the number of those dedicated to terror and turning to terror, perhaps in desperation, perhaps out of some crazed ideology, are increasing. Something isn't working.

Steven comes into the conference room, his sloppy blond hair seems out of place in here. Most men shave their heads or keep their hair short. Even Jake's hair is shorter than it has been since he was a child. He is again locked to the table.

"I obviously can't stay away," Steven says with a smile.

"I suspect it's not true love," Jake responds.

"Give it time, give it time. Listen, the pressure from the Civil Liberties folks – thanks to you – is having an effect. Surprisingly. It looks like you're going to trial. The first hearing will be in three weeks. Preliminary orders will be given, discovery will begin. They'll set a trial date with any luck."

Waves of terror and relief both wash through him, like one of those beaches where the currents run in two directions at the same time and at the point they meet, there is a turmoil of water and spume.

"Finally," is all he manages to say.

"I don't think there's much we need to get sorted, but I wanted to know if you have any questions about the process from here?"

Jake is silent for a moment and then says quietly, "I know we've plead not guilty, but I'd like us to prepare a necessity defence, just in case."

Steven looks at him slightly startled. "We can do that," he says eventually, "but that is a defence we need to discuss at length before we go to trial."

"That's fine," Jake says evenly.

Neither wants to discuss it now because a necessity defence is based on admitting the underlying act and makes pleading not guilty very messy.

"Okay. Discovery is going to be interesting. You know that none of the other Free Radical cases have moved to trial under counter terrorism laws. It means that we may have to test the boundaries of these laws in a number of ways. One of them is the reach of discovery. Historically, evidence secured illegally could not be used by authorities. That is no longer completely true. The authorities are also going to try and prevent us from getting access to any information that exposes how they secured some evidence or data, whatever that may be." Steven pauses. "I don't need to ask whether you're guilty or not but I do need to know if there is anything that might implicate you?"

Jake shapes his answer slowly. "The only thing I am pretty sure of is that they have footage – or maybe a witness – of a blue car. Julie and I have a blue car. They know that I visited Frank – the farmer with the CSG well – last year with Six Degrees. That's all I can think of but they can't be basing my arrest or detention on just that, surely?"

"No," Steven says. "It won't be that thin."

"Also, I have a welder's licence, or did. I told the police I didn't."

"And they know this?"

"No, I don't think they'll find out unless I tell them."

Steven looks unblinkingly at Jake for a moment. "I'll prepare for the worst in any event," he says finally.

*

"He was always the favourite. He did better in school. He was the better athlete. He did law and I did accounting. He found success so easy and even when I found it, it didn't feel successful." Peta is packing her things and talking to Julie who stands in the doorway. "A part of me hated him. A part of me envied him and a part of me adored him. He was a good brother." She suddenly realises that she has put that in the past tense and begins to cry. Julie hugs herself. She can't give comfort, not about this. She will fall apart. She hugs herself to hold herself together and it doesn't feel like it's working. "And now," Peta continues. "I feel as though there must be something I can do for him and instead I am too busy reinventing my life."

"There is nothing you can do for Jake except to live and love and be happy when he comes home." Julie doesn't believe her own words but she can't say more or different.

"Will you come over for my housewarming next weekend?" Peta is going to live on her own for the first time and has rented a small flat in Albion. She's crossing to the north side. Julie suspects there is something symbolic in that.

"I'd love to."

6 September 2016

Dear children

In Sarajevo you must learn to wrestle with the past, many pasts. They are everywhere but always take different shapes, make different sounds. It is like a wilderness or perhaps a zoo, and every creature that lives there has an injury. You must understand both the animal and the injury in order to make sense of where you are and how the different pasts entwine with this moment or the next. That doesn't sound much like an economist!

The war is only the most obvious past, but there are histories within that. Children who died, artefacts that disappeared, permanent injuries, arrests, torture, friends who became enemies and vice versa, flight – and all the horrors that entails. If you stay long enough, care enough, strangers will open this box of histories in front of you, for you. At first, I thought these people who told me their stories were looking for sympathy, but they weren't; they were sharing their survival, and saying you will survive this too.

I think of you Jake in saying this. Here, it is the past that is filled with loss. In your world, it is the future. Rebuilding a life after loss is hard, as I am finding out, but I suspect building a future life in the face of the loss that you know is coming is even harder.

When you were arrested Jake, my heart was ripped from me. I can't imagine that even the death of a child would be worse. But now I have some understanding of the choices you made. I have some sense of the choices that Milos, Janos and Sofia all made.

They understand climate change here. The hills are burning again. Some speak of feeling surrounded by fire, like another kind of siege. The drought is the worst in memory, water restrictions are in place. Many people here planted small gardens during and after The Siege. There is not enough water to maintain them. And so, another history that is really just beginning imprints itself on the life of a city and people.

I am sounding more like you Jake every day.

When Jake reads this, he thinks, my father is a changed man but so am I. I like the man he is becoming but not the one I have become. He stares at his hands. I used to do the same, to wonder if in those hands I could make sense of what I had become and what I had done.

11 September 2016

My dear children

I had a breakthrough today, I think. A horrible one and one that gives hope.

I met Mrs Vanic. She is in a nursing home but used to live two doors down from Sofia. It took days to find this out and then days to find out she was alive and in a home.

She moved into the home in late 1995, around the time that NATO began to bomb the Serbs in and around Sarajevo.

"Such a nice lady," she kept saying about Sofia. At first, I thought she was senile. Her memories are strong – but they drift around unattached to anything in particular. Memories from one time mix with memories from another. Once I figured this out, I pieced together what I think is a story that makes sense.

"Such a nice lady. She would bring me medicine. I have bad circulation, very bad. She would sit with me. He was a nice man too. Nice man. But he didn't bring me medicines. Terrible, terrible what happened to him. He used to stand in the doorway a big smile on his face, asking me if I was ready to dance because Sofia dances so badly. I blushed, I did. Terrible what they did. I didn't see it though."

"What did they do, Mrs Vanic?"

"Once he came in my house with a gun. He apologised though."

The conversation was like this. Eventually, she told me that Janos was killed. He may have been arrested and executed.

Mrs Vanic saw Sofia only once more after that. She came to Mrs Vanic's door and without a word embraced Mrs Vanic then gave her an old jewellery box, which she still has on her dresser in the home.

It is so strange how much power objects can have. It was wood, handmade, simple, using different woods interlocked. It was so similar to one that I once gave Mary. I was stunned. I am not a mystical being but at that moment, I was – and still am – convinced – that Sofia and I shared our beings in ways that go way beyond rational explanations.

I have to assume now that Sofia was leaving or going to attempt to leave Sarajevo. This seems to be not long after her last letter. I must confirm Janos' fate and then I will see if I can determine Sofia's. I now have Janos' surname – Kovac – and so tomorrow will go back to the Book of the Dead.

I have moved out of my hotel now. Almost daily I receive offers to stay with people. It is known that I search for my family and it is as though that makes me family to everyone here.

CHAPTER 44

Julie longs to be home. Peta has moved out. She comes over frequently, but she is for the moment deeply self-absorbed. Julie doesn't resent it, but she finds Peta's presence makes her feel worse not better. She suspects it's because Peta is a little bit too oblivious to what is happening in the lives around her.

It's kind of the same with Mel. Julie doesn't want someone to cheer her up, she wants friendship that is quiet and strong and simply makes surviving the absence of Jake possible.

She goes to the park every day now with Tarek. He is only four months old but she takes him on the swing and goes down the child slide with him. She meets other mothers – and a few fathers – of similar age. They chat – about children of course. They have little else in common, Julie knows.

It's clear she's lonely.

A young man around her age, Daniel, flirts with her one morning. His daughter is old enough to play on her own. She sits on the bench with Tarek still asleep in the pram. He sits close to her and she likes his easy manner and quick smile. He's a bit too hip for Julie, but a nice guy. He smells nice too. He makes it clear quickly that he's single. He touches her now and then on the arm or the shoulder. She flirts back. She can feel the pull of her attraction and the deep horror that it causes her.

It's only Tarek who awakens and decides he's hungry and can't wait another second that pulls her back. He howls loud and long and Julie decides she better feed him at home. She says goodbye hurriedly and prevents Daniel from asking to see her again, which I suspect he would otherwise have done.

How am I going to survive this? she wonders. How are both she and Jake going to survive this? She knows that if Jake loses his case, it will be over. She may never stop loving him, but she can't lead a life of waiting.

But for now, she knows she needs to do more than she is doing. Work? Volunteer? Start a project? Learn Swahili? She sits down one evening and makes a long list of things she might do. She makes another long list of tasks. She stares at the words as they run down the page like dirty rain, like tears.

*

Almost eight months without an act of violence by The Free Radicals ends in two horrible deaths. An oil executive is pulled from his car in the driveway of his home in suburban Perth, bundled into a van and four hours later executed Al Qaeda style, kneeling and sobbing. The video is horrific. The voice on the video is Australian. "This man has committed crimes against humanity and the planet. There is no question of his guilt. While he makes millions of dollars for himself, he is prepared to let a planet burn. His company is prepared to allow millions to die so it can make more and more money at everyone's expense. This must cease. Today we put all of the one percent on notice. It is time for you to change or to be very afraid." The man is then beheaded.

What has Jake unleashed? He watches the video in his cell. Crimes against the planet. A part of him feels the weight of this responsibility. A part of him wonders how difficult it must be to behead a human with a single stroke.

The second death is two days later. A child dies in a house fire set by The Free Radicals. The death is accidental but those responsible don't pull the footage or shut up. They call the child's death unfortunate and then move on.

Jake watches in stony silence.

He knows these attacks can't be by greenies, but that is where the blame will be.

Two days later there are five different arson attacks in national parks – two in Queensland, one in Western Australia and two in New South Wales.

Several offices of green NGOs are trashed in the middle of the night and one poor man working late is beaten badly and hospitalised.

Even the number of accidents involving bicycles being struck by cars are increasing in numbers.

The deep divisions so often spoken of between the haves and the have-nots are getting worse but they are also now being challenged. Unions are changing tack and are now attacking corporate influence and tax evasion. Middle ground seems to be disappearing everywhere and is replaced with chronic conflict, with a kind of bitterness and anger that creates an ugly turbulence in daily life.

It's not surprising during a war, but in a time of relative peace, it's like a warning of the storm that is coming.

The political class makes it worse. Hate politics, politics of terrorism and a zealous devotion to free market extremism seem to be the pillars of governance and in one way or another, their response and answer to everything.

Just Disobey is now a real movement and it swirls in the political maelstrom in ways that Jake can't quite decipher. They are confronting those who deny climate change. They are challenging the laws, they are growing larger by the day and politically they are much more difficult to attack than The Free Radicals. At the same time, it isn't clear what that movement means in the weird landscape that now defines the world of climate change.

There are many more arrests and headlines that daily grow more strident. The counter terrorism laws give virtual carte blanche to arrest and detain anyone on the flimsiest of evidence, but there is also more unrest, more political dissent and more violence than Australia has experienced in a very long time. Both socially and politically, the edges fray and the normal courtesies and casualness are disappearing.

The relocation of a community in the Torres Strait because the rising sea has started reclaiming a village is lost in the madness.

Jake, of course, doesn't see how the society seems to be falling apart, but what he reads suggests this is happening.

He knows this will make his case much more difficult to win. In order to win a jury trial, he will need their sympathy. If they are afraid and he is made to represent one of the reasons they are afraid, he will find the going very difficult. He will fight on the evidence but he is also going to fight on climate change and accuse industry and government of being part of the problem. When people are afraid is one of the few times they turn to government, which is how we got these laws in the first place. A risky time right now, but he no longer has even the smallest level of control over events.

Jake has started playing chess again. He hasn't played since he was a boy. He is trying to train himself to think two, three , even four moves ahead. He imagines the game as an act of war, the battles he is actually fighting. He feels ruthless even though he is only playing against a machine. His soul is on a very short and fragile chain, but it feels as though his mind is becoming dangerous.

He is not only doing extensive legal research on climate law and Australian and international court cases, he is also researching the defence of necessity and reading all the new scientific literature on climate change that he can find.

There is not much cause for optimism. In the Netherlands, a court in 2015 ordered a 25 percent reduction in emissions must be made within five years by the government. Otherwise, there is little that suggests the judiciary understands the urgency any more than the politicians. There have been more legal challenges in Australia than anywhere except the US and almost without exception the climate has lost.

17 September 2016

My dear children

I found Janos in the Book of the Dead. His death was reported by four people. Three of them are now dead. I will now see if I can find the fourth man, Vladic. Janos died in 1994, around the time of Sofia's last letter. I think that must be why she stopped writing. I have no doubt that she was alive then. The Book of the Dead generally gives only a very brief description of the believed cause of death. Janos' has two different possible causes of death –'executed' and 'killed in battle.'

I never met the man and yet I feel I know him, that I would recognise him on the street. It is very odd to feel the loss of someone who was dead before I even knew he existed and yet Sofia's letters painted such a strong picture of their love for each other, I will miss him.

There are several photos of him in my Sarajevo box, but it is one portrait by Sofia that I remember most clearly. It is drawn from slightly below, looking up through that rugged beard to those intense eyes, shaded by his heavy brows. There is the slightest grin visible through the beard, a grin of amusement, the grin of a trickster, who has seen his latest prank succeed completely.

Tomorrow I am meeting a man who was a smuggler during The Siege. He then became a member of Parliament and is now retired. He was well connected and well known during The Siege. I am hoping he knows something – but my clues are becoming increasingly sparse.

Julie and Peta worry about Ian. He has been gone almost two months and he is journeying deeper and deeper without any end in sight, without Sofia in sight. If all he learns is of death and the horrors of this war, he won't find the redemption he needs or perhaps even the strength to return to Jake's trial and the reality of his grief for Mary.

21 September 2016

Dear children

I have learned the story of Janos' death today. As you know he was in the militia. He was captured in a battle protecting the tunnel, which had, in the short time it had been complete, become in many ways the lifeline of the city. The retired smuggler now politician, Davud Guja remembered Janos well. He was wounded first then dragged off by the Serbs. They crossed to their side of the street, took him to the rooftop of a building, shot him in the head and threw him off the building. Davud wept as he told me this. Sofia must have seen this. When they went to recover his body, she was already there and she would not let go of this man. Nothing could make her let go. Janos' friends in the militia stayed there, well into the night while Sofia grieved and tried to stop him from leaving her. Twenty years later and it was still raw. As it is now for me.

13 October 2016

My dear children

Today another horrible, confronting discovery. Sofia wrote several times about a Bosnian assassin, dzelat, the executioner.

Today I found out this man, who is mythologised in Sarajevo, was Tarek. Gentle Tarek. When I was in the Palace yet again going through the Book of the Dead, I was approached by a man with grey eyes and a kind of sadness about him that was hard to bear.

'I am Ahmud', he said and held out his hand as though it weighed a thousand pounds. 'I am an academic. I come here often to look at the Book of the Dead. I have seen you now, three, maybe four times. Are you an academic as well?'

I tell him why I am here. I tell him about Sofia, Janos, Milos and Tarek.

'Tarek Votek' he asks?

'Yes, you know him?'

"Indeed I do. He is dzelat, the executioner. Or was before he was found out. I still do not know how he was found. Whether it was

an informer or good intelligence. It is a story I want to know and still search for. But when he was crossing the border into Macedonia – he travelled extensively – he was arrested. He was travelling under an alias but it seems clear that his secrets had been exposed including the various names he travelled under.

Interesting man, he travelled widely but not always to kill. Not even primarily. He sought money, guns, drugs, medicines. He was tireless. I have calculated he travelled 30 thousand kilometres in 1993 alone, much of that on buses or on foot. He even travelled by donkey once. He twisted arms, he begged, bribed, blackmailed. There was nothing he would not do for his country, his people, but it is hard to know if in doing so he lost his soul."

I am stunned and more horrified than anything. I don't yet know how to process this. My uncle, my gentle funny uncle is a 'zealot', an executioner. In the world of wars and violence was he a good man, a bad man, a necessary man? Was this always within him? Or something created in a time of war? I know these are questions others have grappled with thousands of times, but until now these kinds of questions have always been abstract. No longer.

And so, I am exhumed. No longer the avuncular uncle, I am now and forever the assassin, executioner. Dzelat was not a name I ever used or liked, but there it is, indelible now. I am more sad than anything. Certainly not surprised. The Tarek of those years was never me, at least in my mind. When I was being tortured after being arrested, I admitted to everything, although I betrayed no one. I wasn't proud, I did not want to be remembered this way. I was terrified and admitting my guilt did not stop the torture. I didn't think it would. I admitted it because it was true, because I knew I would not live much longer regardless of what I said.

That's not to say I regret what I did. There are no easy answers in war. You make choices about what is necessary, what is good, what you are capable of, just as Jake has done. Just as Sofia did. All choices at some point are flawed. I knew that. I knew I was undertaking a role that few if any wanted and few could do.

My biggest worry, my largest fear, is that Julie and Jake will want to change the name of their child.

*

It is the least of Julie's worries.

Tarek has been crying for three days now. He isn't feeding well, isn't sleeping well, isn't happy. Julie is looking bedraggled and on edge. She went to the doctor this morning and she could find nothing wrong. Julie is still breastfeeding but Tarek has been on solids for several months now. He's not teething, his ears are clear. Julie worries and the less sleep she gets and the more weary she feels the more she worries. She finally calls Peta who comes over immediately and Julie falls asleep almost instantly. When she awakens, Tarek is asleep too. "My grandmother's recipe, I hope it's okay. A bit of honey and a tiny bit of rum."

Julie starts laughing and then begins to cry. Peta is worried that Julie is angry with her, but that's not it. Julie just sees the life in front of her as too demanding and she too unequipped.

Jake writes to her regularly, brief notes in which he says little. 'It is hard to write anything about this place that is positive, hard to write anything about me that is full of light. Even my desire to be with you, which is enormous, is painful.'

She can't do anything to help him, can only visit him occasionally.

Not for the first time she thinks of going to the States for a little while.

CHAPTER 45

There is another suicide at the prison. A hanging, which is probably the hardest to prevent. He hung himself inside the phone cage, right outside the guard station. One piece of rope for his neck and another to keep the door closed just long enough to die.

It was a guy named Kieran Potts. He brutally murdered his partner and children. He then murdered two inmates in maximum security in Brisbane and so he was transferred here where he was allowed almost no contact with inmates.

There were no sirens, no flurry of activity. A doctor came, confirmed death and the body was quietly and efficiently removed. The news travelled quickly. There are few in here that haven't flirted with suicide. Jake feels no compassion or loss. He does, though, feel the breeze of oblivion and tries not to even consider whether that appeals.

There is virtually no mental health care in the prison. These are considered not only the most dangerous people in Australia but the most evil and they therefore deserve nothing – even before a finding of guilty has been made. Jake doesn't know how many inmates here are waiting for trial. He wants to wear a star on his orange jump suit that says 'Presumed Innocent. LOL'. Steven has said many if not most of the terrorist suspects in Australia are housed here, including before trial. That can be years. If a violent crime is committed by asylum seekers they are often brought here as a kind of additional punishment for daring to flee the threat of death. They are probably the majority of suicides.

Jake thinks of Ian in Sarajevo. We can adapt to war, to prison, to psychopathic capitalism, to histories of abuse. We may be able to adapt to climate change too. Not true, Jake thinks. If we go beyond two, maybe three degrees, then all bets are off. We will be going where no one has gone before. Then it won't be a question of adaptation but survival in conditions that are brutal and unpredictable. There won't be many safe places to go, maybe none.

I won't adapt to a life in here. If I am convicted, I will find a way to die, Jake decides again. It doesn't feel like an emotional decision to him at all, only rational.

*

29 October 2016

Dear children

I am sorry I do not write more often. My days are long and tiring. I follow more leads and suggestions than I can remember. I visit many people, go to many different places and at the end of the day spend time with whatever family I am staying with. Sometimes they don't have internet and often I am simply too fatigued to even think of writing.

I have postponed my flight home. I am too close now to give up. I found nothing for a week. No sign that she'd left the country, no sign that she died. Nothing. I decided to visit all the hospitals in the event she was injured. The records kept during the war weren't always the best. Hospitals were often destroyed or partially destroyed and the records lost. Sometimes they were moved as new temporary hospitals were set up wherever they were needed. Sometimes hospitals sprang up and kept almost no records at all. Of course, if Sofia was injured, she could have gone to a doctor or a small clinic. But I thought I'd try.

It was at the last hospital – the seventh – that I found her. Or found a record of her. It was the State Psychiatric Hospital. She was admitted to the State Hospital a week after Janos was executed. I only had to say I was her brother to get all the help I could wish for. The State Hospital records were partially destroyed so they had a record of her being admitted but none of her medical records or her fate. They think that if she had died at the hospital, those records would likely have been found with her admittance documents. They think. Nothing was as organised as it would have been in a peaceful world.

She tried to suicide. I suspect this was after she gave the jewellery box to Mrs Vanic. I thought it was a present from someone preparing to leave the country, not someone preparing to kill themself. She took a large overdose. She had easy access to some powerful drugs. She was brought to the hospital but no one knows by whom. Usually, the admission papers will have that name, but it is blank, suggesting she was brought and left.

I have found no one who remembers her. I did speak with a doctor from that time. 'There were so many people, so much chaos, such poor records', he said. 'I sometimes sit and try and write about this time, but it is never anything but a trough of memories, words, injuries, cries and the terrible smells of infections so bad that bodies were rotting from the inside.'

The doctor thinks she was probably transferred. If it was during the war, it was because someone paid for her to be transferred or smuggled out of the country. If it was after the war, it is likely she would have stayed in the country – or perhaps Macedonia. Many were transferred if they needed levels of treatment we were no longer able to give in those days, he said.

If it was an official transfer, she would have travelled under her maiden name. Otherwise, who knows.

So, the more I learn the less I know. I have the gift of another mystery or two to uncover.

CHAPTER 46

Julie is having nightmares most nights. When Tarek doesn't waken her, she wakens herself. Last night her parents were in her living room telling her about their deaths. She doesn't remember the stories they told but she knows both in the dream and in her waking that they wanted her to feel guilty. She yelled at them but they ignored her, just kept talking. The night before she dreamed of Jake. He was in a bodybuilder competition. She ran up on stage, 'they've let you go' she cries out but he doesn't recognise her.

She is so tired. She can barely take care of Tarek today and the image of her parents haunts her. She remembers how demurely her mother sat.

She drinks whisky that night and when Tarek wakes her it is clear he has been crying for too long.

The next day, with a terrible hangover and a foul taste in her mouth, she calls Peta. "Peta could you stay with me a few days please? I'm having terrible nightmares, terrible sleeps and Tarek knows something is wrong so he won't settle."

There is a moment's hesitation. "I have something after work, but I'll come right after that if that's okay."

"Thank you Peta," she says with a terrible sense of relief and need.

CHAPTER 47

The hearing is in the federal court in Brisbane. Jake insisted on attending – a right he still has. They have flown him to Brisbane under maximum security conditions – chains and more chains. The first time there was something not only scary but vaguely amusing to Jake about having to wear chains when he could not conceive of himself as a danger to anyone. He appears before the judge in the now traditional garb of a dangerous criminal – a bright orange jump suit and chains. It is not until there is a jury that Jake will be permitted to look human.

Steven is looking immaculate and sits close to Jake to show he isn't afraid. He leans over occasionally and tells a joke. He wants Jake, whose face has become severe and a bit hard, to smile. The pre-trial hearings can go on for months, Steven has told Jake. There will be battles over evidence, over charges, witnesses and discovery.

They have already lost the motion for bail. Under the counter terrorism laws, it is rarely given. Steven decided not to challenge Jake being charged under those laws at a bail hearing. "I'm sorry it means you remain in prison until trial, but I think it's the more strategic way to go." Jake nodded his assent, the terror rising into his throat.

The judge, Stefano di Maio, doesn't fit any of the physical stereotypes of a judge. He has wavy dark hair – long for a judge and a trendy three day growth of facial hair. He wears white framed glasses, very trendy too.

The court is grand, panelled with wood and imposing. Jake remembers sitting in on a variety of court cases through law school. He only came into these courts once.

The Prosecution table has three barristers, all men. They introduce themselves to Steven, but don't even look at Jake. There is a kind of camaraderie that Jake doesn't like. They are about to battle over a man's life and he thinks they should have their swords drawn and chest plates fastened.

The directions hearing though is fiery. Steven is demanding all evidence be identified and provided to the defence.

The prosecution argues that in light of the ongoing activities of The Free Radicals, they want to limit discovery. They provide the judge with details.

"Perhaps then, your Honour, the prosecution would provide the court evidence that this organisation," he looks down at his papers as though he doesn't know the name, "The Free Radicals, even exists."

"Your Honour, they are a declared terrorist organisation," one of the lawyers says immediately, obviously surprised that Steven has raised this.

"There is no requirement in the declaration process that the government consider this question. It is our understanding that there is no evidence of communication between anyone who claims to belong to this organisation. No evidence that they've ever met or spoken. This is a name but nothing more. If the prosecution cannot even demonstrate the existence of this so-called organisation, how can they show, as they must, that public disclosure of putative evidence against my client will provide benefit to the organisation."

"Your Honour, as Counsel knows full well, we can't reveal the details of the investigation into any terrorism organisation. It is our view and the view of the Federal Police that this is a very sophisticated organisation that has learned to avoid the usual means of electronic contact and communication. Their activities are linked by common language, common goals and even references to earlier acts as warnings. As you know in the days leading up to this hearing and impending trial, the activities of The Free Radicals have increased significantly. We do have evidence of their existence, but getting the full picture will take time. During that time, revealing the extent of our evidence will reveal our methods and that is too risky. I'd also add that the listing of a terrorist organisation is not an ad hoc process. The Attorney General must be satisfied that certain criteria are met."

"The criteria, Your Honour, do not actually deal with any organisational reality. They assume the existence of an organisation and so relate solely to the doing, planning or advocating of a terrorist activity. Your Honour, there have now been, what, five arrests of individuals for counter terrorism activities under the name The Free Radicals and a significantly greater number of actions under that same name. It is clear that, despite intensive investigation and questioning, the State has found no links between those arrested and my client. They are clutching at straws Your Honour."

"Thank you, gentlemen," the Judge says. "Mr Wilson, you will provide me with details of the status of the investigation into The Free Radicals as an organisation and the evidentiary basis for any conclusions you have drawn by the 31st of October. I will make a decision on discovery as soon as practicable thereafter. Any other matters?"

Steven stands. "Your Honour, the implications of our allegation that The Free Radicals doesn't exist as an organisation obviously go well beyond discovery. If The Free Radicals are simply a name but not an organisation, then all charges against my client related to his organisational associations must be immediately dropped."

Mr Wilson stands immediately, but Justice Di Maio holds up his hand. "Mr Kaal, should I make a decision that full discovery must be provided to the defence, you may make that argument at that time. Let's not get ahead of ourselves."

"Thank you, Your Honour. One last motion if I may. We would like the courtroom to be open, both to the public and the media."

"Mr Wilson?"

"Your Honour, provided the court is prepared to hear certain matters in a closed courtroom, we would agree, although we would not agree to live broadcasts or, in fact, any cameras in the courtroom."

"Agreed," says Steven.

"So ordered."

And with that the first step in Jake's new life begins.

He and Steven are given a few minutes to speak before Jake is whisked back into more secure facilities.

"Steven, thank you. You were great."

"Thanks Jake, but we're not on very firm ground. Because the AG can make a decision that there is a terrorist organisation based on criteria that can't establish even the existence of an organisation, the Judge may well feel he has to defer to that. He may, though, see it as so unreasonable that he bypasses the legislature or that the AG's decision is not a decision regarding the existence of an organisation only a decision regarding its activities."

"What's next?"

"For you, I'm afraid, more waiting."

*

9 November 2016

Dear children

I am not sure why I am enjoying this so much, when the circumstances of my search are so sad and so grim. But I feel as though I've been reborn as a PI! I know – more strongly than ever – that I am finding things here that make me stronger and more determined to return, not only changed but one who will do a better job of taking care of myself and my family.

I am staying with a family – my fourth. They are lovely. An extended family. Ageing parents, adult children and grandchildren as well. They don't want to speak of the war but they want to help me find my sister. They call the people they know. They take me to people they think can help. They are fantastic – but they do not talk, ever, of their experiences in the war.

We have checked all the private institutions in Sarajevo – there are only two that were operating at the time – and they have no record of Sofia. I am now beginning to cast the net more widely. Italy still seems the most likely. It can be reached from anywhere along the coast or via Trieste. But Greece isn't that far nor Bulgaria. Circumstances may have meant Sofia couldn't get that far and had to risk staying in the Balkans. The Italian Embassy is sending me a list of private psychiatric institutions. Beyond that, I am still trying to find acquaintances or friends who knew Sofia in 1994. The pool gets smaller daily, but each day I meet new, lovely, generous people, with histories that are unique and too often tragic. The resilience of these people amazes me. The willingness to forgive amazes me even more. I want most of all to find Sofia but I also want to embrace the spirit I keep finding here and run home with it.

*

After three days Peta returns to her home. All three have been sleeping in the same bed and Julie sleeps deeply and well. But soon after Peta leaves, the dreams return, worse than ever. Tendrils of memories trail behind Julie during her waking hours. Fatigue stalks her. Fear holds her. Tarek is too often inconsolable – his mother suffers and Tarek knows this at the deepest levels. She woke last night from a dream that she was standing out by the post box waiting for something – a gift or a letter that she was expecting. She must have been around twelve. When the postie arrived, he arrested her, put handcuffs on her and tossed her in the back of a police van.

A few days later Julie dreams she is having sex with Peta, although she never sees Peta's face. All the time she is thinking, 'I'm not bi, what am I doing?' She wakens terrified

She feels more alone than it is human to feel. Her efforts to hold herself together in Jake's absence are dissolving. She can feel all the certainties and assurance of her life deliquesce in front of her like a puddle that was once something more – gentle rain or ice or a field covered in a blanket of snow.

She wants desperately to see Jake. Her next visit is weeks away.

Three pm and she has her first drink. When Tarek awakens an hour later, she decides not to breastfeed. He doesn't need to be drunk too.

*

20 November 2016

Dear children

They are evacuating the northern part of the city because the fires are still burning out of control and yesterday high winds made the fires much more dangerous. Everything smells burnt. It is still extraordinarily hot and dry for November.

Tomorrow I am heading to Italy. An institution near Verona has a woman named Sofia who came from Sarajevo in 1995. It is in the foothills of the Dolomites and is one of those wealthy establishments that is a mix of spa and resort as well as a serious psychiatric institution. This Sofia has a different surname but I am hoping it was a disguise or a clerical error. I suppose that's not likely. I'm also not sure how Sofia could afford such a place, unless she has a benefactor or the institution accepted the occasional indigent or refugee. If this fails, I'm not sure what I can do. I suppose I will get back on the phone and look further away in Italy. Maybe she crossed into Italy by sea further south, near Naples. Or even Greece. I will try there next.

I am filled with doubts. Doubts about finding her and doubts that finding her will be as transformative as I hope.

*

Jake has stopped writing short notes and started writing long letters to Julie instead, writing by hand. He started a week ago, driven by the fear he was losing more than his life and his love but his humanity too. He could feel the hardness in him spreading. I know that feeling. War gives you that. You must grow that hard shell to survive. In war, you stay human by helping others. By learning to love those around you who suffer similar wrongs with a depth and passion that would never happen in peacetime. Like Sofia. But like me, Jake has taken on a different role, one where loving is punished. It is hard enough to do these things on your own, but now Jake must contend with the even greater isolation of prison. So, Jake writes for an hour a day. Some days, many days, he writes about how much he loves Julie, in part to remind himself. 'I never believed in true love. I never believed in a kind of romantic destiny. And instead of making that the centre of my life I gave it away – classic romantic tragedy – one in which the man must die in the end...' He stops. 'Once upon a time' he writes, 'there was a man who had two great loves: a woman and a planet. He needed both those loves to stay alive. Both nurtured his body and spirit but in different ways. One day, the man was approached by a small, wizened man in a suit. Nasty, nasty man. He said, 'I've made a bet with god and the devil and you're part of it. Sorry. You have to choose only one of those loves.' What did you bet on?' asks the young man. The nasty man just laughs. The young man refuses to participate in the bet. He decides to fight to destroy the man instead, but in doing so he inadvertently makes a choice. Inevitably, he ends up with nothing. And the same would be true if he'd chosen the woman he loved, because he could not tear his spirit in half. The end.' He tears the letter up into tiny shreds as he does most days.

One day, he thinks, I will learn to cry again.

That moment of hope, though, makes him angry. He cannot play with hope. It could be that hope is the wizened man who bets with lives.

He gets down on the floor and does one hundred crunchers

and one hundred push ups. He does them in a fury that swarms inside him like a cyclone.

When he collapses, it's not relief he feels, never relief, just emptiness.

CHAPTER 48

November, and the heat is unbearable. Crazy humid with freak storms. Lightning, hail and high winds. Brisbane is feeling precarious but also limp and slow.

At the end of that first week in November Donald Trump was elected President. I remember the first days of the ultra-nationalist leaders in Serbia. Scary times. To see a people so angry and so scared that they will elect anyone who stands out as strong enough to take on the darkness even if in doing so the likelihood of even greater darkness grows much larger.

Julie attends the second directions hearing in Brisbane. The courtroom is packed. Because it is an open courtroom, Jake is out of chains and jumpsuit and wearing his only suit, which is now way too small for his bulked up shoulders and arms.

When he walks in Julie is shocked. He looks as hard as he feels. She can see he is shut down. This kind of public exposure may be good strategy but it's painful for him. He must simply be on display. He can't speak, can't control any of the events that will unfold. His hair is short and she can see the first streaks of grey. He looks around for her and when he sees her he stumbles and simply stops. The bailiff pushes him along but it's as though he has transported himself out of this place and time into Julie's arms. She smiles at him, a genuine and huge smile and when he smiles in return he looks like a little boy. No one else is in the courtroom for those few brief seconds and those few brief seconds are like a lifetime. It's as though both have received a direct injection of love that will sustain them, if they use it wisely, for the next year.

Julie is sitting directly behind the defence table. Jake turns in the moments before the judge appears. "You look so stunning."

Both are kind of speechless. It's a bit awkward – but it's also like those moments of falling in love for the first time. You simply want to stare at each other, touch and perhaps make cooing sounds because that will say everything that needs to be said.

I don't know that I ever loved so deeply. For both of them at this moment, they needed this reminder more than they needed oxygen or water or food.

Everyone is called to stand and the hearing begins.

The judge is brusque, almost angry. "In the matter of the exclusions of evidence under counter terrorism laws, I find that all the evidence must be provided to the defence. Those matters for which the prosecution sought secrecy and exemption do not reveal any information related either to operational matters or secrets or give any indication of the people involved in those matters. I order that the prosecution provide these materials to the defence by 10 January.

"On the matter of whether The Free Radicals is an organisation, I find firstly that the legislation does not provide that the Attorney General address the matter of whether an organisation is an organisation or not. The legislation is only concerned with the activities of an assumed organisation. While there is an implicit finding that an organisation exists, there is no formal determination process. I have reviewed the legislation, the explanatory memorandum and other Parliamentary documents and there is no indication that the issue of ascertaining the existence of an organisation was ever considered. It was presumed, and, in most cases organisational existence seems obvious. But not in relation to The Free Radicals. Therefore, in circumstances where the existence of an organisation is in question, and the Government has not assumed responsibility for answering this question, this determination is a role properly taken by this court. In this case, I find the prosecution has provided no evidence of the existence of The Free Radicals except a number of seemingly disparate and unrelated uses of the name. In the absence of any definition in these laws of an organisation, I am relying on a generally accepted definition of an organisation as a grouping of people for a shared purpose. In my view, a grouping quite clearly suggests membership and communication and contact between those members. While it is arguable that those who have used The Free Radical name have a shared purpose there is no evidence of contact or communication, nor any evidence that there are members or any way of becoming a member of this organisation. Based on the evidence in front of me The Free Radicals is merely a name.

"Mr Kaal, you have indicated in our previous hearing that you would like to move that all charges related to organisational activities be dropped. Mr Wilson, based on this ruling, I personally see no reason to argue these points and unless you have a basis for contesting the issue, I am prepared to rule now."

Wilson knows he's not going to win this one. "We have nothing more to add, at this time Your Honour, except that in the event of additional evidence that supports the existence of an organisation, we will, of course, reserve the right to reinstate those charges."

"Very well. I rule that all charges related to membership, support, and activities of The Free Radicals are dropped as the prosecution has not shown the existence of an organisation to which such charges could attach. According to my assessment Mr Wilson, that leaves five counts of a terrorist act and, let's see, seven counts of assisting or abetting terrorist acts, as well as the criminal charges. Is that correct?"

"Yes, Your Honour."

"Excellent." The judge's mood has improved.

Jake is trying to look pleased, but the reality is that those remaining charges can still put him in prison for several lifetimes.

Julie gets this too. She nods at the judge's words but is not about to start dancing in the aisles.

The media though is already in a frenzy. Dozens of reporters rush – quietly – from the room to call in the story. This will be a major embarrassment for the government and highlights again how poorly constructed the terrorism laws are.

"So, gentlemen, any other motions to be dealt with today?"

Steven stands. "Your Honour, in light of your finding regarding The Free Radicals, we would ask firstly that the Court consider ordering that Mr Votek be transferred out of his maximum security prison to Brisbane so that he can be closer to his partner and young child."

"Your Honour, we oppose any such transfer. Firstly, we would note that which prison Mr Votek is in is not a judicial decision but a departmental one in the absence of any allegation that Mr Votek's rights are being breached."

Steven no doubt knows this, but I suspect he is playing for the media.

"Your Honour, this young man has no history of violence, is not on any watch list and has never been arrested. He was refused bail in good part because of the allegations that these were terrorist acts. That conclusion is now in question. There is no question that the acts and allegations against Mr Votek are criminal, but if that is all, then Mr Votek has been deprived of his rights."

"Your Honour, honourable counsel has not moved that the terrorist charges be dropped. He knows full well that these particular criminal acts can also be acts of terrorism subject to counter terrorism laws."

"I'm inclined to agree with you, Mr Wilson. I will note that Mr Votek's incarceration in NSW does make contact with his family – which is not under suspicion – much more difficult and will ask that the Commonwealth consider a transfer to a maximum security prison here in Brisbane. Okay. Anything else? Excellent. Mr Wilson, when do you expect to be ready to go to trial?"

"Your Honour, we continue to investigate on a number of fronts, but we would expect to be ready for trial by July."

"Your Honour, my client has already been in prison for four months without trial. Another eight months for a man who must be presumed innocent does not satisfy the requirements of natural justice. If the Prosecution is now trying to find evidence to support any unsubstantiated charge – which is what this proposed trial date suggests – then this should not be permitted in setting a trial date. I would also add that not yet having seen the evidence held by the prosecution it is difficult for us to estimate preparation time in response. I would move that we reconvene on 8 December following consideration of discovery materials to agree on a date at that point."

"I would agree with that proposal Mr Kaal. So ordered and on that note, Court is adjourned."

*

Julie and Jake touch hands briefly before Jake is removed from the courtroom, brusquely, almost roughly, by guards. Suddenly Jake turns back to Julie and yells, "I love you Julie and I'll be home soon."

"I love you too Jake, you gorgeous man," Julie yells back and that moment is like breaking out and breaking free for both of them. It's also the moment from that hearing that is most tweeted and liked and reported.

The media knows Jake won this round, but is a long way from being free. The public saw two people who love each other being kept apart. He doesn't look like a terrorist. He doesn't act like one. Not only were Jake and Julie freed from something in that moment, but the world shifted too.

Social media begins to swirl. The various pages Garth set up are now humming with visits and likes. Garth posts a banner – Presumed Innocent! it screams with a photo of the guards dragging him away. There is a photo posted anonymously of Jake and Julie, their fingers touching with the guards beginning to pull Jake away.

Many are now asking questions about laws that can keep a man in super maximum security prison for a year without trial. Questions are asked about whether the prosecution simply charged Jake under counter terrorism laws because it allows them free reign in collecting evidence, withholding evidence and detaining whoever they want to satisfy political imperatives, not imperatives of justice.

The Federal Government is accused of being extremist and the conservatives don't help their cause by continuing to rail against extreme greenies and eco-terrorists.

Steven applies to the Attorney General for Jake to be transferred to Brisbane. It is refused. Photos of Julie and Tarek follow on social media. The mainstream media begins to take an interest. Julie is interviewed. She talks about life as a single mother and a woman kept apart from the love of her life. She's good. Softly spoken, passionate. She talks of her fatigue – working two days, looking after Tarek, trying to help with Jake's trial and looking after a grieving father in law.

Requests to interview Jake begin to pour in. They are all refused and the media starts talking about cover-ups and secrecy.

Steven again asks again for a transfer. It is refused. He asks for Julie to have regular visiting rights. That too is refused. The prosecutor has clearly been given his instructions, but he's not happy. He knows this is hurting his case but the decision has been made much higher up the food chain.

The Murdoch press has found new levels of depravity in its reporting of the case, but other media are now part of a growing and critical public swing.

Things fall apart. I remember Sofia reciting that poem sitting in the cellar listening to the shells come in. Others would yell out – Passover! Short! Close!! Listening to the whistle of the shells and then waiting for the explosion. Sofia would recite in a liturgical voice, kind of a chant, kind of a prayer; 'Mere anarchy is loosed upon the world' or 'Everywhere the ceremony of innocence is drowned' in Bosnian. That's all I remember now of the poem. But I can see Sofia clearly. Sitting against the concrete wall, her legs drawn up, her arms around her knees, a long red skirt spreading out in front of her and her eyes closed, reciting, reciting as though this was the moment the world was going to end and this was how she wanted to go out.

What is happening here, though, is different. Things aren't falling apart yet, but it feels like those hours before a storm. You can feel the gathering of wind, the low pressure sucking life and sound from the air, the smell of rain and something far more powerful behind it. It is coming. Something is coming – and even with all my age and experience I have no idea what it looks like. That poem...how does it end?... The rough beast, its hour come round at last... That's it, that's exactly what it feels like.

CHAPTER 49

30 November 2016

My dear children

Thank you so much Julie for your description of the hearing. I am so sorry I am not there.

What a rabbit hole this has become. Sofia is no longer at the psychiatric institution in Verona despite what they told me when I called. Or what I understood. Yes, they had a number of clients from Sarajevo smuggled across the border. Yes, a woman named Sofia was there, but no longer is. Those who delivered her did not know her surname nor did she. She suffered from dissociative amnesia, a severe form of amnesia brought on by trauma. She knew nothing of her past, how she arrived here, her friends, her address. She knew she was Sofia – probably because she was called that after the execution of Janos and her attempted suicide, but otherwise there was little of her intact. And in the three years she spent in that place, she began to fill those empty spaces with invented or borrowed lives.

I didn't know how to determine if this Sofia was my sister until one of the doctors mentioned that she was a painter and often drew portraits of staff and others who were patients. He showed me the drawing she had done of him and I immediately knew it was hers. She forgot her name but not how to paint and draw – wonderful and amazing.

She painted and she loved the paintings of an American painter, Helen Frankenthaler and like Frankenthaler, apparently, Sofia developed severe migraines. At one point she adopted the name Milena – apparently the name of Franz Kafka's unrequited love – and told all who would listen that she was going to return to Prague very soon. It is common for those with dissociative amnesia to invent new identities but this kind of borrowing hadn't been seen before. She fixed parts of her new identity but other parts of her kept changing. Some characteristics she borrowed, others she invented and she would leave them behind as she needed.

Someone who worked at the Institute, a psychologist by the name of Arturo Antonini, realised she was a very talented painter. He took a number of her paintings to a prestigious gallery in Trieste and they immediately agreed to sell them on commission.

Eventually, Sofia was released to live independently with regular home care, allowing her to paint, the best thing for her. As far as the Institute knows, she is still living in Verona. I have the address and tomorrow I go there. I am incredibly excited and deeply scared.

CHAPTER 50

Julie brings him home. She knows she shouldn't, but he is incredibly cute and it doesn't look like he belongs to anyone. He was just hanging out in the park. Julie went up to him. She expected him to run away, but she got close enough to hold him. Are you lost? The puppy looks at her, head tilts, I don't understand. "I'm Julie," she says pointing to herself. She holds out her hand. He sniffs. Once is enough. He is not scared but also not a dog exuberant with everyone. He is getting to know her first. She likes him immediately. No collar, no tag. A lovely mutt of a dog. She knows right away she wants him. Ian won't mind. I'll keep him in the garage, she thinks. She sits next to him and strokes his head. She waits. Ten minutes. Fifteen. She stands. "Would you like to come home with me?"

She stands behind Tarek's pram. Dog begins to follow, then stops. Finally, Julie simply tucks the little fellow under her arm, where he stays happily, and with the other pushes Tarek home.

Tarek is delighted and dog is happy to find someone closer to his size. She sets him up in the garage, bathes him and then invites him in the house, 'for a little while.'

That evening, dog – still unnamed – is curled on her lap, Tarek on her breast, the television on and she feels a moment of contentment that she hasn't felt in months.

When she rescues a second dog and agrees to take the neighbour's bird – a cockatoo that can't be released – because the neighbour is moving to London, she knows this isn't as simple as it appeared. The fourth and fifth are two kittens abandoned near the childcare centre.

When she next sees Peta it's eight. Three hens. Peta is delighted. "So, you know you're crazy now, right? And you're doing good things as a crazy woman. I love it. I love that you take the horror of what's happening to Jake and it becomes an impulse to rescue. What could be a better, more hopeful and helpful way to deal with the crap you have to deal with? But I think eight is enough? Can you stop now?"

"I'll try, but this has made me realise how many animals are in need and now that I see it, I can't unsee it. I won't go out of my way to rescue more but if they come to me, well..."

"And I hope you don't start on wild animals either."

"I kind of like snakes," Julie says with a laugh, the best laugh she's had in a long time.

*

The Free Radicals strike again after a long hiatus. The attempt to scuttle a coal ship in Fremantle fails though. A stolen motorboat rammed the hull of an old Panamanian coal hulk. Two men were involved – one in the motorboat, one in a dinghy following, to pick up the motorboat driver who leapt from the boat in the last seconds before contact. The hull is damaged but the boat doesn't sink. Fuel leaks into Fremantle Harbour and the media had a field day with 'Greenies Pollute Harbour!' The two men still haven't been found.

Jake read the story and felt almost indifferent. Nothing has changed except that damaging property has become part of the landscape, like acne or privatisation. Even the pious righteousness of the media and politicians has an air of ritual to it now, at least in Jake's mind.

A week later a young man invaded the lobby of a CSG company in Brisbane, doused the foyer and the lift in petrol and set it alight.

He died of his burns. He was only eighteen and was known to have mental health problems.

Fourteen employees were injured. Media reports blamed The Free Radicals, because no one else claimed responsibility.

More recently Just Disobey occupied the Sahan offices in Brisbane. Seven people – including Garth – walked in wearing suits and ties. One of them went up to reception and told the woman they had a meeting with one of the staff. As she called through, the others waited for someone to come out of the offices and simply walked in through an open door. They chained the door shut and began to chain themselves inside various executive offices.

All seven were arrested, nine hours later, including a young man recently returned from Afghanistan as a hero.

*

10 December 2016

Dear children

Sofia is no longer at the address I was given. The neighbours said that Sofia moved away about a year ago, but no one knows where. Someone must know. I have begun to look for a gallery that carries her paintings – made more difficult because I don't know what surname she is using or even, for that matter, that she is using her first name and not Helen or Milena or who knows. I feel quite flat today. I feel like coming home. I will certainly be there when Jake's trial begins. Maybe I will give it another month. That should be more than enough time. The trail cannot keep getting longer. Or so I want to believe.

Although Sofia always had a pad of paper at hand and at least one pencil behind her ear; although she had many paintings in her house and she gave me drawings and paintings that hung in my house, I never thought of her as an artist. I thought of her as niece and activist and nurse. Ian's journey makes me think again. She lost her name, her identity, her country, her husband, even her sanity, but painting remained her voice for that entire journey. She never lost that and it probably saved her.

20 December 2016

Dear children

I found one of her paintings! I'm sure of it. I think. I was in one of the expensive galleries and I asked to see other paintings. Like Helen Frankenthaler, I said, with great assurance, though I'd never heard of her until two days ago!

And there she was.   It was an abstract landscape that reminded me of Sarajevo. Lots of red – I wasn't sure if it was fire or blood or the shelling during The Siege. Deep greens that seemed to bleed like rivers and a landscape littered with shards of darkness. I asked the name of the painter. Martina Antonini – her psychologist's surname! I am on the trail again. I found the painting quite disturbing, but I had to buy it. It is being sent home, so when a large rectangular box arrives, please treat it well!

However, nothing is easy. The gallery's only contact for Sofia is through the bank. If a painting sells, they simply deposit the money into her account. They told me which bank, but warned me that the bank will never give out her address.

I will go to the bank and try and send a message to both of them, but I don't hold out much hope that this will work.

*

The animals are causing chaos. The garage has become a zoo. Fortunately, the cats and dogs get along well. They have no idea what they are. The cockatoo, Lorax, is incredibly loud and roams freely during the day. She is house trained, but can fly only very short distances. She can climb and often does. She likes to perch on doors or curtain rods and jump onto Julie's shoulder when she passes. Julie almost had a heart attack the first few times but now she is battle hardened. Lorax likes to nibble on Julie's ear but is incredibly gentle with Tarek, who is constantly reaching for her.

In fact, Tarek's grizzling seems to have ceased with the endless attraction of these animals, but still, they're a lot of work. Every evening, she hoses down the garage, sweeps it with a stiff broom, cleans out Lorax's cage and feeds all the beasts. They are growing quickly and Julie doesn't know what she's going to do when they are ready to be outside. The yard has no fence and eight animals probably violates a thousand different council bylaws. Inside they are destroyers. The dogs chew and shit and the cats claw and scratch. Disaster areas. She has no idea either of what she's going to do when Ian returns, which is going to be soon.

Julie starts looking for another place to live, but she doesn't know where to go, what to look for, how she can afford anything working only two days a week and now with eight animals. She is feeling the weight of decisions she has made. Good for her spirit but bad in other ways and those costs get higher over time. 'I need to be wiser,' she says, but she just wants to be a little bit wealthier.

She is saved, at least that's what she thinks, by a television interview she does. She talks about Jake and how she has started rescuing animals. "I'm living in my father-in-law's house. He is overseas and the animals are wonderful, but I can't afford them and I can't afford to fix all the damage they are doing to Ian's house." Offers of help, money, housing pour into the television station. As do dozens of requests for Julie to take on animals in need of rescue.

4 January 2017

Dear children

Thank you Peta for your email and all the news. I look forward to meeting Julie's new extended family. I think.

I had a very quiet Christmas and New Year. Not much to celebrate really except the persistence of hope. I hope you have celebrated what you can and found peace wherever it is to be found.

As predicted the bank wouldn't give me any information although they did agree to forward my message.

Now that I had another name to work with, I started calling the various galleries and asking if they carried any paintings by Sofia Blum or Sofia Kovac or Martina Antonini. It is a bit more difficult here as I speak no Italian. They speak more English than the Bosnians but not a lot. And why should they?

I started with the galleries in Trieste, then Venice and Verona. When I found someone who spoke English, I tried to get advice on the best galleries to call. It's a slow process and success is not guaranteed.

I went back to the gallery where I bought Sofia's painting. I forgot to ask them if they had sold other paintings by Sofia in the past and if so, I would like to get in contact with the purchasers. A long bow, I know, but I am now chasing the shadow of Sofia rather than Sofia herself and it feels as though I am getting further and further away. I only have a few more weeks.

The manager looked back as far as their computer records went – around 7 years – and found five paintings that had sold under any of Sofia's names. They agreed to try and contact the owners and see if they are willing to speak with me.

I ended up telling Sylvia – the gallery manager – the short version of why I was here. I should have done that the first time. It's Italy after all. She became very excited and keen to help.

She started looking in all the art journals, online galleries, art blogs for any mention of Sofia in the last three years or so. I didn't even think that she might be known as a painter.

There was so much! She has a fine reputation as a painter and one too as a somewhat mysterious woman. How little they know! Most exciting was a photo of her. I would have recognised her instantly. Her eyes just jump out at you. Intense, as they always were. I felt on the verge of finding her, but based on my journey so far that's probably not true.

Sylvia has printed out all the pages she could find and I will take them to the hotel tonight, read the ones in English and figure out the next steps.

Inch by inch!

CHAPTER 51

When the annual climate figures are published, 2016 has been the hottest year on record, the fourth year in a row that previous annual heat records have fallen and the fifteenth straight month of record breaking heat. There is not even fifteen minutes of ennui from the public and the politicians. When the Great Barrier Reef bleached for the second time in three years, the most severe and widespread ever recorded, there is an uproar – for a tourism industry that now needs help. Both the state and federal governments are still pushing for Sahan's coal mine to proceed. They will find a way to put taxpayer money into the projects. There is more talk of clean coal, more talk of carbon capture and storage and now a clean coal power station.

The Arctic ice cover over winter has been at record lows and is bringing severe weather patterns to the rest of the planet. The open ocean is now absorbing heat rather than the ice reflecting it, and temperatures in the Arctic are soaring. Ten, fifteen, twenty degrees above normal. Jake reads this and thinks that the climate is becoming The Real Free Radicals. It can't be arrested, can't be accused of being a terrorist and can't be stopped by any usual means. He can imagine this government announcing a war on the climate.

Just Disobey has become a serious political force. Three thousand arrests and not once have the new laws been used to imprison anyone. Civil disobedience is occurring at a scale never before seen in Australia. Banks, investors and super funds are all withdrawing support for coal. The Government, of course, insists that coal is needed, but they are trying to navigate what is now a very changed landscape. They would rather demonise asylum seekers than spruik coal.

Jake didn't believe such levels of civil disobedience would ever happen, never argued for it to occur, but he has to admit it is working, working better than his own actions, he adds to himself. 'It might not have happened without The Free Radicals' he thinks, but that will never be known.

The other trend that is now exploding, is that an avalanche of people are going off grid. Battery systems are good enough – and cheap enough – that thousands of people a week are leaving the grid. The effects are enormous. The price of electricity is projected to double as the generators, wholesalers and retailers struggle to get enough revenue from remaining customers. That is driving more people off grid. Even large industries are going fully to renewables. One commentator puts it succinctly: 'The government's policies have been so poor that virtually accidentally Australia became the world leader in rooftop solar and created the circumstances we're seeing now. Going off grid is easy and far cheaper than paying for coal.'

Jake reads all this, daily he reads this, but a part of him doesn't care. He cares about Julie, about his food, his writing, his meetings with Steven, his legal research, his brief exercise in the cage. To think about anything else is to think about a freedom he may never have.

15 January 2016

My dear children

The impossible has happened. I was in my hotel room writing you a completely different letter, when there was a knock on the door. I am expecting dinner. Instead, it was Sofia! She looked at me and said, 'Janos' in a harsh, ghost-like voice, then passed out.

I brought her into the room and tried to revive her but when she opened her eyes, she didn't know anything. She couldn't even speak. There was such fear in her eyes, fear, I think, that the world she had slowly reconstructed after Janos' execution had just disappeared in a puff of smoke and her old world hadn't returned. She was nowhere and nothing.

She is in the hospital now. I explained to staff what I know about her experiences. I am her carer now and won't lose her again, although whether she will ever know me is a question I can't possibly answer.

I feel relief but I'm also afraid. This has been a journey that has no end, a journey that takes as much as it reveals. I am so tired. I want to arrange to bring Sofia home with me. And then I think, that's what I want, what does she want? She cannot say, but I can't imagine that bringing her to a country she doesn't know, to a language she cannot speak, will make her recovery any more likely.

Tomorrow I speak with her doctors.

I am in shock. I have not seen Sofia in many years. I too thought she was dead.

*

Steven has filed a motion for a directed verdict on all terrorism related charges. Steven will argue that the prosecution doesn't have sufficient evidence of guilt on these charges to warrant taking the charges to a jury. He will ask that the judge give a verdict solely on the basis of the evidence the prosecution will be relying on. The jury won't be present. "If we lose on this, we can try again in front of a jury. The drawback is that the prosecution will know the arguments the next time around."

"I think I'd rather have two chances than one," Jake said.

Jake again insists on attending the hearing. The courtroom is packed again. Challenging the scope of the counter terrorism laws is of both legal and political interest – and today there are more law students and lawyers than courtroom tragics.

Judge di Maio looks over the assembly with a slightly quizzical expression, but he betrays no other emotion.

"Counsellor, are you prepared to make oral arguments?"

"Yes, your Honour." Steven stands. "The definition of a terrorist act requires that the perpetrator have the 'intention of advancing a political agenda and the act must cause serious physical harm.' Additionally, the act must involve an attempt to influence or coerce by intimidation the government or the public. Five terrorist acts are alleged and I would like to address each in turn against these three requirements.

"The sabotage of the rail lines was called in by the perpetrator. There were no injuries nor any serious physical harm. The only harm caused was minor damage to the rail lines, which was repaired in a matter of hours. Similarly, the gluing shut of the doors of Mineral House caused minor damage at most. In both these cases it is our submission that these actions do not meet the threshold requirement for a terrorist action.

"In relation to the destruction or damage to the mining equipment, we acknowledge serious damage but not physical harm. We argue that both those words – 'physical' and 'harm' are words specifically intended to refer to personal injury. The primary meaning of physical is of the body. Physical is also used to refer to corporeal matters – such as the physical universe – but is not used in conjunction with 'harm' to describe or be synonymous with property.

"The word 'harm' is the same as injury and is used to describe injury to people, to businesses, even to ecosystems, but not to property. For property we speak of damage not harm. In fact, under the Criminal Law Consolidation Act, the term physical harm is defined as 'unconsciousness, pain, disfigurement or infection with a disease', clearly referring to injuries to persons.

"There is no evidence before the court that in passing counter terrorism legislation, this term was intended to have a different meaning than it currently has both in law and in the plain meaning of the words.

"Additionally, there is no evidence that a political agenda was being advanced. Unlike the first two acts, this act had only the briefest of messages – 'no more destruction.' On its face, this message is directed at the CSG companies not the government. The media release put out on that day by The Free Radicals is entirely in the context of the fourth action, the destruction of Frank Fisher's drilling rig, not this action, so there is no evidence of a political agenda in this act.

"The issue of influencing or coercing government requires careful definition." Steven pauses, takes a drink and continues. The silence in the courtroom is tense, almost brittle. "To influence or coerce are words that by definition require both an object and a subject – influence or coerce government to what?   Unlike the first two acts, there was no political message, no call for the government to act on climate change. Because Your Honour has ruled that there is no evidence of an organisation then each of these actions must be considered separately and on its own merits. The attempted influence that was apparent in the first two acts is not present here. There was a demand – no more destruction – but clearly that is referring to the activities of the CSG company, so it is our submission that this action did not involve an attempt to influence or coerce the government and therefore does not meet the requirements of a terrorist action.

The fourth alleged terrorism offence is the destruction of the CSG rig. With the Court's permission I'd like to play the audio of the video that was made for this act."

The Judge nods and the courtroom fills with the sound of Jake's somewhat disguised voice. "This rig is built on a property owned by a family that has been here for almost 200 years. Last year, six months after the rig had started up, their infant died. Cause of death unknown, but the parents asked for an autopsy and it revealed a child with lesions, disease and toxins throughout her body." He steps through the hole in the fence. "A month later, the water coming from the kitchen sink was so contaminated that the father put a match to it and it exploded in flames. The water was tested. It cannot be drunk. They don't know all the chemicals that are in it. The health department refuses to conclude it's because of this rig, even though they admit they don't know which chemicals are being used by the CSG company.

Steven stops the tape. He knows this is the trickiest argument to make and he is taking his time. Jake watches with intensity and also admiration. Steven's demeanour is compelling in ways Jake can't describe. It's incredibly subtle but he feels the strength of his arguments not only through his words but his gestures, movements, intonations and rhythms. It is the first time since he was in his first year of law school that he feels as though he would like to be a lawyer, one who could control a room in such nuanced ways.

"Your Honour, the language used here is critical. The perpetrator is clearly acting on behalf of a farmer he feels has been wronged. Rather than demanding that the government act he is accusing the company of a crime and accusing the government of a failure to act. There is no call for cancellation of the licence, no attempt to coerce the government to stop the rig – the perpetrator has already done that. There is no attempt to do anything more than an act of justice – what others might call vengeance – for what the perpetrator sees as a wrong. To influence, intimidate or coerce needs a subject. We submit that it is not enough to simply infer a subject from the Act but there must be evidence of that subject. What did the perpetrators want or attempt to coerce from either government or the public engaging in this act? We don't know because there is no evidence to tell us. Similarly, the means of influence or coercion in the Act is by intimidation. This means through fear. Let's be clear: the Act requires that an act attempts to influence or coerce by creating fear in the public or the government. The public had no reason to be afraid because this act was directed at a very specific and very personal target. There is additionally no evidence that this act created fear in the public. Anger, yes. Support yes, but no evidence of fear. Nor, I would submit, did the Government exhibit any of the generally recognised symptoms of fear. They did not lock down roads, did not close off areas. They did not bring out additional troops or police. There were no helicopters hovering over any area in response to this act. While this was clearly an act that caused property damage, clearly an act that would justify criminal charges, there is no basis for finding this is an act of terrorism.

"Finally, Your Honour, the sinking of the tugs at Bowen. There is no question of significant damage, but once again there is no physical harm to persons. No media release was issued for this act but a video was made and distributed through social media networks. That video again makes no demands of government. It simply accuses the companies involved in the coal industry of crimes against the planet and clearly indicates that the perpetrator will continue to hold them accountable. One could call this act a vigilante act, an act where an individual decides to impose his or her own version of justice, but a vigilante is easily and importantly distinguished from a terrorist. There is no attempt to coerce. The implication of coercion, we submit, is not sufficient. There must be specific steps of coercion – of forcing the government to do something, take some action. That has not occurred. Thank you, Your Honour."

Someone in the audience starts to applaud. Steven grimaces. He doesn't need such theatre.

Judge di Maio stares the man down. "Thank you, Counsellor. Mr Wilson?"

Wilson stands. He is a tall man. Jake likes his looks. Thoughtful is the word that comes to mind.

"As Mr Kaal has done, I will address the defence arguments in turn. The Act does not define 'serious physical harm'. In cases of harm to property, how does one proceed? Was there harm? Contrary to Mr Kaal's attempts to use a very narrow definition of harm, the Oxford Dictionary includes 'material damage' as a type of harm. So, clearly there was harm. Was the harm physical? Mr Kaal would also have you take a narrow definition of 'physical' so that physical harm relates only to people. The plain meaning of 'physical' however relates to things as well as people. The physical world refers to the material world. So, the question then becomes what is serious harm? Even the defence is likely to agree that permanent damage or destruction is serious. When an act occurs that results in the halting of a train carrying over a million dollars' worth of coal. When an act occurs that requires immediate transportation of police and railway experts out to the site to assess and repair the damage. When the delays themselves result in disruption along the rail line and at the Port and mean that ships awaiting the coal are forced to remain at berth for far longer than intended, we submit this is serious physical harm.

"I remind the court of other legislation such as the Queensland Environment Protection Act. That Act defines 'serious' using either the extent and nature of the damage or a cost figure that acts as a surrogate. That Act defines environmental harm as serious if the damage exceeds $50,000 dollars. The damage in this instance far exceeds that. The estimated cost, Your Honour, of this harm was over $200,000 dollars.

"The gluing of the doors, similarly resulted in damages of $72,000." Wilson hands over to Steven and the bailiff the sheet on which these amounts are itemised.

"The defence argues that the third, fourth and fifth actions don't meet the standard of trying to influence or coerce. In good part, the defence relies on the separation of the five actions in order to make this argument. While his Honour has concluded there is no evidence of an organisation, there is evidence, which we are prepared to present at trial, that the five acts in question were done by the same person. That means that the political agenda reflected in the public statements made by the perpetrator or perpetrators surrounding the first two acts can and legitimately should be seen as reflecting the purpose of the third, fourth and fifth acts. That is clearly the way the media understood it and we submit is the way any reasonable person would understand these acts. Thank you, your Honour."

"Mr Kaal, any rebuttal?"

"Yes, Your Honour. In relation to the damage argument made by the prosecution, the Act clearly requires significant physical damage. This is not the language used in the Environment Protection Act, which only refers to environmental harm not physical harm. We submit that financial harm cannot in these circumstances be used as a proxy for physical harm. In relation to the meaning of 'physical' Mr Wilson has separated that word from 'harm' in the legislation and that separation is critical. When we speak of property damage no one says 'physical harm' to a building, they say 'physical damage.' Indeed 'to harm' is defined as harm to a person.

"Regarding the linking together of the five acts, we submit that even if the acts were committed by the same person, the intent was significantly different in the third and fourth acts. These clearly related to the effects of drilling on an individual farmer – motivations not evident at all in the previous two acts. That is all, Your Honour."

Wilson stands even before di Maio turns to him. "Your Honour, all five acts were done under the banner of The Free Radicals. While accepting the Court's decision, that banner nonetheless expresses and represents clear political views and a clear political agenda. If all four actions are carried out by the same person, under the same banner, other motivations may indeed by in play, but we maintain that the original motivations expressed in public statements remains. We would add, Your Honour, that these are no longer questions of law but questions of fact and they are best left to the jury."

"Thank you, gentlemen. I have read your submissions and listened to your arguments and am prepared to rule on the matter now." There is a buzz in the courtroom. No one expected an immediate decision, but it's coming. "On the matter of acts one and two, I find no case has been made that the threshold test of 'significant physical harm' has been met. I therefore make a directed verdict for the defence. On acts three, four and five, I find, as Mr Wilson has argued that these are not matters of law but of fact and these charges will be heard by the jury at trial. Court adjourned." And he's gone. It all happens so quickly, that there is this kind of hiatus in the courtroom. Julie jumps over the rail and then jumps into Jake's arms. Their embrace is electric. It's as though within seconds everyone in that room turns towards those two heavenly bodies with gravity greater than gods! Photos are taken, video is taken, loud applause breaks out. The bailiff runs over and tries to pull them apart – a very bad look. Jake is now so strong that a single man won't make him let go. When three guards come over, one of them, wisely, says, "Mr Votek, you need to let go now. Please let us do our jobs."

Jake looks up as though he had no idea he was in a courtroom, or is a prisoner accused of terrorist acts. He looks at the guard who spoke and nods and then gives Julie a long kiss. He holds his arms behind him as he does, so they can handcuff him. They don't. They wait. He will be strip-searched tonight, but it will be worth every second.

CHAPTER 52

25 January 2016

Dear children

This may be my last letter from Europe. Today I met with Sofia and her doctors. She recognised me immediately as a familiar face. Once again, she called me Janos and I simply embraced her. She embraced me in return with a strength and ferocity that shocked me. A part of her seems to know that she is a bit lost.

The doctors – and there are three – are all acting in an advisory capacity. Because she is no longer a ward of the state, she is free to go if I can establish to the satisfaction of the Italian Government that I am her lawful guardian. All agree that Sofia can be moved; that she is best off with family or friends familiar to her (even if she has the wrong familiar) and that getting her settled as quickly as possible is absolutely the best thing for her. They have urged ongoing care, which I know will be necessary. And so – it amazes me to say or to believe – I am bringing my sister home.

I have arranged an emergency visa with the Australian Embassy – shockingly easy!

The Italian Government requires a DNA test to prove we are closely related and gave me the name of a lab that can conduct the test in 24 hours. As she is not an Italian citizen, they really don't seem too concerned.

What is not so easy is Sofia's stuff. She has a house full of furniture and possessions and I'm not sure what has meaning, what might have meaning – and neither is Sofia. Even worse is her studio. Since Arturo's death, painting seems to have been all she has done and there are dozens of paintings, hundreds of drawings, easels, brushes, palettes all of which need to be packed and sent. Sofia's Italian is better than mine and she – I hope – will arrange this part of our departure.

I hope my dearest Julie that the spare room hasn't been completely taken over by snakes or bats or other lovely creatures, although I'm sure, in time, Sofia, will be their friend.

*

The discovery documents have come through. Jake speaks briefly with Steven on the phone. He says the evidence looks mainly circumstantial. Their witness list is brief. "A fair bit of forensic testimony but I haven't seen anything damning," he says. "Bank account and phone records and the evidence of your flight to Sydney and the car rental, although I suspect that the criminal charge for Canberra will be dropped now that it isn't an act of terrorism. We need to go through those together. They'll hammer your visit to Frank's place and they've tracked down your welding ticket. We are now looking into what we need to counter and whether we need an investigator. They haven't included the records relating to the use of the tracker in the car, so we'll seek that as well as all materials relating to the search of your computer."

"Steven, what can I do? I want to stay involved to the extent I'm useful."

"I need to talk with you about the importance of the evidence they're presenting – but I need a bit more time with the materials. And you said you may want to use the necessity defence. Begin to do your research on that."

"Almost done. I have a bit of time on my hands."

Waiting is painful.

The hearing to set a trial date is brief. The trial will begin in April.

*

Julie feels a deep level of panic. Not only is Jake going to trial, but Ian is returning with his sister and she is going to be homeless. She is afraid to ask Peta for help, afraid to ask Ian if she can stay and she can't afford her own place. Her zoo is increasingly dear to her. Lorax is a constant companion. She rides on the top of the pram when Julie and Tarek go out and she terrorises the local dogs if they come anywhere near. Julie needs these creatures. They have saved her.

The last thing she wants is sudden changes, loss of control, but it's coming. She gets an urgent meeting with her Counsellor Amanda.

Julie is restless, flighty, irritable. "Ian is coming home with his sister. She will need his care and attention. Jake's trial is beginning and I have a house full of animals I love. I need to keep them confined and I have nowhere to go. I'm terrified I'll start getting the nightmares again and that I'll never find a place that will accept my animals."

Amanda smiles. "With Jake gone, you need to feel in control – of your brain, your sleep, your life. Let me ask you Julie, what would be the ideal solution?"

Julie looks at Amanda as though she is being led into a trap, which she is. "Jake would come home, we would have another baby, we'd find a house in the bush somewhere and rescue animals. Something like that."

"Indeed," Amanda says smiling. "You want things that represent a massive change from where you are now and perhaps have ever been. Maybe it's not about control, but something else, something more specific."

Julie gets it but doesn't have an answer.

"You're afraid – understandably. You've learned a lot in the last few months about how to deal with Jake being away, Mary's death, Ian's journey. Change – particularly change you can't control – makes you afraid that this somewhat tenuous hold you have will disappear. Why don't you believe you can cope with a change that isn't that large? You're living in someone else's house, with an absent father and absent love – and you're worried about moving. That's what it amounts to. I understand you don't want to go – but it's not clear to me that even that is necessary. Why is this making you so crazy?"

Julie looks at Amanda and then out the window.

"Julie, you have gone through several hells in the last year – and you've survived them all – and even begun to conquer them. Moving out of a house that was never yours is not a big deal for you. It's not a straw that breaks a camel's back. It's just your lovely father in law returning. And he's returning with something he's rescued. Do you understand how big that is?"

Julie nods. She's a bit embarrassed and somewhat flattened by how little she has thought this through.

"Do you think I can stay then?"

"Julie, I have no idea. Is there room? Room for you, Sofia, Ian and many animals?"

"I could set up a room in the garage if that's okay with Ian."

"Ian hasn't asked you to be out when he returns?"

Julie shakes her head.

"Would it be unreasonable to try and set up the house for Ian's return and Sofia's arrival and for you to stay on as long as you need until you find a place?"

Julie looks as though the thought never even crossed her mind.

When Julie returns home, she decides she can set up the garage as a room for her and the animals, even if it's only temporary. She wonders how she can make the spare room a welcoming, warm and comfortable room for Sofia. The answer is so obvious – Sofia's painting, Sofia's drawings.

She has four days before they arrive and with a clear sense of purpose she rushes around like a lunatic.

*

Jake is transferred to Brisbane for the trial. Maximum security but Julie will be allowed to visit. This is as close to elation as Jake gets in his current life. Everything is measured in the most immediate of terms.

He has a roommate. A massive man with tattoos everywhere. Jake shows no fear, although he's terrified. Slam is his name. "I was a wrestler, mate. Fucking dancing fucking bear, mate, nothin' more. I would do the body slam on some poor fuck and then I had to do my little fuckin' dance. What a fuckin' life."

After that, Slam is okay. He likes to laugh.

He can't believe a greenie is in max for being a terrorist. He goes, "You? Are you fuckin' serious? I've never met a fuckin' greenie who wasn't a faggot, fuck me dead. You blew shit up?"

Jake just starts laughing and then Slam joins him.

"A fuckin' greenie," Slam finally says. "Fuck me dead. I'll look after you mate. You are one fuckin' endangered species in this place!" He breaks into this rumptious laugh, infectious.

*

Ian has tried to prepare Sofia for the flight home. She calls him Janos still, but you can hear in the way she says it that there is doubt there. They are on a Qantas flight, and Sofia speaks Italian first and then Bosnian and when no one understands her, she becomes agitated. "Janos, where are we going?" First Singapore and then Brisbane. Another twenty hours. He wants to wait a bit before he offers her a sleeping tablet. He is so tired. Elated but tired. She is uprooted again and he understands why she is so restless. He tries to get her to watch a movie, but she knows something is changing, something is shifting. She stands, walks to the back of the plane and asks in Italian, where is Arturo, "Dov'e Arturo?"

They understand, but they don't have an Arturo on this flight. She has forgotten that Arturo has died. She begins to panic, they can see it. She turns, turns back. She stands. Ian calls her. She turns, looks at him and says "Janos," and then forgets what it was she meant to say. She is utterly confused. Arturo, Janos. Where am I? Ian leads her back to her seat and says you must take this and gives her the sleeping tablet.

Twenty minutes later she is asleep and Ian breathes. Another twelve hours to Singapore. He tries to sleep too, but he can't. He speaks to the staff. She is not well. I may fall asleep. If she becomes distressed, please wake me immediately. Yes, yes, they say. But he can't sleep. He watches a movie. He has no idea what he has watched a minute after it is finished. He is beyond exhaustion.

*

Peta and Julie and Tarek are there to meet them at the airport. Ian and Sofia emerge from customs like two alien beings. Ian looks shattered and barely able to fight gravity. And Sofia. It's hard to describe. She is frantic with worry, completely confused by circumstances that make no sense in any world she knows, and hanging on to Ian, who is Janos in her head – although that too is a tenuous reality.

When two young women she has never seen her embrace her and speak in a language she knows is English but doesn't understand, she suspects something is seriously amiss. She starts to rave in Bosnian that they cannot move her. No, not under any circumstances. Janos is due back soon. Medicines need distributing. And there are people in the cellar waiting for her. Peta looks on in confusion. Julie takes her hand and says in Italian, 'non fa fretta, Sofia.' Sofia understands the words – don't worry – but doesn't recognise the woman. For a brief moment, though, those words are enough. Sofia then begins to babble in Italian. Julie is immediately lost. She holds on to this lovely woman even tighter. Ian comes over and embraces Julie and Sofia at the same time. "Let's go home," he says.

In the taxi, Julie tries to tell Ian what she has done at home, but Ian is so distracted and so fatigued that he clearly hasn't heard.

Sofia sits between Ian and Julie and she hangs onto both of them, silent and beyond scared, beyond confused.

*

Sofia's bedroom wall is covered in drawings that Julie has had framed and one large painting. Ian tells Julie that many more are on the way. Sofia walks in and stops dead. Slowly she moves clockwise around the room, examining each one intently. Julie imagines she sees recognition, then confusion, then something close to determination. When she comes to the first drawing of Janos it is different. She looks at Ian, then back to the drawing. She bites her lower lip and narrows her eyes.

Ian comes up to Julie and gives her a hug. "Thanks," he whispers.

At the second drawing of Janos, the one where his head is thrown back in laughter, she looks at Ian again, small shake of the head, then she mutters something in Bosnian.

Julie looks to Ian. "She just said 'impossible'," he whispers.

Sofia smiles at a still life and laughs when she sees the portrait of round-faced Milos. You can see she knows him but can't remember his name. She looks more closely and there it is 'Milos' at the bottom of the drawing. She stands back and puts her hands on her hips. She is recognising a disconnection and it doesn't make her happy.

She comes to a drawing of me. It is hanging above the chest of drawers.

She takes the drawing down, reads the name at the bottom. "Tarek," then looks at Tarek the younger. "Tarek?" she asks. Julie nods and Tarek begins to grizzle. Sensitive child. "Tarek, Tarek, Tarek." She rolls the name around on her tongue as though she is close to remembering or understanding. "Tarek, Tarek, Tarek." She puts the drawing back on the wall.

I ache to have her know me. It is hard to be forgotten. It is hard to be invisible. It is hard to be thought a killer when there is no part of me that sees my life that way. Sofia most of all knows me. Or did.

It takes Sofia fifteen minutes to inspect every drawing. She then turns to Ian and tells him she must have a shower and go to bed. She is given the tour of the house and meets the menagerie. Lorax lands on her shoulder and Sofia claps her hands with delight and screeches with laughter when Lorax nibbles on her ear.

Ian just shakes his head at the madness that is going to be his life. No quiet life of contemplation for this retired academic.

Sofia sleeps through the night. When she wakes, she marches into the kitchen, where Ian is nursing a coffee that isn't close to strong enough. "I want to know what is going on," she says. "Who are you? And why have you brought me here?"

"I am your brother Ivan. I brought you here because I read the letters you wrote to me during The Siege and I wanted you to forgive me."

Sofia deflates instantly and collapses into the nearest chair. "My brother?"

Ian nods as gently as he can. Peta, who is watching from the sink doesn't need to understand the words. She brings Sofia a coffee. Sofia looks up at her as though she hasn't seen her before. "And this is my niece?" Ian nods again.

Sofia sips her coffee with both hands. "This morning I looked at those drawings again. They are mine, no?" Ian nods. "I looked at them again. The one labelled Janos. You are not Janos or the drawing is not Janos. This is obvious. Then Tarek. Who is Tarek?"

"Tarek is, was, our uncle."

"And you say you are my brother?"

Ian nods.

"I am sure I have no brother."

"I left Sarajevo many years before The Siege. We fought and did not speak again until I found you in Italy."

"Stop. This is too much for me now. One shock at a time."

"Your name?" Sofia looks at Peta.

"Peta," says Ian.

"She speaks no Bosnian?"

"None."

Sofia nods and returns to inspecting her coffee.

Ian hasn't thought about the psychiatric care that Sofia will need, but it turns out Julie has. Amanda has found a Bosnian speaking psychologist in Brisbane. He hasn't done a lot of work with trauma and amnesia, but for the moment he will have to do.

Julie comes in with a howling Tarek and two dogs and two cats all chasing each other and chaos descends.

Later she speaks with Ian about moving out and he refuses to even consider it. "I'll get used to the animals," he says, "and I don't think I would manage here without you – and I've been back less than a day."

Julie gives him a hug that is so deep and long that Ian begins to realise there is a story here that at some point he needs to know. But not today.

He tries doing some work in the study, but that is no longer where he needs to be. He tries to make sense of all the animals. He has never had a pet much less eight. He tries to process their presence logically. He has no idea whether he wants them around or not. He doesn't want to take care of them. He knows that. They are living primarily in the garage. He doesn't want that either. There is currently no outdoor space for them. He looks at the lawn. How long ago was it that he looked out of the office window and wondered why he had made such a fuss about maintaining the lawn when the children were growing up? He calls a fencing company. They will come next week. He can see Sofia out on the verandah drawing. Julie bought her a pad and pencils and Ian assumes this is the way she is trying to process what is going on both inside and outside her body.

She suddenly stops and calls, "Janos....I mean Ivan..." There is mild panic in her voice.

Ian rushes out.

"What's my name?"

"Your name is Sofia. You were born Sofia Votek." The time for telling her about Janos is clearly not here.

"And all those drawings are mine?"

"Yes, and there are more."

"I would like to see them some time."

"Any time Sofia."

She returns to drawing the backyard Jacaranda so beloved by Mary. Ian takes all Sofia's drawing notebooks and puts them in her room.

Later, both Julie and Peta sit with her. She points. She wants to know the word for 'tree' in English and the word for 'bird'. She repeats the words once and then nods and returns to her drawing.

Lorax joins her. Sits on her shoulder and watches her draw. Finally, Sofia turns to a blank page, offers Lorax a pencil and holds out the pad. She immediately tries to use the pencil but misses the page. Tries again. Eventually, she manages one squiggly line. "A very good start," Sofia says and adds a line of her own. Lorax tilts his head and looks at the two lines with one intense eye. Then draws another line – much more assured.

When Julie comes out, Sofia asks, "Is bird?"

"Yes, a bird. Lorax."

"Low racks?"

Julie smiles and nods.

"What is low racks?"

Julie laughs. There is no way she can explain this. "Ian," she yells, "would you come and explain to Sofia the story of the Lorax!"

For a woman whose identify is fluid and uncertain, she has a force to her character and spirit that even Lorax finds attractive.

PART 4

We should never forget that everything Adolf Hitler did in Germany was 'legal' and everything the Hungarian freedom fighters did in Hungary was 'illegal'.

Martin Luther King Jr.

CHAPTER 53

"The prosecution calls Officer William Fell." So, day one of Jake's trial begins.

The courtroom is packed. Media, friends, courtroom tragics, law students, lawyers. The buzz is intense. The sense that more than any of the terrorism trials to date, this one will define how broadly the terrorism laws are used, will define the future of the environment movement, will set evidentiary precedents in counter terrorism proceedings. In fact, lawyers are already saying Steven's win on the question of an organisation's existence was a major setback for those who promote these laws. The Coalition quickly introduced legislation to neutralise that decision, but the Senate made it clear that proving the existence of an organisation before declaring it a terrorist body is an obvious and necessary step and calls into question the rigour with which the laws were drafted.

Fell is a forensic investigator in the department and examined Jake's car. He is balding but has a pleasant face, one that looks at the world through a microscope, tweezers and bits and pieces of the world that may have a story to tell.

Wilson establishes Fell's expertise and then walks through the report he prepared following examination of the car. Jake has read this.

"You indicate in your report, paragraph 24, that you removed soil samples from all four tires. What was the purpose of taking those samples?"

"We were hoping that something in the samples would identify where the car had been. It's a bit hit and miss, but soil can often be identified as belonging to a particular area or it can contain materials that may indicate, for example, that it comes from an agricultural area."

"At the time you examined these samples, there had been five acts in five different places. How does that affect your analysis?"

"It all depends on what is found and what those findings suggest."

"Okay, so what did you find in your analyses?"

"One of the tests we conducted was for agricultural chemicals. In particular, we were asked to look for chemicals used in the Darling Downs. We didn't test for the most common chemicals – like roundup or glyphosate – because it is used everywhere and wouldn't tell us anything. We tested for heptachlor, diuron, atrazine and simazine. We found minute traces of diuron and simazine."

"And what did those finding suggest?"

"Because these chemicals are used in agricultural areas and not in urban weed control or households, it suggests that the car has been in agricultural areas in recent times."

"Objection, Your Honour. While we accept Mr Fell's expertise as a forensic investigator, there was nothing in his stated expertise involving the use and distribution of agricultural chemicals."

"Your Honour, as an investigator and police officer, investigating where chemicals are used is well within the bounds of the expected expertise of an officer."

"Overruled."

"So, the car has been in agricultural areas. Can you be more specific than that?"

"For those particular tests, no. But we were also asked to test for the presence of fracking chemicals. These are chemicals used by the CSG industry. And we also tested for soil types. There are markers in soils that allow some determination of location."

"And what did you find?"

"We found CSG chemicals consistent with the chemicals being used in the Darling Downs and we found the soil type is consistent with the high loam soils of the Downs. We also found traces of coal dust. We analysed this for sulphur and other chemical content. It is consistent with the coal found at the Acland mine in the Downs."

Fell goes on to claim that sand was also found and while consistent with sand found in Bowen, it was simply not possible to distinguish between sand in Bowen or pretty much anywhere else.

On cross–examination, Steven secures admissions from Fell that the presence of the materials in the tires, even if it could be narrowed down to a specific location, doesn't mean the car was there, only that it was somewhere where these materials were picked up.

On the CSG chemicals, Fell admitted he didn't know what chemicals were being used in other CSG wells in Australia. Nor did Fell know how many CSG wells there are in Australia.

"Would approximately 40,000 surprise you?"

"Yes, a little."

"And are you aware that these wells are all over the state and all over NSW?"

"No sir, I'm not aware of the locations of the wells."

"So, when you find CSG chemicals in soil you can't tell where they are from, can you?"

"No, except that the soil type is consistent with the Darling Downs."

"Since you don't know the location of the other wells, are you able to tell us which soil types in areas where CSG is drilled are consistent with this kind of soil."

"No sir, I cannot."

"Now, could you tell us the name of the CSG chemicals you identified?"

"I'm sorry I'm not permitted to. It was a condition of getting the names that we would not disclose them."

Steven looks shocked although he knew this was coming. He turns to the judge, "Your Honour, I ask that Mr Fell's testimony regarding the CSG chemicals be struck out. We cannot properly cross-examine the witness on the uses and scale of these chemicals if they aren't named. "

The judge immediately agrees and instructs the jury that the testimony is to be ignored. Steven then asks, "Are the chemicals identified by the CSG company dangerous?"

"Objection Your Honour, relevance. You've just struck out testimony regarding the chemicals and any question about those chemicals has no relevance."

"May we approach Your Honour?"

Steven and Wilson approach and hold a brief whispered conversation. Sofia is drawing madly. She knows it's a trial but has no idea what's going on. It doesn't matter; she has already drawn members of the jury, the judge, the bailiff and the lawyers. She saw Jake's face only briefly, when he walked in. She waved to him shyly.

The sidebar concludes and di Maio announces the question will be permitted.

"So, Mr Fell, are these chemicals you identified as being used by the CSG company dangerous to human health?"

"I'm going to give you an unsatisfying answer. All chemicals can be dangerous if misused or if exposure is too great."

"Are you aware of any specific health issues associated with the chemicals you identified?"

"Two are probable carcinogens although there is not a lot of data relating to human carcinogenicity. There is insufficient evidence relating to two others to make any claim regarding their safety to humans.

"For all these chemicals, are they likely to harm the environment, including the water table?"

"My understanding is that their effects on the environment are unknown."

"No further questions Your Honour."

Fell is followed by a voice expert who has examined the video of the destruction of the CSG rig. His analysis is that, while there is some uncertainty because of the voice alteration technology used, there is a reasonable likelihood that the person speaking on that video was Jake.

The only counter that Steven is able to elicit is that based on the patterns of the voice that are ascertainable in light of the alteration of the voice, the voice could belong to others. "So, basically you're saying that there is a chance that the voice belongs to someone else. How many others might it belong to?"

"My estimate is that there is a 1 in 100,000 chance it belongs to someone else."

"So, in Australia that means approximately 250 people would have similar voice patterns using this technology and globally approximately 70,000 people?"

"Yes, that's about right."

Frank is on next and reluctantly he testifies that he knows Jake, that Jake has visited his farm, that they had many discussions about the rig and both expressed a desire to destroy it.

On cross, he tells the story of the inflammable water and of how his infant daughter died a slow but inexorable death. Wilson tries briefly to prevent this testimony as irrelevant but he knows he can't be seen fighting too hard for its exclusion. Frank has tears streaming down his face as he speaks. He doesn't wipe a single tear away. Jake cries, the jury cries.

"And you blamed – blame – this death on the CSG company?" Steven asks.

"I do. But the company has been protected by the government, which refuses to reveal the chemicals used in fracking. But I know my tap water has never been flammable before. We're still pursuing this legally," he adds, "but it's incredibly hard to take the company on – especially when your own government doesn't help but actively hinders you. I'm pretty much broke now and can't keep fighting."

"So, you have testified that you and Jake talked about destroying the drilling rig. Did you have similar conversations with friends and other acquaintances?"

"All the time. It was just talk. Although after Amy died, I came this close to doing it myself."

"Did you ever see in Jake any hint of violence or likelihood that he would act to destroy the rig?"

"None at all. I always saw him and still do as a thoughtful and peaceful man."

When court is adjourned, Jake immediately turns to his family and kisses Julie before the guards can intervene. Jake then introduces himself to Sofia. "Zdravo, kako si."

Sofia blushes with pleasure. "Znate neki bosanski!"

Jake guesses – actually he guessed yesterday in front of the computer – what Sofia said. "Naučio sam da je juče. I learned that yesterday." She turns to Ian and starts babbling and Jake is hauled away by the forces of order. "I love you Julie," he says. "Vidimo se sutra." See you tomorrow.

He and Steven are given a few minutes in the court conference room. Steven is relatively happy. "They are focusing on the equipment and the rig. They seem to have little evidence so far relating to the burning of the tugs and I suspect they will simply drop the other charges – the rail line and the building. Their evidence is highly circumstantial, but it does gain weight the more evidence they produce. I think we countered it as well as we could."

*

Sofia seems to have accepted that her identity is fluid. Her past both intrigues and eludes her but she doesn't appear haunted by those absences.

She has decided she wants to learn English at the dinner table. "When we eat, break bread, share stories. Perhaps everyone can help teach me."

She occasionally asks questions, like "who is Milos?" and slots the answer into the shifting self she is. After dinner she shows everyone her drawings from the courtroom. It is clear that this is part of the core of who she is, something she could not forget how to do even if she wanted.

*

Court doesn't sit on that first Friday and Julie goes to visit Jake at the Brisbane Correctional Centre. It's a scary place. Like the other one. Sterile, metallic, industrial. Everything is ordered, systematic, robotic. That's the word Julie was looking for as she walks into the reception area where she is searched and scanned. It's a place that would feel like a factory even if it was empty.

Jake is already sitting, chained to the floor at a table in the meeting room. A large open space with a few other prisoners there. It is eerily quiet. Julie has only thirty minutes but she needs to look at this man, needs to remember his touch, hear his voice, smell him, as does he.

Finally, she summons the courage to say, "Jake I need to tell you something."

Jake is filled with dread. He knows she is leaving him or maybe she is seeing someone else. He looks at her intently and waits.

The impetuous man who went to prison has become far more self-contained, far more patient, perhaps resigned.

"I have someone new in my life."

Jake waits although he feels the abyss open before him.

"More than one, really. Eight"

Jake looks at Julie more intently and slightly quizzically.

"One cockatoo, two dogs, two cats and three hens." Julie smiles at her joke. She conceived it on the way to the prison, then decided against it, then changed her mind. Humour is in short supply, she thought.

"You're cruel. Your twisted sense of humour is only redeemed because you left me suffering for seconds." Now that he has moved away from the edge, he can enjoy the joke.

"How's Ian putting up with them? He never let us have pets when we were growing up."

"He's been great. One of the kittens has started curling up on his lap and he's funny. He doesn't know what to do. A bit like he was with Tarek at first. And Lorax the cockatoo is in love with Sofia. It's a bit of a madhouse."

"A madhouse would be nice," Jake says quietly.

Julie cannot stop herself. She leans over the table and hugs this man she refuses to believe will be lost to her. She holds on to her life by holding on to him and he does the same. A guard is tugging at her. She can't let go. He is speaking to her, but she doesn't understand him. Then another guard is there and slowly they are pulled apart and Julie is escorted from the room and both Julie and Jake are yelling, again, "I love you" at the tops of their voices over and over. This isn't the usual scene in a maximum security prison and at least one of the guards is amused by the exhibition. Both are strip searched.

*

The second week of trial looms. The wind has been wild since last night. There are trees and wires down and in some suburbs rubbish swirls through the streets like a modern incubus. Jake's drive to the courthouse is eerie. The roads are empty. After thirty minutes, the van turns back. "Trial cancelled mate. Bunch of jurors can't get there."

"Bloody climate change," Jake says, an attempt at humour or getting a rise out of someone. No one even bothers looking at him.

*

When the trial resumes, the prosecution continues to build its circumstantial case. They call an investigator who examined tire imprints at the two Darling Downs sites. He testifies that there was only one set of tires that didn't belong to a four wheel drive or a truck at both sites and that those prints exactly matched Jake's car, both at the storage shed and at Frank's farm.

On the data projector he shows the prints taken from the site and overlays them on the tires themselves. They match, of course.

Wilson tries to pre-empt the obvious cross. "What make of tire are these?"

"Goodyear radials. 195, 55, 16. Those are the width, profile and rim size."

"And that's a common tire, is that correct."

"Yes it is. Goodyear estimates that it sells 100,000 such tires every year in Australia."

"Now were there any identifiable marks, flaws, or signatures in the tires on Mr Votek's car?"

"There were a few anomalies. On the front right tire, there was a bit of metal wedged in the tire tread." The image on the screen isn't very clear. "On the rear left tire there is a tack stuck in the tire." The image of the tack is shown.

"So, these anomalies are a bit like identifying features when you analyse tire tracks, is that correct?"

"Yes, that's right."

"Now Mr Crane, in the tire prints you examined at the site, was there any evidence of either of these two anomalies?"

"Yes, there was. This print was taken from the rig site. You can see," and he uses a pointer to identify a spot on the screen, "that the tread is interrupted here. That interruption is consistent with the tack, both in its circular shape and diameter. Similarly, for this print taken at the yard where the machinery was stored, you see the same shape again. And on this one, also from the yard, this print shows a pattern consistent with the piece of metal, both in its angle and width."

On cross Steven wants to try and neutralise the combined effect of the circumstantial evidence. "Mr Cane, you used the term 'consistent with' to describe the similarities in shape. Statistically, what does that mean?"

"I don't understand."

"What are the chances that these similarities or consistencies in the tire prints are in fact created by the tack and the piece of metal?"

"Well, I don't know. There could be any number of other explanations but I did reach the conclusion that the prints are consistent with both of those shapes at both of the sites on the Darling Downs."

"So, a stone on the ground could have resulted in that consistency?"

"Yes."

"Or something dropped on the ground by a worker?"

"Yes."

"Or tires with other 'consistent' objects in their tires?"

"Yes, but less likely."

"Ah, less likely. How much less?"

"I couldn't quantify it."

"Could you quantify the chances of other objects that have similar shape leaving a consistent print such as the ones you have shown us?"

"No sir, I couldn't."

"And could you quantify the chances of those shapes being found in those particular locations?"

"No sir, I couldn't."

"On the screen, Mr Crane, there is an image of a stone. This was found at the rig site. In this photo it is placed next to a tack. Based on the similarity in size and shape, would you agree that such a stone might leave a similar anomaly on a print taken from the ground?"

"It might."

"Would you agree that your conclusion that the marks are consistent with the tires on Mr Votek's car is a bit like saying it's possible that Mr Votek was there but the same could be said for an unknown number of other people, maybe thousands?"

"I wouldn't go that far."

"You testified that each year 100,000 of the same tires are sold in Australia. Can you tell me how many are currently on the road?"

"No sir, I can't."

"So, would it be correct to say that you cannot quantify the chances that those prints come from another car nor can you quantify the number of objects that would be consistent with marks you found?"

"Yes sir, that is correct."

"How old was the oldest tire print that you identified at both sites?"

"I don't understand."

"You indicated there were a number of tire prints at the sites. How long had they been there?"

"We have no way of knowing."

"So, prints could be weeks old or even older?"

"I suppose."

"So, do you have any way of ascertaining whether the vehicle prints you have analysed were produced on the day in question?"

"No sir, we don't."

"No further questions."

Wilson then calls an investigator who examined hours of CCTV footage from dozens of cameras. There are nine photos they exhibit. Several are near Bowen and show a sedan, four are from the Darling Downs and show a similar sedan. The investigator testifies that based on his analysis, the car in the photos is the same, a Toyota hatchback, an early 2000 model.

In all the images, no licence plate can be discerned and a silhouette of the driver is all that can be seen. The gender of the driver can't be determined.

On the screen, Schenk the investigator, has reduced the images to outlines and compares it to outlines of particular makes and models of cars. He concludes that the car in the photos is more likely than not to be a Toyota hatch. Steven stands.

"Mr Schenk, how many registered Toyota hatches are there in Brisbane from, say 2000 to 2005?"

"Approximately 7000."

"7000?"

"That's correct."

"And how many of the owners of those 7000 vehicles have you investigated and questioned?"

"None sir."

"None?"

"Asked and answered," Wilson interjects.

"So, you have no idea if any of these cars have gone to Bowen or the Darling Downs in the period we are talking about?"

"No sir."

"No further questions." Steven shakes his head in wonder and contempt and then sits down.

The problem, as Steven knows, is that this evidence, no matter how weak on its own, is beginning to pile up.

CHAPTER 54

Today the State of the Climate Report was released. Green Earth has reviewed the findings and sent out an appeal for money. And although it's grim reading it barely causes a tremor in the fabric of space or time. Sea ice levels in both the Arctic and Antarctic are at record lows. This is dramatically increasing temperatures in those regions as the exposed oceans absorb more and more heat. Carbon dioxide levels surpassed 400 parts per million. Extreme weather events are increasing, deaths from extreme weather events are increasing exponentially, including 19 firefighters in the US who lost their lives in the unprecedented fires in Yellowstone. Typhoons in Asia are significantly stronger than they used to be. The number of category four or five storms has quadrupled. Help us make change...

The same newsletter celebrates that the International Criminal Court in The Hague has agreed to hear a case against Australia for the criminal harm being inflicted by its leaders and fossil fuel companies. Abbott, Turnbull and others are accused of being climate criminals. Jake has no doubt it will lead to nothing, but at least someone is bearing witness.

When Jake is dragged out of the courtroom each day, chained in the back of an unmarked van and returned to prison, there is no one inside those walls who donated to the Libs or the ALP, no one there who is a politician or a CEO who exploited or even killed children in order to increase his bottom line. When did it become a condition of our laws that only the powerless can be convicted of crimes.

I am judged for being a dzelat, for killing killers, for killing thieves who took from all of us. That judgement against me is fair, but only if the judgements themselves are made fairly. Milosevic eventually paid a price, but what about all the others? What about Bush for going to war with Iraq, a war that is still killing thousands of civilians. Or Kissinger's murderous bombing of Cambodia. How should citizens respond to this? Violence committed by states against others – greenies or asylum seekers or tribes halfway across the world is still violence. Calling it legal doesn't change that. I understand better than I have before my young nephew and his trauma, his anger, his decisions.

*

The strange family that is taking shape in Ian's house comforts Ian in ways he would never have believed. Peta is there almost daily. "It's much more interesting than being alone at home," she says.

Sofia is learning English by putting post-it notes all over the house – on coffee pots, tables, windows, mirrors, shoes, keys, toilets. Everything, everywhere. And she interrupts conversations with an emphatic, "What is?" and demanding a word be explained before the conversation can continue. She is teaching Lorax Bosnian curse words, much to her amusement.

She doesn't want to go back to court. "Ugly place," she says in English. She has drawn all the participants. Julie looks at the jurors over and over. It's as though Sofia has seen how they are going to vote in these portraits and a part of Julie is convinced that this is true. She hands the notebook to Steven and says to him. "Sofia did these. Look at them and you'll see the jurors you need to work on."

Steven and Jake look at them together and Steven later returns the notebook with a contemplative, "Thanks."

At the moment Sofia asks few questions about her past. "I do not have enough present yet to have a past," she says to Ian somewhat enigmatically.

One day she asks, "Did I have pet in other life?"

Ian responds in Bosnian. "I don't know Sofia. You never mentioned a pet in your letters and never drew one that I know of."

Sofia nods and then goes back to considering something she hasn't yet spoken. Lorax nibbles on her ear. Those two are inseparable. She never had a pet. She was too busy or careless. She never wanted children, but this bird is imprinting itself on Sofia's identity and being.

The fence has been built and now the dogs and cats are free to roam. Sofia comes home one day from a daily wander with three baby chicks in a carry cage. She lets them go in the yard. The dogs are used to the fully grown chickens but the chicks they see as food until Sofia kicks both of them a few times and yells at them in Bosnian. Eventually, she sits on the grass with the chicks and the dogs and introduces them properly. Lorax leaves her shoulder to introduce herself and hangs out with them for the afternoon. When Flotsam tries to have a go at the chickens after Sofia has gone inside, Lorax jumps on his back and screeches. Flotsam behaves – they all do – after that.

Sofia drags Ian outside to help her build a chicken coop, which fails utterly. Ian buys one on Gumtree instead.

Julie is feeling the weight of the trial. She is at the courthouse every day, all day. She sees Jake's fatigue and his worry. It doesn't seem that the evidence is that strong but it keeps growing. There is nothing she can do to help except be there and that is far harder than being actively involved. Poor Tarek is being left with sitters or family for court days and he's pissed off. He's sick of bottles, sick of fake mothers, sick of his mother falling asleep when she does breastfeed. He is not shy about telling everyone that he's not happy.

Tarek is walking now and a whole new world of trouble has opened up. He is fearless and adventurous. Child-proofing the house from this young man takes a full day. He will not be told he can't explore and when he encounters doors or drawers that don't open, he tries to solve the problem with force first and then reason and then, if he fails, loudly asking for help. He spends much time out in the yard with the animals and Sofia.

You can see that he is growing on her. He is a handful but it's because he wants to know and experience everything. Sofia won't hold him at first, but one day she asks him if he'd like to learn to draw. Not just children's drawings. Sofia wants to teach him perspective and shading from the beginning. She guides his hand. They are drawing Lorax. When he sees that the image on the paper is like the image of the bird, he stares at it in wonderment. Every day after that he insists that Sofia draw with him. He tells her what he wants to draw. She agrees. Soon Sofia is telling everyone of his exploits in her mangled English and Tarek has adopted Sofia as his second or third mother.

Ian wants to write about Sarajevo, but it is Jake and climate change that are occupying him now. He has no idea how he can help him. There is no research he can do, no contacts he can use, no comfort he can give. He goes to court with Julie and sometimes Peta and feels a deep uselessness, as though his inability to help is somehow a character defect.

He wants to stand up, walk over to the jury and tell all of them what a fine young man his son is. If he did this, he did it to protect us all. But he doesn't, can't do that. He has to watch and nothing more.

*

After the second week of the trial, the prosecution is perhaps halfway through its case. It has put most of its forensic evidence on the table. Witnesses and colleagues of Jake's will testify next week as will the police officers who interviewed him.

Court is adjourned until Tuesday. On the Saturday the nine year old son of a CSG executive is kidnapped from a soccer game. His parents rarely attended the games. He was brought to the games by the mother of a friend. During half time a man came up to the boy and said something and the boy walked off with him. They were laughing about something. Lisa, the friend, saw him walk off and stupidly assumed it was someone Zak knew. When he didn't reappear for the second half, she went to look for him and he was gone.

She can barely remember what the man looks like. Around thirty. Jeans. Slight build. Blond or maybe brown hair. Useless.

The Free Radicals demand the release of Jake in exchange for the boy. The demand is accompanied by a diatribe about the Paris Agreement, the continued burning of coal and the claim that this nine year old boy will suffer far worse than kidnapping if the corporate and political interests aren't called to account.

Jake doesn't hear about the kidnapping until that evening. He knows it's big trouble. He calls Steven right away. "I want to put out a public statement, repudiating the kidnapping. And I want to say I will not agree to be released, do not want to be released as part of any deal with kidnappers."

"Okay. Listen, I'll put out a brief statement, but you know this is going to stick to you in any event."

"Should we ask for a mistrial?"

"Highly unlikely you'd get one. We'll ask the judge next week to tell the jurors that there is no evidence that the organisation exists – that it is individuals using the name only and that there is no evidence that you know the people or are involved in any way. But it's still going to stick."

"How about a delay until the boy is found. Surely, the judge will understand the prejudicial nature of this for me."

"We'll give it a try."

That evening police release CCTV footage and a composite drawing, pieced together from numerous disparate and very uncertain descriptions. The man was wearing sunglasses and a hat, clean-cut, running shoes, might have had a tattoo on his forearm and that's about it. They know he drove off in a Subaru. The random nature of the attacks from a random collection of disgruntled people is causing the police all sorts of problems. Intelligence hasn't been of much use. These aren't people with a history – or not the histories that the police have used to predict and prevent this kind of crime.

On the Sunday, arsonists burn down the office of a green group in Brisbane, an old Queenslander. No one is injured but the building wasn't empty. Some students were in the art studio there, but managed to get out from the first floor quickly. There is a handwritten note on the streetlamp just outside the building: "Greenies out!"

Another fire follows that evening in Sydney. A petrol bomb thrown through the first floor window of Wild Life, an organisation that buys and protects habitat. No one is inside but there is considerable damage.

Jake's statement is lost in the bedlam. Politicians, who were on the 'I hate greenies' band-wagon yesterday are now calling for calm. But there is no calm. Violence simmers just below the surface like that great ocean of methane slowly bubbling to the surface as the frozen tundra begins to melt. Violence is now normalising and it means more and more people will feel they are entitled to be violent too.

Jake knows he is in part responsible – but he is also convinced that a government that endorses hatred, tortures those seeking asylum, participates in war and violence against countries that are no threat, that promotes the wealthy at the expense of the planet, as this one has done, has responsibility too.

He realises too, this unravelling isn't going to come in a progressive kind of way. It will lurch, stop, start, explode, hide, reappear in random ways – as it has been doing for almost a year now.

The timing sucks though. Jake stays awake into the early hours on Monday night, dreading the trial's resumption in yet another way.

Jake can feel the difference in the courtroom immediately. Eyes everywhere, burning a hole in his skin. Steven's motion to adjourn because of the prejudicial effect of the kidnapping and the demand for his release, is denied, although the judge, for what it's worth, instructs the jury that there is no evidence that Jake knows or has had any communication with those responsible for the kidnapping, and that nothing can be inferred regarding the current case from that event. The faces of the jurors tell Jake he's in trouble. "We need to delay," he says to Steven. "Even for just a few days." Steven nods in agreement.

And during the day he objects to as much as possible. He dithers and loses his place, repeats questions, asks endless and irrelevant questions, makes unwinnable motions to dismiss and generally makes himself almost as hated as Jake. Only one witness is heard during the entire day. It is one of the police officers who interviewed Jake.

Officer Stern testifies regarding Jake's alibis. Jake has claimed he was home with Julie on all the relevant dates. The notes from those interviews are entered into evidence – over Steven's objections, of course. The interviews with Julie, in which she also claimed that she was home the entire night, are the problem. She wasn't home the entire time. Her bank records show she used her card on two of the nights in question. A restaurant bill paid at 8:30 pm on one of the nights and a withdrawal from a city pub ATM at a bit after 9 pm on another night. Jake feels a moment of dread – not that their lie has been discovered but that Julie had an affair. He feels it with a certainty that is visceral. He wants to turn around but can't. Julie is looking down. I cannot see her face.

The officer also testifies that they examined Jake's phone and EFTPOS records and on the nights of the various attacks, his phone was not used for between 1 and 3 days before and after each attack.

"And do you have a view of why that might have occurred?"

"The phone registers location, so our belief is that Mr Votek didn't take his phone with him on any of these trips."

"How long were these phone silences?"

"The rail line, over 24 hours. Canberra three days. Bowen just under three days. The two actions on the Downs, around 35 hours."

"Did Mr Votek's phone records show similar silences outside of those days and times?"

"No, several hours – not including overnight – was the longest."

"And over how long a period did you examine the records?"

"We went back 18 months. The anomalies began with the sabotaging of the rail line and ended shortly after the tugs in Bowen were destroyed."

"In relation to the EFTPOS, did those records reveal any unusual use patterns?"

"Yes, like with his phone, there is no use of the card during any of the attacks and for a bit of time before and after. Also, either one or two days before each of the four attacks, Mr Votek withdrew several hundred dollars cash. Outside of these times, he was very consistent. He took $250 out every Monday."

"And why would he have taken out cash before the attacks?"

"The same reason. His location can be identified from where he uses his card, so he was careful never to use the card when he travelled for these activities. So, we surmise it was used to pay for petrol and food while he was away."

During this testimony Steven makes numerous spurious objections, seeks sidebars, slows the testimony down to a snail's pace.

When it's time to cross examine, he dithers, becomes clumsy – dropping entire folders of papers and asking for brief recesses, which he then extends as long as possible. All while trying to counter the officer's damaging testimony.

"Officer, how long was Ms Harber out on the nights in question?"

"I'm afraid we don't know that."

"And what do her absences tell you about Jake's whereabouts?"

"I don't understand."

"You're implying that Ms Harber's failure to tell you about these instances out of the house suggests that she is lying about being home with Mr Votek. Do her absences tell you that she didn't spend the night at home?"

"No, they don't."

"And do you have any evidence that she didn't spend her nights and the following mornings at home?"

"No, sir, I don't."

"Did Mr Votek ever claim that Ms Harber was home every hour that he was?"

"I'd have to check."

"Here's his statement Officer Stern."

Stern reads, but he knows as the jury knows, he isn't going to find any such statement from Jake.

When he looks up, he gives a small shake of his head, his sallow eyes like puddles beneath a street lamp. "No, sir, Mr Votek did not ever make that claim.".

"So, once more Mr Stern, what do these EFTPOS records actually tell you? Do they tell you anything more than Ms Harber wasn't with Mr Votek 24 hours a day on the days in question?"

"Not on their own, no, they don't."

"Now in relation to these phone silences, which you attribute to Jake's devious mind; is it possible that Mr Votek was ill during the period when the silences occurred? Is it possible the phone was broken, the bill not paid, or the battery flat?

"Possible, yes, but the coincidence is pretty telling."

"Did you investigate any of the multiple possible explanations for both the phone silence and the extra withdrawals?"

"No sir, we felt no need to do so."

*

That evening the kidnapper releases a photo of the child locked in a cellar, barefoot and obviously distressed. In addition to Jake's release, they are now demanding a million dollars ransom.

In the courtroom the next day Jake doesn't know where to look. He is being judged and he's afraid.

Officer Stern continues to testify. Jake, in his first interview with police, denied having a welder's ticket. The police found it and Wilson is hammering the fact that both Julie and Jake have been caught out in lies.

They didn't find the welding equipment but the lie hurts.

A neighbour from Highgate Hill, William Tyre testifies that several years ago, he saw Jake welding in the garage – fixing a bed head. Jake had totally forgotten.

The most damning piece of evidence though comes on the last day of the week and the last day of the prosecution case.

Detective Ingrid Balke takes the stand.

"Detective, what was your role in the investigation into the various attacks?"

"Two of the attacks used hydrochloric acid to destroy equipment. My role was to find who purchased it and where."

"Now is hydrochloric acid restricted at all?"

"No, it's commonly available and currently there are no restrictions on its sale except that those selling it must have their chemical handling ticket."

"When you say it's commonly available, what are its most common uses?"

"It's used in industry. It's used to make chlorides, refine ores and in the production of some metals."

"What kind of businesses sell hydrochloric acid?"

"Generally, chemical business geared towards industry, but in smaller quantities hardware outlets like Bunnings carry it as well."

"And what did you discover?"

"Well, we began with hardware stores and we began with the assumption that the acid would have been purchased with cash. We had ascertained that Mr Votek was very careful not to use electronic cards. We didn't detect a large withdrawal in the days prior to the use of the acid, so we deduced he had purchased smaller quantities and had sufficient available cash. We then identified the hardware outlets closest to Mr Votek's home that carried the acid. There were two in Rocklea that we thought were the most likely. We interviewed staff, checked sale records and finally when that didn't uncover anything useful, we went through security camera footage for five days before the attacks, assuming that Mr Votek would not want the acid around his home for very long. We found him, both taking the acid off the shelves and purchasing it and leaving with two five litre bottles of acid."

Wilson shows the footage. It's clearly Jake. He's not wearing a hat or sunglasses and the jury can see Jake staring at the image of himself in what is close to horror.

"Now, Inspector, when you questioned Mr Votek, was he asked whether he had purchased hydrochloric acid?"

"Yes we did and Mr Votek denied purchasing any acid."

"I have no further questions Your Honour."

Steven is going to have his work cut out. He approaches Inspector Balke slowly.

"Inspector, what are the home uses of hydrochloric acid?"

"It's not generally recommended for home use because it's so powerful."

"On the bottles sold by Bunnings, what home uses are noted?"

"I don't know, sir."

Steven hands a photocopy of the label to the bailiff.

"So, you weren't aware it can be used to clean stains off metal?"

"No sir I wasn't."

"Or that diluted it can be used to clean bricks?"

"No sir, I wasn't."

"Or that it can be used to clean tiles and grout?"

"I wasn't aware of any of those uses."

"Do you have any evidence regarding how the hydrochloric acid was used by Mr Votek?"

"No sir, I don't, but..."

"And are you able to determine whether the hydrochloric acid used to damage machinery was the same as the hydrochloric acid sold by Bunnings?"

"No sir, we weren't, but,"

"Thank you, Inspector, you've answered the question." Steven turns to the judge. "No further questions."

The prosecution case closes and once the jury is excused and leaves, Jake closes his eyes and tries to still the chaos that is buffeting him. Steven looks troubled. "We need to look at plan B," he says quietly. "Today hurt."

CHAPTER 55

Ian sits in his office and stares at the gum tree that is flowering outside his window. How strange it seems that a tree offers itself to the world in order to propagate. In economics that would make no sense he thinks. But the tree flowers and the insects and birds come and not only does the plant propagate but it feeds the world around it.

He remembers Jake telling him how the coordination of flowering, migrations, seasons and the appearance of birds and insects was getting out of sync. Some trees flowering early and pollen eating birds not being there and so plant and bird both suffer.

Ian's life feels horribly out of sync.

Ian didn't attend court today but Julie told him what happened, that the evidence is mounting even though it's circumstantial. He feels the shadow of loss move over him again. After Mary's death, finding Sofia was as close to a cure as he was going to find. If he loses Jake... He can't finish the thought.

Julie has taken sleeping tablets and gone to bed. Tarek started crying but Julie didn't awaken. Sofia takes Tarek and walks outside into the shadows of moonlight. She begins to sing and Tarek calms. It isn't hunger that wakens him, but the disturbances around him. Tarek picks up every vibration, every arrhythmia, but doesn't understand them yet. Sofia sings a Czech song of the moon. She has a lovely husky tone and soon Tarek sleeps part in shadow, part in light, wholly in song.

Who am I, lovely Tarek? Sofia asks the sleeping child sprawled on her lap like the moonlight itself. Am I what I have forgotten as well as what I invent? You are the only Tarek I know, although I know I knew another Tarek long ago. He is the faintest of shadows. A face I have on my wall. That is all. He may become real that way. Does forgetting matter? Does knowing matter? Can we replace the holes in our spirit with stories or drawings or songs or moonlight? Is that good enough? Ivan tells me about climate change and Jake and Mary who was a physicist who never spoke of her passion. I lost my past. She put hers away.

Why do babies never remember their life as babies? Do they forget? Need to forget? They remember so many things that they learn – how to walk, crawl, eat, speak, recognise faces, love, paint, but most do not remember any events at all until they are three or four. Sofia smiles at this young trusting child. She has already drawn many portraits of him, but she will remember the image of the moment before sleep, his blue eyes looking outward at the sky or moon or the branches of the jacaranda, blond hair partially bathed in the light of a yellow moon and partially from the light coming through the window. It is quiet except for the rustle of a few night creatures.

Poor Jake. His face is hard, she says to Tarek. That reminds her of something, but she cannot catch it. Her capreolate memory. So many tendrils so tantalisingly close to something. I have seen hard men like that she says – to herself now – and knows it must have been in Sarajevo. Ivan told her about Sarajevo, told her some things anyway. The house where they grew up. The hills around the city. How they went for picnics there once long ago. None of that rang any bells but now it's stored in the artificial memory house that is her mind. Artificial? Real? Memories are not that simple.

But it's true that memory matters, knowing matters, just as loving matters. She forgot everything but still speaks Bosnian, still knows how to draw and paint. She has changed even though she may never know that. She is gentler, less certain, more willing to embrace perspectives that are new. She was such a difficult woman to disagree with in Sarajevo. Too smart, too certain. Funny to think that I, the dzelat, was not as zealous as Sofia, not by a long shot.

Odd, that so many people want to forget things, want to not know and Sofia has no choice but to have that kind of emptiness. And in the emptiness, she is building a new history out of bits and pieces she finds lying around. Perhaps it is like a painting and Sofia will reinvent her life one layer at a time, a mix of memory and invention and something deeper, more elemental.

What does it mean to invent a life? Is this 'history' a lie? How can it be a lie when it is real? Sofia is real. She touches Tarek's hair, his foot. So real.

Belief matters too. But belief doesn't make something real. It makes it matter, it makes it something to be cared for, but it is not the reality itself. It is like the gossamer threads of a giant net that links the branches of a tree, that connects leaf to leaf and perhaps even moonlight to root.

Tarek sleeps in her arms. "I don't need belief or memory to feel you draped with moonlight, to know that you trust me lovely Tarek," she whispers to the sleeping child.

I feel a deep sadness tonight. Being dead isn't so hard, but being aware that you no longer are, that your being is only to see and hear and experience, like an echo, the lives of others, that is sometimes hard to bear.

For so long, I thought I had a purpose in being here – to be Jake's guide, a small voice in his head. I thought I had a certain wisdom that war and death taught me that I could pass to Jake, particularly when he decided he must act.

There was no purpose and my wisdom was wishful thinking. I fell into a role and in the chaos of war it seemed important and now, in the chaos of history, it seems meaningless. I picked up a gun. I killed. I saw death that I caused. I pretend this wasn't me. That I was always someone else. I killed one woman during the war. She was a spy for the Serbs and I strangled her. She stared at me the whole time. Not afraid, not angry, resigned and looking into my soul to see if anything remained. I didn't care. I didn't really like killing but I liked feeling powerful, liked feeling so important that I had been made a keeper of life and death. I liked to think I treated that power well and with respect. But I don't know. I thought I found myself here because I was an honourable soul and I was to help Jake. Now I don't know that either. I suspect now I was being punished, am being punished.

*

Steven, Jake and Wilson are seated in Judge di Maio's chambers. Judge di Maio turns to Steven, "Your call counsellor."

"Your Honour, Mr Votek would like to change his plea in relation to two charges. The destruction of mining equipment and the destruction of the oil rig, he would like to plead guilty to only the criminal, not the terrorism charges. We will however argue the defence of necessity."

Judge di Maio looks at Steven severely.

"I presume this means that you will argue that the prosecution hasn't made a case of a terrorist act in relation to those charges and necessity will only be plead for the criminal charges?"

"That's correct, Your Honour. We'd also ask that you instruct the jury on the required elements of a necessity defence prior to us presenting the defence as it will otherwise simply confuse them."

"Counsellor, you do realise that the necessity defence is rarely successful outside a very limited range of activities? Does your client understand the risks associated with this defence?"

"He does, Your Honour." Steven isn't exactly thrilled with this plan B. The necessity defence is highly risky.

"Will you be calling any additional witnesses?" Wilson asks.

"None that aren't already on the witness list," Steven replies.

When court reconvenes, Judge di Maio instructs the jury on the change in circumstances. "Mr Votek is now pleading guilty to the two criminal charges related to the destruction of drilling equipment and destruction of the rig on the Darling Downs. He is not pleading guilty to the other three charges, nor is he pleading guilty to any of the charges that his actions were terrorist acts. In pleading guilty, Mr Votek is going to be arguing what is called the necessity defence. I want to out-line the requirements of that defence to you now so that you will understand the reason for the testimony you will be hearing. The necessity defence is used when a defendant believes in acting as he did he prevented a greater crime or loss. A classic example is breaking into a house – a criminal act – that is on fire, in order to save someone. To demonstrate necessity the defence must show, one, that a situation of imminent peril exists; two, that the defendant honestly believes on reasonable grounds that it is necessary for him to do the acts alleged in order to avoid the threatened danger or harm. Finally, the acts must be proportionate to the threat."

Jake watches the jury as they receive these instructions. He can see that pleading guilty proves that he's a liar to some of the jurors. No one will give him credit for coming clean this late.

The basis for the necessity defence is going to be climate change.

Wilson tries to short circuit the defence by agreeing to stipulate to the existence of anthropogenic climate change, but Steven is prepared for this.

"Your Honour, the issue is not simply whether climate change occurs but whether it represents an imminent peril. I assume that Mr Wilson won't stipulate to that."

Di Maio turns to Wilson who shakes his head. "No, Your Honour, we won't stipulate imminent peril."

The first witness is Professor Arno Hensen from ANU, a leading expert on climate change. He was once a sceptic, even received funds from the Institute of Public Policy, a conservative American think tank. He explains that he used the money to reevaluate all the original data upon which claims of climate change were based. It took two years and it was simply inescapable that the measurements of the accumulation of carbon dioxide were correct; that they correlated absolutely with industrial activity and that these gases were the only explanation for the warming that had occurred. He explained too that the heat is not only in the atmosphere but is absorbed by the oceans, which is causing not only climate instability but fears that the oceans will change in unpredictable ways, including the loss of most of the world's reefs, including our Great Barrier Reef.

He's a good witness. His conversion is compelling and he is clear and concise. He keeps his explanations simple without making it simple. He's also a nice looking guy.

He moves on to the predictions associated with climate change. "This is more difficult because we are talking about an incredibly large and complex system that has many forces acting on it. But if we go back to the 1980s when the first predictions were being made, there are two things to keep in mind. The predictions have all been correct in the main and every prediction has underestimated the speed with which change would come and the severity of the change. When I say they have been mainly true, there are more detailed predictions that have been wrong, but the big ones: warming climate, more severe weather, less stability in the system, sea level rise, sea temperature rising, melting of ice at the poles and slowing of calcification rates in corals as levels of ocean CO_2 rise have all been shown to be true – except without exception the rate and severity have been greater than predicted. The models are tweaked constantly so the predictions are becoming more accurate as more and more data comes to hand. We don't simply create a model and act as though we have every setting right."

Hensen explains why this human induced warming is significantly and dangerously different from historical warming periods.

"So Professor, what is our current position?"

"We are currently on track for a 4-6 degree increase in temperature based on current emissions and current trends. This is well beyond our worst case modelling that has been generally looking at the impacts of a 2.5-4 degree increase. We need to remember that our current status is reflecting the emissions released twenty years ago. We have twenty years of increases we cannot prevent even if we stopped emissions today."

"What are the imminent threats, Professor, associated with climate change?"

Hensen exhales deeply. "There are a number of existing harms that are being driven by climate change that will become significantly worse without immediate action. These risks are imminent even though they may not fully play out for several decades. That's because within a few years, they will be locked into the climate system. We can't undo them. These are already causing both human and other deaths. Extreme weather events have increased fourfold globally and the number of deaths is on a similar trajectory. In Australia, drought, bush fire and flooding in the last decade have all reached unprecedented frequency and scale. But it will get worse unless we act now. These are existing as well as imminent threats.

"The worst for me is the threat that the Great Barrier Reef will not survive the next decade.

"Other imminent threats are equally concerning. Recent research strongly indicates that the projected linear progression of Antarctic ice melt may be wrong and that we may be facing a three to six meter sea level rise within several decades. Most of our population lives in that narrow lowlying coastal strip."

"Would you agree Professor that we are already living in a changed climate?"

"There is no question about it. Now, climates change all the time, but the changes we are seeing are not a natural and gradual change but a rapid shift and that's part of the reason it is so dangerous. It's a bit like driving on a motorway and one truck, two, ten suddenly cut across four lanes of traffic without signalling or looking. Rapid shifts bring rapid and usually chaotic responses and many, many parts of the system can't respond or don't respond in a way that will work."

"Can you give an example Professor?"

"Polar bears. Smart creatures, but the pack ice, which they depend on, is disappearing. Their response is to travel and swim further and further to find pack ice and food. They will almost certainly go extinct in our lifetimes."

"Is there anything that can be done to prevent these risks from becoming real?"

"Yes. First, we must move away from fossil fuels immediately. The technology is already here for power and transport. We could become 100% renewable within ten years if there was any commitment from those who rule us. Secondly, scientists believe we can increase the capacity of the land to store carbon that is already in the atmosphere by changing farming and land use practices. That means maintaining forests, planting millions of trees, making the soils healthy, using fewer, much fewer chemicals and synthetic fertilisers."

When Hensen finishes testifying, Jake watches the jury. Some are looking stricken. Others conflicted – as though what they have just heard contradicts so much that they believe or have heard elsewhere and they are adrift. A few are openly disbelieving.

Wilson is well prepared. He knows that the weakness in the picture painted by Hensen is uncertainty.

"Professor, you have testified that the models are tweaked as new data comes in. Would you agree that another way of saying this is that as errors appear, miscalculations are shown, you correct them?"

"Yes, that's basically correct."

"In other words, there are enormous uncertainties in our understanding as well as enormous gaps in our knowledge."

"That's true, although..."

"Thank you, Professor. Isn't it correct that in the 60s and 70s scientists predicted an ice age was coming as a result of climatic shifts?"

"That's true. A long time ago now."

"And didn't Professor Paul Erlich at Stanford predict in 1971 that England wouldn't even exist in the year 2000?"

"Yes, I'm familiar with that bet."

"In its most recent report, the International Panel on Climate Change looked at 73 different models of what the climate might do. Would you agree that 73 different models, using different data and making different predictions, is almost by definition an admission that no one knows what's going to happen?"

"Yes, but...."

"And if no one knows what's going to happen, then how can you speak of imminent dangers?"

"Can I use an analogy to answer that? Imagine releasing all the dangerous animals from Taronga zoo. You have pretty good information on lions, tigers, elephants, snakes, bears, wolves, but you have no accurate way of predicting what they will do, where they will go or who they'll attack. But you know they are dangerous and that is not uncertain at all."

"Professor, would you agree that identifying something as dangerous is not the same as an imminent threat? In other words, the fact that wild and potentially dangerous animals have escaped doesn't tell you anything about an imminent danger."

"That's true, but I'd argue that lacking knowledge of the specific danger doesn't make it any less imminent."

"No further questions."

Steven calls Jennifer Blake next, a Professor of Politics at the University of Sydney. She describes the strange political response to climate change. The moments of concern mixed with the political calculations that ultimately decided the issue. The policies and reversals, the incentives and the refusal to stop subsidising fossil fuels with billions of dollars a year.

"In some ways, it's understandable. Who in politics that wants to remain in politics is going to tell voters that life as they know it has to end? And who amongst them is going to say, we're going to make hard decisions now, really hard decisions so you don't face a completely altered and unstable world in the future. A future contested by the fossil fuel industry and many denialists, a future, which in its details is unknowable. If things fall apart because of climate change that's better than us having to legislate radical changes to the way people live, travel and consume. We will never occupy office again. And so, almost nothing happens. In fact, worse, our emissions are increasing. We agreed in Paris to act to keep temperatures below a 1.5-2 degree increase and we've approved – this year – the largest coal mine in the country. We are not only facing a crisis of climate but a political crisis because this, climate change, is beyond the current capacity of our politicians and our political system to address."

"Would you agree, Professor, that climate change represents an existential – in a political and social sense – crisis?"

"No question."

"What are some of the existential risks to the social and political system that you're most concerned about?"

"There are many but the most immediate is the social instability we're already seeing. The level of civil disobedience and acts of violence against the society are at levels I've never seen in Australia. That is happening now and the risks it brings are imminent but also unpredictable."

"The most concerning risk though, for me, are those forces that will lead to large migrations, very large migrations of people. Sea level rise alone will result in the displacement of enormous numbers of people. A three meter sea level rise will see millions in the Pacific made homeless. We don't know where they'll go because no one has even begun that discussion. Millions in Australia could be displaced by a three meter rise in sea levels. This map shows projected new boundaries of Australia. This is based on a four degree increase but does not account for a rapid rise in sea level due to ice melt. Over 600,000 people will lose their homes, primarily here in Brisbane, Sydney and Adelaide. If this happens rapidly, we simply don't have any means of responding to either the human or structural catastrophe that represents. Trains, roads, power stations, ports, airports all gone. If it happens quickly, political and social instability will be extreme. If climate refugees begin to come here in large numbers – which is likely – we won't be able to stop them all, we won't be able to send them anywhere, Nauru will be under water." She takes a deep breath. "I have two children. I don't want them to live in fear, but I am terrified for them."

"Thank you, Professor, I have nothing more."

Wilson stands wearily, as though this is such a waste of his time. "Professor," – exasperation drips from his voice – "you call this an existential crisis. Are we all going to die?"

"Not all of us."

"So, many of us will die? How many? Who and when?"

"Objection."

"I'll rephrase. Professor how many people will die in this country because of climate change?"

"I don't know."

"Who is in imminent danger of death in this country because of climate change?"

"The poorest are the most at risk."

"You mean the so-called 99%?" Wilson is almost mocking her.

"No, I mean the poorest. Probably around 15% of the population."

"All of them?"

"I don't know."

"And what are they going to die of? Neglect? Mosquitoes? Heat rash?"

"Medical experts have identified a number of different health risks associated with climate change, including heat, mosquito borne diseases and extreme weather."

"When will these deaths start to occur?"

"They are occurring now."

"Ah, so who has died from climate change?"

"I'm afraid I don't have specific names, but..."

"No further questions."

CHAPTER 56

That night, the young kidnapped boy is found safe and well and the kidnapper – a former coal activist who disappeared from the movement several years ago, a young man Jake met several times – is arrested. By morning the police have informed the prosecution that Jake was not involved in any way. When the judge informs the jury of this – on Steven's request – all eyes turn towards him. Jake has no idea where to look or what to do. He leans over towards Steven and whispers, "Should I smile? Laugh? Steven smiles and gives him a hug, paternal. "This will do nicely," Steven whispers back and rubs Jake's head as though he is a young boy.

The final expert witness is Michelle Lindley, another Professor – of psychology, sociology and statistics. She has returned from a posting at Princeton to testify.

Steven knows he needs to handle this testimony carefully. If it's done well, it will confront the jury but not alienate them. This is a calculated risk. Those in denial don't want to be confronted, but those with open minds need to know and recognise denial at work.

"Professor, your recent expertise is in the nature of denial with a focus on climate change, is that correct?"

"Yes, that's right."

Lindley is another well-chosen witness. She has a round, avuncular face, grey hair and looks completely unthreatening. She laughs at herself easily and comes across as gentle, even harmless.

"Professor, can you tell us a bit about the psychology of denial?

"Absolutely not." She laughs. "My idea of a joke." She laughs again. Not all of the jury get it. "Denial is a defence mechanism we all use. It's a mechanism used to protect us from information we find too difficult to process or believe. We see denial in many trauma cases, sexual abuse cases, war zones, dysfunctional families – those are the ones that are clinically common, but denial is everywhere. We all fail to see things that we don't want to see. My sister, bless her socks, is in denial about the world. She finds it all too much. She can't listen to news about murders, or politics or automobile accidents. She refuses to read newspapers or watch the news. She doesn't want to know because it hurts too much so she shuts it out. And that's fine. It means she doesn't have much to do with being a citizen, but she is happier for that choice. That's denial too. So, we all have it and we all do it to varying degrees."

"Climate denial is then one form of denial."

"Absolutely. Climate change has psychologists more engaged than they've been in years. This is in some ways the mother of all denials. It is both personal and cultural. We saw this to some extent during the Holocaust – the refusal of many, including many, many Jews to believe that Jews were being carted off to death camps. We've seen it recently with the Inquiry into sexual abuse in schools and churches here in Australia. A willing blindness that is both cultural and personal and we're seeing it now with climate change."

"Why do you call it the mother of all denials?"

"We deny for many reasons: ideology, fear, worldviews, paranoia, guilt, faith, beliefs, a brain that doesn't easily recognise future danger very well. A Harvard psychologist calls them dragons. And climate change has many, many dragons. Many different mechanisms working together in many different ways mean that convincing those who are in denial is incredibly hard. And in psychology it's pretty axiomatic that in order to fix a 'problem' it first has to be recognised as one. And you see in the world of climate change there is little personal or even cultural recognition that denial is a problem."

"Professor, have you worked then with those who not only believe in climate change but are trying at a social level to convince those with power to do something about it?"

"I have. It is a familiar psychological issue. It has been called the Cassandra Complex – those who possess knowledge and belief that many refuse to believe. Being believed matters, whether it's family, friends or your community, not being believed is psychologically profoundly difficult and often traumatic. You see two classic responses – internalising, suppression, repression, forgetting and all sorts of traumas arising from that. Or you see anger, lashing out, even acting out."

"Professor, you had the chance to examine my client, Jake Votek?"

"I have," and she nods and gives a small smile – seen by all – to Jake.

"Could you tell us your assessment?"

"Gladly. I sat down with Jake in prison and spent 2 hours, both questioning Jake and simply discussing his life and beliefs. Jake is a smart, passionate young man. He is deeply in love with his partner Julie – and he has a similar passion for the planet. Speaking with him, even after so much time in prison, you can hear that he sees the living world around him as his companions, friends, source of his strength, a place to hide or love. I am not like that – and most aren't – but for those who are, nature becomes like a family. Psychology is only just learning about this world of love, which until recently has been invisible to us. A kind of denial too, I suspect. Climate change is for Jake something that threatens that family in real – and current – ways. He has no doubts about climate change at all; he is clear that his belief is backed by a thorough reading of the science and an understanding of the shortcomings and mistakes of the current science. As the effects of climate change become more visible and for him more horrible, and as nothing is done, he has become incredibly angry. So, to go back to the Holocaust example, he is one of the Jews who decided he had to take up arms to protect his family and people."

"So would you agree that Jake had a belief that he must act in order to protect himself and his family?"

"Absolutely."

"And was that belief reasonable?"

"It's funny you know...I was going to say, 'if you believe in climate change, of course it's reasonable.' But like Jake I have no doubt at all that climate change is occurring now – and the kind of self-censorship that I just engaged in, demonstrates how deeply this issue has divided us and how much harder it has made it for all of us to speak the truth. Yes, in the world we live in where climate change is occurring now and where no action is being taken by those charged with responsibility and power to do so, his actions were based on a reasonable belief that such action as he took was necessary. And can I add that it's important to remember that reasonable belief, in my view, means a belief based on knowledge. Denial of climate change is a belief, but by any psychological standard it's not reasonable."

Wilson stands and then remains for a moment, head down behind the prosecution table. Finally, he moves forward. "Professor, if I believe that fluoride has been put in the water to poison us and that belief is based on the fact that fluoride is a by-product of building nuclear weapons, and no one in power listens to me, and I resort to acts of violence, I destroy a fluoride plant or blow up a dam, is that based on a reasonable belief that my actions were necessary?"

"It's arguable, yes."

"And if one hundred years ago I had destroyed machinery because it would be responsible for bringing us climate change, would that belief have been reasonable?"

"Probably not one hundred years ago."

"In your assessment of Mr Votek, did Mr Votek indicate whether he thought his actions would succeed in protecting us? In other words, would his actions convince the world and those in power to act on climate change?"

"Not really. He acted consciously. He grappled with what it would take to make the world respond. He took those actions he thought might lead there."

"In other words, he took actions that he did not believe would accomplish what he knew needed to happen."

"He knew he couldn't accomplish this on his own and he hoped that the steps he took would lead to it being accomplished. If I could use the burning house metaphor, imagine the house is very large and he knows he won't have the time to search every room, but he can break down the door and perhaps find and rescue someone before others arrive."

"I have nothing further."

Wilson knew he was treading a fine line. He didn't want to give oxygen to arguments which significantly broaden the necessity defence, but he does want to make it clear that the uncertainties and scale of the threat that Jake is supposed to have been responding to are way too large to accommodate the real purpose of a necessity defence.

Court is adjourned. Tomorrow, character witnesses and the defence will then rest. Then closing arguments and summaries and the jury will retire.

Steven looks very tired. He doesn't quite know what to say to Jake. He has done well, but he can't know if he has done enough. Jake feels as though each day of trial is a step closer to the abyss, the rest of his life abyss.

Ian attended today and he too is showing the signs of wear. Julie and Ian sat close, shoulders touching. They are leaning on each other and soon neither will have the strength to support the other. They were so unprepared for this.

In Sarajevo we had warning, we had years of drumbeating and chest banging and then we had war – a very different reality. All of us struggled with making a place, forging an identity and life in those circumstances. Some failed. Many failed. But I have to say, this is worse. This is waiting for the hand of Justice – or injustice – to fall. Words are the only tool one has and no one has control over their own destiny or even the illusion of control.

I remember days where everything went wrong, or it felt that way or it felt as though one small incident was that last straw and you wanted to simply give up, to sleep, to shed your skin and melt into a peaceful earth. That is how Ian and Julie look today.

That is kind of how I feel too. I'm dead. It's hard to care about climate change, or burning houses or the stupid choices we make as a species, but I care about Jake and I care about who I was, what I did, the choices I made. I became a dzelat only because I could narrow my view to the needs of today and tomorrow, to the needs of me and my family and community. But I wonder if – like Janos – I had seen the larger picture I would have chosen differently? I suspect I would have seen this as one more brutal war with no victors and fled to an island in Greece. Jake never had that choice. If you're not a billionaire building a spaceship and biosphere somewhere on another planet, the choices are few. You must stay here and this 'war' is everywhere.

*

The character witnesses are all very similar. They all say nice things as expected and probably have as much weight as ashen fluff. Garth testifies. He testified looking and speaking directly at Jake. "You're an important man," he said. "We all know that the world we live and work in isn't healthy. It's not a healthy political system, it's not a healthy ecosystem and it's not a healthy society. And you challenge us, force us to confront things that are incredibly hard to confront. That's pretty special. Thanks."

Wilson doesn't cross examine and spends most of the time reading a document or whispering to his colleagues.

The courtroom is tense on the day of closing arguments.

The prosecution begins. "It began with five acts. With the sabotage of a rail line, the gluing shut of doors at Mineral House, the burning and destruction of the tugs in Bowen, the destruction of drilling equipment and destruction of a rig. Those acts committed by the defendant Jake Votek have led to many, many more acts, all done in the name of protecting the climate, protecting the planet. Those subsequent acts have seen people die, people with children and wives. Those first five acts lead directly to those others and while Mr Votek is not charged yet with any subsequent act, I lay those at his door too. They would not have occurred absent Mr Votek's acts of terrorism.

"Those five acts were not random. They were not done for personal profit or from any personal motives. They were done to further an ideology, a belief, to force governments and industry to change to suit him. This is the definition of acts of terrorism. They are criminal acts, too, make no mistake about it – they damaged or destroyed millions of dollars' worth of property, but first and foremost, this was an attempt by Mr Jake Votek to bring down the state, to end the exploitation of fossil fuels, to put an end to governments supporting fossil fuels.

"Some of you may agree that needs to occur, but we are a democracy. We have ways to make that happen.

Wilson then summarises the evidence against Jake. He walks through every crime, every piece of circumstantial evidence, repeating again and again, 'But there's more'. It is hard to believe that anyone else could have committed these acts.

He paints the necessity defence as proof that Jake is a liar. "He wants to stand on the high moral ground as one who would protect the planet, but doesn't have the moral fortitude to admit to what he has done supposedly to protect all of us."

I watch the jury. I cannot read their faces, but there is a prickly silence in the courtroom, a tension with many different arms. Ian leans forward, an intensity in him that, in truth, scares me.

Wilson reminds the jury of all the holes in his alibis, the radio silence each time a crime was committed.

"Jake Votek may love his partner, he may love the planet, but unlike most of us, unlike you, he is capable not only of lying but of acts of violence, acts of terrorism.

"Mr Votek has, in an act of desperation, argued the necessity defence. This defence is normally used when someone is charged for a crime committed while saving someone's life. Necessity is immediate, definite. It is about preventing an imminent and clear harm that will otherwise occur. His defence is like that of a cult that believes the end is nigh and uses that belief to justify whatever actions they want to take. A necessity defence cannot be used that way.

"I ask you to reject this defence and to find Mr Votek guilty on all charges – both criminal and terrorist." Wilson looks over the jury again and gives them all the smallest of nods, as though to say, 'I trust you all'.

Steven looks energised. Yesterday he was old, today he is angry. A good angry. Or at least that's what I hope. I am nervous. Jake watched Wilson's closing arguments with an intensity and bewilderment that left me mourning for him. The man Wilson was describing isn't Jake, wasn't even vaguely familiar to Jake. How does the law manage to do that? I suppose we all do that – reinvent ourselves and others in ways that fit our needs.

I can't say who Jake is anymore, only how I know Jake.

Steven faces the jury quietly. "When I first started this case, I took it on because I am interested in the rights of the disenfranchised, in the rights of protestors and environmental issues. I took it on, in other words, as a lawyer. I am standing here today somewhat differently. I am here to argue for the life of a young man I have grown to like enormously, a young man whose passion for protecting the world we all live in has left me feeling ashamed at how little I do. I consider Jake a friend. He is not a violent man. He is not a man driven by hate, but by love. When I heard Mr Wilson call Jake a terrorist, I thought this isn't true. It isn't true legally and it isn't true in a personal sense either. This is an odd way to begin closing arguments. I planned to begin differently. But I am changed because of my association with Jake, changed for the better, and I want you to understand this man as I do. I will come back to this soon."

"I want to remind you of the definition of a terrorist act in our laws. Before I do, I want to say that in my view the laws are so poorly conceived and drafted that they are intended to cast this gigantic net that makes millions of us – and I would include me – suspect. It's important that you understand that this law has been used to imprison people simply for where they travel, for their religion, for associations with bad people. For having a brother who does wrong. Remember Dr Haneef? David Hicks? These are people held, tortured or convicted wrongly. Sometimes for their looks, their culture or poor choices they made – but not violence; sometimes for simply being an object of suspicion. In prison Jake helped a prisoner who was serving 15 years because his brother planned a terrorism act which his brother was never aware of. I want you to remember this as you deliberate. You cannot change the laws but you can understand how poorly they work and you can reject them in this case."

Steven then walks through what the law requires and the circumstantial nature of the evidence. "How many times did you hear the prosecution witnesses say, 'consistent with' – a term that tells you so little it shouldn't even be called evidence."

Last, Steven deals with the necessity defence. "I had a case not long ago representing a family in detention on Nauru. Their son was seven years old. He was showing a variety of signs of mental illness that were expressing as physical problems and self-abuse, which were getting worse. They received no help. The father became so desperate that he beat up a guard, took his keys and gun and broke out of the centre and checked his son into the underequipped hospital in Nauru. He left the gun in a field. He was arrested sitting by his son's side. The hospital refused to let the child go. The father was charged with a criminal act. The necessity defence was used in that case and he was found innocent.

"Jake was a desperate man too. He has worked for years on trying to get government to do something about climate change but nothing changed. In fact, it became worse. You have heard the evidence. The building is burning. When a house burns, you don't have lawyers come in first and say, well, you know we don't have exact knowledge of where it will burn first or hottest. You act."

"Imagine Jake's dilemma. There is no single answer to climate change, no single act that any individual can do to rescue us – but that doesn't mean one doesn't act. You do what you can as an individual. Imagine you're in the burning house and a door is locked and you don't know if the child is in there so you obliterate the door with an axe. The child isn't in there. Would anyone even think of arresting you for property damage?

"You have seen how much Jake has to lose. Every day his partner has been in this courtroom. It is hard to miss how much he loves that woman and she loves him. He made a choice to take a step that put all of that at risk. He made a choice hoping and believing it would matter. Jake acted to protect himself, his family and all of us.

The question isn't whether he succeeded – because he hasn't – but whether he was acting out of a reasonable belief not only that this was right but necessary."

"I urge you to find Jake Votek innocent."

And so it ends. The packed courtroom empties slowly. Like the tide in a river emptying quickly through the heads in a medley of currents. Voices are kind of hushed. The jury is gone. The judge is gone. Julie once again steals an embrace with Jake. Steven watches the shuffling of the crowd with a kind of sadness. He hasn't felt such weight from a case in a long time. Ian listens to the conversations that pass by him as he stands there like an emptied vessel. "Good closings," someone says. As though this is only theatre.

I am bone tired. Impossible, but still true.

EPILOGUE

CHAPTER 57

There is a rose gum outside Ian's window. It glows pink in the morning light and Ian insists on watching his tree at dawn with a coffee in his hand. He is outside this morning. It's cooler here than in Brisbane and he is still not used to the quiet. Actually, it's not quiet at all, but there are no sounds of the city here. Birds mainly. He loves the whip birds. The call and response that always comes.

He can hear Tarek talking to Julie. Tarek comes out with a bowl full of seed. He feeds the birds every morning. The finches and doves. Sometimes he gets mealworms and feeds the robins by hand. When they land on his hand he is utterly still, a stillness that seems remarkable for a two year old boy. Julie watches him adoringly.

Julie suggested moving down here. She was the only one working. Sofia can sell her paintings anywhere. They are in Sydney, Byron and Brisbane and in high demand. They moved nine months ago.

Since they moved here, after the trial and verdict, Julie is working two or three days a week at different centres. She has started a veggie garden, which is now a fortress, keeping out wallabies, pademelons and possums.

She gives Ian a hug. She sometimes calls him dad now. He built the garden beds – a level of technical accomplishment beyond anything he'd ever done. He was so excited that Julie had little plaques made for each of the three beds, 'Lovingly and expertly constructed by Ian Votek'.

Sofia comes out with a walking stick. She is too afraid of snakes to walk in the bush or even along the trails, but every morning she walks three kilometres down to the intersection with Dead Man's Road. She still doesn't believe that's the name of the road, but it's true. She knows all the neighbours in her fashion. And speaks with them all – in her fashion. Her English remains...uneven. A bit like a cubist painting, with fragments of reality scattered between fragments of the imagined.

After her walk she will paint. She often sets the easel up in front of the house, near the creek, facing a wonderful grove of brush box and tallow wood. Most of her paintings, though, are still in one way or another about Sarajevo.

Sofia and Ian are incredibly close. Ian likes to say they are both reimagined beings, nothing like what they once were or ever thought they'd be. They sit together on the swinging chair in the evening drinking a wine, their shoulders touching, and speak in Bosnian. Sofia has remembered little of her past and Ian has told her little of what she described in her letters. She doesn't need that history now, maybe not ever.

Both watch Julie and Jake with concern. They both feel there is little they can say that would help, except to embrace them often.

Jake has been up since dawn, as he has every day for the two weeks he has been home. He pulled lantana for several hours – as he has done most days – and is now sitting down at the end of the paddock by the creek. He often sits there alone staring at the water, watching the turtles surface thinking Jake is no longer there.

Climate change doesn't feel real here – although it is. The life he once had doesn't feel real and the person he once was is neither here nor gone. He has lost something. He calls it his fire spirit. Something that drove him, cursed him, inspired him, incinerated him. It has been replaced by a chasm and as he sits here, he is hoping that space fills with beauty, with mysteries, with love, with sounds. 'The abyss of birds' he thinks. He suddenly hears the piece – long forgotten – in his head. A lone clarinet singing from the depths of an abyss, from the depths of his memory. A call of utter loneliness that no other voice hears or responds to. A piece written in a concentration camp.

His return has been hard. He is a changed man in so many ways. He is not haunted by memories, but he has served two years in a prison that has sucked the soul and life from him. He was convicted of two criminal offences which he will carry with him for the rest of his life. He saw a jury convict him, but also to say to the judge – we accept the necessity of what he did. They didn't accept it as a complete defence, but a court for the first time in Australia's history said climate change is putting us in imminent danger.

That story still lives. The environment movement and Just Disobey were catalysed by the judgement and there is a new vitality in the demands for change.

The Government has desperately tried to rally political support for changing the laws to protect the fossil fuel industry, but the headwinds are now strong.

There is also a more radical reality. The Free Radicals are now a real group. Organised, loud, violent. They have openly advocated attacks on privilege including the issuing of death sentences. They printed and posted online 'Wanted for Murder' signs for the CEOs of 50 companies, held by them to have killed people both here and overseas. Three of those CEOs have died, four left the country. One shot, several poisoned, one found dead in water. One was floating in Sydney Harbour on a burning barge with the sound of Wagner blasting across the water until the barge, the fire and the music sank beneath the sea. Many arrests have been made but the organisation continues to attract new members. Things fall apart.

Not that Jake derives much pleasure or satisfaction from that. He had to endure one more year in prison. The judge didn't want to encourage more violent acts, but he turned to Jake when sentencing him and said, "Mr Votek, it is a rare event when I feel I am putting in jail an honourable man, but that is what I feel I must do. But I want it known that you – and your lawyer and your family – have taught us something that must go beyond this courtroom."

He remembers all of this with a flatness that haunts him. He watches The Free Radicals with a distance that feels almost infinite. He can just feel the stirrings of life since being freed, but it is like watching a tiny halo of light as one surfaces from the deepest parts of the sea. A part of him knows that acting alone was wrong. It wronged Julie and it wronged the people he worked with. If we're going to dismantle something big, we need to do it together and if we're going to build something new that has to be together too. Those words have many meanings and many roads to follow, but Jake already knows they are true, if only, next time, he chooses more wisely.

When he was released and Julie brought him down here, a place Ian bought for Jake as much as anyone – a wild, beautiful block of subtropical rainforest far away – he felt none of the joy or gratitude he knew he should feel. Ian and Julie both know it is a place that Jake desperately needs if he wants to shed the hard skin he has built around himself. Julie, though, worries there may only be a shell underneath.

At first, he just wanted to go away with Julie. Not even Tarek, not yet, just Julie. She can still reach him, with ease, with a word, a gesture. But even that isn't easy, is often as painful as it is amazing.

"I think we need to make sure you're healthy and as whole as you can be before we go anywhere," she says. It's clear she doesn't want to go, not yet. She struggles with his moodiness but doesn't always recognise her own. She struggles with what he has done, and what he has done to everyone she now loves. Everyone has suffered with Jake and because of Jake. She doesn't feel that his trial and conviction has taught her anything, given her anything. But that's not entirely true either.

She and Jake both need time – but for different things. She has already been waiting far longer than she would ever have chosen. Waiting for him to be free, waiting for him to be Jake again. He has forgotten how to touch her. He has forgotten how to kiss and to make love with her – not just to her. He is still absorbed in his own world and she is still angry, doesn't feel ready to let that go. She doesn't see that she can simply reach deeply into his spirit and wait there, instead of here, at a distance.

She doesn't see her own anger. She doesn't see how his acts have given her a family she has never had before, how Ian has been transformed, in good part by Jake's decisions. He didn't do that, she thinks. Ian did that and Peta did that. I did that. He chose for all of them but never asked. But, and she knows this well, no matter what he's done and how angry she feels, her love for him doesn't change. The landscape around it is different – denser, harder to navigate, thorny – but at its core is this wondrous love that has barely changed shape at all in the last three years. This miracle she will remember soon enough, but not yet.

When he arrived at this place called Morelia, Jake looked around at the giant trees, swimming holes and deep peace with no expression, except perhaps waiting to see what it was about. A wariness that has become sharper the more his senses have blunted.

She watches him by the clear running water. Once, she would have been next to him. She watches him and it's always the same. He pulls the lantana with a fury that is deep and meticulous. He breaks the branches, stacks them, then pulls out the plant by the roots and makes sure the roots don't touch the ground. He has cleared more in two weeks than anyone has done in the nine months that they've owned this land.

She watches him by the creek. He sits and stares, sometimes as long as an hour, as still as a stump. When he stands, he always drinks deeply from the creek before coming back to the house. Sometimes she thinks the water will magically restore him because she thinks she can't.

Sometimes when he is in the garden, he holds handfuls of soil in his cupped hands. He looks at it, smells it, watches it. She can't begin to penetrate what is happening in his mind.

There is stillness in him that is incredibly deep but also incredibly dark. The line between the still waters and hard stone is very, very thin.

Sofia painted a portrait of Jake after he'd been home a week. Jake had no idea. Sofia showed it to Julie only this morning and she broke out crying. It captured much more of Jake than Julie had been willing to see. His pain and the hardness, yes, but also his losses and his love, still as strong as ever. It's not only Jake that needs to change, she realises, but she does too. She has to forgive this man the impossible burden he carried – and perhaps carries still – in his passion for a planet in such deep trouble. She has to embrace both the love she has and the love he gives. She hugs Sofia. In her still muddled English, Sofia says, "No make like me and Ivan. No lose good man."

Jake finally comes and joins them on the verandah. "Sorry, have to wrestle the demons before coffee," he says with an uncertain smile. Even after two weeks he isn't used to being with family, isn't used to freedom. He is only used to himself and his self-hatred is still quite intense.

He suddenly sees his portrait. Sofia brought the easel and painting out while Jake was weeding. She decided it was time for him to see himself as well. He sits utterly still and stares at himself, tears streaming from his eyes. He has no words for what she has shown him. He looks at Sofia, thanks imprinted on his entire body. She gives him a small smile and a small nod.

Tarek comes and sits next to him, delicately, as though he knows this man is fragile. He has been seeing Jake twice a week for a year while he finished his sentence in Brisbane and Jake has slowly warmed to this little man whose heart is so open. When Tarek sees the painting, he puts his head on Jake's shoulder without a word. It's more than enough. Ian watches his son and knows with a level of intuition he's never felt before that something good has finally broken open inside Jake. A lock or a door. For the first time since Jake arrived back, he feels a deep sense of hope. He's going to be okay.

For the first time since he's returned Julie wants to be alone with him.

Tarek hands Jake the skull of a bird. "I found it by the creek," he says. "Next to a rock and a little tree. I can show you if you want."

"I think I'm happy just sitting here with you."

He stares out at a place that feels as old as time. He knows it was once a dairy property and then a failed intentional community. It has been wilding for twenty, maybe thirty years and he knows that it isn't even close to what it once was, but it feels more wild than tame.

Since his release, which was televised and widely reported, he has received hundreds of emails wishing him well, many from people he doesn't know. He has also had a few death threats. He has been invited to speak at a law school in Brisbane. The Anarchist Society has invited him to Melbourne. At the moment though he simply needs to be here.

He ponders this. He knows he can't go back to any environment organisation and work the way that he once did. He knows that environmental collapse, climate disasters and social breakdown are part of the same problem, but what he doesn't know is whether he has the strength to approach his working life in an entirely new way. The door that he felt he pried open feels as though it is many doors, behind which are many voices, angry, loud, and all speaking different languages. What does he do with that? The politics haven't improved at all. The far right dominates behind the scenes and while Just Disobey continues to grow, little seems to change or it changes too slowly. Corporations still own the planet. Jake says this now matter-of-factly. None of the rage remains.

Garth came down for a day last week to see him. He was effusive and lovely, but Jake was cold. Not personal, but he is wary of everything that moves outside the narrow band of emotion and life he allows himself. Garth spent most of the time with Julie and Peta.

Jake likes Tarek. He isn't yet his son, loved unreservedly and joyfully, but he likes him. He likes his gentleness and his intuition. He knows when to stay away from Jake and when to sit with him. When to bring him a little gift and when to be a silent companion.

It has to change soon. I have to fight to be well, he thinks. I have to figure out how to do that. That's first. I will pull lantana. I will contemplate by the creek. I will learn to give a little more each day. I will learn to love a bit more each day.

I know he will heal. This place and his family will grow into each other like the entwined roots and branches of so many trees along this creek. I am not sure I will be here, although I will try to stay. Things are getting a bit hazy. I'm getting a bit dimmer as though I am being forgotten by the world I occupy. I feel cold too and very tired.

Jake has started keeping a journal. It's not about him but about trees and birds and insects. He has named the goannas around the house. He is learning to name trees, recognise birds, identify weeds. Tarek is teaching him to recognise bird calls.

After breakfast he and Julie and Tarek go for a walk up the creek. They swim in pools along the way. Collect pods and feathers. They clamber over stones and there are times when certain things – an epiphyte growing out of a giant stone in the middle of the creek, a tree leaning out over a wide part of the creek like its guardian – make his heart sing out to him. This, Jake, is where you find love and meaning. He's just not sure how to make that happen regularly.

They reach a flat area where the creek broadens out and the light becomes more generous and warm. Tarek sits in a shallow pool and plays with stones and floating sticks. Jake and Julie embrace. No words, just light and wind and the opportunity to feel peace, quiet, serenity. Jake closes his eyes. Closes his eyes and hears Tarek talking to the world, hears black cockatoos with their gentle and melancholy call, hears Julie's breath, feels it on his neck. Something more opens in him, a small slash of light on the floor of his spirit where it has been dark for a very long time. He can actually see it, feel it. The tendrils of light, the motes of light, warmth.

He holds on a bit harder. Julie feels that, of course, but more too. If they stay here, right here in this magical spot with its magical light for as long as they can, it will be well, all will be well. Jake laughs quietly but neither Jake nor Julie opens their eyes.

ABOUT THE AUTHOR

JEREMY TAGER

Jeremy Tager has been an environmental activist for many years, working both here and overseas on a wide variety of some of the biggest issues that face all of us, such as climate change, widespread species extinction, land clearing, ocean protection, forestry, food and agriculture, and emerging technologies. He is widely published in non-fiction journals, including Nature Biotechnology and The Alternative Law Journal.

He has worked as a campaigner for Friends of the Earth, the Greens, Greenpeace, and others.

E: jeremytager@gmail.com

ACKNOWLEDGEMENT

The Siege of Sarajevo, the longest conflict in Europe since WWII, was a war that the major powers wanted to forget, deny, ignore. I knew nothing about the Siege when I began this novel and the idea to include it came out of a subconscious that somehow knew that I too had ignored this war. Like all people – and probably other living beings as well – all of us ignore, forget, deny. It can be an essential form of self-protection, but also, particularly in a time of climate change or war a very dangerous choice.

The Siege was ignored because it wasn't convenient to the European and American powers - not until the countries of the Balkans were exhausted and impoverished and ripe for plunder.

So, I read widely about the Siege and disaster capitalism – the same capitalism that now continues to profit from climate change without doing anything to protect the planet.

Any errors are mine alone.

Jeremy Tager's Shaking the Trees is a gripping and emotionally charged novel that intertwines the deeply personal struggles of one family with the vast, inescapable crises of our time—climate change and the lingering scars of war. Through evocative prose and layered storytelling, Tager explores love, loss, denial, and the weight of past trauma, delivering a novel that is both intimate and urgent.

At its core, Shaking the Trees is about choices—the sacrifices we make for our convictions and the unintended consequences of our actions. Jake, driven by desperation to fight climate change, turns to vandalism, believing he can protect both his cause and his partner, Julie. But as lies unravel and his actions escalate to arrest and trial, the personal and political collide, threatening not just his freedom but also his relationship and impending fatherhood. Meanwhile, his father, Ian, retreats into intellectual detachment, unable to face his wife's mortality or the global crisis unfolding around him. His eventual journey to uncover the fate of his sister, who survived the Siege of Sarajevo, forces him to confront not only family history but also his own complicity in turning away from the world's harsh realities.

Jeremy's writing is unflinching, tackling complex moral dilemmas with a sharp, thoughtful perspective. He doesn't offer easy answers—Shaking the Trees is not a novel of simple resolutions, but one that asks difficult questions about responsibility, activism, and the cost of change. The novel's exploration of climate action and civil disobedience is especially compelling, reflecting the anxieties and passions of the present moment.

Deeply affecting and thought-provoking, Shaking the Trees is both a love story and a reckoning, a novel that lingers in the mind long after the last page.

Congratulations, Jeremy, on the publication of Shaking the Trees. It has been a privilege to help bring this heart-wrenching and timely novel to life.

Crystal Leonardi
Bowerbird Publishing
www.crystalleonardi.com

www.ingramcontent.com/pod-product-compliance
Lightning Source LLC
Chambersburg PA
CBHW050608170726
48283CB00001B/160